BREAKING FREE

'Through the lives of three generations of women, Vaasanthi, a magical storyteller, has presented a living picture of the cruelty and injustices of the devadasi system. Equally skilfully she depicts the passion, pain and courage of artistes who, inspired by India's freedom struggle, learn to break free.'

— SHASHI DESHPANDE, author of *Strangers to Ourselves*

'The writer opens the vein into the story of a horrific tradition in which girls are specially chosen to be married to God. It actually meant that they served the "needs" of high priests of the temple, and of the raja who was the temple patron. A powerful story, told with clarity and insight, about some of the young girls who suffered and the few who fought back.'

— KAVERY NAMBISAN, author of
The Story that Must Not Be Told

'*Breaking Free* plunges the reader into the varied and turbulent world of devadasis, bringing the complexities of their history to life.'

— GITANJALI KOLANAD, author of *Girl Made of Gold*

BREAKING FREE

A NOVEL

VAASANTHI

Translated from the Tamil by
N. KALYAN RAMAN

HARPERPERENNIAL

An Imprint of HarperCollins *Publishers*

First published in English in India by Harper Perennial 2022
An imprint of HarperCollins *Publishers*
4th Floor, Tower A, Building No. 10, Phase II, DLF Cyber City,
Gurugram, Haryana – 122002
www.harpercollins.co.in

2 4 6 8 10 9 7 5 3 1

Originally published in Tamil as *Vittu Viduthalaiyagi* © Vaasanthi 2012
English translation copyright © N. Kalyan Raman 2022

P-ISBN: 978-93-9440-759-6
E-ISBN: 978-93-9440-767-1

Typeset in 10.5/13.7 Adobe Caslon Pro at
Manipal Technologies Limited, Manipal

Printed and bound at
Thomson Press (India) Ltd

BREAKING FREE

1

Boisterous laughter floated in from somewhere. Not a lone burst, but an endless uproar, like a long string of firecrackers going off, as if a whole army was laughing. Startled, I looked up from the book I was reading. A short distance away, under a sun umbrella set on a grassy knoll adjoining the lake, a group of men and women sat on a bench or lounged nearby, chatting among themselves. Everyone had a can of Pepsi or Coke in their hand. Mostly young; tourists perhaps, or colleagues from the same office. Repeating whatever had triggered their uncontrollable laughter, they laughed again: carefree, uninhibited, joyous, explosive laughter.

What could have caused so much mirth, I wondered. I was amazed by people who could laugh with such abandon, so freely, as if there was nothing on their minds except the present moment, not even the shadow of any other. If they tore their chests open like Lord Hanuman and revealed what was inside, they would prove that there was no burden in their hearts. As a child, when I had gone to my friend Uma's house, I saw a large portrait of Hanuman in their puja room. A monkey with pink, bloated cheeks. He stood tall and upright, tearing his chest open with his hairy hands. Lord Rama and his wife, Sita, were visible inside his torn chest.

'Shall we keep a picture like that in our house too?' I had suggested.

'No,' Amma said, smiling.

'Why not?'

'Because we don't need such things. All we need is good thoughts in our minds.'

'But they are not god, Amma.'

I remember Amma pulling me close in a tight hug. I can still recall the fragrance of her body.

'For us, they are our only god.'

In what form would good thoughts appear? I was confused. The next day, on her way back from work, Amma bought a figurine as if to offer me an explanation. It had three monkeys. One had covered its ears. One sat with its mouth shut. The third had closed its eyes. Luckily, Amma didn't say that it was god.

'Speak no evil. Hear no evil. See no evil. That's the message of this figurine,' she said. 'If you follow it, you will always be happy.'

I didn't know if she actually lived by those maxims. She must have tried and failed.

At the age of five, I realized that our family was different. When I told Uma that there was no god in our house, she stared at me with wide eyes, as if to say, 'How sad. You're an orphan.'

'In that case, I'll pray for you too before our exams,' she said.

Uma created the illusion that it was through her prayers that I had cleared every exam up to twelfth standard. I lost touch with her after school. During my first-year exams in college, I was afraid that I had truly become an orphan.

For some of my classmates in the hostel, temple prasadam arrived from home to reassure them. During the exam season, those who always loitered around with their foreheads bare would smear their faces with vermilion, sandalwood paste and sacred ash in a drastic makeover of their identities. Some kept a palm-size picture of their god at their bedside. Christians wore a cross at their necks as though they were born with it. They kissed it often. Having no such sacred object, I felt anxious. I feared that god would surely reject me because I didn't know how to pray. I was annoyed that Amma was not one of those mothers who said 'I will pray for you, don't worry'; a mother who expressed her love by sending me bottles of Chyawanprash and Complan to boost my energy.

But Amma did call me without fail on the eve of every exam. 'Have you prepared well?' she asked, like a class teacher.

For some reason, I felt a lump in my throat. 'No matter how much I study, I think it's not enough. I am afraid I might forget everything.'

I could imagine Amma smiling at the other end. 'That's how you feel now, but once the exam begins, you'll remember everything.'

'I am really scared, Amma.'

'But an exam is not a devil or a demon, is it?'

'That's how it feels, though—as if a demon is strangling my neck.' I still remember how I had burst out in despair once. 'Others in my class are confident. Their mothers pray for them, send prasadam from the temple.'

I couldn't tell whether there was a change in Amma's expression. But moments later, she said quietly, 'Let's not discuss what others do. If a person doesn't work hard and lacks confidence, no god can save them. Haven't you done well in class so far? Why do you feel scared now, suddenly? You should be confident of your worth. Then all the demons will run away and leave you alone. Best of luck.'

I got very angry with Amma that day. I was furious that she had offered me no sympathy or solace. I didn't raise the topic again with her for the exams that followed. Determined to shun both god's and Amma's kindness, I focused my attention on studying. When I told Amma a few years later how I had felt then, she laughed. 'If I hadn't reacted like that, you wouldn't have grown into an independent girl. You would be looking for a crutch even today.'

A sudden gust of wind made me feel cold. It penetrated my bones and made me shiver. I pulled the woollen shawl tight around me. Only then did I notice the wetness on my cheeks. Whenever I thought of Amma, my eyes welled up involuntarily; there must be a direct connection between my thoughts and tear ducts. Stemming their flow was beyond me.

Black clouds were forming in the distant sky. Fearing them, a mass of white clouds overhead was rolling away like a bale of cotton. From a white cloud, Amma waved and smiled.

Amma was different. It was her distinct character that had alienated me in some ways from the normal run of people. I couldn't burst into loud, hearty laughter; I had never seen Amma laugh that way. Her smile was the only permanent feature of her demeanour. Sometimes I felt guilty because even that smile had begun to recede from my memory.

There was no sign of the frolicking tourists. They were probably laughing and partying somewhere else. Creatures who believed that life was one big celebration. Their mothers must be normal people. I realized only now that Amma had been neither normal nor average, that she had had a complex personality. She must have sat in the same reclining chair where I was relaxing now. She must have analysed the black and white clouds that floated overhead. What kind of thoughts had passed through her mind?

If you are confident, no demon can stalk you.

Amma was confidence personified, but some demons must have stalked her too. The very idea that she was unable to fend them off seemed incredible to me.

Feeling dispirited, I got up and strolled aimlessly in the garden. Analysing Amma in minute detail had become my preoccupation lately. I had no other option. My mind told me that it was a way to find answers to my questions. But my feelings got entangled in the process. My eyes shed tears on their own. Amma would certainly not like it. I didn't know how to get out of this predicament. It was like being caught in a quagmire. I couldn't think of a way to extricate myself.

Amma had planned her life to an inordinate extent. Studying, earning a degree, pursuing a career, marrying Appa, sending me to a hostel—she had decided everything on her own. Her neatly planned life must have been like a glass case though, one that crumbled at the slightest touch. Sometimes I thought that she wanted to control not only her own life but also that of others. It must have been what caused those frequent arguments between Amma and Appa. But I was shocked to discover that there was no connection between what was visible and the truth that lay hidden behind a veil. The woman who carried herself with such confidence was in fact a weakling; the pretence was an attempt to drive away the demons that stalked her. Eventually, she had failed in that attempt.

I walked towards the compound gate and opened it. As I closed it behind me, I noticed that the curtains in Appa's room were still drawn. Whenever he was here, Appa got up only at nine. There were still fifteen minutes left. Crossing the road that

ran between the house and the lake, I climbed on to the pathway
that skirted the edge of the water. Watching the little waves
while holding on to the wire-mesh fence was endlessly absorbing.
It could be distressing too. The sun, which had begun to shine
brightly, had scattered diamonds across the lake's surface. A few
pleasure boats had set out. The number of people on the pathway
had increased—boys and girls eager to cover the distance of six and
a half kilometres on their bicycles, and their parents who followed
them, shouting admonitions: 'Keep to the left!' 'Be careful!'

There was a small gap in a section of the fence. Two benches
had been placed on a small mound on the lake's shore for walkers
to sit and relax. I went towards the mound and sat on a bench.
It was warm from the sun's heat. At the edge of the shore, water
lilies were in bloom: pale violet and pink. A little girl ran past,
shouting, 'Look, a lotus!'

I didn't know whether Amma used to come and sit here.
I must ask Appa. She would have come alone. She lived in
her own, special world—one where my father and I were not
admitted. A family went by in a boat, laughing exuberantly. They
were simple people. The three of us had never travelled together
or laughed like them. Their life must be an open book. That must
be why they could laugh so freely. They wouldn't feel the need to
wander alone through dark caves.

But Amma might have had such a need. I felt guilty that
neither Appa nor I had made any effort to understand her.
How much did Appa know? He had stopped talking about her
altogether. Amma had worn a mask and made everyone believe
that it was real. I couldn't decide whether it was a sign of her
intelligence or failure.

Suddenly, an air of serenity settled on the area. The water in
the lake became clear as glass; the blue sky had descended on it.

The limpid water looked as though it might be very deep, as deep as the ocean. Amma's long, curly hair displayed its splendour in the water. Her smiling face appeared perfectly still. Her naturally red lips stretched wide with pleasure on seeing me. 'Did you look at the lotus?' She smiled. 'How many flowers do you want? I'll come back with an armful for you,' she said and dived deeper into the water.

'Amma, no! Don't go! The water's deep, very deep.' I felt an agitation in my chest. I wiped the tears that had begun to flow and stood up, but the tension did not subside. I didn't know why I was running. My feet stumbled on something, I lost my balance and fell. I clutched at the wire fence that ringed the lake for support and felt a stab of pain—I had scraped my palm. As I tried to get up, I saw a boy standing before me. Looking intently at me, he asked with concern, 'Are you hurt? Why did you run like that?'

At those words, for some strange reason, the agitation in my heart began to abate. Without giving him an answer, I smiled gently and said, 'Give me your hand.'

He extended a cheerful hand. I took it and stood up slowly. 'Thank you.'

'Are you able to walk?' he asked shyly.

'Oh yes. That, over there, is my house. I'll manage.'

He glanced in the direction I pointed. Then he looked keenly at me. 'That one?' he said.

I nodded and walked towards the house. I sensed the boy's eyes on my back. I turned around. He was standing in the same spot, gazing at me. I waved to him with a smile and resumed walking.

As the boy faded from my mind, thoughts of Amma overwhelmed me. Her face which had surfaced in the water refused to budge. My friend Joan said that her dead mother visited her frequently in her dreams. Amma never came to me in my dreams, not even once. I felt sad that she seemed to be ignoring me.

When I reached the compound gate, Appa was relaxing in the same chair that I had occupied a little earlier. He looked frail. He saw me and smiled faintly. Suddenly, I felt a surge of anger. I could not return his smile. Instead, fury exploded within me, like a tightly shut container bursting open in a microwave. I hurried over to him and grasped his hands in mine.

'Why did Amma take her own life?'

Appa gave me a distraught look.

'I don't know, 'ma,' he said in a tone of mild irritation. 'How many times are you going to ask me the same question? Let's go away. I don't like it here.'

I stared at him for some time. Then, with a determination I didn't understand myself, I said, 'Yes, let's go, but where? To Delhi again? What can we do once we get there? Here is where we must find the answer.'

Appa covered his eyes with both hands. 'I'll leave. I can't stay here.'

From his heaving shoulders, I could see that he was crying. I did not rush to console him. I was annoyed that he didn't share my zeal.

It seemed like I didn't know much about him either.

2

Subramania Gurukkal woke up suddenly, as though someone had roused him from deep slumber. He sat up with a jolt and glanced at the timepiece next to him. It was five minutes to four. He reckoned that it would be half past four by the time he bathed and got ready to leave for the temple. The lamp in the alcove cast a faint light in the room. By god's mercy, his eyesight had not dimmed even at eighty-seven. Though his joints troubled him now and again, he had not had to seek medical treatment for any ailment so far. Nor had he forgotten the sacred chants with which he offered daily worship to the Lord—his tongue never faltered. He would be glad if life went on in this way until he stopped breathing.

As soon as he opened the door to the backyard, the chill wind of the predawn hour struck him on the face, giving him goosebumps. He was shivering by the time he reached the well and drew a pot of water. Muttering 'Siva, Siva', he scooped water from the pot in a sombu and poured it on his head. He feared his body might go numb from the coldness of the water. After pouring a few more mugs of water on himself, he dried his head with a towel and wiped his body. He pressed three fingers into the tin of vibhuti kept in an alcove and, intoning 'Namachivaya, Namachivaya', drew neat strokes with the sacred ash on his shoulders, chest and upper arms, and finally across his forehead from left to right. By the dim light from inside the house, he picked the neatly washed, ritually pure clothes from the clothes line, removed the wet garments from around his waist and dumped them in a bucket. Once he had worn the dry veshti in the ritual panchakacham style, his body stopped shivering and slowly returned to normal. And after he covered his shoulders and chest with the angavastram, he even felt cosy and warm. He had begun to enjoy these luxuries only recently though. Until five years ago, he had always entered the temple clad in a wet veshti and with his chest bare.

He thought he saw Kamakshi sitting on the floor in the hall, leaning against a pillar. He was taken aback for a moment. She had died ten years ago. Why did I suddenly have this illusion? Was it an illusion, or was it really her? When he stepped out after taking the flashlight from the cupboard, he told Kamu, who was still there leaning against the pillar, 'Latch the door from inside.'

'I have truly lost my mind,' he muttered to himself as he drew the bolt on the outside and locked the door by taking a key from his waist and turning it in the lock that hung from the latch. The flashlight threw a circle of light in front of him that jumped and moved in step with his stride. In the distance, the gopuram appeared like a dark shape. It was a path his feet had traversed ever since he learnt to walk. He remembered running behind his father, wearing nothing but a string around his waist. As soon as his father opened the gigantic doors at the entrance of the temple while intoning shlokas to himself, a colony of bats would take off noisily from within, wings flapping, and fly out. He remembered clinging to his father's legs in panic and his father clasping him with affection. As soon as father and son entered the temple, two yalis would rise from the pillars on either side, as if paying obeisance to his father with folded palms. Even at that age, he knew that his father was the commander of that empire. As a teenager, he was awed and delighted by his father's learning and wisdom. The respect and affection he had for his father did not lessen a whit even after the old man breathed his last.

When he saw the silhouette of the temple's gopuram today, he was reminded of his father, something that had never happened before. The gopuram was not very tall, but its majestic beauty lifted the spirit. Appa had been small of build, but the glow on his face could inspire anyone to bow deferentially with folded palms. No one at the temple had contradicted Appa's words and opinions. 'The times have changed,' he said, as if explaining to his absent father. 'Change is natural, after all. But so long as I am alive, I won't fall short in performing the rites and disciplines you taught me,' he said to himself. 'After I'm gone, anything might happen. Why should I worry about it?'

He was slightly winded by the time he reached the end of the walkway and climbed the steps leading to the temple. 'Easwara.' Piously muttering the Lord's name, he stopped in front of the gigantic doors of the temple. He set the sombu of water on the floor and trained the beam of the flashlight on the mouth of the lock with one hand and tried to insert the key in the lock with the other. Soon his fingers were tired. In despair that he might not be able to open the lock, he groped for the hole again, muttering to himself, 'Lord, it is such a trial.'

'Who is it?'

As soon as he saw Shanmugam, the guard, come up the steps, calling out in a peremptory tone, he calmed down.

'It's me, Shanmugam. I am not able to open the lock.'

'Oh, it's Gurukkal Aiya. Why have you come this early, when it's still dark? Here, I'll open it. Hold the flashlight.' Shanmugam stepped forward and stood in front of the door, leaving enough space for Subramania Gurukkal, clad in ritually pure clothes, to move aside. With the priest shining the torch, he opened the lock, flung both doors open and switched on the electric lamp in the outer pathway along the temple's perimeter. In the soft light, the yalis came alive. Bats wheeled anxiously near the ceiling.

As the priest walked to the deity's chamber, Shanmugam said, 'I asked you, didn't I? Why so early, well before first light?'

'Oh, maybe I got restless,' the priest said as he kept walking. 'I wonder when we'll get the news from Kasturi's house. If it comes, I shouldn't light the lamp for the deity. I can't bear the thought. I came here thinking I'd light the lamp and offer at least two plantains before anything happens.'

As he walked along with the priest but at a distance, Shanmugam muttered, 'Oh, I forgot all about it.' After a brief pause, he ventured delicately, 'I thought those practices are not followed these days, aiya.'

'Not legally, yes. But there's such a thing as temple rules, isn't there?'

'If the woman dies, you say the deity should observe ritual mourning?'

'Yes, as when a wife passes away.'

As Subramania Gurukkal continued in silence towards the chamber of the main deity and opened the door, Shanmugam kept switching on the lights along the way. The oil lamp the priest had lit the previous evening was still burning in the sanctum sanctorum. The lingam had a withered garland of oleander around it.

'Kasturiamma's brother, Sabapathi, might question the need for these rituals. And his son, Senthil, does have a quick temper.'

Without replying, Subramania Gurukkal removed the wilted flowers from the lingam and washed it with his own hands with the sombu of water he had brought, as though bathing a baby.

Then he said gently, as if to the lingam: 'No matter who forgets the bond between Kasturi and the temple, this deity won't. This temple will pay all due respects to Kasturi. I have stayed alive only to ensure that it happens.'

'I told you what crossed my mind, aiya.'

Without a word, Subramania Gurukkal started the puja. Lulled by the melodious tones of the devotional hymn, Shanmugam began to feel sleepy. He was amazed at the sincere attention with which the octogenarian priest performed his duties. The priest rang the bell, offered worship to the deity with the sacred flame and set the plate with the burning camphor on the steps. Shanmugam bent down, swept his fingers above the flame and touched them to his eyes, then took a pinch of sacred ash from a small tin outside and smeared it on his forehead.

'Carry on, Shanmugam,' Subramania Gurukkal said. 'Go back to sleep if you want to. I'll sit here and meditate for a while.'

'Fine, aiya,' Shanmugam said and left.

Gurukkal shut the door of the sanctum sanctorum and walked to the outer pathway. He sat down cross-legged, rested his back against a pillar and closed his eyes.

Behind those closed eyelids, Kasturi appeared and stood before him.

A thrill spread through his body as though she had entered it and possessed him. A smile settled on his lips. What beauty, what grace, what hauteur. His eyes, which had seen her as a child wearing long skirts, had never forgotten that shimmer of youth. Fifteen-year-old Kasturi, with a childlike innocence in her face; eyes like round, black beetles; complexion, fair and shiny like the inside of a plantain stem. Kasturi at twenty, the empress of dance, a picture of elegance. Majestic at twenty-five, with her clear gaze and fierce pride. Teary-eyed Kasturi who had come to him wounded and grieving. 'Suppuni, please, please allow me, just this once, to pay my tribute before the deity in his chamber. For one last time ... I can't bear it, Suppuni ... I feel my heart is about to break ... There's no place for me anywhere, Suppuni ...' He had wanted to take her in his arms then and wipe those tears away.

Subramania Gurukkal's frail body trembled slightly. His eyes welled up. His heart wheeled around at a dizzy pace. And holding his hands, Kasturi whirled around too. Her arms were like strings of flowers. When she laughed, the sound rang out in peals, as if someone was shaking a small bronze bell. He yearned for that laughter. The fragrance that surrounded her—was it sandalwood, or rose, or simply the sweet scent of her body? The silver anklets on her feet that tinkled softly. Her feet, reddened with henna, whirling around in a circle. And in that picturesque scene, Suppuni spun around too.

'Don't cry, Kasturi. Wherever you dance, the Lord will be present.'

Kasturi broke down in great, heaving sobs. 'They won't even let me dance, Suppuni. The deity himself has spurned me.'

Suppuni was shaking. How could this golden idol be reduced to tears? How was he to console her? He could not say 'Don't worry, I am here for you.' It was not allowed. Though his body and heart pulsed with desire, he couldn't even lift her to her feet.

Subramania Gurukkal's body shivered. Opening his eyes, he reminded himself of the present, and then closed them again. It must have been clear to her that day that the god I worshipped was a mere onlooker even though I didn't have the maturity to say it to her; I couldn't hide my weakness. I was upset by her tears but I didn't have the wherewithal to help her either. My wretched heart longed to touch her, to lay her on my lap and comfort her. If my father hadn't come there, something disgraceful might have occurred. Kasturi wouldn't have forgiven me all her life.

'Remember, there is a woman at home who is dependent on you.' It was as if his father stood before him now, chastising him.

Subramania Gurukkal got up immediately. He prostrated himself in the direction of the Lord's chamber.

'Please forgive me. Please forgive me. I never betrayed Kamakshi with this body.'

When he stood up, he was overcome by a fatigue he had never known before. He sat down once more, cross-legged on the floor, leaned against a pillar and closed his eyes.

'Om Namachivaya.'

Lord, please set her free. She has suffered enough. Her life is lingering on for no good reason.

Something had taken hold of him today. He couldn't steady his mind. It seemed to have grown wings of its own will. Two enormous wings and a physique capable of roaming the universe. Like a chowry fanning the idol of the Lord, they flapped slowly and took flight. With every beat they scattered the moments and minutes buried in the dark caves of memory, like tearing off the pages from a calendar. Everything that he had seen and not seen, heard and not heard, understood and not understood, everything that was secret and mysterious assumed a shape as large as the universe and danced before him. Like Sanjaya perceiving the events of the war in the Mahabharata from afar ... the priest gasped for breath. As though he was standing as tall as the sky, laden with the histories of many births on his shoulders, his chest grew wide and his head erect. He imagined that he was at once the blind king Dhritarashtra and his adviser Sanjaya.

This be the gate, this be the gate
where the liturgies of our Saivite faith thrive.'

Kasturi was dancing in front of the deity's chamber. The young priest Suppuni who had come to perform the night puja in his father's stead looked at her with rapture. Was she at all human? Or was she a nymphet from the land of the gods? How could a human be so beautiful and so proficient in her art?

'Chinna gurukkale.'

Suppuni looked up, startled to hear a voice as melodious as the tone of a veena.

'You can call me Suppuni. I am the same age as you.'

She smiled and said teasingly, 'Yes, Suppuni Aiya. Don't you have to light the lamp?'

'Have you finished dancing yet?' said Suppuni, gathering his wits. 'You seem to have skipped a verse.'

Kasturi clapped her hands and giggled. 'You missed it because you were sleepy. Light the lamp and perform the puja. Or the deity himself might fall asleep.'

A spirit of levity entered Suppuni. 'How can he go to sleep? He is still enchanted by your dance.'

She tittered, the sound like the tinkling of a bell. Dimples appeared on her cheeks for a fleeting moment. 'As if you would know! I am feeling sleepy. I'd like to go to bed early.'

Suppuni lit the piece of camphor on the plate, held up the flame before the idol and turned to offer it to Kasturi. His eyes fell on the entrance and his face grew dark. After sweeping her fingers above the flame and raising them to her eyes, Kasturi turned in the direction of Suppuni's gaze. A footman from the palace stood at the door. Suppuni looked intently at her face: a faint trace of sorrow was visible there. Yet when he fetched the plate of votive offerings from the sanctum sanctorum and gave it to her, her face was radiant and smiling as always. She touched the plate piously, then her eyes. Then she walked silently behind the footman from the palace. As he saw her leave, Suppuni felt a blaze flare up in his belly. He locked up the sanctum sanctorum hastily and hurried, half running, to the entrance. The horse-drawn carriage was already on its way, accompanied by the rhythmic sound of ankle bells. It was a closed one with curtains. Wondering if Kasturi, seated behind the curtain, had a smile on her face, Suppuni locked the main door of the temple and walked home.

3

Is IT DAY or night?

Kasturi didn't know.

Where am I?

She was not sure.

Am I still alive?

One moment she seemed to be floating inside a bank of clouds; the next, she had dived to the bottom of the ocean, looking for its treasures—floating and drowning, as if riding a swing.

When she raised her head after a dip, the doors to the chamber were open. The Lord appeared before the devotees dressed in silk robes and draped in garlands of fresh jasmine from head to waist with dots of vermilion and sandalwood paste glinting amid streaks of holy ash on his forehead. As soon as Suppuni Gurukkal intoned 'Om Namachivaya' and commenced the puja by showering the idol with oleander and assorted flowers, she realized that she was standing at the threshold of the sanctum sanctorum. It was a joyous sighting of the deity that was hers alone to experience. A song came gushing forth from her navel.

'May I come by, Lord, to sing and dance in your chamber?' One hand rested on her waist while the other mimed the phrase, 'May I come by?'

'May I come by, Lord ...'

Who is singing now, Thilakam or I?

Kasturi's body was racked by anxiety. Is it Thilakam standing before me? Why have you become so thin and dark, Thilakam? What happened to you? Tears brimmed over in Kasturi's eyes. Grief choked her throat. How many years has it been since I heard you sing? How extraordinary your voice was: the range, the richness, the gift. It was a gift, girl, but you didn't realize it. You didn't understand that you were born to this. Never mind. You are here now, finally. I told you back then, but you ignored me. If you had stayed with me, we would have been queens of our kingdom. You didn't listen. You've come today, when I've lost my legs and voice, when I am without protection, an empty shell. But I am glad you've come at least now. Sing.

Kasturi closed her eyes and whimpered.

May I enter, Lord, to dance and sing in your chamber?

Why is your voice sounding ragged, Thilakam? Have you cut down your practice hours?

'Manjula.'

Hearing that voice which sounded like a clap of thunder, a tremor ran through Kasturi. Who was this Manjula? Kasturi couldn't remember.

'Won't you do as you are told?'

The voice set off a wave of panic in her abdomen. The singing stopped.

'Manjula, how often should I tell you to stop this singing and dancing?'

'What's it to you if I sing? Whenever I sing you tell me to stop. Singing at sunrise is good for the voice, Kasturi Aththai used to say.'

'Let all this song and dance stop with Aththai. We want no more of that.'

'I sing because I feel like singing. Why does it bother you, da?'

'I'll kill you.'

'Aiyo! Amma! Somu is beating me.'

'I'll kill you for real. Be careful.'

Kasturi trembled. Haven't they killed her already? How can the soul survive once the heart is crushed? Now I can't even open my eyes at will. I should run away if I can. I am used to running. How I ran to the Lord's chamber that day like a crazed woman …

They have killed me, Suppuni! They've murdered Thilakam. She didn't die alone; I died along with her. What's left of me to kill now? How many times can a person die?

Grief came surging from below.

What did I do wrong?

Growing up, they told me that I was born only to sing and dance in the Lord's chamber. I never realized there could be another kind of life. Nor did I yearn for one. I didn't know whether it was right or wrong. Those who broke free and went away—did they do well for themselves? We have to ask them. Just one Thilakam is enough to let us know. Swimming upstream requires ability and courage from each person. I had neither. That's why I was killed over and over again, without being conscious of it. It's true, Suppuni. What does Lakshmi call it? She will say it is political scheming. What do I know about politics and whatnot? I thought shouting 'Vande Mataram' was politics.

She heard many thousands of voices at once. 'Vande Mataram! Vande Mataram!' Holding a tricolour flag aloft, she shouted along with the others in the procession, 'Vande Mataram!' Her veins bulged with the effort. It felt like a holy dip. The clamour for freedom was everywhere. While she danced, whirling round and round, he sang, 'Now our sorrows are gone, all gone.' Lakshmi spoke about that too.

The swing went back and forth, and back and forth. So many voices, so many faces. Sweeping everything aside, the swing moved up and down. And as it swayed, people looked like dolls, with doll-like voices. The web of memories wound itself around the swing as it went up and came down. Like a peacock feather, it caressed her softly.

Kasturi as a little girl of six. The street where she was born, where she played, sang and danced. The sound of water being splattered in front of doorways well before daybreak. 'Chathak, chathak.' Water mixed with cattle dung hits the mud floor. 'Charak, charak.' A twig broom moves in brisk strokes to sweep the ground. Kolam powder is dropped through fingers as dots on the wet floor and on the cool earth. Even in that dim light, hands swiftly join the bright dots with lines, bangles tinkle gently like anklets. As the day slowly dawns, flowers bloom and parrots perch before the entrance as though waiting only for the clang of the temple bell. The temple bell rings. She hears Sundaramurthi Mama playing the nadaswaram. Enchanted by his '*Saraguna Palimpa*', hands drawing the kolam presently begin to tap the taalam on the wet floor ... for a deep love of music pervades the air. The gentle drone of the tambura floats in the stir of a breeze.

'Why are you taking so long to draw the kolam, Sengamalam? Don't you have to wake Kasturi and get her ready?'

When she heard Kanagu Paati's words, Sengamalam paused for a moment to admire the kolam and then went inside. 'Get up, Kasturi. It's getting late. Don't come crying to me later that the master rapped your knuckles.'

Kasturi was curled up in deep slumber in the passage next to the courtyard. After a vigorous shake, she woke up immediately and sat upright. Rubbing her eyes, she walked to the courtyard. Sengamalam glanced at her for a moment with delight.

A solid gold figurine she is. At least she should attain a good position in life. 'You'll go places.' When words of praise, rare as pearls, drop from the dance master's lips, they are equal to god's own utterance. Let no evil eye bring her harm, Brahadeeswara. She needs luck. Beauty alone isn't enough to lay the world at one's feet. One has to be smart. This one is naive, though: she thinks all that is white must be milk.

When Kasturi came back after rinsing her mouth and washing her face, Sengamalam gave her a bowl of rice water. While she drank it, Sengamalam combed and braided her thick, curly hair and changed her skirt. 'Enough, 'ma. I'll be off now.' As Kasturi flitted away like a little bird, Sengamalam prayed aloud, 'god, may a new life dawn in this house because of this girl.'

'She hasn't reached puberty yet, and you are already building castles in the air,' Kanagu Paati said.

'I hope she doesn't become a bearer of ill-luck like me.'

'Come on, you stupid woman. Of course Kasturi will be a lucky girl. But if you keep up your daily complaints, even god will get fed up. In his irritation, he might go looking for Lakshmi, Thulasi's daughter, from the opposite street. Do we have singing practice today or not?'

Sengamalam laughed and said, 'All right. Come. We'll try singing that jaavali today.' She fetched the tambura and sat down to practice.

Taking care not to stomp on the kolam at the entrance, Kasturi stepped gingerly on to the street, and, as instructed by her grandmother, looked up at the gopuram and patted her cheeks as a mark of pious devotion. As she headed towards the nattuvanar's house, Dhanam, Meenakshi and Lakshmi joined her and ran alongside.

Nattuvanar Muthulingam looked freshly bathed, with neat streaks of holy ash on his forehead and bare chest, and a long gold chain glittering around his neck. He sat down on a mat spread on the floor with the kattai in front of him. He prayed for a few moments with his eyes closed. Then he grunted softly, prompting everyone to touch the ground, half kneeling, and pay obeisance. The little girls knew that from here on, he would not waste even half a second. Just as they formed a quick row and stood ready for practice, the stick sounded, keeping time as the master sang, 'Thaiya, thaiya.'

It was as though she had been prodded awake; Kasturi's drowsiness left her and her mind became engrossed in the rhythm. The practice of adavu was very important. If any girl slipped up, the master's stick would be hurled with perfect aim at her ankle. The pain of that moment could not be adequately described in words, only in tears.

'Lakshmi,' the master's voice rumbled. The next moment, the stick had smashed into Lakshmi's ankle. She writhed in pain. 'Learn to dance at least by looking at your mate Kasturi. Sit over there and watch her dance.'

Kasturi felt as though he had hit her instead. She experienced a mix of inexplicable fear and shame. As soon as the master commenced the jathi, she began to dance. Whenever the other girls made a mistake, the stick was hurled at them.

'Why does the master get so angry, Paati?' she had once asked her grandmother.

'Who knows!' Kanagu Paati said, sounding somewhat irritated. 'When a man is nursing a disappointment, he snaps at everyone like this.'

'What disappointment?'

Kanagu Paati lost her patience. 'Listen, girl. Every man suffers some disappointment or other. If he can't talk about it, he tends to pounce on people at random.'

'What are you saying to that little girl, Amma?' After Sengamalam had admonished her mother, Kasturi had no way of understanding the reason for the master's anger.

She glanced at the master's wife, Karpagam, who was chopping vegetables in the veranda adjoining the courtyard. She wondered if the master had ever hurled the kattai at his wife. Would she have sat quietly like Lakshmi, her eyes filling with tears? When the master flung the kattai at them, Karpagam looked as if she relished it. Sometimes, she even had a smirk on her face as if to say 'You had it coming, girls. Now, take it.'

As though he was fed up suddenly, the master laid the kattai on the floor. 'That's enough for today. Be off, all of you,' he said. Absorbing this incredible reprieve, the girls bent down to touch the ground and paid obeisance.

'Listen! If you make the same mistakes again tomorrow, I'll finish you off. Watch yourselves. You trudge in like a flock of sheep. Among you, only Kasturi is going to make the grade.'

His praise made Kasturi squirm. The other girls would certainly not like it. They would show their displeasure in time. She was annoyed at the master. Why did he have to say it?

The master went near Lakshmi, pulled her cheek and pinched it. Anger flaring in his eyes, he said, 'If you don't want to dance, what else would you like to do with yourself?'

Lakshmi stood with a pained expression on her face while protectively covering the other cheek. Kasturi couldn't bear to look at her and bowed her head.

The master would not let go of Lakshmi. 'You don't have a voice good enough for singing, either. Girl, what are you even thinking? I hear arrangements for the wedding of our Periya Mirasu's daughter are going on in grand style. Do you imagine he will do the same for you?'

Startled to see a few of the other girls snigger into their hands, Kasturi turned to Lakshmi, who stood with her eyes downcast. Her lips trembled, and her face was red.

Kasturi heard the master's wife say in a somewhat reproachful tone: 'Why do you talk about such things with these girls?'

The master's reply was cruel. 'They'll understand only if I tell them. I'm not giving away a secret, am I?'

Though she could not fully understand his remarks, Kasturi knew that it was demeaning talk. Lakshmi's face was flushed with anger and shame.

As soon as the master said, 'All right, you can go,' Lakshmi and Kasturi fled without taking his leave. Lakshmi ran at a furious pace.

'Wait, I'll come with you,' Kasturi cried as she followed Lakshmi.

When they reached the temple tank, Lakshmi stopped. She retreated to a deserted corner, sat on the steps and buried her face between her knees. It was obvious from Lakshmi's heaving back that she was crying. Kasturi sat beside her and clasped her shoulders. She, too, was close to tears. 'Don't cry, Lakshmi. I don't know why our master gets so angry. I can't bear it when he beats you like that. Does it hurt a lot?'

Without raising her head, Lakshmi said, 'No.'

Kasturi hugged her and said, 'That movement is so easy, di. Come home, I'll show you.'

Lakshmi shook her head vigorously. 'No. I won't come to that class any more.'

'Then …?'

'I don't like dancing. I want to go to school and study.'

Eyes wide in wonder, Kasturi said, 'Really?'

'Yes. I'm going to be a lawyer.'

'Will your amma agree to let you study?'

'I have to persuade her. There's a school in the nearby town.'

'As a lawyer, will you go to court and argue your case?'

'Yes, I will,' Lakshmi said emphatically. 'You know what I am going to do once I become a lawyer? I'll file a case against our dance master for breaking the legs of ten-year-olds.'

Startled, Kasturi looked at Lakshmi. Her chin was up and a smile appeared on her lips. Kasturi felt like laughing too.

'Beat him to a pulp and put him in jail,' Lakshmi said.

'The police should thrash his legs just like he did with us.'

Imagining the prospect filled them with delight. Both girls fell about laughing.

4

Lakshmi had a clear memory of the marriage ceremony. She remembered even more vividly how she had waited for her father to come home that night.

Thulasi cast a troubled glance at Lakshmi, who was sitting alone in the hall, playing a game of pallankuzhi with herself.

'Dear girl, why haven't you gone to bed yet?'

Face brightly adorned, Thulasi was sitting on the swing in the hall dressed in a silk sari and wearing a profusion of fragrant jasmine in her hair.

Carefully depositing tamarind seeds in the pits on the pallankuzhi board, Lakshmi replied without looking at Thulasi, 'I want to meet Appa.'

'Why?'

Ignoring the note of surprise in her mother's voice, Lakshmi said even more assertively, 'Because I want to speak to him, that's why.'

'What will you say to him?' It wasn't clear whether Thulasi was amused or upset; Lakshmi had no interest in finding out.

Suddenly she was angry. 'A daughter can have many things to talk about with her father. Why should I tell anyone?' As she spoke, a lump rose in her throat for no reason.

'But you should tell me. I *must* know,' Thulasi said sternly.

'It's no use letting you know. To make this happen, I need to talk directly to Appa.'

Thulasi gave her daughter a look of alarm. 'What will he make happen for you? Something like his daughter Paapa's wedding, is it?'

'Chee, chee! I don't want a wedding or any other farce.' Even as Lakshmi said it, the shame induced by her mother's apprehension filled her eyes with tears.

Thulasi came and sat next to her. 'What do you want, kannu? You said you don't want to dance or sing, and you stopped taking lessons. The master keeps reminding me whenever I see him.'

Lakshmi felt a sharp pang of fury. 'Don't talk about master aiya.'

'All right, I won't. But what on earth are you going to do with yourself?'

'I'll do whatever I want. What's it to you? That's why I have to talk to Appa in private. I don't want you there.'

'What! Is it a great secret?' Thulasi laughed.

'Yes, it's a secret. I won't tell you.'

Countless questions roiled up in her. Should I be forced to sing just because I am your daughter? Am I obliged to dance too? Should I get dolled up every night and wait for my patron to arrive? Amma wouldn't have the answer to any of those questions. Nothing was in her power. From the food she ate to the clothes she wore—everything was alms from some patron. There was nothing wrong in asking for yet another dole.

Thulasi looked at her daughter with concern. 'By the time he comes in, it'll be late.'

'Never mind. I'll wait. Tell him his daughter wants to speak with him. I'll go to bed after talking to him.'

'How old were you then?'

Lakshmi came back to the present. It felt like an episode from a previous birth. Her age at the time was irrelevant. As she looked at Dharini sitting before her, she thought it must have happened on a different planet. That she had embarked on a very long journey from that place was a great feat in itself, but Dharini wouldn't understand. For her, it was mere history. How could Lakshmi explain that it had been a struggle for the right to choose her livelihood, that she had stood and fought all alone in that struggle? When she thought about it now, she couldn't believe it. She was not yet twelve then. Where had she got that steely resolve from? She was not propelled forward by some supra-human power, as Kasturi seemed to think. Yearnings, rejections and humiliations were enough to make her strong and tenacious. Her mother had not understood it then, because Thulasi believed that the guile she possessed was her sole weapon for self-protection, and she felt no shame in using it. Lakshmi could now analyse the sociological reasons for her mother's actions, but when she was eleven, she had been overcome by an uncontrollable rage—anger so intense that it made her despise her own mother. She was furious at everyone: at Periya Mirasu, her mother's patron; at his daughter Paapa; at her mother and her superbly arrogant gait; at the dance master; at Kasturi, the simpleton. Wrath that would burn everything to ashes.

In those days, a fire had raged in her belly. A blaze fit to scorch the universe. It glowed like red-hot coals in her heart.

Had that little girl's life not changed course, Lakshmi thought now, she would have destroyed herself as well as those around her, like a fighter from a suicide squad.

She recalled vividly the anger that had erupted in her that day, making her want to burn down that pandal, a large, flat-roofed thatched shed temporarily erected for the wedding. It was a giant pandal, with festoons of jasmine dangling from the roof, and tinsel that sparkled amid the chamomile bouquets. Why couldn't she turn into a monkey and rip everything apart? Realizing now that her fervent wish had been a natural instinct, she was moved to self-pity.

Since it was a wedding in Periya Mirasu's family, the whole street bustled with activity. Thulasi had been restless with excitement for the past two days. Spreading out several saris on the bed, she queried her daughter like a little girl, 'Tell me, which one should I wear to the wedding?'

'Wear anything you like. It will look good on you,' Lakshmi replied without betraying her boredom. She thought that her mother's excitement and eagerness made no sense at all.

On the wedding day, Amma woke her well before dawn. 'Get up. Don't you want to bathe and wear a new dress? He has insisted that I should adorn the bride. Get up, quick!' she nagged Lakshmi as she readied her. She had decked herself up to look really special.

'You are the one who looks like a bride.'

'Right. Of course, I am a bride,' Amma said, jerking her chin sideways in a gesture of dismissal, but the smile that lit up her face meant that she had taken it as a compliment.

As Lakshmi walked behind her mother in her rustling long skirt, wearing a dancer's gold earpiece and waist-band at her mother's insistence, she felt a puzzling twinge of shame.

The street wasn't awake yet. Kamalam who came out of her house at the end of the street to clean the front yard looked at them and said, 'Is it Thulasi? Why are you going so early for the wedding? The muhurtam begins only at nine.'

'I know, Akka. They've called me to dress up the bride. We have to start now if we want to get her ready in time for the swing ceremony.'

'Oh, of course. Carry on. When Periya Mirasu has called you, you should be there, right? After all, you are entitled to every privilege.'

As they walked down the street, Thulasi muttered to herself: 'All these women are simply bursting with jealousy.'

'What is privilege, Amma?'

'What do I know? We'll have to ask her,' Amma said, quickening her stride.

Periya Mirasu's residence was huge. It was a house with four bays. There was enough vacant land in front of and behind the house to build four more mansions. There was a thick cluster of mango, jackfruit and plantain trees in the backyard, making it cool and shady. The backyard was the only place familiar to Lakshmi. She could safely lurk unseen in its semi-dark areas. Though it was not yet daylight, the front entrance was illuminated by the glow from the petromax lamps. The compound wall and iron grille gate distinguished the house from the others on the street. Tall plantain trees had been erected on both sides of the gate and a pandal made of coconut thatch had been put up enclosing the open space in front of the house. The roof was covered with white cloth and decorated with silk tassels. Lamps dangled from various points on the roof. Lakshmi had never seen such decorations before. She hesitated even to cross the threshold and enter the house; her steps faltered. Her mother too stood diffidently at the entrance.

In a sudden panic that made her stomach churn, Lakshmi said, 'Come, Amma. Let's go back.'

'Wait. Someone will come for us,' Thulasi said softly.

Just then, as though he had been sent expressly for the purpose, a man came running from inside and addressed her, 'You're Thulasi, right? Please come.'

Lakshmi didn't think he was old enough to call her mother by her name. Instead of the front entrance, they were led through a doorway on the side of the house into the second bay.

'Mami, Thulasi has come,' the man said in a loud voice.

A woman emerged from inside. She was slightly plump. Diamonds and gold glittered on her ears, nose and neck. She was wearing a silk sari with a wide zari border in the traditional Brahmin style. A bunch of keys hung from her waist. She appeared to be Periya Mirasu's wife. Lakshmi wondered if she could laugh or even smile. The woman looked enviously at Thulasi.

'Come. The poor girl has been waiting for more than half an hour,' the mirasdar's wife said listlessly. Noticing Lakshmi's presence, she remarked, 'You've brought your daughter along so early in the morning? No wonder you got delayed.'

Lakshmi squeezed her mother's hand to convey her denial. Being impervious to such slights, Thulasi said with an ingratiating smile, 'We'll do the job in no time. Don't worry,' and walked to where the bride was waiting. The girl was seated on a rug. She had plump cheeks and big, round eyes. To Lakshmi, she too seemed incapable of laughter. Thulasi had told her that the girl was three years older than her. A large brass salver next to her held an assortment of make-up items and jewellery. Lakshmi sat a little apart. Before Thulasi finished adorning the bride, the girl had been offered milk, fruit and snacks two or three times. No one asked Thulasi or Lakshmi if they wanted something to eat. Lakshmi was hungry. She felt drowsy as well. She curled up where she was sitting and went to sleep.

Periya Mirasu appeared in her dream—tall and well built, wearing a silk veshti and a silk stole, like Arjuna in a play enacted from the Mahabharata. 'I am father to you too. Come here,' he said. 'You also have a right in this house.'

She thought of asking him what he had meant by 'right', but did not. Instead, she said, 'I am hungry, Appa.'

'Come closer.'

When she went to him though, he moved away, like Arjuna exiting the stage after the scene was over.

She is hungry. She is waiting with her mother in the backyard for food. The cook who has come to the well says, 'Oh, you're here already?' and goes inside. She is sitting on the washing stone near the well, looking on idly as the squirrels scurry up and down the mango, coconut and jackfruit trees. The cook arrives, finally. He hands over a lidded food pail to Thulasi. Without ornaments, flowers in her hair or a silk sari, her mother looks like a beggar woman. Lakshmi feels like crying. She wants to knock down the pail from her mother's hands: We don't need this food, Amma!

Someone was gently shaking her awake. Lakshmi sat up with a jolt. 'Here is some ginger coffee.' Amma had a bronze tumbler in her hand. 'Eat this too,' she said and held out pongal heaped on a plantain leaf. Beggar's alms. Still, her hands stretched out involuntarily in hunger. Amma led her to a secluded hallway. They sat on a mat there and ate, then washed their hands in the backyard. When they returned to the room, daylight had spread everywhere. The bride sat there like a doll. Amma must have worked some magic, for the girl's face had been transformed: it looked beautiful, as in a painting of a bejewelled goddess.

'Your father is coming to see you all decked out,' Mirasu Mami said.

Lakshmi stood up abruptly. Her heart started pounding for no apparent reason. As if she had been hit by a spray of thick drizzle, she felt suffocated. Periya Mirasu arrived. To her surprise, clad in a silk veshti and silk stole like Arjuna in the Mahabharata play, he looked exactly like her father in the dream, the one who had told her only a short while ago that he was her father too. But this man hardly spared her a glance. It seemed that here, in this house, his whole personality had changed. A sacred thread slid across his bare chest. The double-stringed golden chain around his neck hung down to his navel. This plump-cheeked Paapa couldn't be his daughter, Lakshmi thought.

Periya Mirasu strode in, and gazed steadily at his daughter, the bride, who asked in a tone of mild anxiety, 'How do I look?'

'Like a gold idol,' Mirasu said with tenderness, his expression brimming with love.

Lakshmi observed him with wide eyes and imagined herself in Paapa's place.

'How do you like the get-up?' Mirasu Mami asked, looking proudly at the bride, as if she had been responsible for the girl's adornment.

Without turning to Thulasi, Mirasu said, 'When Thulasi is on the job, do you even have to ask?' Mirasu Mami's face turned dark with disappointment. 'Perform drishti to protect her from evil eyes,' Mirasu said. Then he left without glancing at Lakshmi even once. It was like a tight slap on Lakshmi's face. She felt sad that her father had deceived her. She blinked back the tears threatening to spill from her eyes. She was filled with rage at her mother, who stood by grinning happily, as if someone had just placed a crown on her head. The servant who had brought them inside appeared suddenly. He told Amma, 'There is a place reserved for you two in the pandal. Bring your daughter along and sit there.'

Lakshmi and Thulasi sat in a section of the outer pandal indicated by the servant. They could hear the jubilant music of Sundaramurthi Mama's nadaswaram. Within a short while, all the families from their street had arrived. Lakshmi was somewhat consoled by the presence of Kasturi, Thilakam and Sabapathi. After being ritually persuaded to abandon his plans for a pilgrimage to Kashi as a renunciate and marry the bride instead, the groom entered the pandal area. He had plump cheeks too.

'A good match for Paapa,' Lakshmi whispered to Kasturi. At her answering laugh, she felt mollified to some extent. But she didn't like anything around her. Periya Mirasu sat proudly on the stage, totally oblivious to the presence of Lakshmi and her mother. Whenever his gaze fell on her inadvertently, Lakshmi would feel a thrill of excitement, but she was bewildered to see no flicker of recognition in his eyes. That he seemed to have no recollection of her face made her feel dejected. After the rituals were over, the marriage feast was served to the guests in batches. Sabapathi and Thilakam grumbled about feeling hungry. 'They'll call us only after everyone has had their meal. Don't wail like some famine-struck ghouls,' Kanagu Paati said. Lakshmi remembered standing with her mother daily in Mirasu's backyard under the midday sun. On seeing them, perhaps Paapa too had said, 'Those famine-struck ghouls are here.'

Lakshmi sat hugging her knees, with her face buried between them. In the dark, she could see Mirasu's face as he said, 'Perform drishti to ward off the evil eye.' He moved to the doorway without seeing her. There was a blazing torch in her hand, like the one tied to Hanuman's tail. As if she had sprouted wings suddenly, she flew upward, carrying the torch. She moved through the air, setting fire to the pandal, which stretched all the way from the front entrance to the backyard. The silver-and-gold tassels were singed in the heat. The white roof of the pandal was charred.

'Lakshmi, have you gone to sleep? Come. They are calling us for lunch.' Kasturi shook her awake. When she opened her eyes and stood up, the roof of the pandal was still white, the tassels glittered like gold in the afternoon sun, the wedding guests had finished their meal and gone home ...

Someone was knocking on the front door. The hinges of the swing screeched as Thulasi sprang up and ran eagerly towards the door like a young girl. Lakshmi looked up at the sound. The fragrance of civet musk wafted in even before Periya Mirasu entered the house. Fully prepared, Lakshmi stood leaning against the pillar in the hall in order to catch his eye. Standing in the centre of the hall, he seemed a very different man. He was not the Periya Mirasu who had strutted regally on the wedding stage as though he was the ruler of the whole world. Wearing a silk veshti in the informal wraparound style and a half-sleeved silk shirt, lips reddened by betel juice and a dot of sandal paste on his forehead, he appeared comfortable and relaxed. His eyes betrayed mild fatigue. He was startled at first on seeing her. Recovering quickly, he said softly, 'Is it Lakshmi? Haven't you gone to bed yet?'

As Lakshmi wondered whether he spoke to her with the same tenderness in his voice that he had while talking to Paapa, Thulasi said with a smile, 'I believe she wants to discuss something with you.'

Periya Mirasu gave Thulasi a perplexed look. She stuck out her lower lip as if to say, 'How would I know?'

'I want to speak privately,' Lakshmi reminded her mother. She waited until Thulasi left and went inside.

'Now? At this late hour?'

'But you come only around this time, don't you?' Lakshmi struggled fiercely to hold back her tears. 'I am not Paapa. If I were, I wouldn't have to wait like this until late in the night.'

The confusion on Mirasu's face had not cleared yet. As if to hide it, he smiled gently and said, 'What you say is true. Are you going to fight with me over that?'

'No fight. I need a favour from you.'

Surprised, he looked at her as if for the first time. 'What help do you want? Tell me.'

'I want to study. I want you to arrange for me to attend the school in town.'

At first, Mirasu was taken aback. Then he asked her with a serene smile, 'Are you saying you don't want this music and dance?'

'I won't even look in that direction.'

To her surprise, Mirasu patted her on the shoulder. 'All right. I will make the arrangements. Don't worry. Go to sleep.'

Lakshmi couldn't believe that she had won the battle so easily. She became so emotional that her eyes welled up. She felt like hugging him. 'Do you actually mean it?'

'Yes, I do. Do you think I am lying?'

She wanted to ask him why he hadn't looked at her at all during the wedding, but paused with her head bowed and reflected briefly. Then she said, 'I want to study in college too. I want to be a lawyer.'

He looked at her in amazement and smiled. 'That's the spirit. Well done! My son is loafing around, refusing to study, and you, a dasi's child, want to go to college.'

'You must pay for my entire education.'

'I told you I'd see to it, didn't I?'

'I'll get a job and return the money you spend on me.'

Periya Mirasu laughed heartily. 'Listen, girl. We'll take care of everything. Go to sleep. Send your mother.'

Dharini grinned. 'So, did you return the money to Grandfather?'

Lakshmi didn't reply. Lost in her memories, she gazed in silence through the window at the sky. Of late, many questions had been gnawing at her heart. How I stood fast at that historic juncture and achieved my aim cannot be reduced to a mere transaction. The courage I had mustered was essential during that period. Those were the days when the nation, land, society were subjected to a great, historic upheaval.

'It was a gigantic churning,' she said instead, like someone talking to herself. 'It left everyone gasping for breath. A radiant moment when all that we believed to be true was exposed as a lie. Many were terrified when they saw that light. Yet, in that process, it was Kasturi who lost her balance.'

'Who is Kasturi?'

5

SHE HAD BEEN feeling out of sorts since morning. There was a throbbing pain in her arms and legs. Kasturi was terrified that she would make a mistake in front of the master in the dance class. Had she complained of body ache, her grandmother would have made her stay back. But the master had told them that he was going to teach an important new varnam today, that too in her favourite Mohana raagam. But her heart would not cooperate with her body. Unable to follow the rhythm during the adavus and jathis, she faltered and stumbled.

'What happened to you? Why are you lagging behind the taalam?'

Stung by shame, she was afraid that she might tear up.

The master got up, came to her and pinched her cheek hard. 'Are you becoming another Lakshmi? If you associate with her, you will never amount to anything.'

Afraid that he might have overheard them talking and laughing together the other day, her throat went dry and tears streamed from her eyes.

The master pinched her cheeks even harder.

'Why are you crying and making a scene? You were never punished as hard as the others. Stop your tantrums and dance. Um ... thaam thithaam thai tha thai.'

A rolling pain slashed through her lower abdomen. Unable to keep standing, she clutched her middle and sat down. 'My stomach is paining, aiya,' she groaned.

The master looked intently at her. Then he turned to his wife. She came up to Kasturi, clasped her shoulder and said, 'Get up. Go home. Ask your grandmother to boil dry ginger in water and give it to you.'

After touching the ground and paying obeisance, Kasturi stepped into the street and walked towards her house at a brisk pace. She couldn't run home as she normally did. Her lower abdomen had become limp and both thighs pained terribly, as if from swollen glands. She knocked on the front door of the house. Not wanting to answer any questions from Sengamalam, who had come to open the door, she said, 'Move. I want to take a shit,' and ran to the backyard. When she washed her sticky groin, the water that flowed at her feet was bloody. Her inner thighs were smeared with blood as well. Fear gripped her. She kept bathing her legs, but the bleeding didn't stop. Anxiety set off palpitations in her chest.

'Kasturi! Kasturi!' Kanagu Paati called out as she came to the backyard. When she saw Kasturi sitting on the steps on the outside of the well, holding her knees close and crying, she asked with a hint of agitation in her voice. 'What's the matter, kannu? What happened?'

Kasturi raised her head, hugged her grandmother and started to weep loudly. 'I feel I am going to die, Paati. The master is teaching a new varnam and it seems like I'll never be able to dance, Paati.'

Paati was taken aback. 'What happened, kannu?'

'I am bleeding, Paati. My skirt is soaked. There's severe pain in my stomach. My thighs are aching.'

Instead of flying into a panic as Kasturi had expected, her grandmother broke into a wide grin. She swept her hands over Kasturi's cheeks and then cracked her knuckles in a gesture intended to ward off the evil eye.

'Why would anyone weep over becoming a woman? It's something to celebrate, kannu. Come and sit here in this sheltered spot. I'll prepare warm water and pour it on your head. Don't be afraid,' Paati said. Standing on the steps leading to the backyard, she called out to Sengamalam, who hurried over and embraced Kasturi.

Kasturi could not get up. She experienced a sharp pain that ran from her lower abdomen to the soles of her feet. 'My whole body is aching, Amma, yet you two are being so cruel and laughing at me.'

Sengamalam chuckled again. Stroking Kasturi's head with affection, she said gently, 'It's something that happens to every girl, kannu. The pain will be gone by tomorrow. Don't be afraid.'

'Did this happen to you, too?'

'Yes, it's happened to me and Paati, and it will happen to Thilakam in a few years. It's something all of us have to experience. Every month, you will bleed like this for three days.'

'Aiyaiyo. I am going to die!'

'Hush, silly! We haven't died of it, have we? If the world has to accept you as a woman, a complete woman, you have to suffer this pain. That's how god has created us. Go ahead and fight with Him, why don't you?'

Kasturi felt that if such a god stood before her, she would fight with Him. This was *such* a torture.

Sengamalam talked further about all manner of things. 'Your life is going to really begin today. My princess will look more beautiful than ever. The blood coursing through your body will change completely. When you do the abhinaya for "I was smitten", the phrase will take on newer meanings for you. Just as the sound rises from a plucked tambura string, your body will tremble when you dance with a full understanding of what it means.'

Kasturi couldn't see any connection between her mother's words and the glitch in her body. But she felt that her mother would have 'understood the meaning' and danced with a delighted expression on her face. Every time she danced to the phrase 'I was smitten', she must have discovered new meanings. 'By whom was she smitten?' The question rose suddenly in her mind. Did her mother have someone like Periya Mirasu? A man who visited her after everyone had gone to sleep—who could it be? Suddenly aware that she had never had such thoughts about her mother, she was embarrassed. She thought of Lakshmi. Lakshmi didn't have any doubts about her mother's life. Surprisingly, Lakshmi had a firm opinion about everything. Even Periya Mirasu himself seemed to be afraid of her, of Lakshmi who was beaten regularly by the master! She remembered what Lakshmi told her when she had come home a couple of days ago.

'I won't go to the master's house any more. I am going to attend school. It's been arranged.'

Kasturi looked at her with surprise. 'By whom?'

'Periya Mirasu.'

'Him? Paapa's father?'

Lakshmi spoke with her head bent. 'He is my father too.'

Incredulous, Kasturi looked at her wide-eyed. What a big shot he was! Was he really Lakshmi's father?

'How, di? The other day, at the wedding, didn't you sit with us?'

Lakshmi said coldly, 'Because outsiders shouldn't come to know that I am his daughter. If they do, it would bring him dishonour.' She added with a bitter laugh, 'The joke is that being his daughter is a disgrace for *me*! I was so angry that day, I felt like torching that pandal.'

Kasturi was taken aback. 'Chee, chee. Only jealous people feel angry like that.'

'Yes, I am jealous. I am jealous of that idiot, Paapa. She can get whatever she wants even without asking. She can call him Appa, hold his hand, sit next to him at mealtimes. She can ride with him in the bullock cart in public and go around the village. Because she can do all these things that I can never do, I am jealous of her. My father doesn't even know that I have such desires. He visits us at night like a thief after I've gone to sleep. He leaves before sunrise. He would hardly remember that I exist.'

As she said all this, a note of agitation was evident in her voice. She sounded as if she was holding back tears with great difficulty.

'Why do you talk like this, di?' Kasturi said in an appeasing tone. 'After all, he is sending you to school.'

'I stayed awake and waited for him last night. I asked him and got something like a promise that he would let me study. I told him I didn't want music and dance. I feel like running away from this place.'

'The school is in the neighbouring town, right? The one within walking distance?'

'Yes. But when I study further in high school and college, I will have to leave this place, won't I?'

'Did you tell your father that you were going to study law, become an advocate?'

Lakshmi laughed. 'Yes, I told him. But I didn't tell him who I was going to sue in my first case. Nor did I tell him that my second suit will be against Periya Mirasu.'

'Why against him, di? For letting you study?'

'For not being brave enough to admit that Lakshmi is his daughter.'

'You are a wicked girl, Lakshmi,' Kasturi said in wonder. Lakshmi's talk confused her. Though Lakshmi was only a year older, she seemed to possess a degree of clarity about most things that bewildered Kasturi. Her anger and fury remained beyond Kasturi's understanding.

She still couldn't believe it. Periya Mirasu was Lakshmi's father. Even if he would not admit that she was his daughter, she was able to negotiate with him and have her wishes fulfilled. To the children in that street, 'father' was a metaphor. They had grown up without even realizing the need for one. No one yearned for that abstraction of a person. But when Lakshmi revealed a sign of her longing, questions began to gnaw at Kasturi from within for the first time. She didn't know whether anyone came home the way Lakshmi's father sneaked in like a thief after everyone had gone to sleep.

Kanagu Paati prepared a bowl of warm water into which she threw a bunch of neem leaves and dissolved a pinch of vermilion for the aarti, a ceremony of welcome. Together with Sengamalam, she performed the aarti for Kasturi, the new woman, and symbolically removed the drishti from her. Then she anointed Kasturi's face, waist and stomach with a paste made of finely ground green turmeric and bathed her from head to toe. The warm water soothed her aching body. As she dried Kasturi's hair with a towel, Paati said, 'You mustn't cry, kannu. This is something that happens to every girl.'

As if she wasn't listening, Kasturi looked up at her grandmother's face and said, 'Paati, who is my father?'

Paati was so taken aback that her towelling hand stopped abruptly. 'Why do you bring it up now?'

'I want to know.'

Paati said calmly, 'It's an unnecessary question for people born in this clan, kannu.'

'Lakshmi knows who her father is.'

As she resumed towelling Kasturi's body briskly, Paati said in a tone of mild irritation, 'That Thulasi brags about Periya Mirasu visiting her house, so the whole village has come to know. There is no man from the landowners' quarter who doesn't visit Dasi Street. Their wives know about it; they just pretend not to notice. If it becomes public knowledge, none of the wives will stand for it. Didn't you see how Periya Mirasu's wife demeaned Thulasi at Paapa's wedding? Did she get special treatment as Periya Mirasu's mistress? Didn't Thulasi set off before sunrise, all hurry and bustle, to do the costumes and make-up for Paapa? That woman didn't even buy Thulasi a sari for the occasion.'

Kasturi didn't understand a word of Paati's outburst. But she was clear about one thing: her father must be someone from the landowners' quarter. But it was a secret relationship that no one could know about. She could not claim kinship with her father, whoever he was. If the secret of his identity were revealed, she might feel just as angry as Lakshmi. She might say, 'Chee, chee. Why do you visit only at night, like a thief?'

Paati helped Kasturi into a clean dress. To check the bleeding, she tore off a section from an old sari, folded it several times, drew it over the girl's groin and secured it at her waist. 'Let me know when it's soaked, I'll give you another one,' she said.

Kasturi was frightened by the changes in her body. Throughout the day, her pelvis and thighs throbbed with pain.

She wanted to lie down and never get up. Seeing the blood that soaked and spread on the cloth covering her groin, she felt scared. Though no attention was paid to her agony, snacks were prepared in the kitchen by specially hired cooks as if for a grand function. After three days, she was again given a ceremonial bath from head to toe with turmeric water. She was made to sit on a polished wooden plank and many rites were conducted. Kanagu Paati invited all the residents in the street and served them a fine feast. Everyone ritually swept their hands over her cheeks to ward off the evil eye and gave her money or silk cloth before leaving. Lakshmi didn't come. 'She has gone to school,' Thulasi said.

Lakshmi dropped by in the evening to see Kasturi. She had plaited her hair into twin braids.

'How is school, then?' Kasturi asked her eagerly.

'It's wonderful,' Lakshmi said with zest. 'Just the thought that I won't get beaten by that dance master is such a relief.'

Kasturi wondered for a moment whether she should tell Lakshmi that the master had scolded her too and pinched her cheeks, then decided against it. 'Have you come of age yet, Lakshmi?' she said.

'Not yet. Whenever it happens, I have told my mother not to conduct any rituals.'

'Did she agree?'

'How could she not?'

Kasturi was amazed by her reply.

'These are the customs followed in our clan. We *have* to observe them, Paati says.'

'Such a wretched clan this is.'

'Why do you get so angry, di?'

'I am surprised that you don't, Kasturi.'

Kasturi didn't see a lot of Lakshmi after that. Most of her time was spent in preparing for school lessons, Lakshmi explained. Since she had scored high marks, they had put her in a class two years ahead, she said, using an English word for it. Though Kasturi was glad that Lakshmi seemed to be much happier than before, it felt as if she had travelled to a different world. She realized later that Lakshmi could no longer enjoy a conversation with her.

Now when Lakshmi asked her 'How are you, Kasturi?' she replied in all innocence, 'Oh, I am fine. The master has taught us a new varnam. It's a composition by the legendary Thanjavur brothers. Don't ask how complicated the jathis are. Each one takes an hour to practice. We have to change our dress when we finish; we sweat so much that we are soaked right through. Will you drop by one of these days? I'll perform it for you.'

'I'll take your leave now,' Lakshmi said. She never came again.

Kasturi felt sad that an unbridgeable distance had set in between her and Lakshmi. It had been three years since she last met her friend. As there was no high school in the nearby town, Lakshmi had moved to Thanjavur with her mother.

'The girl has developed all kinds of unseemly habits,' Kamalam Mami complained to Paati. 'Thulasi would have done better to birth a prickly plant instead of this girl.'

Though she didn't understand what it meant, Kasturi developed a permanent dislike for Kamalam Mami.

'There's a cool breeze outside. Come, let's go to the terrace,' Kanagu Paati said to Kasturi.

'Yes, let's go.' Kasturi got up instantly. 'Should I call Thilakam?'

'No need. The evening dew won't suit her. She might catch a sore throat. As dance is for you, singing is Thilakam's fortune.'

'Let me fetch something warm.'

Kasturi picked up a blanket and set out for the terrace. As her reflection appeared in the full-length mirror on the door of the teak wood cupboard, she felt proud for a moment. A slender build, at once voluptuous and elegant, ivory complexion, shapely eyes and nose, long curly hair—hers was a body made for dance. *She* was born to dance. Her own mother, Sengamalam, didn't have such a beautiful face. Kasturi was sired by a person who was faceless to her. It was unlikely that she would ever come to know the secret of his identity. Being curious about it was a futile exercise.

Paati was waiting on the terrace. When she spread the quilt, it was covered by milky white moonlight. The terrace was cool as if it had no connection to the sultriness inside the house.

'Tomorrow is a full moon,' Kanagu Paati said as she sat down on the quilt.

'Shall we eat dinner by moonlight tomorrow, Paati?' Kasturi said, lying down with her head in Kanagu's lap.

'Let's keep it for the next full moon night,' Kanagu Paati said. 'We have another engagement tomorrow.' Her face appeared very gentle. The diamond studs she wore in her ears glinted in the moonlight.

'What function, Paati?'

Kanagu stroked her hair softly. 'It's your wedding day tomorrow, kannu.'

Kasturi sat upright immediately.

'What do you mean, Paati?' she said, taken aback. What Paati said sounded ludicrous.

'It's a marriage between you and god, kannu, as per the custom of our clan.'

'What! Kasturi laughed. 'Is it the god in our temple?'

'Yes.'

'But it's only an idol.'

'For us, it's real.'

Paati seemed to have journeyed to some other world. She continued to talk, lost in her own depths.

'Once you stand in the deity's chamber, say, "I am your slave," and wear the bottu, you will have a higher status than the priest who performs worship for the deity. You will attain that position only when you excel in the arts. Remember, the temple trustees held a dance competition? It was a test by which experts selected the best after a lot of scrutiny. That position is yours now. It's your good fortune—and ours. God is your husband. You will always be an auspicious woman, auspicious forever. There will be no ill fortune in your life. It's a position that everyone born in this clan aspires to.'

Kasturi could not understand anything. 'Lakshmi says ours is a despicable clan.'

Kanagu Paati felt a stab of fury. 'She goes to school and studies English, doesn't she? She would talk like that. She has no taste or flair for the arts. You were born to pursue this art, child. Never mind Lakshmi. Go stand in the deity's chamber and dance. You'll see that no thought occurs to you but that you are His servant. "This be the gate, this be the gate"—when you dance to this line, the gates of heaven will open for you. What I'm saying is the sacred truth.' Tears fell from Paati's eyes.

On that cool moonlit night, Kasturi felt that every word Paati had spoken was true. Paati started to sing then. With her voice mellow and soothing, eyes streaming with tears, face glowing and radiant, it seemed to Kasturi that Kanagu Paati was truly immersed in the ecstasy of standing before the gates of heaven.

6

After the sudden thunderstorm last night, the weather had turned colder today. When I drew back the heavy curtains covering the glass window and looked out, the world was swathed in a blanket of mist. The flowering plants in the garden were not visible. In a short while, the mist would begin to lift, like a shadow receding gradually.

When the rain began to pelt down yesterday, I rushed to the window and looked outside. The watery expanse of the lake glittered as if countless diamonds had been sprinkled on it. In the light from the Carlton Hotel, the raindrops falling from above appeared to fly into the lake like silver arrows, spreading ripples of white foam and scattering a profusion of stars.

It must have rained like this on that day as well. The last line that Amma wrote in her diary: 'Rain is pouring down like wires drawn between the sky and the earth … no, not wires, but arrows flying.'

Why did the sentence end there? What had stopped her from writing further?

I had asked Appa many times, in many different ways. 'I didn't know she wrote in a diary,' he had said. Now that I thought about it, that seemed possible too. When the diary was discovered, it was strange to find only this page with her writing on it. Among the preceding pages, some were blank; a few others seemed to have been ripped out. Who had torn them? Had she done it herself before seeking an end to her life? Yes … she must have. What secrets did they hold that she didn't want others to know? How many things could there be that Appa and I didn't know about her? The question induced a feeling of guilt. I wondered whether it was at all possible to know a person fully, even someone who was very close. While I was bewildered by such reflections about Amma, I also felt that her memory might be fading for both me and Appa. That in itself might be the reason for our confusion. On many occasions, Appa just blinked, unable to respond to my reminiscences about Amma.

'Leave me alone,' he would plead, as if he wanted to erase the very memory of Amma whereas I agonized over the prospect of her memory disappearing entirely from our lives one day.

'Nothing can be as tragic as the memories of those close to us fading away,' Joan, my classmate in New York, often said. After her boyfriend Mark died suddenly in an accident, she said that she was haunted by a feeling of emptiness, of no longer having a life. I know that she had taken medication for a long time to ward off depression.

'I've stopped taking medicines now,' she said when we ran into each other one day.

'Good,' I said. 'It means that you have reconciled.'

She was quick to deny it. 'This is not a grief with which one can be easily reconciled. I was afraid that those pills were blunting my memory. One day I found myself wondering about the colour of the shirt that Mark had worn on the day he died. I couldn't remember. I had loved him deeply. I had given him that shirt myself to wear that day. Yet, for the life of me, I couldn't remember the colour of that shirt. How disgraceful!'

She seemed on the verge of an emotional collapse. I was worried.

'Have you had any problems since you stopped the medication? Does your doctor know?'

There was no sign that she had heard the question. She seemed to be immersed in her own thoughts.

'I woke up before I became a total slave to those pills, Maya. You'll be surprised if I tell you what I've been doing these days.'

'Are you learning yoga? Have you been snared by some Indian godman?'

'No.' She laughed. 'Yoga is good, isn't it? But I heard it requires a lot of time. Where is the time in our daily rush, Maya! No, I sing in a choir now.'

'In a church?' I asked, amazed.

'Yes,' she said with a smile. 'It gives me peace of mind. At night, I fall asleep like a baby.'

I was genuinely taken aback by the change in Joan. Until Mark's death, she had never indulged in any kind of religious belief. She never even went to church.

'I am of a different blood,' Joan had said one day.

'How? Has your blood changed?' I laughed.

'No.' She beamed. 'Until now, I believed only my mother's blood flowed in my veins. Now I realize that I carry my father's genes as well.'

I didn't understand a word of what she was saying. She laughed suddenly. 'My mother used to say that we are born carrying a burden. As if I wanted to challenge her, I told her that she was the one who carried a burden; I had none.'

I walked with her in silence. We were strolling in New York City's Central Park. Some distance away, a few children were kicking a ball around. Some others were looking curiously at a horse-drawn buggy. A young black couple sat on a bench. A group of white tourists was relaxing on another bench.

'My poor mother carried a burden all her life. She believed that some lives were cursed, and *that* became her burden, I think. She could not free herself from memories of the past.'

'What memories?'

Instead of replying immediately, she picked up a small pebble from the ground and threw it in the artificial pond nearby, as if to rid herself of something that was weighing on her. For some time, we watched the water eddy and flow outward.

Keeping her eyes on the pond, she said, 'My mother migrated to this country from Germany. While studying in a college here, she met my father and married him. But she didn't reveal one thing: she was born in a gypsy tribe. She kept it a closely guarded secret. When it was revealed by chance, there was an uproar. My father left home.'

I was startled. 'Why?'

'My father is a Catholic who is intensely attached to his faith. He should have become a priest. Getting married was a mistake.'

'I still don't understand, Joan,' I said in confusion. I remembered the witches in Shakespeare's *Macbeth*. Had the shadow of those symbols followed us in this century too?

'Haven't you heard about gypsies?' Joan said, and continued without waiting for a reply. 'Through the ages, they've been branded as sorcerers, sinners and mortal enemies of Christians. The bigotry continues to this day. Though some of them converted to Christianity, majority didn't adopt it as their religion; they still worshipped different gods, followed other rituals. There are plenty of stories about how Christians threw stones at the very sight of them and chased them away. They've been put in prison, even murdered. There are obviously no records left of the horrors inflicted on them. Though the people and their lifestyle have changed altogether, Christian society still treats them in a disgraceful way, worse than the Jews. Do you know something ironic? Even Jews are hostile to gypsies and chase them away. They're not even issued identity cards in many European countries.'

What Joan said sounded incredible to me. Whenever news about the caste atrocities that happened routinely in India even today were brought to light in American newspapers, I felt humiliated by the shameful reality that formed the backdrop to such incidents. Learning that similar bigotry and prejudice existed even in developed countries stunned me.

'Someone from my mother's town came visiting one day and betrayed the secret while we were at dinner. My father was beside himself with rage.'

My surprise wouldn't subside. Nowhere else in the world was society as hybrid as it was in America. To think that this couple—who had fallen in love, unmindful of differences in religion, language and geography, and got married—could separate for such a conventional reason shocked me even more.

'More than her being a gypsy, I think he couldn't forgive the fact that she had hidden the truth from him,' Joan said.

I fell silent. I remembered Appa's inexplicable bouts of anger. Though they were people of different tastes, Appa and Amma had no major differences in matters of principle. That's why they could still live together, I thought.

'"Why did you hide it from him?" I asked my mother,' Joan said. '"I loved him and I was afraid he would reject me if he knew the truth," she said.' She laughed. 'What a fool she was! She lived a false life because of that, walked around with a burden. Unable to bear its weight, she would have dropped and broken it herself, or taken her own life.'

Joan's claim that singing in the church choir brought her peace of mind seemed like an attempt to forget her gypsy ancestry. However, during the same period Joan also undertook the task of researching her roots. I watched her check out a large number of books from the library and immerse herself in studying them. She even chose the same subject as the topic for her PhD thesis.

'Do you know something? My gypsy ancestors migrated from western India to Europe!' she had told me enthusiastically once.

'Both of us carry the same set of genes,' she had added after deep reflection. 'Scientists say that all human communities are in fact descended from the same primitive mother. Yet we keep dividing people like idiots. When I meet my father some day, I will try my best to demolish his foolish ideas. Even if he is angry that my mother had hidden the truth from him, he should understand why she felt compelled to hide it.'

These days she seldom spoke about Mark. She seemed to have almost forgotten him. I thought it was a good sign. I wonder why I suddenly remembered Joan today. My mind had jumped from memories of Amma to thinking of Joan. It was she who had said: there was nothing more tragic than the memories of those closest to us fading away.

I opened the curtains wide. Outside, the mist had lifted. Laden with the weight of dewdrops, the roses near the window had closed their petals. There was water on the glass windowpanes, as if sprayed by the drizzle. The lake was visible in the distance, glittering under the mild sun. It had a persona all its own. Its character changed with the time of day. It occurred to me, oddly enough, that Amma would have thought so too.

I exercised a little and put on my walking shoes. When I stepped out of the room, I saw Ganesan in the kitchen. He was a young man who cooked and did the housework for us. On seeing me, he said, 'Tea is ready, 'ma. Drink it before you set out.'

Moments later, he brought a steaming cup of tea on a tray and offered it to me courteously. Too courteously, I thought, feeling awkward. Though I had told him time and again that he could walk around the house in slippers, he preferred being barefoot. 'Not used to it,' he would say with a smile.

Even on the streets, in this biting cold, many people of his community who worked in the tea gardens here walked around in their bare feet. It troubled me to see them, but he would explain cheerfully, 'It's not because of poverty, 'ma. We cover our heads with a woollen blanket but leave our feet bare. The earth should touch our feet. Something would be amiss only if we let the dew fall on our heads.'

What he said seemed like an attractive philosophy. I never spoke to him about slippers after that.

The hot tea was refreshing and filled me with cheer. 'What are you going to make for tiffin?'

'I am planning on making idiyappam.'

Delighted, I said, 'Great! Will there be stew to go with it?'

'Of course, madam.'

'Excellent!' I laughed and started out.

The moment I stepped beyond the doorway, a gust of cold wind embraced me. The sun shone brightly, splintering through the clouds. Muffler tied around his head, Kuppusamy, the gardener, was busy weeding the lawn. He saw me and said, 'Vanakkam, 'ma.' I nodded at him, opened the gate and walked towards the lake. Just like ours, the neighbouring houses were also independent bungalows with a large compound. If someone was killed within, no outsider would know. There were no permanent residents here. People visited only during the season. Why did my mother, who worked in the north, want to come south for her vacations? 'I was born there. I want to die there too,' she had once told me. 'Don't talk about dying,' I retorted, my eyes filling with tears. Amma had laughed and hugged me. 'Silly! It was only in a manner of speaking. Everyone must die some day. When I grow old, you must take me there.'

I still remember her hugging me and the warmth from that embrace. Her smell, too. Somehow, a sweet fragrance always lingered around Amma. I could never tell whether the fragrance came from her body or her clothes. Now, when I open her cupboard, the same fragrance wafts out, as if she is there in the flesh.

Amma must have lost confidence in me. That's why she sought her end by herself, without waiting for me to bring her here.

I shook my head to clear it and walked on. I shouldn't be thinking about Amma through all my waking hours; I'll go mad. What I have come here to accomplish won't get done. Though the memories came like puppies snapping at my heels, I shooed them away as I walked. Among the pine trees standing tall on the hillside to my left, there were single, isolated bungalows at many levels. At the very top was a lone, tall mansion that seemed to touch the sky. No one knew who the owner was. Amma had looked at it once and said, 'How nice it would be to live there.' I was ten years old at the time. I remembered the story of Jack and the beanstalk. If one planted a hyacinth seed in the garden of that house, the stalk might actually grow upwards and touch the sky. When I told my mother that if I climbed it like Jack had, it would take me straight to paradise, she stroked my back with affection and smiled. She had looked very beautiful then.

I don't know if she developed an acquaintance with the people in that house later.

Absorbed in my thoughts, I had walked to the wrong part of the lake. By then, a crowd of visitors had begun to arrive in the vicinity of Sims Park. Horse-ride vendors were luring young children with a display of horses. I passed them with quick strides. As I hurried by rows of shops selling woollen wear, fruits and sweets, it felt as if the human energy all around and its vitality had no connection with me. I wanted to escape, to run away from there. It was sheer madness to have wandered to this side of the lake. As I looked around bewildered, my eyes fell on a narrow track that cut across the road and went upward. The steep climb spurred my interest. I took a deep breath and started up that path. Its beauty stunned me. Tall tress stood on either side, so tall that their tops were not visible. I was reminded of my visit to Muir Wood Forest, a nature park maintained by the US government near San Francisco in California that is filled with giant redwood trees that are several hundred years old. These trees, too, might be as old, I thought. They were witnesses to the history of an era. They would know secrets not recorded in the pages of that history, secrets that were embedded in their leaves instead. Since there was not a lot of sunlight in the area, the air was cool. The solitude there was very pleasant. How had I not discovered this path all these days? As I ambled along the path, gazing upward, with no grasp of its beginning or its end, I stumbled on something. I almost fell but someone caught hold of me.

'This is what happens when you walk without looking at the ground.'

I recovered my balance and looked around. A toothless old woman stood there laughing. Standing beside her, holding on to her sari, was a young boy.

'Thank you, Paati,' I said.

The old woman looked at the boy.

'She is saying nandri in English,' he whispered to her.

'For what?' The old woman laughed. Her question was drawn out like a melody. 'Why are you walking alone in this forest area, girl?'

'This spot is very beautiful. I discovered it only today. Why should anyone be afraid to come here?'

'There isn't much light here. We are used to it. You are a city girl. If I talk of spirits and demons, you won't believe me. Anyhow, it's best if you come here with a man. That's all I'll say.'

I found the old woman's warning interesting. The boy was staring at me without taking his eyes away even for a moment.

'Then I'll have to look for a man.' I laughed as though I was talking to someone familiar.

'Are you not married yet?' she enquired fondly.

When I shook my head to say no, she said, 'Why not bring your mother?'

As I tried to come up with a reply, the boy pulled her by the hand, saying, 'Come, Aaththa. Let's go,' and forced her to leave. He must have found our conversation boring. When they had moved out of earshot, he said something to her. The old woman turned abruptly and looked at me with surprise in her eyes. There was something else, too, in those eyes. Then, holding the boy's hand, she walked swiftly down the path.

I resumed my stroll in a state of confusion. What could have caused the dread I had seen in the old woman's eyes? The question stood tall before me, blocking my way.

Suddenly, I remembered.

He was the boy I had met the other day on the lakeshore. I couldn't recognize him in his woollen cap.

7

Suppuni was staring at the performance, transfixed. There was a huge crowd at the temple. They had come not for a darshan of the deity, but to watch Kasturi dance.

'There is no difference between the two,' Suppuni murmured.

He was shocked at himself. If Appa had an inkling of his train of thought, the old man would punch his own forehead to atone for the sacrilege. Suppuni had often witnessed his father torment himself in this fashion, as though he was trying to take on the burden of other people's sins and punish himself for them. Did Appa imagine that such contrition would lead to his own deliverance as well as that of those who had done wrong? There was an obstinate fury in the old man's behaviour that Suppuni found intimidating. While everyone was looking at the stage, his father sat in the sanctum sanctorum where the main deity was installed.

'What is he doing there?' Suppuni wondered wearily. 'There is nothing wrong with my thinking,' he told himself. 'Those who watch Kasturi's dance with an aesthete's delight will certainly feel the joy of seeing god in the flesh.'

When he had said as much to Kamu last night, she had said, 'What is aesthetic delight?'

'Duffer! It's exactly what you don't have.' He mock-punched her cheek. She giggled, because he had his arms around her. Kamu was no Rati, that heavenly epitome of female beauty. But she was a good girl; she treated his mother with love and respect. A simpleton. It wouldn't even occur to her to take anything amiss. She didn't wince when he reached for her at night. He could sense that she too waited eagerly for those nightly pleasures. What more could one want in a wife?

From where he sat, he had a clear view of Kasturi's performance. She was enacting a varnam in Bhairavi raagam. 'The god of Love shoots his arrows.' As her mother and younger sister burnished the line over and over again, Kasturi whirled and swayed, pining for love. Suppuni was sure that every wretched man in the crowd was in a trance, imagining that he was the one she longed for. It made him angry. He worried that some man in his stupor might grab Kasturi's hand. He was itching to put a security ring around her. But this was god's chamber. Nothing untoward would happen here. He knew that Kasturi was in love with the Lord—with all her heart. He could see it. When she touched the ground and then her eyes as a mark of respect for the stage, turned towards the deity's chamber and prayed for a moment with her eyes closed, paying obeisance from her posture in aramandi, and then looked up, a change came over her. It was like a chemical transformation. A divine radiance lit up her face as if the Lord himself had merged with her. Once she started dancing, she traversed a different world. It must be Kailasa, the abode of Siva, or Vaikunth, where Vishnu resided, Suppuni thought. She saw neither the lusty men who ogled her with their tongues hanging out nor the assembly of devotees. Once, a visitor had arrived from the court of Pudukottai. 'That man never took his eyes off you the whole time, Kasturi,' Suppuni told her in a voice tinged with jealousy.

'I don't notice anything, Suppuni.' She had laughed. 'I have eyes only for the Lord.'

And, no matter when she danced at the temple, from the waking ceremony at dawn to the bedchamber ceremony at night, the expressions on her face attested to that truth. It was as if her performance was a conversation solely between her and god, one specially dedicated to him. When the idol was taken in a procession through the streets, she would dance in front of the deity, oblivious to the clusters of people standing around and watching her.

'That may be true during puja, but this is an open assembly, no?'

'How does it matter, Suppuni? The place is not important for me, only the dance is. When I dance, I feel like I am soaring in the sky. As if all kinds of doors are opening. Do you understand what I'm saying?'

He nodded eagerly. 'I do, indeed. But it's an imaginary world, Kasturi.'

She gave him a pretty smile, her teeth shining bright like a string of pearls. 'That's what you think. For me, it's real.'

Before leaving, she turned to him gracefully and said, 'You can ask Sundaramurthi Mama if you wish. Ask him what he feels while playing the naayanam. He might explain it in a way that you can understand.'

'So, you think I don't know anything,' he muttered in dismay.

'No, no. That's sacrilege, Suppuni. You are a great connoisseur, but not an artist.'

Suppuni was silent, stricken by a disappointment he could not name.

Playfully bringing her palms together, she bowed to him with mock deference. 'Respected Suppuni Aiya, please forgive me. Everyone need not be an artist. Connoisseurs are important too. If there is no one to enjoy it, for whom shall we dance?'

'But you say you dance for the gods.'

She burst into peals of laughter. 'I may say it's for god, but I dance only for myself. I am my own connoisseur. I'll say this, Suppuni. I'll dance so long as there's strength left in my body. If I am asked to stop, I'll die.'

He was moved. 'Kasturi, don't talk like that! Not even in jest,' he protested.

She laughed again. 'Is this a time for jest?' She hummed the song and mimed a gesture.

He felt a strong urge to take her in his arms and taste those ruby lips. She came near him suddenly. As the fragrance of sandalwood embraced him, she said, 'I share a bond with the deity in this chamber. I'll never be in such peril.'

He believed that it was true. There really was a spiritual connection between her and the deity. A strange charade—that this bond was enabled only by means of a worldly knot—was enacted in the name of tradition and ritual. The shame of being a witness to that ceremony tormented him for some reason. He still remembered how shocked he had been to watch her marry the deity. Even today, the memory made the roots of his hair tingle.

Kasturi had been adorned like a bride and brought to the temple in a palanquin that day. His father was so busy with temple duties that Suppuni did not dare ask him to explain. The very idea that Kasturi was going to marry some stranger and leave the village made his stomach turn. When he asked someone in the crowd who the groom was, the man laughed. 'Who else will marry a dasi?' Suppuni blinked. 'She is marrying the deity.'

Suppuni was taken aback. 'The deity in the sanctum sanctorum?'

'Yes, but only in name.' The man laughed. 'Though the deity is supposed to tie the bottu, it's the priest who will tie it.'

Stunned, Suppuni moved away and watched the ritual. What the man said was true. After the auspicious cord was placed on the deity for a brief moment, it was his father who fetched it and tied it around Kasturi's neck. Unable to stay there, Suppuni hurried home. Spasms of grief racked him over and over again. He sat on the ground beside the well with his head buried between his knees and sobbed his heart out. His mother, who had come to the backyard for something, saw him and became flustered. 'What happened, da? What is it? Did your father scold you?'

He sat there for some time, without responding to her queries, crying. In truth, even he wasn't sure why he was weeping. He got up and, as if in a frenzy, drew water from the well and poured it over his head repeatedly until he was exhausted. By the time he changed his clothes and went to the temple, the noontime puja was over and his father was locking up. Kasturi and the others had left. He peered intently at his father's face, but could detect no sign of agitation there.

Though the deity is supposed to tie the bottu …

Just as his father often did, Suppuni punched himself on the head for this sacrilegious thought. The following month, his father married off seventeen-year-old Suppuni to ten-year-old Kamakshi. Suppuni suspected that his mother might have told her husband about the scene near the well. He was surprised that his mother wasn't angry at his father.

Now, whenever Kasturi danced in the temple, Appa sat in the sanctum sanctorum as though he had nothing to do with it. But Appa's involvement was over after tying the bottu on that day. Those who came with entitlements were of a different kind. In the front row was the owner of their principality's royal palace, a man addressed simply as 'Raja'. He sat imperiously, wearing a silk robe and a gold-bordered silk stole around his shoulders. Suppuni doubted his ability to appreciate Kasturi's art. That Kasturi might not have such concerns worried him. He found it disappointing that she didn't bother too much about it. A few times, he had noticed her getting into the carriage sent for her from the palace. No expression ever surfaced on that chiselled face. He had brooded over what might happen in the palace. How would Kasturi conduct herself with Raja, a man old enough to be her father? Would she be happy? Imagining her lying in Raja's arms inflamed him. Too restless to sleep, he would toss and turn on the mat. He would masturbate, then go to the well and bathe in cold water from head to toe. He knew that his bathing at unearthly hours didn't escape his father's notice. But Appa never asked him to explain. Fortunately, having attained puberty at eleven, Kamakshi came to lie with him when she was only twelve years old. During many nights, when he slept with Kamakshi, he found it pleasurable to fantasize that he was with Kasturi. Unable to bear his reckless passion, Kamakshi would become weak and drained. 'Enough. Let me go.' Her feeble cry would bring him down to earth. Still, his heart would be full from the satisfaction of sleeping several times with Kasturi.

No one but the deity is present for me ...

Could it be true? When she sang '*So wicked is the ecstasy of lust*', was the desire in her eyes meant only for the deity?

The concert was over. Many among the seated guests gifted purses of cash. Kasturi received them politely and handed them over to her mother. Suppuni was embarrassed to see the elated expression on Sengamalam's face. Raja looked at Sengamalam and made a sign; she nodded.

'She is saying that she will send her daughter,' Suppuni thought.

After the concert, the crowd dispersed quickly. Only a handful went to the main deity's chamber to pay obeisance to the Lord. Sundaramurthi started playing 'pallandu', the verse of benediction in the Tamil Vaishnavite tradition. There must have been something alluring in his nadaswaram. Those who had gone all the way to the entrance came back and sat on the pyol to listen. Suppuni was in the deity's chamber, assisting his father. The devotees had left. Sundaramurthi played mangalam, the coda to the evening's concert.

'Carry on, Suppuni. I'll finish the night puja and come home,' his father said. Since he was not used to asking why or disobeying instructions, Suppuni set out from the chamber. When he came to the outer pathway, Sundaramurthi was getting ready to leave. Wondering whether Kasturi had gone to the palace, Suppuni nodded and smiled at Sundaramurthi.

'Suppuni Thambi. Wait. I'll come with you.'

Sundaramurthi was probably as old as Suppuni's father. But, being from a lower caste, he had never addressed Suppuni informally, not even by mistake. Except for residents of the Brahmins' quarter, everyone in the temple, even people who were much older than him, addressed him only as 'Chinna Gurukkal Aiya'. Suppuni had never given it much thought. Kasturi had also addressed him the same way initially. But after he asked her to, she started addressing him by his name and in familiar terms whenever they were alone together. He was glad of this secret between them.

Both men didn't speak until they had passed the goddess's chamber and crossed the temple's entrance. They went down the steps of the temple tank to wash their hands. In the darkness, the light from a distant lamp fell on the water, spreading out as gold and silver strands across the surface as soon as they dipped their feet.

'Kasturi's dance tonight was incredible,' Suppuni said.

'When is it not?' Sundaramurthi remarked.

'True, indeed,' Suppuni agreed. 'Do you know what makes me feel bad?' he asked a few moments later with some hesitation. 'Not all the people who come to see her dance are there to appreciate the performance.'

Sundaramurthi offered no reply. 'Shall we sit and relax here for some time? Do you have to leave in a hurry?' he said instead.

'No, no,' Suppuni responded eagerly, as if he was Sundaramurthi's cohort now. Because of his temple duties, he never had the opportunity to chat with Sundaramurthi at leisure. All he could do was listen to the older man playing the nadaswaram and enjoy the music. Moreover, the age difference between them would normally inhibit Suppuni from speaking casually with him.

Sundaramurthi took a piece of tobacco from the string pouch at his waist and popped it in his mouth.

'Should we expect everyone who comes to see the dance to be a connoisseur?' he said in an even tone. 'When it is the dancers' vocation by birth, how could they worry about all this?'

'When I look at them, I feel bad.'

Sundaramurthi laughed. 'Kasturi doesn't bother about such things.'

'She has told me that she doesn't even see them,' Suppuni said, as though he was sharing a secret.

Sundaramurthi remained silent for some time. A few stars twinkled in the sky. Suppuni thought it might rain later that night. There was no breeze, and the air was sultry.

'When you are utterly in love with the art, no humiliation can affect you. Kasturi was born only to dance.'

Concealing the emotions that roiled within, Suppuni said, 'Like you are born only to play this naayanam.'

Sundaramurthi didn't say a word. He gazed at the sky again. Suppuni realized that this love must be the reason why the other man was never stung by the indignities inflicted on him.

When he was nine or ten, there was a wedding in Periya Mirasu's house. Sundaramurthi's son, Manickam was four years younger than Suppuni. They used to play marbles on the riverbank. Suppuni remembered how a famished Manickam had curled up in the outer mandapam on the day of the wedding. Periya Mirasu had sent for Appa one day, and he had accompanied his father. Appa did astrological predictions, and selected auspicious days and periods for weddings and other ceremonies.

'Select two of three dates, Gurukkal Aiya. You know that the girl's birth star is Swati,' Periya Mirasu said. He was sitting on a chair in the middle of the courtyard, one ankle resting on the other knee. As he talked, he kept shaking one foot vigorously. A manai was placed in the courtyard for Suppuni's father to sit on. Appa was busy doing some calculations, frequently consulting the almanac. Suppuni looked around with interest. Shining pillars made of teak wood. A swing with its four corners ferruled in silver gleamed in the hall. It was a huge mansion. Going from the entrance to the rear bay took as long as making one round of the spacious inner pathway of the temple.

As soon as Appa gave the dates, Periya Mirasu summoned a farmhand and said, 'Ask Sundaramurthi to come here immediately.'

Sundaramurthi arrived at a trot, breathless and perspiring, in the next ten minutes. Manickam came too. He smiled at Suppuni. When he played the nadaswaram, Sundaramurthi looked regal, but now, as he stood before Periya Mirasu, he seemed a different man: a lowly, bowing servant.

'Come,' Mirasu said. 'There are three auspicious dates for Paapa's wedding. Tell me which one would suit you. You have to play during the jaanavaasam ceremony to welcome the groom on the eve of the wedding. You should definitely play "*Saraguna Palimpa*".'

Sundaramurthi was all smiles. 'Certainly. Of course,' he said and confirmed one of the three dates.

Suppuni remembered how the crowd had stood transfixed during the jaanavaasam, enchanted by the beauty of Sundaramurthi's '*Saraguna Palimpa*'. During dinner that night, Suppuni's father told the man who was serving the food, 'Chandru, give Sundaramurthi two extra scoops of paayasam. For the way he played the Kedaragowlam melody, he deserves an entire kingdom.'

'He'll get what's left over after everyone has finished eating,' Chandru said.

After dinner, Appa said, 'Go home, Suppuni. I'll be late.'

Suppuni took off in a flash. That Appa had, uncharacteristically for him, applauded the musicians today pleased his heart, as though he was the one being praised. He wanted to find Sundaramurthi and tell him that Appa had even asked for extra paayasam to be served to him. But the nadaswaram and thavil players were nowhere to be found. Suppuni walked on, looking for them. All the bustle of the wedding had died down by now. Those who had carried the petromax lamps on their heads for the jaanavaasam had left. Although it was enveloped in darkness, the street was clearly visible in the flickering light from the mud lamps in a few houses here and there.

The musicians were sitting in the mandapam on the riverbank. Manickam was fast asleep.

'Haven't you all had dinner?' Suppuni asked.

'Of course, we will—in a bit.' Sundaramurthi chuckled. 'How was our "*Saraguna Palimpa*"?'

'It was excellent. Appa asked Chandru to give you extra paayasam for playing it so well.'

Sundaramurthi laughed with pleasure. He nodded vigorously and looked at the others.

'Aren't you coming to eat?' Suppuni asked.

'Our food will be brought right here, thambi.'

'When?'

'When all the batches of guests have finished eating,' the thavil player said.

Suppuni didn't ask why. 'But Manickam has gone to sleep.'

'We will wake him up when the food comes. You should go home, thambi.'

Suppuni remained sitting there, making no effort to leave.

Sundaramurthi hummed a melody in a low octave. 'Do you know which raagam this is?'

'Senchurutti,' Suppuni said.

'Excellent!' Sundaramurthi commended him. Immediately, he started singing a kaavadi chindu. He had sung two more songs before a servant rushed in, carrying a pail.

'Food, food,' he hurried them.

They removed the mel thundu and held it in front of them. For each person, the servant scooped up a melange of kari, kootu, appalam, lentil gravy, morkuzhambu and rice on to a plantain leaf and dropped it on to the cloth.

Suppuni stared, his eyes bulging. 'What about paayasam? Didn't you bring some paayasam?'

'Who is that? Suppuni? The paayasam got over, da. You've eaten, haven't you? Then why are you sitting here? Go home. Go on!'

Suppuni started running without a backward glance. He heard Sundaramurthi say, 'Wake up, da. Manickam, the food is here.'

Suppuni couldn't control the tears streaming down his face. He felt like wailing out loud.

His father was waiting at the door. 'Where did you go?'

Suppuni could barely speak. Before he could finish saying, 'There was no paayasam for Sundaramurthi Mama. It got over, they said,' fresh tears began to spill from his eyes.

Sundaramurthi stood up. 'Let's go, thambi. It looks like rain,' he said and hummed a melody. It was Senchurutti.

8

LAKSHMI WAS WAITING.

In the past she would feel exhausted, wondering whether her whole life would be reduced to waiting. Now, waiting didn't make her weary; it had taught her patience instead. As now, she had once stayed awake until midnight for her father to come. That wait turned out to be the one that changed the course of her life. On reflection, it was this incident which taught her that she would have to wait patiently to attain every milestone in her life. And it is that very need that has inspired me all the more, she thought.

Today, she was waiting again for her father's arrival. She expected him to come home tonight. When she had lived in the village, he would visit at night, but only after she had gone to sleep. Her mother would stay up, dressed in her finery, waiting for him. After they moved to the town, his visits became fewer. But he did come at least once a week. Her mother would grow flustered, waiting for him to visit. Amma is afraid that someone else might take her place in his life, Lakshmi thought. Her father was not in the habit of informing them in advance about his visits, but she had reason to believe he would definitely drop by that night. She looked at the clock on the wall. It was already ten. The exuberant happiness and joy of that morning was about to vanish completely. After she got the news, she couldn't sleep a wink the night before, imagining what she would tell her father. She loved to see the rays of happiness spread on his face as he listened to her. A few years earlier, when the results of the matriculation exams were declared and he learnt that she had stood first in the Presidency, he had come home immediately and showered her with praise and appreciation; her pride had known no bounds then. As usual, she had had her demands ready. It was a more daunting task to convince her mother, who was afraid that Lakshmi's demands might dishearten Periya Mirasu.

'Hmm. What, then?' Periya Mirasu said.

'I want to go to college, Appa, and become a graduate.'

'That's an impossible wish, 'ma,' her father said pensively. 'The only college here is for men. They don't admit women.'

Her eyes filled with tears. 'In that case, send me to Madras.'

Startled, her mother intervened: 'What do you mean! Where will you stay in the city? Are you going to get a job after graduation?'

'Yes. That's my plan.'

'Until now, which woman has worked at a job?'

'Why, Amma. Can't I be the first woman to do it?'

A faint smile had appeared on her father's lips. He remained quiet, absorbed in deep thought.

'She is talking nonsense. How could it ever happen!' her mother said dismissively, as if apologizing to him.

That Amma seemed to be making a trifle out of her serious intent angered Lakshmi.

As though he was talking to himself, her father said, 'We'll see. She is a studious child, and it would be wrong to deny her wish. Let me see if I can find a way to educate her in this town.'

'Suppose you are not able to?' Lakshmi asked anxiously.

'I'll make some other arrangement. Don't worry about it.'

She had wanted to hug him then. But she realized with diffidence that she might not be permitted such a liberty. He, too, had never shown his affection by coming closer to ruffle her hair or stroke her cheek. During the wedding Lakshmi had seen him fondly run his hand over Paapa's hair. Deep in her heart, she longed to have him to stroke her hair or look at her some day with affection. With her, his manner was of providing support and encouragement to a highly deserving orphan girl in the village, or so it seemed.

Now her mind was clear. He was Periya Mirasu. She had no legal ties with him. He was merely her patron, and even that patronage was given to her on her insistence. But it was enough. Only education was important to her. His contribution towards that was of immense help. She shouldn't be greedy for more. True to his word, Periya Mirasu had made arrangements for her study. He went to the king of the principality, showed him her marksheet and told him about her desire to study in college. Raja had immediately passed an order to the effect that women would henceforth be admitted in the college. When her father gave her the news, it had felt like a miracle had come to pass. As if by magic, all the grievances she had harboured against Periya Mirasu vanished instantly.

Her father had not arrived yet. Lakshmi was disappointed. She had passed BA in first class. Top rank in college. She was the only woman in a class of men. Departing from custom, her principal had made a special mention at the prayer meeting in the college earlier that day about how Lakshmi had defied convention and aspired to study in the face of many difficulties, and scored marks that had brought distinction to their institution, a great achievement. He couldn't have been unaware of the isolation and harassment she had experienced during the course. The gathering of men bowed their heads and clapped vigorously. To some of them, her attainment of a distinction that should have gone to a man might have been humiliating. The tone of the principal's speech implied that they ought to feel ashamed of themselves.

Lakshmi had no friends in the college. In the classroom, she was allotted a desk and chair that were set apart from the others. Even the lecturers conducted their lessons without ever glancing in her direction. Given such an environment, it hadn't been easy for her to attend college. Feeling alienated, as though she was participating in something that was intended for others, she kept silent and resolved all the doubts that arose in her mind by her own effort, spending long hours in the library. Upon learning that she was in the library, a group of men would turn up like an army, and exchange derisive remarks aloud while pretending to sit there and study. Ignoring their antics, she would focus on her work. Later, they would talk in the playing field, within her earshot.

'What business do prostitutes have here?'

'What else can she do? She can't dance. She can't sing. Her face and features aren't up to the mark either.'

'What's she going to do after a college degree?'

'Why don't you go and ask her yourself? You know her address, don't you?'

'Aha! Do you want the whole town to slander me? My father will cane me.'

In the beginning, she had often felt like crying. She had examined her face and features in the mirror; not so plain and ugly, she assured herself. Then, when she scored more marks than those loafers in the exams that followed, she decided to hold them in contempt.

Hearing a knock on the door, she sprang up and ran to open it. She had already rehearsed several times what she would say to her father.

Kitta was standing in the doorway. She was taken aback. She wondered why he had turned up at an hour when her father usually arrived.

'What is it, Kitta?' she asked gently.

'I came to congratulate you,' he said with some hesitation.

She stood beside the door so he couldn't enter. 'Oh. It's all right.' She smiled. 'You needn't have come all the way home. You could have told me in the college, no?'

'No. Saying it there would have been awkward,' he said. 'I have troubled you a lot. Please forgive me.'

She was surprised that this extremely arrogant fellow was apologizing to her now. She felt that even his standing here in her doorway could be an act of mockery.

'You'll find it humiliating to say this in front of everyone, won't you?' She laughed.

He was silent. She knew that he had failed the exams. Didn't his father cane him for that?

'Please forgive me, Lakshmi,' he said again.

'It's all right. I think it was your harassment that made me even more determined.'

'You're not angry at me, are you?' he said diffidently. There was a look of bewilderment in his eyes. His hair, worn in a tuft, was dark and thick. A moustache had begun to spread like a faint black shadow on his upper lip.

'Not at all,' she said earnestly.

Suddenly, her heart turned hard; his gaze was fixed on her chest. Ignoring his rudeness, she said, 'My only worry is that because of a couple of boys like you, girls might get frightened and keep away from college. They can survive only if they are strong and remain unfazed like me.' She laughed again. Noticing that passers-by on the road had stopped to look at them, she told him urgently, 'Leave now. If you linger at the doorway of this house, you'll spoil your name.'

Not wanting to look at his face, she shut the door in a flash and went inside. Her heart was pounding. Would that arrogant cad remember that those were *his* words?

'Who was that, di?' Amma said.

'A boy who studied with me: Kitta. He is the son of the village chieftain. It seems he wanted to congratulate me.'

Thulasi looked at her with interest. 'The chieftain's son? Why didn't you invite him in?'

Lakshmi was angry. 'Why should I? He gave me so much grief when I was in college. I've told you about him, haven't I?'

'It's natural for boys that age to indulge in mischief. But you can't antagonize a rich man's son over such a small matter.'

Lakshmi found her mother's talk absurd. 'Amma, I don't need any rich man's friendship. Please don't insult me.'

'Oh yes. This arrogance is the only thing that's come out of your studying a couple of books,' Thulasi said with some irritation. 'I don't know where this education is going to land you. As if you'll live like a duchess on a clerk's job that pays fifty or sixty rupees.'

Lakshmi's eyes filled with tears. It felt as if her mother was laying a curse on her. 'I may not live like a duchess, but I'll live with honour,' she said. 'I won't hang about near the back entrance of anybody's house, holding my hands out for food. I won't allow my daughter to be in a situation where she knows who her father is but has no right to call him father.'

Before her mother could reply, Lakshmi sat on the floor, drew up her knees and buried her face between them. She was sad to have hurt her mother. But Amma will develop a sense of shame only if such words fall on her ears often enough, Lakshmi thought.

But there was no sign of any change in Thulasi's mentality. Seated on the swing, she lashed out at Lakshmi: 'You strut around as if you are an extraordinary creature. All of us grew up like this. We never asked to know our father's name. There was no need for that. I never wanted to live like Mirasu's wife. Mirasu likes chatting only with me. *I* am the one who makes him happy. There are women who *envy* me!'

'I don't want this life you have lived,' Lakshmi hit back angrily.

In a flash her mother rose and stood before her. 'Don't shout, di. I don't understand what you think of yourself,' she said in a fearful whisper. 'Are you saying you want to be a housewife? Who will marry you?'

Lakshmi looked at her with hatred. 'In that case, I won't get married. What difference does it make?'

Lakshmi went to her room and sat down. She was surprised that her behaviour had driven her mother into a panic. Didn't she find it demeaning to wait every day in the backyard of Mirasu's house for food? Wasn't it humiliating to be treated by Mirasu's wife and her daughter with scant respect? She was nettled that her mother didn't believe an education would give Lakshmi a livelihood. No girl in that neighbourhood had ever gone to college or got a job. She smiled to herself. I am going to be that first girl.

Her father didn't come home that night. After watching her pace from her room to the front door and back for a long time, her mother said, 'It's delivery time for Paapa. Perhaps she has gone into labour.'

No news came from the village. Nor did her father. She reminded herself that for Periya Mirasu only his immediate family was important, but knowing that she was secondary made her sad.

Two weeks later, her father came one night when they were not expecting him. He looked tired and ill. The stubble on his face made him seem much older now.

'What happened? Are you not well? Has Paapa delivered?' Amma chattered nervously as he walked in.

Periya Mirasu sat down on the swing without a word and, covering his mouth with the stole around his shoulders, began to weep with great heaving sobs. Amma tried to clasp his shoulders and console him.

'What happened, 'pa?'

Periya Mirasu looked at her slowly with tear-filled eyes. 'Paapa is no more.'

'Aiyaiyo! How did it happen?'

'Something went wrong during childbirth. The midwife didn't know what to do. She couldn't stop the bleeding.'

'How atrocious!' Lakshmi exclaimed, genuinely distraught.

'Yes, it really is an atrocity, 'ma. I lost my precious child. We were so happy that she had conceived after many years.'

'And the baby?'

'A boy. He cries all the time. No one has the heart to pick him up and cradle him. We have arranged for a wet nurse to feed him.' He broke down again.

Lakshmi found it hard to believe that Periya Mirasu, who always walked around with a swagger, was so utterly broken. Would he shed tears like this if something happened to her or

Amma? She was troubled all night by memories of Paapa's plump cheeks, round eyes and her bridal get-up.

The next morning, she was heartened to see that her father, after spending the night, had stayed until she woke up. His face, too, had cleared up a little by now. Must have been Amma's doing. This was what she meant when she had said, 'I am the one who makes him happy.'

'I heard that you have come first in your college in the BA exams. Very good. Well done,' Appa said with a gentle smile. 'What do you want to do after this?'

'At first I thought I'd study to become a lawyer. But after what you told us yesterday, I've decided to become a doctor.'

He looked at her, startled. 'But you have to go to Madras for that.'

'Yes, I will. I'll get a seat. I'll also get a scholarship. It'll be enough if you can make arrangements for my accommodation.'

Amma was in the kitchen. Fortunately, she didn't start an argument.

'What happened to Paapa must not happen to any other girl, Appa.'

'It's fate, 'ma. Just fate,' he said sorrowfully.

'I don't believe in fate.' Lakshmi was firm. 'Had there been a good hospital or a trained lady doctor, you wouldn't have had to rely on that midwife. Deaths during childbirth are caused by lack of proper medical facilities, not fate.'

'Are you saying that Paapa would have survived?'

'Definitely.'

'Then her death was indeed an atrocity.'

'An outrage,' she said with passion. 'It's like murder. I want to become a doctor for women, Appa. I want to save the lives of many women.'

Periya Mirasu remained pensive for some time. Finally he told Thulasi who had joined them, 'Thulasi, get ready to go to Madras with Lakshmi. She is going to study to become a doctor.'

Lakshmi then did something she had never done before. She hugged her father and sobbed her heart out. When he stroked her head fondly, a feeling of incredible happiness and satisfaction enveloped her. For a long time after he left, the lingering warmth of his affection made her giddy. Thulasi was speechless.

A daughter born to Thulasi need not become another Thulasi, Lakshmi said to herself. It was heartbreaking that the people of Dasi Street still believed that living by their tradition was their only fate. When they chose to wallow in that condition without ever realizing that it was a disgraceful way of life, she didn't know what she could do to create awareness. She grew weary whenever she thought of Kasturi. When she learnt that Kasturi's bottu-tying ceremony had been completed, she was shocked—as though she had received news of a calamity. She was angry at Kasturi for having submitted to that ritual for no good reason. The ecstasy she experienced while dancing was keeping her entranced. When she came out of that trance, she would realize that she was trapped in a terrible conspiracy.

Lakshmi nodded intensely to herself. Bringing that conspiracy to an end would be her mission for the future.

9

'PEOPLE LOVE IT when you perform a jaavali. Do you really need a thillana?'

An hour into her daily practice by now, Kasturi bristled, 'Of course, we must include the thillana in the programme. I can't keep performing an endless series of jaavalis and padams. Why can't the crowd learn to appreciate the thillana? Why should I dance for people who have no taste?'

'Akka is right,' Sabapathi said, tapping once on his mridangam. A faint blackness had appeared on his upper lip, indicating the impending arrival of a moustache. His voice had broken and become deep and husky.

'Right! You are a big man now. You have to give your opinion on everything,' Sengamalam snapped.

'You need me to play the mridangam, so why shouldn't I give my opinion? Ask Thilakam. She will say the same thing.'

'I agree. How can there be a dance concert without a thillana?'

'Fine! Do whatever you want. Remember, you have to perform a varnam too. It will drag on for an hour. You must be good enough to keep the crowd from melting away.'

'When Akka is dancing, you don't have to worry about the crowd going anywhere,' Sabapathi said cheekily.

Kasturi felt like laughing.

'Akka, people *will* stay and watch you dance, but let me tell you something else. I hear there is a poet called Subramania Bharathi who writes a lot of songs. His patriotic songs are becoming wildly popular, Akka. They are wonderful to listen to.'

'Where did you hear them, da?' Thilakam asked eagerly.

'Sundaramurthi Mama was singing a few. Last week, when I had gone to buy semolina powder for my mridangam, I met a man called Singaram. What a fine singer! Even though he is an achari by caste, from a community of sculptors.'

'Never mind that, but do you remember the song?'

Sabapathi stood up immediately, raised his right hand, closed his eyes and sang in a ringing voice: '*Vande Mataram is our chant / We salute the mother of our great land.*'

Thilakam and Kasturi looked at him with interest.

'We can perform it like a padam, Akka. Even the cadence sounds good. Thakita thaka thimi, thakita thaka thimi ...'

Kasturi laughed. 'It will be a novelty, da. Our nattuvanar would say that only the emotion of love appeals to the audience.'

'People everywhere are singing Bharathi's songs, Akka. If you dance to them, the audience will definitely appreciate it, you'll see.'

Sengamalam scowled. 'It'll land us deeper in trouble. Look where your mind is going! As it is, times are bad. If you dance to these songs, you will be put behind bars immediately.'

'White men don't understand Tamil.'

'Don't underestimate their intelligence. Why should we invite trouble? When there are so many padams, why should we perform something written by a lunatic?'

'If you don't want to, that's fine. But why call that man a lunatic?'

'Well, I heard someone say he is a madman,' Sengamalam said defiantly.

Kanagu Paati peeped in.

'Come in, Paati. You can also watch this. I am going to perform a thillana.'

'Take off your salangai, kannu. The carriage from the palace is here.'

'Oh,' Kasturi said, suddenly dispirited. 'Why at this hour today?'

Sabapathi got up and checked the timepiece in the little alcove. 'It's not even eight yet.'

'Why not let her finish the thillana, Paati?' Thilakam said.

'Adi, she can dance in the morning. He needs to speak to her, it seems. Could be about a concert or something. Who knows?'

Assuming this was an imaginative explanation Paati had come up with, Kasturi removed the salangai, touched it to her eyes piously, and said in a gentle voice, 'We can do this tomorrow, Thilakam.'

'Chat!'

Ignoring Sabapathi's cluck of disapproval, Kasturi went to change her clothes.

She washed her face and dusted it lightly with the powder Raja had brought for her from abroad. After lining her eyes with kohl, she drew a tilak on her forehead, draped her silk sari, rubbed a drop of civet perfume behind her ears and finally looked at herself in the mirror. Everything is fine, she told herself. She remembered how Sabapathi had clucked wearily at her. I too felt like reacting the same way, she confessed to her reflection. When Kasturi stepped out of the room, Thilakam gave her a quick glance and then bowed her head. Sabapathi didn't look up at all. Kasturi gave him an affectionate pat on the back and walked on.

It was quite dark outside. Without letting her eyes wander, she climbed into the carriage. Her departure was observed from many neighbouring houses. There was a high-speed information network in the street through which everyone found out who had visited which house. Sometimes, when she listened to Paati and Sengamalam talk among themselves, she marvelled at how much they knew in spite of being confined to the house. Usually, the carriage from the palace came only after ten. Sabapathi would be asleep by then. Even Thilakam would have gone to bed. Kanagu and Sengamalam would help Kasturi get ready and send her away in complete silence, as if in secret. Before she climbed into the carriage, they would station themselves on either side like bodyguards and help her get in.

'Some woman might cast her burning evil eye,' Sengamalam would say. 'None of them knows that this Raja is just a bit player, with no real value. He is dependent on the British for his daily needs.'

The carriage glided smoothly on the road. Inside, the seat was soft, appointed with bolsters cased in silk fabric, and the silk curtains kept her presence hidden from view. The horse had no idea whether Raja was a dummy or a slave to British rulers. Like me, Kasturi thought to herself. She recalled vividly the day she had first travelled to the palace and the advice that Paati had given her the previous night.

'From now on, the carriage from the palace will come here often to fetch you, kannu,' Paati told Kasturi as though she was sharing a secret.

By then, the flood of all-round praise for her dance performance after the bottu-tying ritual had subsided.

In a stupor from the repeated rehearsals of a new padam the nattuvanar had taught her that day, Kasturi asked, 'What for?'

Kanagu shut the door and sat beside her on the bed.

'To someone like you who was born in this clan, do I need to explain why a man would seek your company?'

Not having given it much thought all these years, Kasturi was gripped by an inexplicable panic. Her eyes filled with tears, as if someone had stopped her dance midway.

'No, Paati! You told me that god is my husband. Now you want me to go to this Raja.'

Paati hugged her. 'God *is* our husband. But we are not Andal, kannu. We are not housewives. We are born for the pursuit of art. We need a rich man to take care of us. If we are to develop and safeguard these arts, we shouldn't have to face problems in running our household. That's why we have this custom in our community. We are not going to make any claims on that rich man. Think of it merely as an arrangement, but one that we must engage in without any reservation. Bear in mind that this too is an art.'

Thereafter, Paati proceeded to give her lessons in that art for a long time: how to laugh, how to walk, how to talk, how to embrace, what gave the most pleasure ...

Kasturi understood that this art form was far more intricate than the mimed hand gestures taught by the nattuvanar. Her grandmother had made it seem like a simple acting exercise.

Paati had also added, as if to remind Kasturi, 'This is an arrangement. You have already dedicated yourself to the Lord. Only dance and music are your god. You stand at the entrance to god's chamber. This body is merely a costume, a block of wood, the sages say. Sleeping with Raja will bring no dishonour to you or to your soul.'

Paati had a knack for bringing Kasturi completely under her spell. There was a magical power in her words. Kasturi told herself that the arrangement with Raja was meant solely to nurture dance, a cause for which she was willing to do anything. She would give only her body to Raja, not her soul. Her soul, which was pervaded by dance, belonged only to her.

As she travelled in the carriage from the palace, she remembered Lakshmi's words.

It's a wretched clan.

When Raja embraced her eagerly on their first meeting and his hot breath grazed her budding breasts, she recalled those words; her stomach twisted in revulsion, as if she had stepped into a gutter, and her vagina contracted in fear.

'Are you feeling scared? Didn't Kanagam train you?'

Hearing Raja's words, she recovered her wits. This is merely an arrangement, she reminded herself. She forced herself to relax.

'Won't the subject be afraid of the ruler?' She laughed.

Raja was bewitched. Stroking her cheeks fondly, he said in a light-hearted manner, 'In this room, I am not the king, and you are not my subject. I am a slave to an angel called Kasturi.'

As the night progressed, Kasturi could not remember any of the ruses that Paati had taught her. It was Raja who was the true expert in this game. He dispelled her fears with ease, the same ease with which he removed all her clothes, one by one. He seemed to think deflowering her was his birthright. When it happened, her body shook as if an earthquake had exploded inside her. Bursts of stars scattered before her eyes. The pain in her legs and thighs made her tear up.

When she curled up and turned over to the other side, she heard Raja say, 'Hmm, Kanagu didn't deceive me.'

She didn't know what he meant.

All of a sudden, she thought of Lakshmi. Of what Lakshmi might think if she saw her in that condition. She hadn't imagined that it would be so horrible. It felt as if a knife had been stuck into her groin and pulled out. Her thighs ached for two whole days. Her eyes streamed with tears of fright. Kanagu had massaged her body with oil and bathed her in warm water. 'It's always painful at first, kannu,' she consoled Kasturi.

Thoughts of Lakshmi surfaced occasionally and tormented her. Many years had passed since their last meeting. Someone had said she was in Madras. Kasturi worried whether Lakshmi was leading a comfortable life. She remembered Lakshmi now. If someone told her that the body was only a costume, Lakshmi would certainly laugh at the idea.

Suddenly she heard a loud commotion. Some people were shouting slogans. The carriage slowed down and came to a halt on the edge of the street. She moved the curtain aside slightly and peered out. A group of men was marching down the street in a procession, shouting slogans. They wore white caps and khaddar shirts. Holding a flag in one hand and freely swinging the other, they shouted, 'Vande Mataram.'

Forgetting to close the curtain, she watched the procession for some time as if under a spell. Abruptly, the carriage lurched forward and entered a lane on the left and gathered speed. The voices of the marching group were audible behind them; then they faded gradually.

'What happened, Arumugam?' she asked the carriage driver. The bumps and jolts of the carriage made her voice tremble.

Arumugam drove for some time without stopping. When the noise died down, he slowed the carriage. Crouching to look inside, he said, 'They are freedom fighters, thangachi. There is a big group in the town now. "Vande Mataram" is a slogan started by one Gandhi. He had come to Mayavaram recently. My! What a huge crowd turned out to hear him speak! Even though he doesn't know Tamil. Just what they heard from someone translating his speech fired them up. From that day on, this slogan has become very popular here. The cap they are wearing is called Gandhi cap. Many of our people have joined them now. They get beaten and thrown in jail by the British. How can they fight with the white man and win? To me it seems like a futile struggle.'

Kasturi listened eagerly. Even the song Sabapathi had sung began with 'Vande Mataram'. Was Sundaramurthi part of the procession just now? She knew they were under British rule and that Raja himself received a grant from the government, but beyond that she didn't know anything about politics. That she had evinced no interest in it made her feel guilty. A great churn seemed to be occurring in the world outside. She didn't know whether it was good or bad. Becoming free meant that they had to drive the British away. How were they going to do it? She would have to ask Mama. What kind of fight would it be? Would Raja take part in it? How could such weaklings as they win that fight?

But the slogan did something to her.

'Vande Mataram.'

They were Sanskrit words. Because she had formally studied Sanskrit along with Tamil, she knew it meant 'Salutations to mother.' Mother India? That's what the song said.

Vande Mataram is our chant / We salute the mother of our great land.

She tried repeating the slogan: 'Vande Mataram.' Her whole body felt charged, but she couldn't understand why.

The carriage slowed down again. Addressing the interior, Arumugam said: 'We are trapped, thangachi. It looks like the procession is heading towards the palace gates. I'll drive faster. We'll take a short cut and reach the palace before they see us.'

Kasturi could sense the fear and urgency in the way Arumugam drove the horse. As the carriage raced forward at tremendous speed, she clutched her seat in panic. The cries sounded all around them.

'Vande Mataram!'

'Quit India, white man!'

The curtain that covered the window flapped in the wind. She could see young men in the crowd passionately raising slogans. She spotted Sundaramurthi Mama marching in the front row, and immediately drew the curtain. There was a young man beside Sundaramurthi Mama. Though she couldn't recognize him, he seemed familiar. That must be the young man Sabapathi had told her about. She hadn't known until then that Sundaramurthi Mama was a freedom fighter. He gave the impression that he knew little else besides playing the naayanam.

Overtaking the procession, the carriage speedily entered the palace gates. As soon as it was safely inside, the guards hurriedly closed the iron grille gate and locked it. You cowards, she thought, if you are so afraid of our own people, how are you going to defeat the British?

She climbed the stairs to Raja's chamber. He appeared to have let his patience slip away. Still, on seeing the smile she flashed at him, he faltered momentarily.

'What took you so long? I had sent the carriage quite a while back,' he demanded, recovering his ill humour.

Wondering why he was so anxious today, she said, smiling, 'But I am here, aren't I? There was a procession that got in our way. The carriage had to wait by the side of the road for some time.'

'That's why I had sent the carriage early.'

'It seems the procession started even earlier,' she said gently, as if to appease him. She still couldn't understand why he was agitated. 'Freedom fighters, they say. Even now, they are standing in front of the palace gates.'

'Never mind them, those rebellious layabouts! The guards will chase them away. If they continue to make noise, it won't take me long to inform the Collector. If you oppose the British, do you think they will just stand around and watch? You'll be thrashed ruthlessly. And they'll throw you in jail without a second thought.'

Kasturi was startled by the intensity of Raja's anger. She prayed that the slogan-shouting group would disperse soon before anything happened. Knowing it would be pointless to mention the people in the procession to Raja—and foolhardy—she became cautious. But the king, who moved around in public with a majestic bearing, looked rattled. She understood everything in a flash. It was the march of freedom fighters that had upset him. He was afraid that the Collector might think he was also one of them.

Raja didn't know what his situation would be if the country became independent. It wasn't certain, either, that the nation would become free. The struggle for freedom could not be won merely by raising slogans and writing songs. The white man was in power today. Raja could survive only if he supported the British.

Raja being such a coward would have angered even Sabapathi. But she didn't have the credentials to share her personal opinions with Raja. He was her patron. Life in her household was sustained by their relationship; it walked the streets wrapped in the protective blanket of social prestige.

One rule in Kanagu Paati's rulebook was very important: one must not clash with the patron's ideas or enter into an argument. 'Remember this. It's only to forget all his problems that he comes to you. Like applying fomentation to a sore, you must give him comfort and ease his heart. That's what he needs.'

The sound of slogans outside had ceased. In the silence that followed, she prepared to give fomentation to his wound.

10

GENTLE DARKNESS HAD spread all around me; the tall pine trees and other giants of unknown genus had adopted me as their own. A cool fragrant breeze folded me in its embrace. There was a strange smell of green herbs, a very strong aroma, like a blend of myrtle, cinnamon, worm wood and eucalyptus. Suddenly I was afraid that it might send me into a stupor.

I wondered why that fear had surfaced today. It must have been the impact of the book I was reading last night: Murakami's *Kafka on the Shore*. In the novel, there is a description of a strange forest like this one. Those who walk into it cannot find their way out; trees intertwined with one another obscure the paths. Those who enter are swallowed up by an incomprehensible, recursive path resembling a labyrinth or maze. But the labyrinth is a metaphor. There is another world configured as equidistant and parallel to ours. One can enter it up to a point and come back if one is careful. This is what the boy Kafka Tamura is told by Oshima, the man who comes forward to help him.

Do you know where the idea of a labyrinth first came from?' Oshima explains. 'It was the ancient Mesopotamians. They pulled out animal intestines—sometimes human intestines, I expect—and used the shape to predict the future. They admired the complex shape of the intestines. So, the prototype for labyrinths is, in a word, guts. Which means the principle for labyrinths is inside you. And that correlates to the labyrinth *outside*. Things outside are a projection of what's inside you, and what's inside you is a projection of what's outside. So, when you step into the labyrinth outside you, at the same time you're stepping into the labyrinth inside. Most definitely a risky business. The forest has set a trap, and no matter what you do, no matter how careful you are, some sharp-eyed birds are going to eat up all your breadcrumbs.

It was on this page that I had closed the book and put it away. I felt dizzy, as if the story itself was progressing through a labyrinth. Magical realism that wove imagination, philosophy and lust together. I thought that the lust was beyond definition. It wasn't clear if it was lust or longing. To escape the labyrinth inside him, Kafka is prepared to travel through the maze inside the forest. I wasn't trying to break free from the grip of any lust. Was it longing then? Perhaps. This was a journey I had undertaken to solve a puzzle. But to my surprise, I had entered such a forest today. Might it also have laid a trap for me?

A little earlier, the old woman had said something odd: 'You are a city girl. You don't believe in spirits and ghosts.'

Believing aside, I couldn't even understand what she was saying. Perhaps she had wanted to tell me that ghosts roamed around in the area. Ghosts had no shape. They would blow like the wind, or sit in a corner, dressed in black, and weep. When I lived in a hostel, some of the senior students would cook up such stories to frighten the junior girls. They would wander around at night, disguised as ghosts. One junior girl came down with a galloping fever and had to be admitted to hospital. My mother had prepared me for all that.

'Ghosts and sprits. Such nonsense! I am confident that my daughter won't develop such stupid beliefs,' she had said when I told her about it.

At the time, I could accept it only half-heartedly. M. Night Shyamalan's *The Sixth Sense* had been released then. The film conveyed the message that ghosts really wandered around. Dead people appear before a little boy. Each time, he is terrified. Everyone shuns him, mocks him, calling him a freak, an unnatural boy. A dozen girls from the hostel went together to see the film. No one slept that night. We screamed even at the slightest stir of a breeze. Hearing the sound of a steel tumbler dropped on the floor by accident, we held our breath. They say you don't feel afraid in a group. That day, we were afraid as a group. One person's fear infected the others. I couldn't confess all this to Amma. She would refuse to believe that her daughter could be such a coward. She would feel ashamed. It was an important credo of hers: There is nothing to fear except fear itself. Fear is a delusion of cowards, imagining the existence of what doesn't exist.

I was startled. I thought I heard Amma's voice. There was darkness all around me. Though it was not pitch-black, it obscured my vision and spread like a fog in front of me. Was it real or an illusion? Dark clouds must have gathered above and hidden the sun completely. Suddenly there was a gust of cold wind. Like smoke, the mist spread very quickly, merged with the surrounding darkness and smothered me. I stood rooted to the spot, gasping for breath. I couldn't see the path at all. I thought I was stranded in the labyrinth described by Murakami. Wondering how I would get out, I was seized by panic. I realized that the old woman had warned me with good reason. She and the little boy—by which path had they arrived there? Had they even been real? Even in that cold weather, I broke into a sweat. Whom could I call for help? god. Does god have a name? I couldn't remember the name of a single god. A non-believer herself, Amma had also denied me the opportunity to accept god. She did not believe god would come to our aid where no human help was available. She had forced that idea on me. The epic story in which the Kauravas attempt to disrobe Draupadi in the court and Lord Krishna sends thousands of saris and saves her honour is merely a fabricated myth, she had laughingly insisted. That I stood here now without any protector or succour, unable to call out to any god for help, was because of her; she was responsible for my state. If I had been born, like Joan's mother, in a tribe of gypsies, some angel would have come to my aid. I was distressed to think that my mother had left me stranded without any protection. An indescribable sorrow and anger welled up in me.

'Amma—'

'Amma—'

The word was flung back at me with great fury.

A ball of fire came rolling up from the bottom of my belly. 'Amma, why did you die? How could you forget me? Answer me!'

Squatting down, I began to moan and wail. Grief that had lain buried within me for two years because I couldn't weep even in privacy came gushing out of me in great, heaving sobs. Once again, I was afraid that I might even forget Amma's face. I didn't know how she looked before she died. I had last seen her a year before she died. During my college days, I didn't have the money to buy a ticket on a whim. 'Focus on your studies. Come after you've finished your thesis,' she would tell me. She had insisted that academics was more important than affection. I often felt sad that she was such an unusual mother. She died without ever knowing how I had longed to be with her.

When Amma died, I got the news days later. Appa might have deliberately kept it from me. It was around the submission deadline for my PhD thesis. I was busily preparing to defend it. Amma was very excited. She was the one who had encouraged me, insisting that the doctoral degree I would receive from Columbia University in the US would propel me forward in my career and life. I defended my thesis successfully. Everyone congratulated me. After my doctoral degree was confirmed, in high spirits at the end of the champagne party and dinner that had followed, I tried to telephone Amma, but the number in our Delhi house kept on ringing. I could not connect to either my mother's or my father's mobile number. On both, I got the message that the number was outside the service area. I decided that I would call after some time. They might have gone on holiday to a location where there was no signal. I went to sleep, happy to imagine how delighted my parents would be at my success. Amma appeared in my dreams. I gave her a bunch of red roses. Smiling, she extended her hand and received it. She spread the flowers on herself, like a young girl. As the red roses were placed on the yellow sari draped over her body, the petals fell away and turned into patches of blood. Crimson-red blood. I woke with a start. The telephone was ringing. Thinking it had to be her, I answered.

'Amma?'

'This is Appa speaking,' was the reply. There was a tremor in his voice.

I looked at the clock. It was two at night.

'What's the matter, Appa? Aren't you both in Delhi?' I said, worried.

'No. We came to Kodaikanal. Amma would've have sent you an email, right?'

'I haven't checked my mail. I was preparing for my viva.'

There was no response from Appa. I wondered if he had forgotten about my PhD. Amma would have asked me about it right away.

'Why are you calling me at this hour, Appa?'

'I was able to connect only today. I've been trying for the past three days. It's raining very heavily here. All phone lines were dead. They were restored just now.'

I felt my stomach churn. I remembered the dream. 'What has happened to Amma?' I asked, assailed by a vague fear.

'She's gone, 'ma. She has passed away.'

My heart broke and fell apart. As if it had anticipated the news, it beat like a kettledrum. My eyes widened and bulged out.

'What? No. I won't believe it.'

'I can't believe it either, 'ma.' Appa's voice cracked.

'What happened, Appa? Was something wrong with her health?'

'She wasn't ill. I just didn't expect this.'

'When did it happen?'

'It's been three days.'

I was furious. 'Three days! And you took so long to inform your own daughter?'

'I told you, didn't I? All the lines here were dead.'

'Along with Amma?'

'What?'

I had not imagined India was such a backward country. How was it possible that the news of a death could not be communicated immediately? It didn't occur to me then that even in certain mountainous regions of America, communication was difficult. Grief came bursting out of me. 'Is everything over, then?' I couldn't bring myself to ask if they were waiting for me to reach before cremating the body. That Amma had turned into a lifeless object during that three-minute conversation left me stunned.

'Yes.'

I cried for a while, without making a sound. Then the line got disconnected. I wrote down the number from the caller-ID and tried to call back. After several attempts, I was finally able to hear Appa's faint voice.

'Where should I come—Kodaikanal or Delhi?' I asked.

'Don't come now,' Appa said. 'In four days, I have to travel to Japan for a conference. I'll be away for three weeks. I haven't cancelled it. I need some change too. Otherwise I'll go mad. Come at your convenience. What can you do here anyway?'

'Then write me a detailed letter.'

Before Appa could answer, the line went dead again.

Appa never wrote that detailed letter. Whenever we spoke on the phone, we carefully avoided talking about Amma; or, to be precise, I did. I believed my memory of Amma was private; Appa wouldn't understand this. All kinds of things had happened before I saw Appa again. In the new job that I had taken up, a hundred thousand problems cropped up and I couldn't get leave when I asked for it. After a bereavement, two years was a shamefully long interval. But I was hesitant to visit that house bereft of Amma; it could be because I had never been close to Appa. When I finally came home, I realized that two years was indeed a very long gap. Appa had changed. His eyes were clouded over. He stumbled about as though he had lost his crutch. That Amma was the reason why he had turned this way and I was trapped in the maze now made me angry. Like someone crazed, I banged my head against my knees and cried out, 'Why did you die? Did you not want us any more? Were you that selfish?'

In my anger, I began to weep once again. In that deserted forest with nary a human or sound, grief continued to pour out, unrestrained.

I felt someone touch my shoulder. Taken aback, I sat upright. I couldn't see anyone. I was surrounded by mist. It was like sitting inside a bale of cotton. But I was certain that someone had touched me.

'Who is it?' I said.

In fact, I only thought I said it; the sound never rose from my throat. My chest throbbed with fear. My legs shook as I slowly stood up. I rubbed my eyes clear and looked around.

Amma was standing just a short distance away.

I was startled. Was it Amma? How was it possible? She was wearing a yellow sari and a red blouse, but there was no smile on her radiant face. I remembered that she had worn a yellow sari in my dream too. This too must be a dream. Was it possible to dream with my eyes open? Could someone stand before me as in real life? In the surrounding mist, Amma alone was starkly visible. Then she turned and started walking ahead. As if in a dream, I followed her. Miraculously, I couldn't see a maze. My feet didn't stumble on anything. In that mist-laden forest, it was like walking blindfolded. As though being guided by a thread, I followed Amma's figure. My brain had ceased functioning. At times it seemed that I could catch up with Amma in just a couple of strides. But as I kept advancing, that figure also continued without looking back even once.

'Amma, stop. Please stop, Amma.'

My voice was dead. My mouth had gone dry.

I didn't know if I was walking or floating. I was barely conscious of it. The urgent need to catch up with Amma propelled me forward. Walking through the fog and semi-darkness as if moving among clouds or tearing through empty space, I followed that yellow sari. But Amma walked faster than me. I yearned for her to turn around at least once. Running at that pace, I became breathless. Amma didn't seem to be tired. Amma had always been physically strong. She practised yoga and pranayama daily, without fail.

'Amma, stop for a few minutes. I want to ask you something. Please answer me before you go.'

In the stillness of the forest, my words sounded as though they had been amplified by a loudspeaker. They startled even me. I stopped abruptly. The mist had cleared completely. The sun's rays filtered down through the trees, spreading light in patches. A neat, narrow foot-trail was visible in front of me. Amma had disappeared. Wailing 'Amma! Amma!' I began to run down that path like a crazed woman.

After some time, the trees became fewer and the ground became level. Light shone brightly. I came upon a house. At its entrance, an old couple sat in a patch of sunlight. I hurried over and stood before them, panting for breath.

'Who are you? Why are you running as if you've seen some kaathu karuppu?' The old man laughed.

I was confused for a moment but recovering quickly, I asked him, 'Did an elderly lady in a yellow sari pass this way?'

From the way they exchanged glances, they appeared to be talking in private code. I was certain they had seen Amma.

'So she came, didn't she?'

'No, we didn't see anyone like that.'

'Where did you see her last?'

'Inside the forest. There was fog and mist all over; I couldn't see a thing. I couldn't find the way out. Then a lady appeared, wearing a yellow sari. I kept pleading with her to stop, but she kept walking. I followed her out.'

Both of them exchanged meaningful glances again. 'So, that explains it. I was wondering how you went into the forest and managed to come out. Why did you come alone, child? Where do you live?'

'You haven't answered my question,' I said testily. 'She must have walked by on this route. You would have seen her.'

The old woman laughed. 'You don't know about this forest. That you have emerged safely is quite a miracle. You should know that. Don't come here any more. It's your luck that brought you out today. Otherwise, you would've been struck down.'

I was taken aback. What was she saying?

The old man added in a stern voice, 'The woman is right. Wherever you want to go from here, there is a shortcut to go down on this side. Come, I will show you the way.'

The old man picked up his staff and stood up.

I was still hesitant. 'Are you sure you never saw her?'

The old woman said impatiently. 'Look, can't you understand if you are told once? No one like that came this way. Just mind your business and leave.'

The old man started, 'Two years ago, at that lake—'

'Hey! Why are you talking about it to this girl?' the wife interrupted. She added, 'You go ahead, child.'

After scanning the surroundings once again, I said to the old man, 'Escort me out of here, thatha. You will also show me the way home, won't you?'

'Show her the way and come right back,' the old woman said.

11

Lakshmi heard people talking on the terrace of the neighbouring house. Female voices. Natarajaiyer's wife had told her that a tenant family had moved in there recently. They were from near Tirunelveli, as Lakshmi recalled. Though it was just eleven in the morning, the sun was scorching hot. What were they doing?

In Natarajaiyer's house, only the front portion of the terrace was open to the sky; a tiled roof offered shade over the remaining portion. On holidays, once the morning brunch was over at ten, Lakshmi would come to the terrace, sit down with a book and study, leaning against the parapet wall. From as early as three-thirty in the afternoon, a gentle sea breeze would begin to blow. At three, Mami would call her for coffee and snacks. If she sat down again after eating the snack, she could study until the light began to fade. Holding on to the parapet wall, she could idly watch the city below.

The ocean was visible in the distance. As far as the eye could see, the dark blue expanse of water kept moving forward and back in endless waves. Its natural splendour captivated the heart and evoked feelings of awe and wonder. In the early days, after she moved to this house, simply looking at the ocean would give her immense joy. Even now, she never tired of gazing at it. She could see two worlds there, worlds that never touched one another. On the seashore, local fishermen's children at play were visible as black dots. Dark or brown Indians huddled in clusters here and there on the sandy expanse. As if totally unrelated to them, white men and women strolled hand in hand on the pavement adjoining the road, appearing like dolls. Their automobiles were parked on the near side of the shore. There weren't many women among the Indians. Men and women didn't hold hands while walking like white people did. If a couple were to, onlookers would certainly find it odd. Lakshmi felt like laughing. Back in their village it was acceptable for a man with a wife and children at home to visit Dasi Street, spend the night there and return home like a thief in the morning. But if he were to walk down the road clasping his legally wedded wife's hand, everyone would tease him. When the poet Bharathi did so deliberately, people called him a lunatic, clapped their hands and mocked him, according to Natarajaiyer.

'Why did they laugh, Mama? You should also hold Mami's hand and walk on the street, like our revolutionary poet,' Lakshmi said, giggling.

'If Mami agrees, I am ready,' Mama responded.

Mami pulled a face and said scornfully, 'Sounds ridiculous! How can a wife behave like a prostitute?'

Lakshmi was aghast.

Natarajaiyer moved quickly to appease his wife. 'Shall we go to the beach this Sunday, all three of us? We'll pack something to eat, Karpagam. It's a full moon night too. What do you say?'

'Yes, we can. But I won't be holding your hand or your feet!' Mami smiled.

At the beach on Sunday, Mami's personality was completely transformed. She laughed like an adolescent girl. She marvelled at the British couples. It lifted Lakshmi's spirits to stand in the water with Mama and Mami, and to see how lovingly Mami edged closer to her husband and how she laughed heartily at the sensation of the water eroding the sand beneath her feet as it receded. The hem of Mami's sari was around her knees. Smooth as plantain stems, her legs gleamed above the water.

'If your mother knew how you're carrying on, she would kill me,' Mami whined indulgently to Mama and laughed. Her eyes sparkled with mischief. Lakshmi imagined Mami's mother-in-law might well ask: What's this whorish behaviour? The tamarind rice, curd rice, plantain chips and mango pickle that Mami had brought were as delectable as nectar. Lakshmi had never been so happy in her life. In her dream that night, Periya Mirasu and her mother were at the beach, standing hand in hand in the water. Lakshmi stayed on the shore, built a house of sand and wrote 'Our House' in the sand. In one swoop, a big wave rolled in and carried it away.

Try as she might, she could not suppress the desire to tell her mother about the dream. 'Mama, Mami and I went to Marina Beach yesterday. Have you ever seen the ocean? Mami must be your age. She enjoyed herself like a child. Last night I dreamt that you and Appa were standing together in the water. But the dream collapsed like a sand castle. I'll get a job in this city, no? I will bring you here then.' These days, she could not talk to her father whenever she wanted to.

Lakshmi didn't know whether the aspiration in her dream was intelligible to her mother. Even her frustration would be beyond her mother's grasp. Amma had tried her best to prevent Lakshmi from entering medical college. 'How can we live in Madras?' she had complained. It was clear to Lakshmi that

Amma's biggest worry was losing Periya Mirasu. She could not make out whether her mother actually loved the man or was merely afraid that she might lose his patronage. Periya Mirasu's assurance that he would find them a house in Madras sent her into a panic.

'Where do you get such ideas?' she snapped at Lakshmi. 'I am hoping to pass my days in peace till it's time for me to mount the bier, and you want me to set up house in Madras and do things I've never done before. How long can I stay there without seeing him? Other women are only waiting for the day when I'll be gone.'

That night they had to wait for her father's arrival, again for another negotiation. These days her initial hesitancy with her father had disappeared. As in the past, Appa accepted her demands. Amma would go back to the village and live in the old house, and Lakshmi would stay in his close friend Natarajaiyer's house till she completed her studies in medical college. She sensed that her father had come with his mind made up. Appa could not go for very long without seeing her mother.

'A request, Appa,' she had said.

Her father laughed. 'What now, child?'

'Amma won't wait like a beggar in your backyard. You should arrange to send food to her house.'

As Amma looked at him in alarm, Appa said with bowed head, 'We'll do that, child.' Then he looked at Amma and smiled. 'Is she really your daughter? She even gets the better of me.' Then he did something he had never done before. He pulled Lakshmi close to him and stroked her head fondly. 'Thulasi, don't worry about this girl. She will survive. It seems she will be the one to bring honour to my name. The boy is loitering around like an oaf.'

Even later, when he took his leave after bringing her to Natarajaiyer's house, his eyes had welled up with tears.

'Yogu, open out the veshti and spread it wide, di. Bring that kundaan over here. Fetch that sevai press also. God! Why are you so lazy and dull!' A woman's sharp-toned voice could be heard clearly from the terrace of the neighbouring house.

After her move to Madras, there had been no opportunity for Lakshmi to interact with women other than Mami. There was not a single woman in the medical college. The men kept away from her, as though she were an unearthly creature. The college itself seemed to encourage that impression. Here too, in the classroom, she was allotted a separate table and chair placed in a corner of the front section. Inured to the teasing from the men back in her college, she erected of her own volition a fence around herself. Though she didn't need to talk with anyone, having to hold her tongue and remain silent in that environment did leave her feeling lonely. For some days now she had yearned for an opportunity to talk to girls her own age. Those she saw walking by on the roads were nearly all men; women were seen only in the vicinity of Kapaleeswarar temple or Parthasarathy temple, sitting in the front pyols of their houses, exchanging gossip.

Lakshmi got up slowly and looked around. She could see two women on the terrace of the neighbouring house. Sitting under the hot sun, they were making vadagam. The younger of the two had a tonsured head and was draped in a plain cotton sari. The other wore a bright silk sari and had diamonds glittering in her earrings and nosepin. She reminded Lakshmi of Periya Mirasu's wife. Lakshmi could see that the younger woman was finding it difficult to lift the heavy kundaan. As she set the kundaan down, straightened up and massaged her back to ease the strain, Lakshmi was shocked to realize she was a young girl—no older than fourteen or fifteen—in a widow's garb, her forehead unmarked, ears and neck bare. Her beautiful face had wilted and turned dark under the sun's heat, and her eyes filled with unshed tears.

'Why have you stopped? Come, roll the batter into little balls. Press the sevai also.'

As though she had sensed Lakshmi's presence, the girl turned around and looked at her. Overcome by shock and distress at having stumbled upon the girl's wide eyes brimming with tears, Lakshmi stepped back quickly and sat down on the floor, close to the wall. The girl was so young. Why inflict such terrible cruelty on her? Lakshmi's heart was pounding. The woman adorned in diamonds and silk can't be the girl's mother, Lakshmi thought. She was relentlessly chastising and scolding the young one about this and that.

'The batter is too hot to touch,' the girl said.

'Aha! The unlucky wretch needs comfort now, does she?'

'Aiyo! Aiyo!' the girl cried out. The woman seemed to have slapped her.

Unable to sit there any more, Lakshmi got up and briskly went downstairs.

Mami, who was relaxing on the indoor swing and reading a magazine, said, 'Why is your face red? Did you stand in the sun?'

Lakshmi was breathless with anger and unable to speak for some time. She went to her room, drank water from a pot, and came back. As she sat down in the hall, and leaned against a pillar, Mami asked her, 'What's the matter, Lakshmi? What happened?'

For a moment, Lakshmi didn't know what to say.

'Some ladies are making vadagam on the terrace of our neighbour's house,' she said eventually.

'And why not? It's the right season, isn't it? We are not yet in Chithirai though, when the sun is scorching hot. Did that woman ask you to press the batter?' Mami laughed.

Lakshmi's anger had calmed down. But she could not bring herself to smile.

'She has a servant to do all that. A very young girl, Mami, practically a child. It is horrible, Mami. Her head is shorn and she is wearing a rough cotton sari. A nine-yard sari at that. The woman is constantly scolding the girl, asking her to fetch the kundaan, the press ... When the girl said the batter was too hot, the woman beat her, saying, "Why do you need to pamper yourself?"'

'Really?' Mami said, suddenly pensive. 'That girl is the woman's daughter-in-law. She told me that her son died of typhoid. "The girl's family is quite poor. Her mother is no more. Father has a second wife. Who knows what hardships they're facing? If she were my own daughter, would I abandon her? That's why I've kept her with me," she said.'

Lakshmi wondered whether Mami hadn't quite believed her account of the woman's cruelty. 'That may be true, but if you heard the woman speak, it wouldn't appear so. Would anyone abuse their own daughter as an unlucky wretch, ask her to lift a scalding hot kundaan, and then beat her for saying that the batter is too hot?'

'But why are you so angry?' Mami said. 'At her parents' place, the girl would have suffered far worse at her stepmother's hands. When the husband dies at a young age, life becomes hard for a woman. What can we do?'

Lakshmi was disappointed to see Mami consider the matter quite normal.

'She is a child, Mami,' Lakshmi protested, sounding helpless. 'It's not clear how long she might have lived with her husband.

Her body is so young she could wear a skirt and blouse. But they've shaved her head, disfigured her, made her wear a sari too heavy for her, left her ears, wrists and neck bare ... Why such a harsh punishment for a child, Mami?' Before Lakshmi could finish speaking, tears spilled from her eyes.

'It's so strange, what you're saying,' Mami said wearily. 'It's our custom. Women are not used to asking why and what for.'

'But we must ask questions, Mami! People should realize what a huge travesty this is.'

'Who are you going to ask? The woman in the next house?' Mami said with a note of concern. 'Don't do anything of that sort. She has already enquired many times about who you are and where you are from. If a serious quarrel breaks out with the people next door, life will become very difficult.'

Lakshmi composed herself. She understood what Mami was telling her indirectly: 'You have sought shelter here yourself. You don't have the right to create any problems here.'

'Look here,' Mami continued. 'Don't get involved in all this. Your education is what is important. Once it's over, you're going to leave.'

'I will never behave in a way that might cause you trouble, Mami,' Lakshmi said gently.

Mami didn't reply. When Lakshmi gathered her books and returned to her room, grief came spiralling up from the bottom of her stomach. She was not so stupid that she couldn't grasp Mami's warning. Nor could she fault Mami. It was Lakshmi's good fortune that Natarajaiyer and his wife had agreed to help her out. Mami's personality was shaped by her birth, upbringing and circumstances. Although the main reason Natarajaiyer had agreed to provide her accommodation and food was his generosity of spirit, Mami's willingness to respect his word and behave accordingly deserved appreciation. Lakshmi didn't mind that she was expressly prohibited from entering the kitchen. As Mami had reminded her, only her studies were important. Once they were over, she was 'going to leave'. In the meantime, as someone who had sought shelter in their house, she could not create a problem over incidents next door. Besides, nothing was happening there that was not a common occurrence in the world, Mami had said, as if in justification.

It saddened Lakshmi that Mami, Amma and Kasturi, along with their whole community, were caught in a maze where they couldn't distinguish just from unjust. A maze which instilled a dread of asking questions because it was dangerous. They worried that instead of yielding benefits, asking questions might add to the burden of one's sins. It was like being afraid to set foot on an unfamiliar path. Over generations, their minds had become blunt to the extent that they believed they did not need deliverance from this maze. They were fools in spite of their brains, blind in spite of their eyes, deaf in spite of their ears. The eyes must become sharp. The ears must detect unheard sounds. The minds must resist. Only then would the seeing eye, listening ear and the resisting brain ask questions.

'We must question,' Lakshmi had said.

'How?' Mami had laughed dismissively. 'Do you have the necessary status, position and power?'

Lakshmi had goosebumps. She would acquire them. No human was born with those credentials. They were societal constructs put in place by men. Paths that they had laid. Limits which they had set. Rules that they had prescribed. It was their kingdom, their fortress. How could she demolish it and bring it down? She told herself that there was no need for demolition. It was their complacency that had to be smashed. They had to be made aware, to admit that these were atrocities. Laws must be enacted. It was a task for the men in the administration. But how could she make them do it? Theirs was a domain of power. She was not qualified even to enter it. The whole world was against her. There was an enormous burden on her back. She had to set it down.

How?

12

'Vande Mataram.'

The words fell on Kasturi's ears clear as rain. Her body tingled all over even now. All the birds, flowers and trees in the natural world shouted the slogan in unison.

'Vande Mataram.'

The cry reverberated in the soil, water and sky, making the whole universe tremble. Kasturi scanned the avenue of memories with her clouded eyes and sharpened her dulled ears. The voice rang out loud and clear.

Vande Mataram is our chant / We salute the mother of our great land.

What a marvellous voice. Equal in its beauty to the music from Sundaramurthi's nadaswaram, it sounded clear as bronze, unmarred by any discordant note.

All I know is only what I've heard.

If such virtuosity could be achieved from just listening, he must be a born genius. He had an immensely subtle mind and a proud heart. His strength came from his determination to raise his voice for the nation. Though he shouted slogans with eyes blazing, he also knew how to sing '*Chinnanchiru kiliye*' (My pet parakeet) in a voice tender with love. A faint smile appeared on Kasturi's wrinkled face.

Singaram stood before her. Kasturi was beside him, holding a tricolour flag. When both of them shouted 'Vande Mataram' together, new gates flew open. It felt like this was indeed the gateway to heaven.

'Police. Kasturi, we have to run. Take my hand. Let's run.' His hand feels like iron. Like a ball of flowers, her hand takes shelter in his. Kasturi runs with him. It's an endless flight. It feels like the whole world is running along with them. They are running at a feverish pace. The tumult raises a cloud of dust. Beatings, kicks, revolt, sacrifice, betrayal, disappointment and spilt blood ... She is at the very centre, eyes bulging in fear, orphaned ... even the deity's chamber has disappeared ... it is a figment of the imagination ... she has suffered enough.

'Aththai laughs to herself, then she cries,' Manjula said.

'They say all the old memories return at the moment of death.'

'Poor Aththai, Paati.'

'She is doing poorly, sure. But aren't we the ones who bear that burden?'

'Come on, Paati. You're also talking like Somu.'

'You won't understand it now. It's the burden of lifelong stigma.'

Without continuing the conversation with her grandmother, Manjula went to the room where Kasturi lay. When she was unconscious, did memories of the past pass through Aththai's mind? Though she was older than Paati, Kasturi was Aththai to everyone in the family. No one ever called her Paati. Manjula believed that there were secret troves inside Aththai. They must hold many interesting treasures. Heart-rending stories. Moments that reached the limits of rapture. Manjula was sad that she couldn't listen to them when Aththai was still in good health. She also wondered whether Aththai would have narrated all those stories and incidents. Perhaps not. No one allowed her to open her mouth about the past. Manjula had learnt that her own grandfather was a mridangam player only when Aththai happened to mention it one day.

'Sabapathi was a born genius, did you know that? He was such a marvellous mridangam player when he was just sixteen.'

When she asked her father about it, he snapped angrily, 'It's all lies.' Then he went to Aththai and scolded her. Not wanting to get Aththai into trouble, Manjula never broached the topic again.

Certain memories of the past were prohibited in that house. Now, with her consciousness adrift, Aththai seemed to be travelling freely through that past.

Sweat flowed like a rivulet from Kasturi's forehead. With Thilakam singing vocals and Sabapathi on the mridangam, dancing in step with them was a huge challenge for her. She was afraid that enchanted by Thilakam's voice she might miss the taalam. Her body felt charged, eager to throw a challenge at the figure tapped by Sabapathi's fingers. Confident that this combination would last forever, her feet danced and leapt, scarcely touching the ground. Once the varnam was over, Thilakam started singing the new padam they had choreographed. After drawing out the melody of Bhairavi raagam once, when Thilakam started with '*Chinnanchiru kiliye, kannamma*', Kasturi experienced a fresh burst of energy. Sabapathi had learnt the song in Sundaramurthi Mama's house from his new friend, Singaram.

Singaram was six or seven years older than Sabapathi. It was he who had been raising slogans with Mama the other day. Her gaze couldn't have settled on him for more than a few seconds—the carriage had passed in a flash—yet his teak-brown body and face were imprinted on her mind. Every now and then she would tingle in anticipation, wondering when she would get an opportunity to hear that song again.

'This is the Bharathiar song that Singaram sings everywhere, isn't it?'

Kasturi turned when she heard the voice and saw Sundaramurthi Mama sitting in the hall.

'Ah, when did you come, Mama?' she said, beaming.

His smile reddened by betel juice, he said, 'Don't interrupt your practice. I was already here during the varnam.'

'Bale,' he said in appreciation after Kasturi finished her zestful performance of the padam.

'That's enough for the day, Amma. My legs are aching,' Kasturi said as she sat on the floor.

'What's with the intense practice? Do you have any concerts coming up?' Sundaramurthi said.

'Yes, Sundaram. We have been invited to perform at a house-warming ceremony in Perungudi Zameen's house.'

'Perungudi Zameen, is it?' Sundaramurthi said thoughtfully. His tone and the fleeting shadow in his eyes made Kasturi uneasy.

'What's it, Mama? Do you know anything about them?' she asked.

'I've heard that they don't have a good reputation.'

'In that case, let's turn them down, Akka,' Sabapathi said.

Sengamalam slapped her forehead in annoyance. 'Look at this fellow talking out of turn! Why should we care about their character? We are going to dance, collect our money and come back right away,' she said.

'If they are not decent people, we won't go, Amma,' Kasturi said, still troubled.

Sengamalam was angry. 'A wealthy gentleman says, "I'll give you a lot of money if you dance just for two hours." After the performance, we need not linger for even a minute. How will it dent our honour? Hey Sundaram, did you come here only to create trouble?'

Sundaramurthi smiled awkwardly. 'No, Akka. I just told you what I've heard, so that Kasturi can be a little careful. A man called Gopalaiyer from Madras will come here. He runs a music sabha. He has heard of Kasturi's dance, it seems, and wants to organize a performance there. If she starts dancing in Madras, you won't need to perform for any zameen.'

'Let the man approach us first. We'll take it from there,' Sengamalam said.

Still not convinced, Kasturi, Thilakam and Sabapathi exchanged glances and cast their eyes down.

Pretending not to notice their mood, Sengamalam told them sharply, 'Get on with your work.' Everyone got up and went inside.

'She is blinded by money,' Thilakam muttered.

'Akka, why do you agree to everything Amma says, as if you are an ordinary dancer? Brother Singaram was right about you.'

Kasturi looked at Sabapathi with surprise. 'And what did your Singaram say?'

'He said, "Your sister is totally unaware of what a great dancer she is."'

Kasturi laughed. 'How can he say this? I haven't even met him.'

'So what if you haven't met him? He attends every time you perform in the temple.'

'When he is not busy shouting "Vande Mataram", is that it?'

Sabapathi chuckled. 'He is not a jobless fellow with nothing to do, Akka. He makes idols using aimpon, the alloy of five metals. He sings well too.'

'My, my! I am sure the man won't get another admirer like you. Bring him over some day. We'll also listen to him,' Thilakam said cheerfully.

'Oh well. He is an achari, so Amma won't let him in. Unless he comes disguised as an upper-caste zameendar, there is no hope,' Sabapathi said flatly.

The pragmatism in his words and his world-weary tone made Kasturi cringe. Thilakam's gaze seemed to indicate that Kasturi herself was responsible for it. Well, what do they expect me to do?

Sengamalam could not accompany them to the Perungudi Zameen's mansion. When they received word that the carriage sent by the zameen had broken down on the way, they readied their own cart for travel. After Thilakam and Sabapathi had taken their seats with their shruti box and mridangam, there was room left only for Kasturi. Cart driver Muthu assured Sengamalam: 'Don't worry, Akka. I will bring them back safely.'

When they arrived at the mansion, the hall was already full.

'Zameendar is about to flare up. What took you so long?' A scowling man led them inside through the back entrance.

'The carriage you sent us didn't arrive in time. So we had to come in our cart,' Sabapathi said curtly.

'All right. You must start right away. All the important sahibs are waiting. Did you know that the Durai is also here?' the man said.

Sabapathi started to say something, but Kasturi grabbed his hand and silenced him.

They had erected a stage in a big hall. Many people were already sitting in the chairs arranged in the hall. A liveried attendant was serving fruit juice or alcoholic drinks to everyone. Once Thilakam and Sabapathi had sat down on one side of the stage, Kasturi went up, greeted the audience, touched the ground and raised her head. Enthusiastic applause broke out in the room. In the front row, a white British officer was seated next to the zameendar.

Kasturi remembered that stranger, Singaram. 'Why should your sister dance in front of a white man who considers us slaves?' he might ask. When Thilakam started with '*Gajananam*', the opening hymn to Lord Ganesha, she came back to her senses. As Amma had told them, this was her vocation; she must dance for the money they would be paid and leave at once without stopping even for a moment. How did it matter who was sitting in the front row?

After she had danced the alarippu, Thilakam started singing a padam. They had decided that only padams would be suitable for this audience. Once she started dancing, Kasturi forgot the people sitting in the audience.

When they had finished performing Kshetraiyer's padam and jaavali, Thilakam sang '*Chinnanchiru kiliye, kannamma*', her voice dripping with love; melting in its tenderness, Kasturi danced as though she was smitten. Suddenly she found the Durai standing on the stage in front of her. He was in an obviously inebriated state. As Kasturi froze in astonishment, he muttered something in English and grabbed her waist and hand. Sabapathi stopped playing the mridangam; Thilakam's singing came to a halt. The audience, though, was not shocked at the Durai's behaviour. It roared its approval and broke into applause. Kasturi's face turned red with humiliation.

'Chee! Let go of my hand.' She flung his hand aside. Seething with anger, she turned to the zameendar seated in the front row, 'Why did you allow him to come up on the stage?'

'Hey, what is wrong?' the Durai said as he lurched towards her again.

'Don't come near me,' she said sternly.

The zameendar stood up and said, 'Are you going to melt if he touches you? Why are you acting shy, as if you are a chaste woman?'

The crowd clapped and laughed raucously.

Kasturi was on the verge of breaking down. Blinking back her tears, she exploded, 'We may not be chaste women who never step out of their homes. But we are artists. I made a mistake in coming to dance here, where there is no respect for our art.'

'And how does Raja show you respect?' someone heckled.

The crowd tittered again.

After glaring in fury at the heckler, Kasturi gave Thilakam and Sabapathi the sign to leave immediately and hurried towards the back entrance. Picking up the shruti box, kattai and mridangam, Thilakam and Sabapathi fled from the hall. They could hear the Durai screaming incoherently in anger. There was a big commotion among the audience. They ran to the cart which was stationed in the backyard, and as soon as they climbed aboard, Muthu demonstrated great presence of mind and rode away in a flash. Kasturi found it consoling that he never asked them what had happened. Her heart was pounding; her earlobes and cheeks were hot with rage. It was a good thing that the zameen's carriage had not turned up that day and Sengamalam could not accompany them. If Amma had been present, she would have mollified Kasturi, telling her that all this was quite normal.

As though even Muthu's horse had understood the situation, it flew like the wind. Men from the zameen came chasing after the cart for some distance, but unable to catch up, they got tired and headed back, spewing a stream of abuse. So long as their pursuers' heads were visible, no one in the cart looked up or spoke a word. Suddenly, Thilakam buried her face between her knees and started to cry. Trying to hide his own tears on seeing Thilakam break down, Sabapathi turned away to face the road. Kasturi remained silent. She felt that those two should not have been born in this clan. They were people who valued their honour, dignity and self-respect. In this aspect, there was no difference between Lakshmi and Thilakam. But unlike Lakshmi, Thilakam lacked the courage to take a firm stand. And even if she were to take a stand, she couldn't approach a man she could call her father and demand her right to be looked after, as Lakshmi had done with Periya Mirasu. Their father could be anyone, even someone among the crowd they had faced that afternoon. Chee, chee, she would prefer to remain ignorant than learn his identity.

After some time, Thilakam calmed down. She raised her head and firmly wiped her face with the free end of her sari. Kasturi embraced her and stroked her hair.

Sabapathi said, 'Brother Muthu, our honour was saved today because of you.'

'Thambi, the Collector's men are tricksters. They may cut across the fields and attack us. We should give them the slip,' Muthu said without slowing down.

Suddenly they heard voices. 'Vande Mataram!'

Sabapathi's body tingled reflexively. A procession of freedom fighters was marching down the street. Sabapathi's expression changed instantly.

'Vande Mataram!'

Hearing Sabapathi's cry, Kasturi smiled and shouted, 'Vande Mataram!'

'Akka, I want to join the procession and march with them. May I?'

'No, Sabapathi. If something goes wrong, how will I explain it to Amma?'

'Mama will be there. Brother Singaram, too.'

'Where?' Kasturi looked out eagerly.

'Brother Muthu, how about slowing down a little?' Sabapathi said.

'Thambi, we don't know when the police will turn up here. Your nadaswaram player is standing over there. He signalled me to get out of here fast. He knows that all of you are inside.'

Kasturi couldn't tell whether Muthu was speaking the truth or spinning a yarn. She was curious to see if she could spot Singaram in the crowd. She had the strong urge herself to get down and join them. Yet, her heart was fearful. 'What's happened to me?' she wondered, mortified.

'I can't see that achari, brother,' Muthu told Sabapathi.

Kasturi was surprised that Muthu knew about Singaram.

'Muthu is right, Sabapathi. It won't do us any good to get caught by the police.'

Muthu drove the cart faster. Suddenly they heard a police whistle. The sloganeers' cries became even louder. There was noise and confusion everywhere. Muthu entered a lane and stopped the cart in the backyard of a small house.

'Everyone, get down. Go inside and sit down. This house belongs to a friend of mine.'

All three got down and walked in the direction Muthu had pointed. It was not a house, but a workshop with a thatched roof. In the light from the mud lamps placed in different spots, Singaram and two other men were putting the final touches on a few sculptures. Kasturi stood bewildered, feeling a mix of joy and alarm. It was evident that Singaram too was taken aback by their sudden arrival.

Muthu told him urgently, 'Brother, let them sit safely somewhere. It looks like the police are coming after us. They could be the Durai's men who had come to the zameen's house earlier today.'

Kasturi looked at Muthu in amazement. She didn't know how he could see what was invisible to them.

Moving briskly, Singaram said, 'This is not a palace, da. They will have to wait in the kitchen. Come this way.' He led them to a covered enclosure adjoining the shed, spread out a tattered mat and bade them to sit. Saying nothing more, he shut the door to the enclosure and hurried back to the workshop. Though they were hiding precariously in that dark corner, which held nothing but a few burnt sticks of firewood, ash and an open mud stove, Kasturi felt at peace. Sabapathi and Thilakam looked at each other and smiled, as though they were participants in a game.

They could hear the sound of boots and voices outside. Suddenly, Singaram's voice rang out from the shed, singing a kaavadi chindu tune:

'*Even the sages who know everything that happened in ancient times / Cannot divine the year of her birth; such is our mother's glory.*'

In the kitchen on the other side of the partition, Kasturi and the others could hear it clearly. Suddenly energized, the three of them sat upright, and nodded their heads to the song in enjoyment.

'This too is Bharathi's song,' Sabapathi muttered.

They heard the clatter of booted feet entering the workshop. The song continued as before.

'Oi, achari. Stop singing! Our Durai wants to know whether two dasi girls and a young boy came here by any chance.'

Singaram's singing didn't cease. He must have shook his head: No, I don't know.

'This fellow is a lunatic. Come, let's go. Anyway, that arrogant bitch will never step into this achari's workshop.'

Someone said something in English.

'No way. She won't come here even to hide. This fellow is from a low caste, brother. You should tell our Durai.'

Kasturi's face turned red with shame. There were further arguments, but in the meantime, Singaram continued to sing. She thought his singing was a slap on their faces.

The sound of boots faded away.

Without stopping his singing, Singaram came to where they were sitting, removed the partition and signalled for them to step out. They laughed at his antics as they emerged from the enclosure.

When his song was over, he bowed his head and greeted Kasturi.

Entirely without her permission, her heart dropped at his feet.

13

'THE SKY IS darkening, child. It's going to rain in ten minutes,' the old man said.

I looked up. Far away, a mass of black clouds was beginning to gather. The air had cooled. I was disappointed. The urge to chat with him for some more time was making me restless.

'Don't dawdle. Walk fast. Where is your house?'

I was reluctant to tell him where I lived. I worried that he too would raise his eyebrows and say 'Oh, *that* house?' and go away quietly, just like the little boy and his grandmother had done. He seemed to be in a hurry, as if he had taken his wife's instruction to 'come right back' as gospel.

'I think we have to go a little further,' I dissembled. 'Since entering the forest this morning, I've lost my sense of direction, thatha. If you take me to a spot from where I can see the lake, I'll find my way.'

'Why would you do such a thing? How can you enter an unfamiliar forest all by yourself? Come on. Keep up,' the old man said and walked faster.

'Thatha, what do they mean by "kaathu karuppu"?'

He turned around abruptly and looked at me.

'What a question!' He shook his head as if to say: You are a real idiot. 'How did you come out of that forest today? When you came to us, looking as if someone had dragged you there, I knew right away it was thanks to that thing.'

'Thanks to what thing?'

'What we call ghosts and spirits, child. They may do a person good, or they may also strike them dead.'

His words made my stomach turn. What would he say if I told him that I had seen my mother? Amma would never strike anyone dead. She was a protector. When I had thought the forest was going to swallow me, she had appeared to save me, shown me the way out and disappeared.

'Has it killed anyone before this?'

'Yes. I am coming with you only because it has. In the past two years, three men were found dead with their necks broken.'

I was startled. 'How can you say they were struck down by a spirit? Someone could have murdered them.'

'Only educated people talk like this,' the old man said irascibly. 'Until two years ago, that forest was peaceful. We were not afraid to walk there with our children. From the day they found that corpse in the lake, the forest changed. Mist and an overcast sky are permanent now. Those who go in cannot come out. If they enter regardless, they end up dead with their necks broken.'

I was worried that he might hear the pounding of my heart.

'Whose corpse was found in the lake?' I asked cautiously. I saw a change in the old man's body language.

He said, 'I heard it was a woman. Was she in some trouble? Was she angry about something? Who knows?'

I walked in silence for some time, trying to hide the impact of his words on me. Those questions had tormented not only me, but troubled the whole town. My eyes filled with tears. Grief entered my throat and choked my vocal cords.

Recovering my wits, I asked him, 'Do you know who that woman was?'

'I heard it was a woman who lived in a bungalow by the lake. How would I know? These rich people might have a hundred issues.'

The old man walked without saying a word. Perhaps he did not wish to talk about what he knew. How much did he know, really? Perhaps he knew more than what Appa had told me. I was dying to find out.

After a long pause, he started speaking as though he was talking to himself.

'For the poor, survival is the only hardship. Whether it is a row between husband and wife, or a quarrel with children, everything comes out in the open. People say, "Calm down. Why are you fighting over such a petty issue?" and help them reunite. Some fights never end, of course. I am telling you because there are few secrets among the poor. Look here, though. At every level on the mountain slope, there are bungalows like separate kingdoms. No one knows what secrets lie buried inside them. Even if someone is killed, no one in the next bungalow will realize what has happened. Whatever it is will be quietly buried, without revealing a name or place. Only when a corpse is found floating on the lake do we learn that this house that stands like a stone fortress is resting on a decayed foundation. But no information would ever come out.'

I walked without responding, hoping that he would say more on his own.

'Money, wealth, education, status and whatnot—these things alone won't help you live in peace. They all turn into burdens.'

'Are you saying that they are not necessary for a human being, thatha?'

'If I say they aren't, you'll call me a lunatic. Overall, I'd say something more is also necessary. I am not educated. What would I know? When ghosts wander around like this, my heart pines for that something. Do you know a place called Coakers Walk?'

'I know, thatha. A beautiful mountain peak where they've laid a path for walkers, right?'

'It was laid by the British. Elegant women would stroll there, holding hands. I have stood there with my mouth open, watching white durais taking a stroll. When a lady who was fondly holding someone's hand fell from the top one day, I was shocked. After her, many others jumped from there and died. They said it was love. What do you gain by listing a hundred reasons after the person has died? Now they have built a tall fence. When there was no fence, it was easy to die or be killed. Whenever I heard about those deaths, I used to think they were idiots who didn't know how to live. If you keep making small knots into big ones, they will end up strangling you—or someone else.'

'Do you think something like that must have happened to the woman who fell into the lake?' The old man didn't notice the tremor in my voice.

He turned abruptly and looked at me. 'Who knows whether she fell in or was found lying there?'

Shocked, I stopped walking and stared at him. 'Do you think someone might have dumped the corpse there?'

Recovering quickly, the old man gave me a cold glare. 'Look here, child. I don't know anything. See, we have reached the lake. Find your way home. Why do you need all these old tales?'

The old man turned around abruptly and walked away without a backward glance. He didn't even give me the opportunity to thank him. I found myself unable to continue walking. Both my legs were shaking and unsteady. I sat down at the edge of the high walkway. My mind remained unsettled for a long time. It was astonishment from going through several incredible experiences on the same day. I didn't think it would calm down any time soon.

Who knows whether she fell in or was found lying there?

It was only his assumption. A suspicion that came naturally to an unlettered villager. A grotesque fantasy about an unfamiliar world. Why should I let it upset me? I began to console myself. Amma had no enemy who might have wanted to kill her. Appa was the one most affected by her death. Though the reason for her suicide was still a mystery, it could have been caused by a burden unknown to the outside world. Appa was afraid that the world might think she had killed herself because of him. I felt ashamed that I, a PhD and a university professor resident in the United States, had become so agitated after listening to the ramblings of an uneducated old man who still believed in ghosts and spirits.

I sat there for a while, watching the vehicles and bicycles passing by on the road. Off the path that ran upward, I saw a sign on the right that said 'Church of South India Retreat Centre'. The campus was spread out like a huge estate. Inside the campus, at the end of a long walkway, there were buildings at many levels. It seemed to be a place where people of the church came for spiritual relaxation. A funny thing about 'Retreat' (Amma had given the bungalow she bought here the same name): Appa and Amma came here only to relax, wanting to rest mind and body, seeking peace. But they might not have found it. Amma must have nursed the desire for an intense quest. She alone knew what she was searching for. It had drowned along with her in this lake with a surface area of six and a half square kilometres and depth of eighty feet.

The old man had said that it might have been anxiety or anger. What was Amma anxious or angry about? Disappointment, panic, humiliation, unfulfilled desire—it could have been any of those factors. Mountain, clouds, air and flowers constituted only the external environment. They didn't have the strength to drive away the struggle that took place within the mind. Because she didn't know how to unburden herself to anyone, Amma couldn't find a resolution to her inner conflict. She wasn't even in the habit of appealing to god. 'Are you just made of stone? All these days I thought you were a guardian deity—was I a madwoman?' The heroine or the heroine's mother in many Tamil or Hindi films will, at some stage, stand before a temple idol and shed copious tears. Whatever it is—superstition or imagination—god is an effective load-bearing platform. Both are true, perhaps. When I think about it now, god is nothing but the psychotherapy we need. When we bang our heads in despair and weep before the Almighty, He becomes an outlet that lightens our burdens. Even when things get out of hand, if we lay the responsibility on god, we are unlikely to take a disastrous decision on our own. But there is no guarantee that people who believe in god and spirituality won't kill themselves.

This train of thought was boring even to myself.

Money, wealth, education, status and whatnot—they all turn into burdens.

What a simple explanation. What was Amma's burden? She had killed herself without leaving any clue as to why she could no longer bear her burden, such as it was. I have read about people who made meticulous arrangements before they took their own life. In works of fiction, people died after writing elaborate letters, blaming some people for their decision or clarifying that certain others were not responsible. Amma hadn't left even a small piece of paper, just an incomplete note that said, 'Rain is pouring down like wires drawn between the sky and the earth.'

Breaking out of my reverie, I stood up instantly. Since the sky was growing darker, I started walking towards home. I would reach the house in ten or fifteen minutes. Suddenly I felt hungry. The time for breakfast had passed. I wondered if Appa, after rising and not finding me in the house, was waiting for me. Ganesan had told me that he would make aapam and stew today. Remembering his words made me even more hungry. As I continued with rapid strides, I had the illusion that the path I was on was getting longer. So many bends and turns? Had I lost my way again? A cloud of mist began to spread like smoke on the lake. I felt as though I had entered a world of illusions. I walked faster. The rain began to pour down, and together with the mist, made it difficult for me to see ahead. Amma was toying with me today.

Amma? I was taken aback. What was wrong with me? If I told Appa that I had seen Amma today, he would wonder whether I had lost my sanity. But in my mind, I believed that I had actually seen her. I didn't even bother to ask myself how I could have seen her. Amma's figure—the one wearing a yellow sari and red blouse—was imprinted so deeply in my mind that I never wondered whether it was illusion or magic. The miracle by which the mist had parted before me, as if by a magic wand, and made me follow Amma out of the forest was not something I had dreamt; it was my actual experience. Would Appa believe it? He would coax me to go away with him to Delhi.

Long ago, Appa used to sing an old film song: '*Vazhve maayam*' (Life is an illusion). The old man might say that this lament was idle chatter by those who didn't know how to live. If his life of hunger and poverty was true, so were ghosts and demons. He had learnt to accept and coexist with them. Hence, he was free of confusion. He was certainly wiser than Appa or Amma, who were both educated and held high positions at work. I decided to tell Joan about him.

It had started to rain heavily. Coping with its ferocity as best as I could, I ran.

'Chinnamma, Chinnamma.' I heard Ganesan's voice behind me. He was running towards me with two umbrellas in his hand. 'Where are you going? You have passed the house,' he said as he unfurled an umbrella and handed it to me.

'Really?' I looked around me in confusion. 'In this rain, I couldn't even see the pathway.'

He ran ahead and opened the gate as though I had arrived in a car. We had to walk half a kilometre from the gate to reach the house. Since my jeans and sweater were drenched and clinging to my body, I ran behind him. 'Careful. You might trip on something,' he cried as he hurried. When I climbed the steps into the house, he was standing there with a towel. 'Dry your hair first,' he instructed me. 'Change your clothes and come down for breakfast. Aiya is waiting for you.'

'Ask him to start eating. I'll be there in two minutes.'

I took the staircase on the side of the house and reached my room. By the time I took my wet clothes off, I had a cramp in my leg. When I stood under the shower which sprayed hot water on my body, when I changed into fresh clothes, and when I dried my hair with the hairdryer, Amma's image sat inside my eyelids. It was there when I looked in the mirror. Startled, I turned around and checked—it was only an illusion. By the time I forcefully pushed it away and rushed downstairs, Appa had finished eating; now he was popping vitamin pills into his mouth.

'Where did you go, 'ma? You didn't even take your mobile with you,' he said in a tone of mild reproach.

'Sorry, Appa. I forgot. I went for a walk. I thought I'd skip the usual route and started walking on a new trail that went up the hill. It led me into a forest. It was so dense. As I kept walking, I lost my way. It was as if I was circling around to the same spot. On top of that, darkness and mist—I couldn't see a thing. '

'How did it happen?'

'I don't know, Appa. I wondered if I was ever going to come back.'

'Then?'

Just then Ganesan brought hot aapams and stew to the table. I waited until he had left.

I considered telling Appa that Amma had brought me out of the forest, but I was afraid it would sound absurd even to me now.

'I don't know how I came out. Once I was outside, I didn't know which area it was. Finally, an old man escorted me all the way to the lake. As I was heading home, it started to rain.'

'Don't go off on adventures like this, 'ma. I've heard about people going up a hill and accidentally falling down a chasm on the other side. If you fell down in some deserted place, where would we even search for you?'

Appa covered his face suddenly and began to cry. His shoulders heaved.

'What's the matter, Appa?' I said.

'You are all I have, 'ma.'

I had never seen him so fragile. I had never imagined that he would feel so close to me. I experienced an unexpected, unfamiliar tenderness towards him. I was supposed to have been close to my mother, but she had never exposed her weakness to me even once. I got up quickly and hugged him with my left arm.

'I won't go off anywhere, Appa. I'll be careful from now on.'

Recovering his composure, he said, 'Go and eat.'

Ganesan, who had watched everything with another batch of aapams in his hand, said for his part, 'Aiya was very worried, Chinnamma.'

'I won't make him worry any more, I promise. Here, keep giving me aapams till I say "No, I've had enough",' I said, laughing. 'Super, Ganesan,' I added.

A faint smile appeared on Appa's face.

When I looked from my room upstairs, I could see Appa strolling in the garden. No doubt several strange things had happened to me today. Though I was quite stunned when I saw Amma's figure in the forest, Appa breaking down in front of me had astonished me even more. Would Amma have considered how helpless Appa would become because of her death, I wondered. For the first time, I felt a measure of sympathy towards Appa. Amma's suicide seemed to be a revenge on Appa. It seemed to be a challenge that said: The world will suspect only you; it is a black mark that will stain your life till your last breath. 'Who knows what anger,' the old man had said. I remembered reading in a psychology text that some kind of rage was the reason behind all suicides.

Amma would never have killed herself from rage. If she was angry, she would fight it out and win rather than jump into a lake like a coward or a wounded egoist. The more I thought about it, the more I began to suspect that Amma might not have killed herself. I knew that Appa wouldn't be of any help to me. He was much too bewildered himself. He did not want to talk about it at all. I would make no progress unless Amma herself turned up to assist me, like those ghosts who supplied clues to the boy in *The Sixth Sense.*

I was amused by my own crazy thoughts. If ghosts were so ready to supply clues, how convenient it would be for the police department.

For no particular reason, I went to the library that Amma had built with great passion. She had maintained the room with meticulous care. The lake was visible through all the glass windows in the room. A rosewood easy chair was available for one to sit and read by the windows. I glanced at the shelves, picked up a book at random and sank into the chair. *The House of Blue Mangoes* by David Davidar. The copy was inscribed by the author; the year was 2003. I was idly turning the pages. When I closed the book, I found that on an empty page at the end of the book, a few names and addresses were listed in Amma's handwriting.

The first one to catch my eye was 'C.S.I. Retreat Centre'.

The next one read: 'Sabapathi, Aranmanai Street, Thanjavur'.

14

THEY HEARD SOUNDS of a fresh disturbance outside. Though the Durai's men had left, the procession must have taken the same route. 'Vande Mataram.' Hearing the slogan, Sabapathi got up immediately and went to the entrance, but Singaram hastily pulled him back inside and said, 'You can't go now, thambi. The police are heading this way.' Everyone stayed silent for some time. They could hear the police chasing and beating the protesters, and the feeble cries of the injured.

None of this registered with Kasturi. Her gaze was fixed on Singaram, the man who had bowed his head and greeted her. Imagining the beautiful aimpon sculptures, finished and half-done, come to life in the light from the mud lamps, and possess her in that unearthly ambience gave Kasturi goosebumps. The great artist who had sculpted them had stood before her and bowed to her. She was overwhelmed by the dignity and majesty of his gesture; it was a majesty that she had never before witnessed in any man. She recalled how a faceless guard, a slave to the English, had abused him shamefully as 'a lower-caste fellow'. The lackey might step outside and call her a whore, too. He might say a lot more, even. Her whole being cringed in humiliation.

There were more agitated voices outside. Singaram secured the workshop's wooden gates with iron rings. At the sounds of police firing, Sabapathi's eyes bulged in shock and outrage. He raced up a ladder placed against the wall, looked out of the latticed window high above and cried out, 'Aiyaiyo! They've killed a man, Akka.'

'Thambi. Get down. No talking.'

Ordered thus in Singaram's deep, low voice, Sabapathi climbed down immediately and sat on the floor close to the wall. He looked like he had been struck by a ghost. His eyes welled up. Singaram climbed up the ladder, had a look and descended quietly. Grief and rage were etched on his face. Everyone sat huddled in silence. Panic was writ large on the faces of the sculptors there.

After a brief spell of clamour and confusion, the street fell silent again. The marchers must have scattered and fled after the police firing. Singaram sat with his head bowed and knees drawn up. Kasturi was aghast to be meeting him at such an inopportune moment. They heard the rumble of thunder. It looked like it might rain too. They couldn't think of staying any longer; they *had* to leave.

Singaram, who had gone up the ladder to have another look, came back and said angrily, 'Wretched dogs! They are dragging the dead man along the ground.'

Kasturi was startled back to her senses.

'How cruel!' she said gently. 'Do they shoot recklessly all the time? You and Sundaramurthi Mama march in a procession every day.'

Singaram said gravely, 'Thousands of people like us have hit the streets. The Britishers think that we will be frightened by their bullets. We are not afraid of guns or of going to jail. If we want freedom, we will have to fight for it.'

She wondered nervously whether their struggle could ever be successful. How could the unarmed fight and win against those who had guns? Sabapathi's face was still frozen in panic.

At the sound of a thunderclap, Singaram told Muthu, 'Leave at once, brother. There is no one outside now. It looks like it's going to rain heavily.'

'Yes, we should go. Thambi, get up. Come, Akka. It will be a nuisance if it starts raining.'

Kasturi noted that Singaram never asked them why the Durai's men had come looking for them.

'We'll leave, then,' she said with a faint smile. 'We must thank you for giving us a place to hide. Along with that, we had a chance to listen to your wonderful singing.'

Singaram bowed his head and said, 'I am not a learned person like you. All I know is only what I've heard.'

Kasturi gave a soft smile. 'That's learning, too, isn't it?'

'All right, let's go,' Muthu called out to them from the cart.

'Have you seen my dance performance?'

'Never miss it.'

Throughout their journey home, a smile sat on Kasturi's lips. *Never miss it.* Four syllables. Just four. Sprouting wings, her heart soared in the sky. A crown sat on her head. When he had raised his head and looked at her while saying them, his eyes had held high esteem and boundless respect for her. The humiliation she had experienced earlier that evening was forgotten. Sabapathi and Thilakam, though, sat glumly, as if they were weighed down by a huge burden.

Sengamalam was surprised to see them when they entered the house.

'What happened, di? Why have you come back so soon?'

'Don't ask me about anything,' Thilakam snapped in exhaustion and anger as she ran inside.

Sengamalam looked at Sabapathi and said, 'What's the matter?'

Sabapathi broke down. He exploded through angry tears: 'When Akka was midway through her performance, an Englishman got up on the stage and grabbed her hand. He said lewd things to her.'

The stiffness in Sengamalam's facial muscles relaxed instantly.

'Oh, I was worried, wondering what it could be. All right, come inside and tell me everything,' she said. Once they had passed the doorway and entered the hall, she asked nervously, 'Did you kick up a row and leave?'

Kasturi had expected her mother to be angry, but the way Sengamalam spoke, without an iota of self-respect, felt humiliating and repulsive. She recalled Lakshmi's term for their ignominy: 'wretched clan'.

'Are we to do nothing when random men grab Akka's hand?'

'*What* did you do?' Sengamalam asked in dismay.

'I pushed his hand away and left immediately,' Kasturi said.

'We got the whole amount in advance from the zameendar. If people come to know that you left in the middle, no one will invite us any more.'

'That would suit me fine. I'll never go to such places again,' Kasturi said.

'I wanted to die right there. I still do,' Thilakam said.

Paati, who was relaxing on the swing, said, 'Hush, you stupid woman. Learn to dust yourself off and get back on your feet again.' Then she added, 'They are right too, Sengamalam. From now on, we shouldn't accept invitations without making proper enquiries. Performing in a shady venue can only mean trouble.'

'I'll tell you just how shady,' Kasturi said angrily. 'I had finished three items. The moment we started the padam, this man came up on the stage. The stench of alcohol was unbearable. He grabbed my waist and said, "Let's dance."'

'Akka must never perform in a venue where British men are present. Dancing before them is treason against the country,' Sabapathi thundered. 'They are recklessly shooting our freedom fighters. I saw it today with my own eyes, Paati.'

Kanagu Paati looked with concern at their faces, which were flushed red with high emotion. 'All right. Have some tiffin and change your clothes,' she said in a conciliatory tone.

Sengamalam kept grumbling about something for a long time.

By the time Kasturi took off her jewellery, changed her clothes and came to eat tiffin, she had forgotten the incident. Singaram's tender eyes and shapely physique occupied her thoughts.

'Be honest, Akka. Don't you feel what happened today was disgraceful?'

Hearing Thilakam's voice, Kasturi turned to her. 'What should I think of as disgraceful?' she asked, paying her scant attention.

'What's wrong with you? The incident at the zameen's place today, what else?'

'Oh, you are talking about that. Yes, it was disgraceful. We registered our protest and came away, didn't we? Awful people! But their talk won't affect me. Even if they hawk and spit, it won't fall on me.'

'It falls on me,' Thilakam said angrily. 'I don't like this profession, Akka. I feel like running away somewhere.'

Kasturi looked at her, startled. There were tears in Thilakam's eyes. 'What do you mean? Where can we run to?' She went to Thilakam, hugged her and said, 'Hush, you stupid girl,' in Kanagu Paati's voice. A wan smile appeared on Thilakam's lips.

'I am not a sage. Nor am I a block of wood. There is only one thing that enables me to stand with my head held high: my dance. It gives me standing. A man who mocks me has no such status. He is a fool, a brute who knows nothing about art. If he creates trouble, we have to deal with it then and there. But to say that I won't dance or sing because of him, that I'll run away, is to be a coward. Singing will give you that stature. You must have confidence, Thilakam. You will definitely become a famous singer one day.'

'I don't want all that, Akka.'

'But you want to sing, don't you?'

'Of course. I'll die if I am not allowed to sing.'

'Then you have to forget what these imbeciles do and say.'

'That's what's impossible for me.'

'Hush, you stupid girl.'

That night, Kasturi was troubled alternately by thoughts of Singaram and worry about Thilakam. Her heart filled with pride when she recalled the courageous way he had said, 'We are not afraid of guns or of going to jail.' But she prayed that he and Mama would somehow escape the bullets of the British rulers, who shot down people indiscriminately out of reckless cruelty.

Whenever Kasturi heard Thilakam say, as she did often these days, 'I feel like dying,' it made her queasy in the stomach. Why were Sabapathi and Thilakam so touchy and angry about not being respected? She recalled how angry Lakshmi would get back when she was even younger than Thilakam was now.

Lakshmi had reproached her once: 'I don't understand why you never get angry, Kasturi.'

Unable to sleep, Kasturi tossed and turned in her bed. The suggestion that she lacked self-respect confused her. If I lacked self-respect, I wouldn't have scorned that Englishman whom everybody fawned over, stopped my performance and walked away.

Did you kick up a row and leave?

I'll never be capable of Amma's shamelessness. I will never insult my art for money. Just because I have an arrangement of sleeping with Raja out of respect for the fact that he is our family's patron, I won't be branded a prostitute. Whether I am living a life of honour or disgrace is determined by the rules I have set for myself. No random scoundrel can enter this house. Dance is what occupies my life. For dancing, I need my own space. I happen to have that. I am not bothered about anything else.

Of late, she had begun to feel that she was different from others around her. She realized, sometimes with trepidation, that changes were taking place within her too. Raja's arrogance, his constant mockery of the leaders of the freedom movement and his ingratiating behaviour with the Durai annoyed her no end. She couldn't just distance herself from his attitude, pretending that it had no connection with her. One day, after Gandhi had delivered a speech in Pudukkottai, Raja had sneered at him. 'Beggar. Mendicant. I hear he wants to launch a struggle over salt. Does he think the British will feel offended and hand over the country to him?' It had made her livid. 'Do you think our fellows can ever match the white man's intelligence? The country will surely go to ruin.' He had continued in the same vein for some time, and by the end of the evening, Kasturi was seething with rage.

There was something in the air tonight. 'How much longer shall we remain mute, not realizing that the men who have entrenched themselves in our land, who have prospered by robbing us, are now enslaving all of us?' When those wearing

Gandhi caps marched through the streets spreading this message, it drew even Sundaramurthi Mama, who thought about nothing but his naayanam, into the struggle and made him raise slogans. The magic chant of 'Vande Mataram!' had begun to shake up ordinary Indians. When she heard it, she got goosebumps all over. The days of fearing the white man were gone. 'There are thousands like us,' Singaram said. 'We are not afraid of guns or of going to jail.'

The air had changed. Rage filled the air now. The wrath of freedom fighters. Lakshmi's rage. The anger of Thilakam and Sabapathi. The fury she had felt against the Durai. All of it had mingled in the air, making it a weapon of battle now. She felt that there was one idea that was drawing everyone together—the yearning for freedom. Perhaps it was within all of us. 'Leaving this village is my only route to deliverance,' Lakshmi had said. 'I feel like running away,' Thilakam had told her. 'If we want freedom, we will have to fight for it,' Singaram had declared. Earlier, one needed status just to get angry. Now, everyone was angry. Pallars, Paraiyars, even women. They had developed the resolve to fight at all costs. It was an era where people had begun to realize that theirs was a world without justice. This was a churning of the mythical ocean of milk. It was highly volatile. She was stranded alone on the shore, wondering whether it was nectar or poison that would rise from the churning.

Singaram appeared and sang in her dreams. Singing themmangu, like a gentle breeze from the south, and 'Chinnanchiru kiliye', dripping with love, he enchanted her. 'How marvellously you sing,' she said. 'All I know is only what I've heard,' he said politely. The sound of gunshots rent the air. Singaram ran, shouting 'Vande Mataram'. 'Don't go. Don't go.'

In the morning, the world had returned to normal. She had to resume her dance practice. Sabapathi had come and taken his seat. As he applied semolina powder to the faces of his mridangam, Thilakam sat down to sing. Kanagu Paati lounged contentedly on the swing with her betel box. Just after Kasturi had finished performing a varnam with furious intensity, someone clapped: 'Superb, 'ma.' Surprised, Kasturi turned to look in that direction. A middle-aged man and a youth were sitting a little away, hidden from view. It seemed that Sengamalam and Kanagu Paati had been aware of their presence.

Kasturi recalled her experience from the previous day. 'Thank you, aiya. Who might you be?' she said warily.

'Remember, Sundaramurthi said that someone was going to come from Madras?' Sengamalam said brightly. 'They had come in while you were performing the refrain. "No need to disturb her. We will also get a chance to watch her dance," they said. That's why I didn't tell you.'

'Come, aiya. Sit on this swing here,' she invited them courteously.

Once they sat down, Thilakam and Sabapathi got ready to go back inside.

'Thambi, you played so well,' the older man praised Sabapathi.

'You too, 'ma. Your singing is remarkably good. I was stunned,' the youth said.

Blushing, Thilakam smiled at him and said, 'Thank you, aiya.'

Kasturi was glad that they had appreciated Thilakam.

'Though she is an accompanist for my dance now, she is destined to become a great singer.'

'We can create opportunities for her as well. I've come here to organize a concert for you in Madras. Shouldn't the people of Madras also get to appreciate such a marvellous dancer? If you dance in the city, you will earn not only fame but also material rewards. I forgot. My name is Gopalaiyer. He is my son, Kalyanaraman.'

'Greetings, aiya,' Kasturi said gently. 'We don't know anything about the city. I don't have any objection to dancing there either. But the party must have a good reputation. The audience should come there for the art.'

Gopalaiyer looked at her with surprise.

Sengamalam was quick to intervene. 'Girl, don't speak without knowing who our guest is.'

Gopalaiyer signalled to her to be quiet. 'Kasturi hasn't said anything wrong, really. I am happy she thinks so,' he said. 'The average person doesn't have a good opinion about sadir dancers. Only those who know how to appreciate dance and music will show them respect. Kasturi is right to be worried. Even in Madras, arranging a sadir concert is bound to attract opposition. I want to try and change that. I am going to start a new sabha. Kasturi must dance at the opening ceremony on the upcoming Pongal day.'

Sengamalam responded immediately. 'We are very happy, aiya. She is really fortunate to be able to perform in front of a discerning audience in Madras. You would of course know how it works. Around here, the dance master takes her to a concert. Three-fourths of the fees go to him.'

Kasturi sat with her head bowed. She kept away from the conversation, considering it a business negotiation between Gopalaiyer and Sengamalam. She was anxious that Amma should not appear too greedy.

'You need not worry,' Gopalaiyer said. 'Travel arrangements to Madras and back, accommodation for your stay, and fees for the performance—we will pay for everything. I will give the advance amount right now. Here is three hundred rupees. I will send the first-class train tickets by post or through a messenger. Is that all right?'

Taking the money from him, Sengamalam said, 'Fine, aiya. We will need five tickets. My mother will also come with us.'

'Of course, she is most welcome. I will make arrangements for all the amenities. Please prepare for the performance without worrying about anything. You may dance for two and a half to three hours.'

Kasturi was satisfied that their visitors were indeed respectable. Usually, it was the attendants who came to talk with them about arranging concerts in the houses of the big landlords and zameendars around Thanjavur. These servants behaved as if they themselves were the masters. They would demand buttermilk and tiffin, and eat heartily before leaving.

'Good. We will take your leave now.' Gopalaiyer got up.

'Why are you leaving already? Please have something to eat,' Sengamalam said.

'I don't eat anything outside my home, 'ma,' Gopalaiyer said.

Kalyanaraman said to Kasturi and Thilakam, 'I am really happy that I am going to see your dance and hear her singing very soon.'

Thilakam blushed again.

After the men left, it started raining heavily. 'This is a good omen,' Kanagu Paati said.

'Akka, do we resume practice or not?' Sabapathi said to Kasturi.

'How could we not?' Kasturi laughed, tucking the free end of her sari at the waist, and preparing for practice. 'Later, we will draw up a list of items for the concert in Madras. What do you say, Thilakam?'

Thilakam seemed to be afloat in some daydream.

'Here, I am talking to you. Why do you look lost? I asked you about drawing up a list.'

Thilakam collected herself quickly and said, 'Yes, we can, Akka. Doesn't Lakshmi Akka live in Madras? I wondered whether we could meet her,' she said.

'I'll go and get the address from her mother,' Sabapathi said.

After a very long time, Kasturi had thought about Lakshmi. She feared that the chasm between them had grown even wider. But she certainly didn't think that a time would come when Lakshmi would become her enemy.

15

LAKSHMI SAT UPRIGHT with a jolt. Someone was calling out to her, but she couldn't see anyone. On the terrace, the sun's heat had subsided a little. It was probably four-thirty; a gentle sea breeze had started up. At three she had gone downstairs, savoured Mami's adai and coffee, and come up again. The aroma of the jaggery and ghee she had eaten with the adais still lingered on her hands. Mami's adais were special. They were at once crunchy and soft. The ones she had consumed back home were dry and thick, hard to chew and swallow; if she ate half an adai in the afternoon, she couldn't eat anything at night. Mami was immensely flattered by Lakshmi's appetite for her adais. They made Lakshmi's taste buds and belly shamelessly ask for more, but stopping at two was good for her dignity—and her belly.

Smiling to herself, Lakshmi returned to the book she was studying. There was only a month left for her final-year exam. She was confident that she would pass with a first class. After graduation, she could immediately take up a job in a government hospital. While working, she wanted to pursue specialist post-graduate studies in obstetrics and gynaecology. She could rent a new accommodation and bring Amma to the city—only if she agreed to come. Amma said that she was comfortable in the village. Food was brought to her doorstep every day.

'I live like a queen, di,' Thulasi had said during Lakshmi's last visit to the village on an unusually long four-day vacation. After Paapa died, Lakshmi's father seemed to crave her mother's company. She saw her mother's relationship with Periya Mirasu as an emotional bond. One night, while they waited for Appa, Amma had talked to her about this and that.

'You call this a wretched clan, and you're right. But I didn't ask to be born here. And there was no way for me to rebel and go away. I didn't even think that I could fight. But I can say this for sure: I don't earn my living as a prostitute. It's my good luck that Periya Mirasu has taken a liking to me. Otherwise, I would have suffered worse than a dog. I may not be his legally wedded wife, but in my heart, he is the one I think of as my husband. He is faithful to me. How many men would do so much for the daughter of a mistress?'

Lakshmi didn't reply. Amma was trying to justify her way of life. Pointing out that she and her daughter had no legal rights as a family would make no difference to her. That she had been made to wait in Mirasu's backyard for her bowl of food for years didn't strike her as humiliation. Her sense of honour was not violated, nor was she angry that society had ostracized her entire clan and kept them in a disgraceful condition. That she wanted her daughter, too, to be shameless like her seemed like a major betrayal to Lakshmi, one she still felt angry about. Amma had no dreams about Lakshmi's future. She thought it would be perfectly normal for her daughter to spend her life as a zameendar's mistress. She did not want any changes in their lives. She was frightened of change, seeing it as a menace.

'With your strong will and stubbornness, I wondered where you would end up. I never imagined that you would make something of yourself some day.'

Lakshmi sat quietly with a faint smile on her lips. Amma was still uncertain about her own future. She had a different yardstick for honour. At times, Lakshmi felt frustrated that she had been unable to change her mother; she thought of it as a personal failure. But these days her mother seemed to be slightly wary of her—afraid she might say something inappropriate to Lakshmi.

'You are angry with me for not having self-respect. But even for self-respect, you'll need resources, no? I was worried that if I insisted on respect, Mirasu would stop coming here. But you don't understand that.'

'Enough, Amma,' Lakshmi said, losing patience finally. 'Why talk about the past now? I'm not asking you why you lived your life like that. What makes me angry is how afraid you are of change. The world cannot stay the same forever. It *must* change, at least in your children's time. It's only when we realize that injustice is happening that some of us will feel outraged enough to bring about change. You need not be afraid. I will become a doctor in six months. I will take you to Madras. You can hold your head high and live like a queen.'

Amma had laughed prettily, like a young girl. 'I still can't believe it. It feels like a dream. You know I am living like a queen already; do you want me to leave your father and come with you?'

Lakshmi was silent. She understood that living apart from Periya Mirasu would be really hard for her mother. He was lucky to have landed such a loyal mistress. As she reined in her wandering mind and returned her attention to the book, someone called out to her again, 'Akka!' She raised her head and looked around. 'Over here!' she heard a voice from the terrace of the neighbour's house. 'Are you hard of hearing? I've been calling you forever.'

She got up and went to the parapet wall. That girl Yogu's veiled head was visible.

'Akka!' Yogu greeted her cheerfully.

Lakshmi saw a childlike eagerness in the girl's large, beautiful eyes. Her dark, thick, curving eyelashes enhanced the blackness of her eyes. She wore a streak of vibhuti on her bare forehead, like Adi Sankara.

Pleased to see her, Lakshmi said, 'Yogu, how are you?'

'How did you know my name?' Yogu demanded, her eyes widening. The ascetic look was totally unsuitable for Yogu's face. Suppressing her anger at this atrocity, Lakshmi told her with a smile, 'Do you see that crow flying over there? It came and told me.'

'You know the language of crows, do you? It steals all the vadagam we work so hard to make. Put in a word with that crow.'

'Sure I will.' Lakshmi laughed. 'But I'd want compensation.'

'Come home. I'll ask my mother-in-law to deep-fry some vadagam for you.'

Without replying, Lakshmi gazed at the childlike face. It was heartening that Yogu was smarter than she had imagined. Her tonsured head and nine-yard sari hurt the eye, making it impossible to imagine her in a long skirt and blouse, with her hair in a braid.

'You're always reading something. What is it, Akka?'

'I am studying for my exam, Yogu.'

'Oh, I know. My mother-in-law says you are studying to be a doctor. Don't you ever read storybooks?'

'Do you?'

'Yes, whenever I can find some,' Yogu said with a laugh. It felt like a secret Yogu was sharing with her. 'But in this house, there are only prayer books.'

'I might have a few storybooks. I'll give them to you tomorrow.'

'Definitely?'

'Yes, definitely. Same time, tomorrow.'

'I called you a little while ago. You didn't hear me.'

'Did you ever go to school?' Lakshmi asked, somewhat hesitantly.

'Oh yes. I studied up to eighth class. Then they got me married.'

With her head bowed, Yogu said, 'I pleaded and cried that I didn't want to get married, Akka.'

'How old were you then?'

'Thirteen.'

When Yogu looked up again, her eyes were filled with tears. 'Since they were a rich family, Appa borrowed money from all over and performed the marriage in a hurry. Before I could move to my in-laws' house, my husband died.'

Lakshmi listened in disbelief to the child who was talking like a very old woman; she didn't know what to say in response.

All of a sudden, Yogu's body language changed. Someone was calling her from inside. A look of alarm crossed her face. She wiped her eyes quickly.

'I'm coming, 'ma.' She fled without a backward glance and disappeared into the house.

Lakshmi worried that she would trip over the folds of her nine-yard sari.

Later, she could not concentrate on her studies. She could not bear the absurd contradiction between Yogu's laughter, her banter, her water-lily eyes, and the life she was forced to lead. What a colossal waste! Yogu was probably unaware of the injustice done to her. She was sad only about having missed school.

One day, Mami had generally observed about someone: 'For a widow without shelter, having a mouth is dangerous.'

A widow without shelter—what a terrible description. Lakshmi remembered Yogu's innocent face and her naughty smile when she had said 'There are only prayer books here.' The tonsured head and rough cloth—such cruel punishment for a crime she had not even committed. Lakshmi wanted to whisk her away from that house and enrol her in a school; instead of that sari which weighed her down, dress her in a skirt and blouse; let her hair grow long and tie it with a ribbon.

Ribbons of many colours unfurl from Yogu's hair. Red, white, blue … 'Akka, Akka!' Back from school, she laughs exuberantly and whirls round and round holding Lakshmi's hands.

'Will you tell the crow, "You can gobble up the vadagams; I am not bothered"?'

Lakshmi's eyes filled with tears. She wanted to wail out loud. If she could do that someday, she would find a release for all the anger, shocks and sorrows that had lain buried within her for as long as she could remember. When she realized that merely crying would not help her find a solution to these problems, she felt even more powerless.

Lakshmi knew that releasing Yogu from her cage was not something she could achieve on her own, as a lone individual. If she were to say 'Yogu, I'll enrol you in a school. Want to come?', the young girl would spring up like a little sparrow. But there was a huge barrier around her—surmounting which was akin to crossing the seven seas of the mythical Vikramaditya tales. The couple next door would have neither the desire nor the affection to facilitate that mission.

When she thought about it, all women seemed tangled up in knots either of their own making or society's. They moved around mutely, as if being tied up was a pleasure in itself, fabricating justifications for injustice. Why did no one think or say that tonsuring a young girl's head and making her wear a nine-yard sari was cruel and unjust? Yogu would have struggled and fought; at the very least, she would have cried. Yet, when they disfigured her, they would have told her sternly that it was her fate. Inauspicious wretch, destitute widow … for a woman deemed unfit to live, being given shelter and food to eat was something to be grateful for.

Tears welled up again in Lakshmi's eyes.

She wondered if Yogu would ever be free. If we wait for other people to come by and rescue us, she thought, we will have to wait all our lives. Don't we need to think differently to even take the first step towards a solution? There are many kinds of humiliation. But how can we shake up people who don't even recognize the humiliation? *Nothing will affect me. I was born to serve god.* If everyone is like that idiot Kasturi, how can there be any change?

The helpless rage that she felt whenever she thought of Kasturi overwhelmed her again. Kasturi was still a foolish girl who lived by deceiving herself. She realized Kasturi's fears were real only when she met Kasturi during her visit to the village.

When she went over to Kasturi's house, the family was preparing to leave for Madras. Kasturi's mother said that a concert had been arranged in a new sabha. The joy on Kasturi's face upon seeing her warmed Lakshmi's heart. Kasturi looked more beautiful than ever. She was lit up by the glow of something pristine within her.

Lakshmi noticed that Sengamalam Aththai and Kanagu Paati were quite aloof when she met them. She would not be surprised if they were wary of her, thinking of her as a rebel who had come to make trouble.

When her mother told Lakshmi that the whole village called her a shrew and a slut, she had laughed. 'A very accurate description, Amma,' she said. 'Yes, I am a shrew. This life where you keep your mouth shut and wait forever in this street, wondering who will give you alms, where you sit for hours watching who has come to which house, is not for me. I ran away; I refused to be kept down. Slut. It's a very accurate word. These people do know how to choose their words!'

Just then she recalled what her mother had reported to her and burst out laughing.

'Your mother told us that you were pursuing higher studies. What do you study?'

'I am studying to be a doctor, Aththai.'

Kasturi was holding Lakshmi's hands with affection.

'A doctor?' Kanagu Paati said eagerly. 'You've come at the right time, di. I have a terrible ache in this joint. Give me your usual treatment.'

Lakshmi laughed. 'My studies aren't over, Paati. But I have an ointment you can apply. I'll bring it for you,' she said.

Kasturi led her to the terrace. 'You've changed a lot, Lakshmi, like a proper city dweller. Even in a plain cotton sari you look so modern. How is life in the city?' she enquired lovingly.

'I like it there. The world is very big, Kasturi. It is only when we interact with other people and see how they live that we realize how much suffering and injustice they have endured,' Lakshmi said. 'How are you?'

Kasturi laughed brightly. 'I am fine. I dance a lot. What could I lack, really?'

Lakshmi was surprised. 'I heard a white man misbehaved with you.'

'Forget him, the bloody swine,' Kasturi said with a laugh. 'Didn't you hear about how we dealt with him and came out safely?'

Lakshmi looked at her with concern. 'Doesn't this life strike you as shameful?'

'I just don't think about it.'

Lakshmi wanted to shake Kasturi by her beautiful shoulders. 'How can you *not* think about it?'

'Adi, you won't understand. I am an artist. That's the only thing that matters to me. If some man misbehaves with me, then something is wrong with him, not me.'

'But why does he behave like that? Because he knows you are a devadasi. Because he believes that you would sleep with anyone who grabs your hand.'

'In that case, isn't he a proper fool?' Kasturi said, all innocence. 'I am a servant of the Lord—that is the only truth. All the rest is a lie. These zameendars and durais can't do anything to me. My art will protect me.'

Lakshmi wanted to punch her own forehead in despair. 'Nonsense! You are deceiving yourself.'

'No, it is the sacred truth!' Kasturi said ardently. Her face was flushed with emotion. 'I have self-respect too, Lakshmi. Don't think I am a shameless person. I see all this as trivial. Within this living arrangement, I have freedom. I can keep dancing for hours. No controlling man can tell me, "You've danced enough." I need this space. Without it, I'll die. Art cannot flourish in a regimented environment. For me, that's what is most important.'

Looking at her with concern, Lakshmi said gently, 'You are content to think only about yourself. If you had suffered the humiliations that my mother and I had to bear when I was a child, you wouldn't talk like this. As soon as I finish my studies, I am going to start a movement.'

'What do you mean by "movement"?'

'A law abolishing the devadasi system must be passed. We must bring together all those who would support this law. A nationwide struggle for independence is on now. Even if freedom comes to the country, it will be of no use if we are not liberated from this system. Deliverance and honour for this clan is possible only if such a law comes into force.'

'Do you think society will treat us with respect if this law is enacted?'

'It will—by and by.'

'And by honour do you mean that everyone will be able to marry and have children?' Kasturi asked in confusion.

'Yes. Why not?'

Kasturi laughed in disbelief. 'Adi, how many people do you think would be ready to marry someone from this clan?'

'Once there is a law, it will happen automatically.'

Kasturi shook her head vigorously to indicate strong disagreement. 'Do you know what will happen if singers and dancers get married? They will forget Bilahari and Todi, and spend their days making poriyal and dosai instead.'

She chuckled as if it was a big joke. 'Whenever I want, I can braid the jathi for the varnam in Mohana raagam, practise the abhinayas for the jaavali in Senchurutti raagam. If a man were to ask "Girl, have you finished cooking?" from inside, I would feel as if my wings had been clipped. Aiyo, I don't want honour and whatnot, di!'

Lakshmi found Kasturi's attitude offensive. 'How many people do you imagine think like you? So many women are disgraced every day just because they were born in this clan. They are forced to behave in ways that invite dishonour. If the devadasi system is abolished, there won't be any scope for such atrocities.'

'It also means there won't be any women artists. They would all be imprisoned in the kitchen,' Kasturi retorted. Suddenly, in evident panic, she asked, 'Will your law say that I shouldn't dance?'

'It will ban dancing in temples.'

'Aiyo, what wrong has the deity done?'

Lakshmi began patiently. 'It's not the deity, but others … the people who behave badly in His name. How can I make you understand?' She had not expected Kasturi to be so inflamed with rage.

'You need not explain anything to me! You are the kind who burns the house down to get rid of bed bugs. You don't know what devotion to the Lord is. Honour and the rest come from how we conduct ourselves. I am not bothered about other people. You will never understand the joy I experience when I dance in the Lord's chamber. Don't come here again talking about laws and whatnot. Please leave!'

Kasturi's face had been flushed with anger and tears glistened in her beautiful eyes. Whenever she thought of Kasturi these days, it was that tearful face that surfaced in Lakshmi's mind.

16

Suppuni was restless with anxiety. He wondered how his father remained detached from everything. When he looked at Appa, sometimes he felt inexplicably afraid; on many occasions, he was annoyed too.

He heard Kamu sobbing in the backyard as he left for the temple. Up until that morning they had been riding the chariot of fantasies. Last night, with her face buried in his chest, she had tweaked his nose fondly and said, 'Our Sundu will have the same nose and the same thick tuft of hair.'

'Who is this Sundu?' he asked with raised eyebrows. She had mentioned a different name earlier.

Twisting his ear, she said, 'The idiot about to be born to this imbecile.'

'A woman who calls her husband an imbecile will surely go to hell,' he said with affection, folding her in a tight embrace.

'Let someone who has been to hell tell me that and I will take it back.'

'So, are you calling me an imbecile?'

'From now on, don't ask me, "Who is Sundu?"'

'You said Gopu or Thyagu yesterday.'

She looked away bashfully and laughed. 'How does it matter what name we give to our child?'

The morning had dawned with Kamu wailing about a severe stomach ache. Amma prepared a remedy and gave it to her, and massaged her stomach with oil. Finally, within the next hour, the castles they had dreamt about were buried in a pit in their backyard. After weeping for some time, an exhausted Kamu lay curled up on a palm-leaf mat inside the thatched enclosure where she stayed during her periods. Suppuni had to leave for the temple immediately, with no time even to visit her. He yearned to take her sobbing body in his arms and soothe her with consoling words. He wanted to carry her out of that dark shed and have her lie down in the airy front hall. If she caught a fever and became delirious in the shed, no one at home would come to know. Only centipedes and scorpions kept her company there.

'After the defilement, she has to stay in the shed,' Amma said firmly.

Appa heard her, but didn't say anything. 'Join me in the temple,' he told Suppuni and left.

As he stood there, shocked and diffident, Amma tried to console him. 'All this is routine in the life of a woman. Why do you look terrified? Her body is weak. She will be all right the next time. Don't worry. I'll cook separate meals for her and make sure she eats properly. Go and attend to your work at the temple.'

Suppuni departed reluctantly. Kamu would be disappointed that he hadn't even asked how she was doing. But since he had bathed and worn ritually pure clothes, custom dictated that he shouldn't even look in the direction of a menstruating woman. 'Cha!' He felt disgusted at these conventions, customs and observances: exclusions bereft of humanity. But he was powerless to oppose them. Menstruation was considered unclean. Those who performed services to the deity had to be ritually pure according to the scriptures. To be lax in one's observance of purity was sacrilege, equal to blaspheming the gods. There was no room to question who had prescribed these rules. If a man who worked in the deity's chamber didn't comply with them, it was a taint upon his birth itself.

Chanting the hymns of ritual worship in clear, ringing tones, Appa was immersed in the puja. After collecting plates of votive offerings from the devotees, Suppuni joined his father in reciting the hymns in an attempt to calm his mind. After the deity had been worshipped with the sacred flame, he picked up the plate. In the blaze from the burning camphor, the foetus lay in a heap of blood and flesh. The unborn child. The child that refused to be born. He put the plate away. Sitting in a corner of the sanctum sanctorum, he began to weep with great heaving sobs.

His father was taken aback. He waited for the crowd to disperse, then he asked gently, 'What happened, Suppuni? Why are you crying?'

Racked by sorrow, Suppuni cried harder, unable to speak.

'Look here. You must not sit in god's chamber and cry.'

'If I can't cry out to Him, where can I go?' he said, mildly angry.

'All is god's will. It's not as if He will know your pain only if you cry. Get up, wash your face and come back.'

There was a note of sternness in Appa's voice. Suppuni was dismayed by his father's seeming lack of compassion. He got up, drew water from the well in the outer pathway of the temple and washed his face. His crying bout seemed juvenile to him now. Yet his eyes filled with tears again.

When he returned to the main deity's chamber, the crowd had left. An eerie silence prevailed in the temple. Without saying anything, Suppuni crumpled next to a stone pillar. He drew his knees up and buried his face between them.

'Our Sundu will have the same nose and kudumi,' Kamu whispered gently in his ear.

Why did Sundu deceive them?

'What's the matter, Suppuni? Why are you crying?'

Suppuni looked up with a start. His father was sitting next to him with an arm around his shoulders. He had no memory of ever being touched by his father. He cringed as though his father had done something forbidden. His father's touch sent a current through his whole body.

'Why did we lose the baby in the womb?'

'We can't seek reasons for all the births and deaths in this world. The baby was destined to live only for so long. It didn't survive. What can you and I do about it? This is far better than losing a grown child after a few years. It was gone before it had a chance to grow. Your mother had four children after you; none survived beyond three or four years. What happened today—is it worse than that? Then why are you so upset?'

Suppuni was silent. He remembered them well, the three brothers and one sister who were born after him. The dull sister with a shrunken belly who whined all the time. But she was pretty, like a doll. She was down with fever for two whole days. The traditional healer's powder didn't cure her. His parents were helpless. They asked a sorcerer to come and chant. On the third day, her doll-like face became lifeless. Burying her face in her hands, Amma wept for days. His younger brothers dying one after another was sheer agony. They had played with him, climbed on to his back to ride horses. Each time the fever would last a couple of days. On top of the medicine given by the doctor, Amma prepared a concoction and gave it to them. Nothing worked. When his mother cried, he cried along with her.

'God has taken them away,' Appa had said, wiping his eyes. 'He granted them only a short life. What can we do about it?'

For a long time, the Almighty's sport had bewildered him. When he realized that if his parents fell ill nothing might save them, he was terrified. He came to believe that the three of them had survived only by the mercy of god. Fortunately, his mother did not have any more children.

If Kamu conceived again, would the foetus survive until she was ready to give birth? He was worried. When he recalled his mother saying that childbirth for a woman was like coming back to life after dying, he was afraid that Kamu might not survive the delivery. News about Periya Mirasu's daughter dying during childbirth was still circulating. There was a hospital in town run by Christian missionaries. His father wouldn't allow them set foot there.

'Even Mirasu didn't go there. The midwife in attendance assisted Mirasu's wife with *her* delivery. They couldn't stop the bleeding after the delivery. It cost the girl her life. I heard that blood flowed in the gutter next to Mirasu's house for two days,' Amma said.

Appa spoke to him in an appeasing tone. 'It happens routinely in the world. She will be ill for two days. Then she will become all right. I have asked the Konar to bring milk for the deity's anointment. I have also asked his wife to sleep next to Kamu for three nights.'

It was as if a spring had opened up in Suppuni's heart. He had never heard his father being so tender.

'A baby will arrive in due course. Kamu is just fifteen, isn't she? By god's will, everything will be fine.'

By the time he reached home, his mind had calmed a little. *God's will.*

If it's true, he thought, can we achieve anything at all by our effort? If someone takes ill, should we leave it to god to let them live or die, and just stand by, doing nothing?

For the next few days, Kamu lay in bed like a corpse. The very sight of the gutter was frightening. It gave off the stench of blood.

On the fourth day, Kamu had a head bath, entered the house and resumed her normal routine. Just before going to sleep, she told him in the manner of a seasoned old woman, 'It seems the baby was destined to live only so long.'

He decided not to trouble her for at least another month.

'Only after your body has completely recovered should we think about another baby,' he told her. By then she had fallen asleep. She slept for many hours in the daytime as well. Amma seemed to allow it.

Today, not wanting to go home from the temple, Suppuni walked to the riverside. The river was in spate due to the recent rains. A few children were swimming in the river. Suppuni sat on the steps, staring blankly at the water. For some days now, his mind had been in turmoil over the many confusing developments around him. Cries of 'Vande Mataram' had become louder and more frequent. Violence perpetrated by the police and the screams of the protesters filled him with dread. Many young boys his age had joined the marches, which grew bigger each day. When Somu from the neighbouring street spoke fervently about a great man called Gandhi who had delivered a speech in nearby Mayavaram, Suppuni felt a strong urge to see this Mahatma.

Gandhi didn't know a word of Tamil, though. He spoke in English and a language called Hindustani. Someone had interpreted his speech in Tamil.

'Even then, his speech was stirring. I was all fired up,' Somu said. 'How much longer shall we remain slaves to the British? They are treating us worse than dogs. They have carried away all our wealth to their country and made beggars out of us. And now they have levied a tax on salt, which is just lying around! To oppose the salt tax, Gandhi is going to lead a big march in a town called Dandi. In our area, a Brahmin called Rajagopalachari is going to walk to Vedaranyam near the sea. Why don't you come along, da?'

Suppuni was bound by his duties at the temple and his father's priestly obligations. He couldn't even speak about it to Appa. There was no use discussing the freedom struggle with a man who said, 'What does it matter who rules us? We are slaves only to god.' Besides, many different communities and castes had joined hands in that struggle, people like nadaswaram player Sundaramurthi and the achari who made aimpon sculptures. It was unthinkable that Appa would allow him to participate along with them.

Then Somu narrated another incident. His blood had boiled when he heard about the Durai's callous behaviour. Even now, merely recalling it made him angry.

'Who is that, our junior priest?'

Startled, Suppuni turned around. Sundaramurthi's son, Manickam, stood there.

'Come, Manickam. Sit down,' Suppuni said with a smile. Manickam's arrival soothed his troubled heart.

'It's all right, aiya,' Manickam said with some hesitation.

'It doesn't matter, Manickam. Sit here. I have finished my work at the temple. Appa will attend to the night's puja. I came because it is a bit cool here. How is your father?'

Manickam sat down a few feet away from Suppuni. 'They have arrested Appa and put him in jail.'

'Aiyaiyo! When?' Suppuni cried in shock.

'He had joined the march last night. I told him I wanted to go too, but he stopped me.'

Manickam appeared sadder about not having marched with them than about his father going to jail. He was around seventeen years old. The dark line of his moustache was clearly visible now. He had begun to play the oththu, providing tonic support to his father's nadaswaram. 'When I listen to Appa playing the instrument so well, I want to play it too. I am learning now. But to be able to play like him, I should have earned enough merit in my previous births,' Manickam had said to Suppuni the week before while standing in the deity's chamber. The boy had seemed like a grown man then. Now he sounded like a child, perhaps because he was anxious about his father.

'He told me to stay at home and help Amma,' Manickam said. 'For temple duties, Appa's cousin Chockalingam Mama will come in his place. Should I come to play the oththu?'

'Of course. Why do you need to ask? I'll tell my father,' Suppuni said. 'Who else have they arrested?'

'As far as I know, they have arrested Brother Singaram too and taken him away.'

'Who is Singaram?'

'The achari who makes aimpon sculptures. Don't you know him?'

Suppuni had no recollection of having seen him. 'Oh yes, I've heard of him. I believe he is also taking part in the freedom struggle.'

'Yes. Like my father, he is also very committed. Appa was the one who pulled him into the movement. Brother Singaram sings Bharathi's songs very well.'

Suppuni felt ashamed; he seemed to be the world's biggest ignoramus. 'Bharathi?' he asked.

'Subramania Bharathi. He is a revolutionary poet who has composed many songs praising Bharat Mata, mother of our land. Listening to them gives me goosebumps. I get angry at the very sight of white men. It doesn't matter if I am beaten up and sent to jail, I must oppose them.'

Suppuni looked at Manickam in amazement. He couldn't help but feel that he was stagnating in life, believing that the temple precinct and the well in his backyard made up his whole world and detaching himself from everything else.

'Oh my. Why don't you sing a song? Let's hear it.'

'I can't sing as well as Brother Singaram.' Even though he felt diffident, Manickam began to sing.

'The finest nation in the world / Is our Indian nation …'

There was a trace of the feminine in Manickam's voice. As he continued to sing, the lyrics mingled with the wind and reverberated; Suppuni felt an electric charge course through his blood vessels. Inexplicably, tears streamed from his eyes.

When the song was over, Manickam began another in a clear, ringing tone:

'Vande Mataram is our chant / We salute the mother of our great land …'

After singing four lines, Manickam buried his face between his knees and began to weep.

Awestruck by the song, Suppuni looked at the other boy in shock. 'Manickam, why are you crying?'

Manickam raised his head, wiped his eyes with the back of his palm and said in a quiet voice, 'I don't know when they will release my father. They beat him up and dragged him away. His back was torn and bloody. Brother Singaram was also thrashed.'

'Aiyaiyo. How vicious! Why must they take part in such dangerous activities?'

'According to Appa if we want independence, we must fight for it. Brother Singaram is even more extreme. After hearing Gandhi speak in Mayavaram, they have turned into proper devotees. They are determined to kick the British out.'

'But how can we fight the British? They are too powerful.'

'Gandhi says we can throw them out without fighting with them.'

'Is it possible? They have an army. They wield authority over us.'

'This is a just war, aiya. We must believe in it. As Brother Singaram says, this is a struggle for freedom, which is everyone's right. He says, once we are free, all Indians will live as equals. Bharathi even has a song about it.'

'I want to hear it.'

'*Freedom! Freedom! Freedom for the Paraiyars and the Pulaiyars!*' Manickam sang. 'Bharathi is a Brahmin, did you know that?'

Suppuni was astonished. With no knowledge of these things, he felt he was groping in the dark. Suddenly he remembered what Somu had told him—about another Brahmin, and another incident too. Would Manickam know more?

'You have kept up with so many things, Manickam. I am confined to the temple and my house, so I don't know half of what goes on around us. I happened to hear that a British Durai insulted Kasturi recently.'

'Yes, aiya. How else would a rascal like him behave? As soon as Appa heard that Kasturi Akka was going to dance in that zameendar's house, he told them it was not a respectable venue. "What's the harm? We are going to dance, collect the money and come back," Aththai said and sent them off.'

'Then?'

'Midway through the performance, the Durai got up on the stage in a drunken state and grabbed Akka's hand.'

'The scoundrel! Did the others simply watch?'

'He was a British Durai, and these people were slavish cowards. They kept laughing, and according to Brother Sabapathi, made obscene remarks.'

Suppuni spat in disgust.

'Akka pushed his hand away, gathered everyone who'd gone with her and left immediately.'

Suppuni felt relieved. Somu had told him a more ominous tale.

'The Durai had chased after them along with his men, but the cart driver Muthu cleverly took them to Brother Singaram's house and hid them there. It's providence that Akka escaped unhurt that day. Appa was livid when he heard about it. He was still upset over the incident and shouted angrily during yesterday's march. That's why they arrested him and took him away.'

It was dark now. The air was cold. But Suppuni was outraged having heard the incidents narrated by Manickam. At a time when such massive upheavals were taking place, he had been upset over fifteen-year-old Kamu miscarrying her first pregnancy. He felt ashamed of himself.

'Hey Manickam!' someone shouted. 'Your father has come back.'

At that Manickam took his leave and ran off.

Suppuni got up. Instead of going home, he went to the temple again.

As his father was offering worship to the deity with lit camphor at the end of the night puja, Suppuni saw Kasturi standing in the deity's chamber. It had been four days since her last visit to the temple. Someone said that she had gone to Madras for a concert. She smiled at him.

A mild thrill ran through his body at the warmth in that smile.

'How was your trip to Madras?' he asked.

'It was good, Suppuni. But I feel fulfilled only when I dance in the temple. Where is Mama? Isn't he going to play mangalam for the day?'

'He was arrested by the police.'

'Aiyaiyo!' Kasturi said, her eyes widening in shock. 'Only him ... or ...?'

'Someone called Singaram, I hear. They took him away too. I hear both of them were beaten up badly.'

'Aiyaiyo!'

'I heard they are back home now.' He was startled by how quickly her expression changed; she ran towards the entrance without a backward glance and rushed out.

17

Kasturi's heart was pounding so hard that she felt it might break in two.

I hear both of them were beaten up badly.

Suppuni wouldn't have said that without being sure of it. 'The times are bad, Kasturi. I can't tell what is wrong or right any more. The British cannot be taken lightly. Their kicks can kill. This achari is a bachelor, they say, but Sundaramurthi is a family man.'

Before the young priest had finished speaking, she had reached the entrance. It seemed he said something further. Though she didn't have the patience to stop and listen, his words came chasing after her. They dashed against the pillars of the outer pathway that she had run across and travelled up to the rafters. Mixing with the flapping noise of the bats whose sleep had been disrupted, they scattered and fell inside the temple and near the entrance, echoing frightfully.

'They got thrashed ... badly thrashed.'

In panic, her feet faltered. Fortunately, Muthu had driven her to the temple in the cart. He had told her nearly the same thing: 'The times are bad, Akka. You shouldn't go to the temple alone like you used to.'

'Oh Lord, why should things turn out this way?'

Earlier that day, news that Raja was not in town had brought her great relief. She had planned to go directly to bed after returning from the temple. The feeling of exhaustion from the trip to Madras had not left her yet. She had wanted to meet Singaram the next day and tell him about her inaugural concert in the city, though she had no idea how it might be possible.

Then Suppuni had told her the terrible news. The moment she heard it, she experienced severe anguish. She couldn't understand why she was feeling so agitated. What was the connection between her and Singaram? Thus far, she had barely spoken to him. He did not even look at her directly while addressing her. If she asked him a question, he answered with his eyes on the ground. Suppuni's words—*beaten up badly*—invaded her brain and paralysed her.

On seeing her running towards him, gasping for breath, Muthu was alarmed. 'What's wrong, Akka?' he said.

Steadying herself, she said, 'I heard that Sundaramurthi Mama and that man were beaten up during the procession yesterday. After arresting them, the police took them away because they were seriously injured.'

Muthu was surprised. 'Aiyaiyo! How did I not know this? Let's go to Mama's house. Brother Singaram will be there for sure.'

It seemed Muthu said it in all innocence. Without a word, she climbed into the cart quickly and sat down.

'Both of them are very strong mentally. No matter how badly he was beaten, Mama stood up again, holding the flag. Singaram is his true disciple. No one knows when this struggle might end.

The British are sitting tight. Inspired by that man Gandhi, these people have dared to oppose them.'

Why won't he shut up for some time, Kasturi thought.

Singaram stands before her with a blood-smeared face. 'How can we win freedom if we are afraid to die?' he says. 'Don't talk about dying. I've just got to know you.' She puts a hand over his mouth. The heat of his lips touches her palm and pervades her entire body. Lord Brahadeeswara, may no harm come his way.

The street was pitch-dark. Everyone had gone to sleep. The day's tumult must have frightened them. She couldn't even hear a baby's cry.

'Can't tell right from wrong any more.' She recalls what Suppuni told her. The times are bad. Is this the era of evil? Is that why we are facing such turmoil? When she hears Sundaramurthi's 'Vande Mataram' and Bharathiar songs, she feels charged and her heart swells with pride. Her eyes grow moist as if the dawn is very near. The spot where the Durai touched her still burns.

Meanwhile Lakshmi says, 'You are born in this despicable clan. I am going to destroy it.'

'You must become free first. Only then will the nation's freedom have any meaning,' Lakshmi continues. 'Why aren't you angry like me? Why do you lack a sense of honour? Why didn't you say, like Thilakam, that you would rather die?'

The more she thought about it, the more perplexed she felt. Even now, she could hear what a heckler in the auditorium in Madras had shouted before her concert began.

This Gopalaiyer has surely gone mad. It is a travesty—inviting a whore to perform sadir before a gathering of respectable people. A sadir concert for an auspicious inauguration? It won't end well.

Words that had pierced her heart like sharp needles. As Thilakam bowed her head and bit her lower lip, it seemed she might burst into tears. When the connoisseurs in Madras displayed an anger they had never encountered in their village, they were taken aback. It seemed like a different world. Was it even possible for them to set foot here? Besieged by her distress and the uncertainty of whether she was going to dance or return in humiliation to the railway station, she brought her palms together and greeted the audience.

'Gentlemen. My salutations. I beg all of you to forgive me. I don't know the custom followed in this city. In our village, it is the devadasis who inaugurate all auspicious functions. I am a dancer; I have learnt my art as per the ancient treatises and perform in the Lord's chamber as per agama rules. I believe that god is present wherever I dance. If you don't wish to watch me perform, please tell me. I will leave.'

When a couple of men stood up and started to speak, Gopalaiyer bade them to sit once more. 'Everyone, please calm down. Kasturi is an eminent artist. It is not civilized on our part to express our opinion even before watching her dance. Don't oppose it simply because no sadir concert has been performed here before this. Art is divine. You'll understand how exceptionally skilled she is when you see the performance.'

Somehow, at long last, peace returned to the auditorium again.

When she began the day's concert, she was anxious for the audience to be satisfied with her performance by the time it ended. But at the close, when she received an ovation loud enough to shake the rafters, she was moved to tears. It felt as though she had been granted an unexpected sighting of the deity. She alone could understand the ecstasy of that experience. How did it matter what anyone said? She felt serene, a sign that she had attained the maturity to stay aloof from all the turmoil.

'Had Gopalaiyer Mama and his son not been present, we would have had to go back.'

Kasturi detected a note of unusual zest in Thilakam's voice. She wondered what contribution Gopalaiyer's son had made to the situation. 'You are being prickly.' She laughed. 'Until they see us perform, it's natural for them to express their personal opinion. From now on, we won't face any opposition here, Thilakam. Invitations to perform will arrive regularly, as you'll see.'

'Let's accept concerts organized by Gopalaiyer, Akka,' Thilakam said.

An unprecedented exuberance was evident on Thilakam's face. For reasons that eluded her, Kasturi felt a knot of fear in the pit of her stomach. Some kind of stealth seemed to have entered Thilakam. Even in the middle of the dance she had noticed Gopalaiyer's son gazing steadily at Thilakam.

Kasturi was sure that being attracted to an upper-caste boy would do Thilakam no good. As someone who was intent on honour and respect, did Thilakam imagine that he would give her a respectable life? Don't trust him because you will surely be betrayed, Kasturi wanted to tell her. There was Lakshmi in one-half of Thilakam. If she were told that we were born to serve art, she would turn her back on it. But what a virtuoso she was! What a rich voice! Would she give all that away for honour and self-respect? Would that Aiyer boy treat her with respect?

Kasturi came back to the present. She felt like a fool, imagining a relationship between Thilakam and Gopalaiyer's son, a man her sister had met only for a few minutes. But the change she noticed in Thilakam worried her. For that matter, even her own feeling of agitation upset her. What has happened to me?

If Sengamalam learnt that Kasturi was friendly with Singaram, a low-caste boy, she would not merely be alarmed, there would be an uproar. She would accept Gopalaiyer's son, but she wouldn't let Singaram step across their threshold. What she would do instead was not beyond Kasturi's imagination.

More importantly, her final salvo would be: 'A woman who dances in the temple before the deity cannot have relations with a low-caste man, don't you know that? If people find out, not only will you lose your position, but they will also make you an outcaste, di. They'll break not just his legs but yours too.'

Kasturi buried her face between her knees.

What should I do? What should I do? She could not control her mind.

There were many people who broke legs these days. The police did. The British did. And Raja would do it tomorrow.

Singaram approaches her, hobbling on his broken legs dripping blood. 'Don't,' he says. 'Why would you want this hardship? Go away. Don't come here.'

'Akka, we have arrived.'

She got down in a flash and dashed towards Sundaramurthi's house. When she bent low in the doorway and entered, she found the house engulfed in darkness. It was shrouded by an even heavier silence. Once her eyes adjusted to the darkness, she noticed a small mud lamp burning in a corner of the veranda that skirted the courtyard. The dark silhouette of a figure seated on the swing was visible.

'Mama!' she called out hesitantly.

'Is that Kasturi?' Sundaramurthi said without getting up. 'Why did you come here now, 'ma?' Along with anxiety, there was also a trace of mild irritation in his voice.

'The head priest's son told me that you were hurt. I couldn't bear it, Mama. I couldn't not come to see you. How bad is the injury, Mama?'

Sundaramurthi didn't reply at once.

'Muthu, put the cart in the backyard. Shut the front door.'

'I came in only after doing both, aiya.'

Their exchange and precautions sent Kasturi into a panic. 'Mama, tell me! Are you badly injured?' Peering into the dark, she saw another figure lying on its side on a mat near Mama. The thought that it might be Singaram made her heart tremble.

'I don't think the injury is severe. The country doctor who lives nearby ground some leaves and herbs into a paste and bandaged the leg with the salve. "It will pain in the night; just put up with it," he had said. In this struggle where we risk our lives, how can we avoid pain, child?'

Sundaramurthi's voice was feeble. She worried that he might have lost a lot of blood. The figure on the mat didn't stir at all.

'Someone seems to be lying down over there?' she ventured cautiously.

'It's that achari boy, Singaram. He was beaten very badly. As they kept on beating him, he raised his hand and shouted "Vande Mataram". It provoked the police even more. They flayed him good and proper.'

'Aiyaiyo! What happened then?' Kasturi's eyes had filled with tears.

'When we came, there was no one here. Luckily, the doctor's house is nearby. I hobbled over and brought him here. The doctor applied some herbal plaster on Singaram's leg and bandaged it. He has given Singaram medicine to sleep. He is resting. The doctor said he will be all right in a couple of days.'

Sundaramurthi spoke in a low whisper. She felt she should stay back and look after them. There was no one else around.

'Where is your wife, Mama?'

'I sent her away to the village, thinking there could be trouble here.'

'How will you manage all by yourself, Mama? With no one around to make even some food? Should I stay back?'

She longed for him to say: Yes, please stay.

'Cha cha. You should leave right away. Coming here was a mistake. I'll manage somehow. I am not seriously injured.'

She was sure he was lying. That Singaram had lain still throughout their conversation made her nervous.

Muthu stepped close to her. 'Akka, let's go. I will take you home and then come here to spend the night. I know how to make hot water and ginger decoction. What do you say, aiya?'

'All right. But first, take Kasturi home safely.'

Neither of them spoke on the way back, weighed down by silence and the fear that the men had been hurt far worse than Mama had revealed. Instead of stopping in front of the house, Muthu drove the cart quietly to a corner of the backyard. As though it had understood the situation, the bull didn't even turn its neck.

'Muthu, take care,' she said in a hoarse voice. 'I believe nothing untoward will happen,' she added a moment later, in a secret whisper.

'This doctor is famously lucky for his patients. Don't worry, Akka,' Muthu said soothingly.

Kasturi was afraid she was going to burst into tears. Determined not to betray her feelings in front of Muthu, she quickly gave him a sign: 'Leave now.' She turned to enter the house after seeing Muthu off, and stopped abruptly in mild shock.

In the backyard, amid the shadows under the mango tree, she saw two silhouettes standing together. Despite the darkness, she could see that one was a man, and the other was Thilakam.

She looked around nervously to check whether Muthu might have seen them. He had vanished from sight. The two of them were speaking in low whispers. Kasturi had no doubt that the man was Gopalaiyer's son. Thilakam never looked directly at any man, but he seemed to have used some magic powder and cast a spell on her. She had changed completely from the day she met him. Kasturi found it baffling that he should come secretly at night to meet Thilakam. This could be a tryst planned in advance. Had the couple become so intimate in the two days their troupe had stayed in Madras? Or, had the affair started a month ago, when he had come with Gopalaiyer to their house? Kasturi was sad to see the deceit that had seeped into Thilakam's character.

She was wondering how much longer she would have to stand outside the house, waiting for him to leave, when she saw him hurrying away. After giving Thilakam enough time to go into the house, Kasturi went and knocked on the back door, which was bolted now. It was Kanagu Paati who let her in.

'Paati? Haven't you gone to sleep yet? Where are the others?'

'They are all asleep. Tired from the trip to Madras. But why are *you* coming through the backyard like a burglar?'

Standing in the rear veranda, she spoke in a low whisper. 'It's a long story.'

Watching Paati take in the information with a palm on her cheek and her eyes popping out, Kasturi felt pity for her. She wondered wearily whether Paati would ever understand the series of shocks she had encountered today. When she went to bed, Thilakam seemed to be in deep slumber.

Kasturi didn't know when sleep finally embraced her. Unusually for her, she woke up well after sunrise. Sengamalam and Kanagu Paati were sitting on the veranda as if they were waiting for her to rise, waiting for something to explode. With instinctive alertness, she looked at Thilakam's mattress. It wasn't rolled up yet.

Her throat felt tight and her voice turned hoarse. 'Thilakam? Where is Thilakam, Paati?'

18

I KEPT LOOKING AT the notes beside the names written in English in Amma's beautiful, slanted handwriting for no particular reason—at least none that I could understand. My heart was beating fast. It felt as if Amma wanted to tell me something. At that moment, the feeling seemed both natural and true. I began to believe that Amma was present in that room, a formless apparition observing me from a nook or a narrow gap between the books. I scanned the room urgently. I sensed her movements in the sway of the curtains.

'Amma!'

My voice faded, inaudible to my own ears. Only after some time did I notice that my fingers were trembling. The realization set off a sudden panic in me. Why should someone who had been so close and dear when alive give me such a scare in a formless state after her death? *Ghosts and spirits ... They may do a person good or strike them down ...*

I recovered immediately. It was not surprising that the old man's words perplexed me, but the fact that I had begun to believe in them was definitely odd. Amma was neither a spirit nor a ghost. Even if she were, she would certainly not strike me down. Offering a supernatural explanation to every incident would be a disgrace to my education in science. It was by accident that I had picked up the book and chanced upon these addresses. Now was the time for scientific thinking. No ghost or spirit would present me with documents as clues to my investigation. There was certainly a mystery to Amma's death; I would have to uncover it by myself.

C.S.I. Retreat Centre was the building I had stumbled upon in the morning. It was where Christian priests and nuns came for a spiritual retreat. What could be the connection between Amma and the Retreat Centre? I had always believed Amma was a Hindu. And she certainly was. Though they had kept no pictures or idols of Hindu gods in their house, my parents had Hindu names. She had no Christian relatives; nor did Appa. During one of their vacations down south, my parents had gone on a tour of many Hindu temples. They were temples of art, my mother said. She would stand in front of each pillar and sculpture for hours and appreciate their beauty. And though she was well versed in all the epic and mythological tales behind them and the mythology specific to each place, she remained a rationalist who did not worship any god.

'How did you become an atheist?'

Amma laughed gently. 'My mother was an atheist herself. Is it any surprise that I am one too?'

'Paati?' I said in amazement. I thought all grandmothers were orthodox. 'Why?'

'There is a story here,' she had once said. 'I will tell you some day.'

Appa remained detached from all these matters. He had no interest in them. His own family was traditionally engaged with communist ideology. 'There is absolutely no confusion whether god exists or not.' He was laughing as he said this. 'Man needed a load-bearing culvert on which he could rest his burdens. So he created god. Religions grew around the idea of god and from there came an individual's identity: Hindu, Muslim, Christian. It's enough if we remain human, child.'

Being born to such parents might be the reason for my extreme confusion. How did I forget that I had identified as Hindu in my school certificate, passport, and all other documents?

Perhaps one of Amma's classmates had become a nun, and Amma had gone there to visit her. Why did everything seem so perverse to me? My brain pointed out that nothing that had happened today was normal. Today I entered that forest for the first time. Amma appeared before me, for real, wearing a yellow sari and red blouse. Even that old man confirmed that I couldn't have come out of the mist-shrouded forest without help. *How did you come out of this forest today? When you stood before me as though someone had dragged you there, I knew right away that you were standing there by the grace of that spirit.* Today my eyes fell on that building. Today, just a short while after coming home, I picked up this book in which the building's name and address were recorded in Amma's handwriting. I couldn't believe that all this was mere coincidence. I kept staring at the page for some time. There was another name: Sabapathi. I had never heard Amma or Appa mention that name. The address indicated that he lived in Thanjavur. Who could this Sabapathi be? If he was a relative, then we would have called on him during our two visits there. The only family I knew of was my grandmother, who had lived alone in Chennai till the end; my grandfather died before I was born.

I will tell you some day.

I still remember the eagerness I had felt looking at the deep lines on her face when Amma had said that. She was admiring the splendid tower of the most beautiful temple in Gangaikonda Cholapuram while we sat in a mandapam with carved stone pillars, a place built for pilgrims to rest, situated a little away from the temple. As she gazed at the magnificent sculptures carved on the outer wall of temple, her face radiated the joy of meeting close friends who were kindred souls.

'Have you visited this temple before?'

She stuck out her lower lip as if to say no. 'But it feels as if there is a connection between me and this place. My mother lived in a village not far from here. She must have come here when she was pregnant with me. Like Abhimanyu, who imbibed his father's skill at archery in the womb, I think I remember everything she saw at the time. Every sculpture and pillar here makes me feel as though I have seen them before.'

It was strange to hear a sworn atheist like Amma speak of a connection between her and the Puranas. Perhaps she was not truly an atheist. Maintained by the Department of Archaeology of the Indian government, the temple shone in its high elegance and cleanliness. Its beauty in the fading light of dusk was enchanting.

'Tell me now.'

It seemed she hadn't heard me.

'Amma, why don't you tell me now?' I said, lightly touching her thigh.

She gave me a startled look. Stories spanning several births were buried in the depths of her eyes. 'Tell you what?'

'How you became an atheist.'

Amma laughed.

'Just as Bertrand Russell wrote *Why I Am Not a Christian*, I too will write a book explaining why we are not believers. You'll know then.'

'You can tell *me*. I'll write the book.'

Amma exhaled a long sigh. 'There is a time for that. It's not something that can be told in ten minutes. One day, I'll be retired and relaxed, I'll tell you then. You will be mature enough to understand.'

'Will we come to this temple again?'

Amma laughed gently. 'Of course.'

I riffled through the pages of the book aimlessly. My eyes filled with tears. We never visited the temple after that. She forgot the promise she had given me. Or maybe she decided that there was no need to tell me anything.

Or maybe her life had ended in an unforeseen way.

Once more, I was taken aback. What on earth was happening to me?

I closed the book carefully, kept it on the table and stood up. I was sure that if I stayed at home my brain would go mad in its obsession with certain ideas and wander chaotically. I decided to walk around for a bit until it was time for lunch. The rain had stopped completely now. There was bright sunshine. I put on my walking shoes, and remembered to pick up an umbrella. Just as I was leaving, my father, who was sitting in the front hall and reading *The Hindu*, said to me, 'Are you going out again?'

'I am going to walk for a bit. Close by, around the lake. I'll be back in time for lunch. I am taking my phone with me,' I said with a smile.

I felt sorry for Appa. Amma's death seemed to have upset him terribly.

'I am forgetting a lot, 'ma,' he told me one day, sounding fearful. 'I went out for a walk as usual. But I didn't know how to come back home. This street itself had slipped my mind. Somehow, I walked around blindly and managed to reach home.'

I was stunned. From that day on, I instructed him not to go out alone. To increase his ability to remember, he began spending several hours every day solving crossword puzzles, a crutch he chose for himself. There was a streak of despair in it. I decided to take him to a doctor when we returned to Delhi. I had taken three months' leave of absence from the university; I had to solve the riddle of Amma's death. The changes in Appa's physical movements as well as his disoriented manner made me anxious. I had a hunch that the two were linked.

I had learnt only by chance that there was a riddle buried in Amma's death. I thought she had died of a sudden heart attack. Back then, I couldn't come home immediately upon hearing the news because I had to attend the viva for my doctoral degree. Amma wouldn't have wanted me to skip it. Besides, Appa had said he was travelling to Japan. After that, my trip home kept being postponed for some reason or other. Many factors, such as my new job and the new environment, overturned my world. When I finally came on leave to Delhi two years later, Appa's face had lost all vitality and looked lifeless. The fact that I had not seen him since Amma's death hit me just then. His touch must have set off the sorrow that I had suppressed in my heart, for when I hugged him, I started weeping. He patted my back soothingly.

Unable to control my tears, I said between sobs, 'Appa, why did Amma deceive us like this?'

At once, his hold became limp. 'You're so right, 'ma. It was not an ordinary deception. I can no longer walk with my head held high. Why did she do it, 'ma? What did I do wrong?'

Confused, I let go of his hand and looked at him. 'What do you mean, Appa?'

'Why would she kill herself?'

I was stunned. 'What? Suicide? But you never told me!' I felt a surge of anger as though I had been deceived yet again.

'How could I talk about this to someone who was living in America?'

'Why not? Didn't it strike you that this was important? I would have come immediately, at any cost.'

'And then? You would have grilled me just like those policemen did. I've forgotten everything now. Can't remember a thing.'

The news came as a huge shock to me. I couldn't believe it at all. The police had somehow closed the case, but no matter how many questions I asked Appa, he said, 'I don't remember, 'ma.' A mental block had formed in his mind where Amma was concerned. It was pathetic.

Amma's death. Had she died in a car accident, apart from the grief of losing her, her passing wouldn't have affected me so deeply. Suicide as its probable cause perturbed me. It made me feel that we—Appa and I and many others—were responsible for it. That we had been idiots incapable of understanding the intricacies of Amma's mind was humiliating to me. It was a shame that we perceived people close to us in such superficial ways. A life might have been lost for lack of empathy. How unfair! And now, Amma's death was not the only riddle; her life was beginning to seem like one too. I was annoyed that she had never shared her secrets with me. It felt like an insult.

Why were you a closed book, Amma? Are you giving me clues now only to compensate for that? Please tell me, Amma.

The sun shone brightly after the morning rain. Birds flitted across the sky in exhilaration: white, green, dark blue ... row upon row, one after another. On the road, boys and girls were riding their bicycles again in endless lines, exchanging lively banter, interspersed with sharp giggles. The fog shrouding my mind began to lift. I walked on the pathway around the lake. It was wet from the heavy rain that had poured a short while ago. An old man with a muffler around his head and a walking stick in his hand came from the opposite direction. I was worried that he might slip and fall.

'Careful, uncle,' I said with a smile.

'Thank you,' he said. 'I was born and brought up here, and I haven't slipped so far. It's you who must be careful. Are you a tourist?'

Clearly, the old man was in the mood to talk. I wanted to chat with anyone who was willing.

'No, we have a house nearby. We spend the summer here. I have a job in America.'

'Really? Good. Which house?' the old man said eagerly.

'About a kilometre from here, there is a house called Retreat near the turning?' I looked intently at the old man's face as I waited for his response.

Mild shock flickered in his eyes for a moment. 'You mean—,' he started and then shook his head as if to reject his line of thought. 'Did you buy that house recently?'

'No, we bought it many years ago.'

He gazed at me steadily for some time.

'So the lady who fell into the lake and died—was she your mother?'

'Yes. I was in America at the time.'

'Oh, I am very sorry,' he said. After a brief pause, he added, 'It may rain again. Walk with care.' Then he turned around abruptly and started walking.

I was a little disappointed. More than disappointed, I was confused. Why were people reluctant to talk about Amma's death? Did they believe that some unspoken truth was buried in

it? The lady who fell into the lake and died—was she your mother?
Did he say that it was a suicide or that it was spoken of as one?

As soon as I turned the corner, the sign caught my eye: C.S.I.
Retreat Centre.

As if someone was propelling me forward, I crossed the road,
opened the large wooden gates at the entrance and continued on
the pathway that stretched up the incline.

It was an old colonial-style building. The glass doors opened
into a spacious reception hall. Beyond the reception, there
seemed to be a long corridor with rooms on either side. A few
white people were sitting on the sofas in the hall, talking in low
voices. When I pressed the calling bell, a nun who was poring
over some work on the reception desk looked up. She came to
the door with a smile and said, 'Yes?' A fair, plump face, the very
image of kindness, with eyes that oozed compassion.

Not knowing what to say, I hesitated for a moment before
I told her in English, 'I have come here in connection with an
investigation.'

Her eyes betrayed shock. 'I don't understand, child. Explain
what you want in detail,' she said.

Apologizing hastily, I told her—about Amma's unexpected
demise, my confusion, finding their address written in one of
Amma's handwritten notes, that the purpose of my visit was
to check whether someone who might have known Amma was
living there …

I was surprised to find myself relating all this to a stranger.
Perhaps it was the evident love and compassion on her face that
made me speak so freely. I realized that I had become emotional.

A hint of alarm showed on her face. Clasping my shoulder,
she said in a gentle voice, 'Come in and sit down, child,' and led
me to a sofa in a corner of the hall. For reasons I could scarcely

grasp, I felt like crying. I realized that I hadn't cried for Amma's death in anyone's presence.

'Did you know my mother?' I asked her eagerly. My heart was pounding. I was hoping that my blind conviction about a connection between Amma and this place would not end in disappointment.

'I didn't know her, child,' she said softly. 'I can understand your confusion, but I don't know what help I can offer you.'

'Surely, there must be people here who knew her?'

She replied after thinking it over for a long time. 'Our Mother Superior may have known her. But she passed away.'

I was dejected. 'What do *you* know of my mother?'

She gave me a startled look. 'Nothing at all, child. I had heard of her. She was a woman of immense generosity, I was told. She made large donations to this organization.'

I was astonished, but before I could ask her anything further, the telephone rang. The nun got up immediately. 'Excuse me. I have work to do. Don't grieve so much over the dead. Let their souls attain peace. Your mother was a good soul.'

I was crushed at not being able to talk any further with her. Without realizing it, I pleaded in a raised voice, 'Please, Sister. Help me.'

As she answered the phone, the nun nodded as if taking my leave and saying goodbye. The white people who were sitting in the hall looked at me in surprise.

I walked out, feeling defeated. While coming down the sloping pathway, her words hummed in my ears.

Your mother was a good soul.

How did she know? Was it because of her donations? What was the purpose of those donations?

I reached home like someone walking in a dream. There was still time left to lunch. Appa was discussing something with the

gardener. I went again to Amma's library. I sat in the easy chair
she used to relax in, and closed my eyes. I didn't understand why
Amma had given money to a Christian organization. How many
more secrets was Amma going to reveal to me? It was foolish to
expect that she would tell me anything at all. I got up and, like
someone possessed, frantically riffled through the drawers in the
desk. Pushed to the back of one of them was Amma's diplomatic
passport. I opened it eagerly and cursorily glanced at the details of
her official trips to many countries. In the photograph on the first
page, Amma looked young. It was a face that exuded strength
and confidence. Looking at her sharp eyes, no one would say
that this was a person who might take her own life. I stared at
the photograph for a while. Then, just as I was about to put the
passport away, my eyes fell on:

Place of birth: Kodaikanal

To my astonished eyes, the next two lines meant little.

State: Tamil Nadu

Nationality: Indian

19

THE WAVES ROARED in exhilaration. Retreating swiftly, they leapt forward at a speed a hundred times faster, and dashed against the sand. Yogu stood in the water close to the shoreline, holding Lakshmi's hand, her skirt hitched above the knees. When a wave attacked her and drenched her thighs, Yogu jumped back with a squeal. Her carefree laughter and the happiness that glowed in her eyes infected Lakshmi too. A current of excitement swept through her, as though she was suddenly ten years younger. This Yogu was the one who appeared in her dreams—dressed in a skirt and blouse, her jet-black hair woven into twin braids and adorned with colourful ribbons, and with an auspicious dot on her forehead. Her smooth bronze legs were glistening and wet. Under the hot sun, her body glittered like a copper icon. Yogu, transformed in her identity and persona. Yogu, resplendent with the unblemished purity of an idol in a temple.

They could see fishing boats in the distance and commercial ships even farther away.

'Akka, wouldn't it be fun to travel in that fishing boat?' Yogu said, pushing back unruly strands of hair from her eyes.

Lakshmi laughed. 'Why only boats, we might even travel by ship some day.'

'Really?'

Lakshmi pinched her cheek fondly and smiled. 'Such ambition! It's only now that you've come as far as the seashore.'

At once, Yogu's face turned dark. 'It wouldn't have been possible without you, Akka. Definitely not.' But before Lakshmi could discern the sorrow in her voice, Yogu laughed. 'Had it not been for you, I would still be on the terrace, guarding the vadagam and driving the crows away, my bare head covered and a nine-yard sari wrapped around me.'

Lakshmi hugged her. 'You will study and pass major exams, as you'll see. Then you will go after all those who commit crimes. You will make sure they are punished and sent to jail.'

Yogu's eyes widened in surprise. 'Are you going to make me study law?'

'Yes. There was a time when I wanted to study law. Do you know why? My mother insisted that I should learn dancing, and she would send me to attend classes with a dance master. Even if I made a small mistake in the exercise, that nattuvanar—'

'Oh, you learnt to dance, did you?' Seeing the shock in Yogu's eyes, Lakshmi felt a pang of sorrow. 'Sadir and all—'

'That's a different story,' Lakshmi interrupted. 'Listen to this. Even if I made a small mistake, he would hit me on the ankle with the kattai. Every day! At such times, I'd think to myself: When I become a lawyer I shall put the dance master in jail for violation of human rights and hit *him* on the ankle.'

'Aiyaiyo! Why didn't you do it? You became a doctor instead!' Yogu fell about laughing.

With a wan smile on her lips, Lakshmi gazed in silence at the horizon. She was relieved that Yogu seemed to have forgotten the shock she had experienced a few minutes earlier. The sun had become a golden platter. Periya Mirasu's face appeared at its centre. *Paapa is gone.* He covered his face and sobbed helplessly. Wetness spread on the fabric of the stole that covered his eyes. *During childbirth, from excessive bleeding.* Her father's shoulders were shaking. The figure that strode with regal majesty was devastated. She wanted to clasp his shoulder and console him. She would have liked to bury her face in his broad chest and cry out, 'Appa!' But she didn't have the right that Paapa, who had died before her time, had had. She could only make a request in an insistent voice, like a beggar.

I want to study medicine. Make arrangements for my studies. Other girls shouldn't have to die like Paapa.

'Akka, look over there. How beautiful it looks!'

With her eyes wide and an enchanted smile on her lips, Yogu stood holding Lakshmi's hand. They remained like that, in silence, until the sun finally set.

Lakshmi was taken aback to see tears streaming from Yogu's eyes.

'What's the matter, Yogu?'

'Nothing, Akka. Whenever I see something very beautiful, my eyes well up, as if I've seen god in person. It was like that when I saw this ocean for the first time. I wanted to wail and cry.'

Without saying anything, Lakshmi squeezed her hand tightly. Yogu would be unstoppable now.

'I said a lot of things to the ocean that day, you know? They named me Yogambal, the goddess of good fortune, but in what way am I fortunate? My education came to a stop. There is no one in my native home with the means to look after me. I don't even know what kind of man my husband was. I don't even remember his face, Akka. I got the news that he had died suddenly. Everyone was crying, but somehow I couldn't. I cried only when they shaved my head. "She can live in my house from now on," my mother-in-law said and brought me here. "The whole town says she is a fine woman, so you should live with her from now on," my brother said. Everyone was saying "It's your fate, it's your fate" like it was a magic chant. I began living in an unfamiliar city, among people I had never met before. I had never done any housework before coming here. For every mistake, I was abused and rapped on my shaven head.'

Afraid that Yogu would see the tears filling her eyes, Lakshmi sat with her head bowed. It grieved her to think of all the sorrow this child must have stashed in the folds of her nine-yard sari.

'I asked the ocean that day: What is fate? If it's what is written on one's forehead, who writes it? What did the one who wrote mine have against me? Look at the sore on my head, I said, lowering the free end of my sari. Look at my leg, scalded with a hot iron handle. What did I do wrong? Was I a murderess? An evil woman? Why should I suffer so much?'

Yogu had said all this many, many times before. Still, every time she heard it Lakshmi's heart was stricken as though she was hearing it for the first time.

'What answer did the ocean give you?'

Yogu's face was glowing. It was smeared with the scarlet of the sky at sunset. The faint glimmer of a smile appeared on her lips.

'It was as if the ocean said, don't be afraid; I am your friend. The sun was scorching above, but the water below was cool. I felt a strong urge to submerge my head in it and drown myself. A wave, even bigger than this one, rose. It called out to me: Come, come. I swear, Akka, it really called me.'

'Is it calling you now?'

'No.' Yogu laughed. 'Even if it calls, I won't go.'

'That day ... You must have felt that you had no other option. You foolish girl! Why didn't you tell me?'

'How could I tell you? You were busy studying for your exams. You came and sat on the terrace to study only on Sunday afternoons. So much happened in the meantime.'

Saying nothing, Lakshmi stroked Yogu's head gently. She had asked the same question and heard Yogu's answer many times over. Yet, she wanted to listen to it again and again. She longed to assert to everyone beset by grief that they should not think that they were alone in the world. When Lakshmi told Natarajaiyer and his wife that all the suicides in the world were caused by despair, because people felt there was no one to help them, the couple had understood eventually. Yet, they didn't have the courage to support her in her decision about Yogu.

Lakshmi kept stroking Yogu's thick, curly hair. She was curled up in her lap like a little child. It saddened her to realize that she had been able to rescue this one girl purely by chance; it was not a social revolution. Yet, even for this single act she had had to fight an epic battle.

In many ways, it was a memorable day in her life, one that had been genuinely filled with joy. Her exam results were out. She had secured the second rank in the whole Presidency. She couldn't wait to share the news with her mother—and her father to express her thanks. She planned to pursue higher studies while working in the Government General Hospital for a year. Then, Professor Rudrappa had told her financial support and scholarship would be available for her to earn a postgraduate degree in England. She was not sure her mother would believe it. She was over the moon when her teachers and classmates in the university campus had congratulated her.

As Lakshmi proceeded towards Natarajaiyer's house in Mylapore, her heart was overflowing with gratitude. Like freedom fighters, she wanted to raise both hands above her head and shout, 'Freedom!' She wondered if her mother would understand what a personal victory it was for her or be too frightened to step out of the cage that she believed was her security.

The afternoon sun was scorching as she walked along the beach road. Mami must be taking her afternoon nap. She would get up only at three to make tiffin. Instead of hurrying back, Lakshmi decided to dawdle for another half hour and then reach home. There was very little human traffic on the beach at that hour. As she looked for a shady spot where she could rest for a bit, she heard a big commotion and disturbance. Near a fishing boat on the shoreline, four or five men were shouting in loud voices as they pulled out a body from the water. Lakshmi trembled involuntarily; ignoring the scorching sun, she ran towards the fishing boat and the cluster of fishermen.

'What happened, 'pa? Who fell into the water?'

Hearing her anxious query, one of them clucked his tongue. 'Some Brahmin girl. A widow. She tried to kill herself.'

Taken aback, Lakshmi looked at the figure that lay on the ground like a heap of empty gunnysacks. She was astonished.

Could it be Yogu?

Shocked, she bent down and turned the body over. Shaven head. Childlike face. The small body draped in a rough cotton sari, as though wrapped in a jute sack. The sari had slipped from her shoulders, leaving her young breasts bare. Lakshmi urgently drew the free end of the sari over Yogu's chest.

'Don't come here and get caught up in this, girl. This is a police case,' another man said.

Ignoring him, Lakshmi checked Yogu's pulse. It was faint. She turned her over and pumped her back.

'Move aside. You need strength for that.'

As the man vigorously pressed Yogu's back, water came gushing out of her mouth and nose. But Yogu still did not open her eyes.

'I am a doctor, 'pa. We need to take her to the hospital. I know this girl. Can someone carry her to a rickshaw?' she said.

'Will she survive?'

'Yes, 'pa. Hurry!'

By the time they reached the road, someone had brought a rickshaw.

Because they knew her at the hospital, the nurses gathered around Lakshmi, grasped the particulars of the case and came swiftly to her aid. They summoned the duty doctor and had her attend to the patient immediately. As she looked at Yogu, Lakshmi was overwhelmed by a surge of grief. It was shocking to think that that little girl had come to such a decision. An hour passed before Yogu opened her eyes and blinked in confusion at Lakshmi and the interiors of the hospital.

'How are you, Yogu?' Lakshmi asked tenderly.

Yogu sat up immediately and tried to flee. Lakshmi needed the help of two more people to restrain her. When she was made to lie down on the bed again, Yogu turned to her side and started to cry, shaking with sobs.

Gently stroking her back, Lakshmi said, 'Don't cry, Yogu. What happened today?'

For a long time, Yogu did not speak. Then she turned and held on to Lakshmi's hands. 'Akka, please let me die. I am begging you. Don't I have even the freedom to die?'

'No, Yogu. Legally, it's a crime. If the police come to know, they will put you in jail.'

'You are lying. It's my life. How does it matter to them?'

'That's how it is, Yogu. You are free only to live, not to die.'

Yogu covered her face again and wept. The hem of her sari had ridden up her leg, baring her ankle where the wound from being burnt with a hot iron was visible. Lakshmi had the nurse bring an ointment. As she was applying it over the wound, Yogu said, 'In how many places can you apply it?'

'What happened, Yogu?'

Yogu refused to reply.

'Let's go home,' Lakshmi said gently.

Panic flared in Yogu's eyes. 'Aiyaiyo! No, Akka! Just push me back into the ocean and be on your way. How will I face anyone in that house?'

'I'll talk to them.'

'What will you say? You don't know what happened.'

'How will I know if you don't tell me, Yogu? You can tell me. I won't tell anyone.'

With her head bowed and her eyes downcast, Yogu spoke in a low whisper. 'My father-in-law is not a good man. His devotion to god and religious piety are just an act. When I am sleeping at night, he tries to touch me. I don't know what he did when I was sleeping last night, but when I awoke, my sari had come off completely. I screamed. He slapped me hard on the face. Before I could wrap the sari around me, Mami woke up and came there. "Ask this whore what she had got up to," my father-in-law said. I was aghast. I kept trying to explain that he was the one who approached me, but I got beaten repeatedly. Mami heated the ladle and drew the handle across my leg. "Go die!" she screamed. No one spoke to me in the morning, or asked me to eat. I waited till they retired for their afternoon nap, then left through the back door. I didn't even know where the ocean was. I walked blindly through the streets.'

Lakshmi was frozen in shock and horror. This was far worse than the humiliation suffered by their clan. It made her furious.

'Now tell me, how can I go to that house again?'

Lakshmi finally understood Yogu's predicament. 'You will live with me from now on,' she said immediately.

Startled, Yogu looked at her. 'How, Akka? You live in the house next door. My mother-in-law will kill me.'

'I am not going to live there any more. Anyway, I have passed the exam. I am going to look for a house to rent. Live with me. I will make arrangements for your education. You can get rid of this widow's garb and live a new life.'

Confusion was writ large on Yogu's face. 'Is it possible, Akka? Would my parents, my in-laws accept it? Won't they try to stop me?'

'Do you want to study or not?'

Yogu's eyes lit up suddenly. 'Definitely ... but ...'

'Don't ever say "but" again. Now it's *my* responsibility.'

Until that afternoon, Lakshmi couldn't have anticipated the arrival of a moment when she would decide to change the course of her life. As she wondered who could be entrusted with looking after Yogu for now, she remembered Sister Jane, a nun who had studied with her.

'I will find you a safe shelter today. Then we'll think about what to do,' she told Yogu.

When they went to Sister Jane's chamber, the nun was getting ready to travel out of the city. Lakshmi told her about Yogu and said that she needed refuge for a few days.

The reply came the next moment like a divine blessing. 'I am going to Kodaikanal tomorrow morning. Let her come with me. She can study in the convent there,' the nun said. After looking intently at Yogu for a moment, she said, 'Lakshmi, this child will need a couple of sets of clothes, won't she? I will arrange for woollens.'

Lakshmi smiled. 'Sister, I will never forget your help all my life. I'll take her to a shop right away.'

'What is it, Akka?' Yogu asked, looking perplexed because she couldn't follow their conversation in English.

Lakshmi touched her face affectionately. 'Your life is going to open up now. You are going to another city with Sister here.

You will study in a good school. You will come and stay with me during the holidays,' Lakshmi said.

'But how, Akka?'

'Shush. Without anyone knowing, of course. We are going to change your clothes first. You will throw away this gunny sack, and wear a skirt and half-sari.'

Yogu's eyes widened innocently. 'What about my head?'

'Your hair will grow soon enough. For now, you can tie a scarf around your head. If anyone asks, tell them you were tonsured in Tirupati.'

Yogu laughed like a child, with dimples in her cheeks. The next moment, she hugged Lakshmi and wept.

20

'Amma, that's enough for the day,' Kasturi said wearily.

A bored Sengamalam laid the tambura horizontally on the floor.

'How long will you grieve for that disgusting floozy? Has the world come to an end just because she is gone? Doesn't it suit you if I sing instead of her?' Sengamalam's voice brimmed equally with anger and despair.

Kasturi was annoyed. 'Why are you talking like this, Amma? Was she one of us only because she sang for me?'

Sabapathi remained quiet, his head bowed over his instrument. For some days now, he has been immersed in silence, Kasturi thought. He and Thilakam were close, like twins almost. The same dazzling talent. The same prickly sense of honour. His fingers kept tapping the mridangam, as though he was stroking it gently. *Thakita thakathimi thakita thakathimi.*

Suddenly Sengamalam burst out in anger.

'Little did that bitch care about family bonds and relationships! She fell for that Brahmin boy's promises and ran away, deceiving all of us. How my womb burns when I think of her!'

When Sengamalam was angry, no one could control her. The civilized language that Kanagu Paati had taught her simply disappeared. Sabapathi was still tapping a figure on his mridangam, following his own whim: *thakita thakathimi thakita thakathimi ...*

Kasturi drew her knees up and buried her face between them. In the darkness that engulfed her mind, she saw their backyard ... Thilakam standing in the shadows, the silhouette of a man beside her, talking to each other in secretive whispers. Kasturi was assailed once again by the shock and grief she had felt that day when she understood the latent meaning of that scene. In the four months that had elapsed since Thilakam's departure, like a rolled-up picture unfurling constantly, the scene confronted her at every moment. Disbelief sat like a ball of fire in her belly. Sengamalam's anger was just. Thilakam had dismissed her relationship with them in a few lines.

I am going to lead a respectable life. I've got the opportunity.
No one should feel bad about it.

Big, round letters inscribed on a sheet that was kept next to Kanagu Paati's pillow. A sheet torn from a notebook for writing notes and songs. Kasturi could not bear to see those non-committal, unfeeling words. Words that felt like a slap on the face.

I am going to lead a respectable life.

You people are leading despicable lives, she was saying, just as Lakshmi once had. Lakshmi was born to someone else. She had learnt to stand on her own. But this girl was Kasturi's *sister*. Her personality was different. Like a delicate creeper, she needed a pole to support her.

Grief surged within her. 'You fool!' She wanted to slap her own head and weep. She was heartbroken that Thilakam, whom she had treated with boundless affection, had run away without telling her. Did her hand tremble when she tore off a sheet from the songbook? It was a book she had worshipped like god. Every day, after she had finished singing, Thilakam would piously touch the book to her eyes before keeping it inside.

I'll die if I am told to stop singing, you used to say. Does your husband ask you to sing?

Sengamalam was still ranting with undiminished fury. Sabapathi continued tapping, as if to avoid listening to her.

Suddenly Sengamalam burst out, 'Elei, won't you stop it now?'

Kasturi looked up with a jolt.

Sabapathi stopped playing. He locked eyes with his mother for a moment, then got up, strode to the doorway and went out. His stare and silent defiance made Kasturi's stomach churn.

Watching him leave, Sengamalam screamed again. 'Go away! Some devil has possessed all of you.' She continued talking to Kasturi: 'He praised her to the skies, didn't he? But whenever we perform in Madras these days, he gives some lame excuse to say that Thilakam can't come. He is telling us indirectly that his family will be shamed if Thilakam sings for us. Well, your sister ran away thinking that life with them was respectable. Why are you pining for her? For us, she is as good as dead.'

'Amma!' Kasturi cried out in anguish as tears streamed from her eyes. 'How can you say that?'

A dejected Kanagu Paati, lounging quietly on the swing, said in a gentle voice, 'Leave it, Sengamalam. Let her live a happy life wherever she is. If that is the life she wants, why don't you let her be? The times are changing. We should understand that.'

Sengamalam calmed down a little. 'So long as she is happy,' she said, with a dismissive jerk of her chin. 'She hasn't even dropped us a line. She must think writing a letter is beneath her.'

Was there some truth in what her mother had just said? Thilakam had signed off with a three-line letter. Could their relationship really turn so bitter? Was it even possible? Or was she no longer free to write letters?

After Thilakam ran away—Chee! what a ghastly word. Kasturi was embarrassed at herself. Four days later, they had received a letter from Gopalaiyer.

Your daughter Thilakam is now the daughter-in-law of my family. Even I am unhappy that my son took her to the temple in Thiruneermalai and married her without telling anyone. I didn't expect this either. But she will lead a happy and comfortable life here. There's no need to worry.

They sat together in the backyard and read the tersely worded letter under the sunlit sky. Tears flowed from their eyes as if they had just received news of a bereavement. Recovering his composure, Sabapathi wiped his eyes and said, 'I am glad that Akka found a way out of her troubles.' His sharp glance seemed to accuse Kasturi of something.

In a street where residents could gather intelligence without ever leaving the house, Kasturi didn't know who said what about Thilakam going away or how Sengamalam managed them. People who were vicious even about Lakshmi going to school wouldn't refrain from gossiping about Thilakam.

'What is all this about prestige and whatnot?'

'Why would any man keep a prostitute's daughter on his head?'

'He is going to rap her on the head and put her down, I'll give it to you in writing ...'

Muthu was shocked when he learnt about Thilakam from Sabapathi. Perhaps his opinion was no different from the others'; yet, he seemed to understand Kasturi's distress. As if to console her, he said, 'Thilakam is a smart girl, Akka. Though I was worried about her, I never imagined that she would sever all ties with the family. But she has married into an affluent household. She will be well off. Don't worry about her.'

Sundaramurthi Mama was highly perturbed.

'Will it do her good or harm, Mama?' Kasturi asked him in despair.

'Can't say, 'ma,' he said wearily. 'We don't know what kind of person that boy is. If he is mature, she will have got the resolution she wanted.'

'As a husband, will he respect her mastery of music?'

'Life is not music alone, 'ma.'

She looked at him in confusion. 'Do you feel that way, too?'

'Yes, 'ma. The very air we breathe now is different. It stirs our blood and makes us contemplate things we have never done before. Earlier, music was my whole world. Now I think that music is bigger than me, and this nation is greater than music. In the past, things like human rights and humiliation didn't affect me. We didn't really mind when those who had graciously invited us to play the nadaswaram at their wedding asked us to sit in a mandapam outside the village and brought us the leftover food after the last batch of guests had finished their meal. We were so used to thinking that the hierarchies in society had been put in place by our elders that our minds had become dull. And now? It is as if fresh blood has entered our bodies, 'ma. I feel like asking questions. I feel that if there's no freedom for the country and the common man, my personal happiness would have no meaning. Do you know what Gandhi said? If there is no freedom for the Paraiyars, Pulaiyars and women, our freedom, even if we get it, will be pointless.'

She looked at him, perplexed. 'If Thilakam is not free to sing, what kind of freedom is it, Mama?'

'Hers is a problem of honour and respect. As the wife of a man from a respectable family, she would get respect, wouldn't she? That boy must have told her that he would give her that status. She must have believed it was worth any sacrifice.'

As Kasturi thought about it, her eyes filled with tears. She could not understand why.

'Thilakam once said that if someone ordered her not to sing, she would die.'

'It must have been before she met this boy.'

Kasturi could not remember. Had the sweet trance of love made Thilakam forget everything? Could it happen to Kasturi too? Singaram appeared before her, smiling. Would she want to elope with him, forsaking dance and god? When he sang '*Chinnachiru kiliye, kannamma*', his voice tender with love, would she not want to spend a whole lifetime in his embrace? The thought made her blush.

'Sengamalam told me that you are giving a performance in Madras on the twentieth?'

Coming back to her senses, she nodded. 'Yes.'

They had received invitations for two performances in Madras; Gopalaiyer had organized them. When asked if Thilakam would sing for them, he refused politely. For unknown reasons, the date kept getting postponed. At present, it was fixed for the twentieth of the month. Kasturi was certain she would meet Thilakam once they reached Madras. Wouldn't she come to watch Kasturi dance?

'I forgot to tell you something,' Sundaramurthi said. 'I met Thulasi yesterday. She told me your friend Lakshmi has passed her exams. She is a doctor now. She wants to work in the same hospital for a year and earn an advanced degree. She may even go abroad for higher studies.'

Kasturi looked at him in awe. 'Really! Then she has achieved what she had set her mind on, Mama. She was only ten when said she didn't want this life. She went away to study because that was the only way to escape. But she couldn't have done it without Periya Mirasu's support.'

'True. But Thulasi is a real weakling. "I don't know whether it's good or bad, Sundaram," she tells me. She hasn't realized the greatness of Lakshmi's achievement.'

Mama has changed, Kasturi noted. Like he said, this air itself had that quality. But she was reluctant to tell Mama about Lakshmi's 'movement'. She wondered if he would understand the panic that it had set off in her. Even if he did, would he still support the movement?

Sabapathi, who had gone out, was not back yet.

'His ways are quite erratic these days,' Sengamalam said.

Kasturi had a pleasant hunch that he might have gone to Singaram's house.

As dusk was falling, Sengamalam came to her and said, 'Get up, Kasturi. The carriage has come for you.'

Kasturi was tired, but she could only whisper, 'Why has it come so early today?'

Once she was in the carriage, she closed the curtains, leaned back on the bolster and shut her eyes. Images kept appearing in her mind like shards. 'I am leading an honourable life. Why are you debasing yourself?' Thilakam said. 'Kasturi doesn't know what honour is.' Lakshmi laughed. 'If someone grabs my hand, the disgrace is his, not mine.' Wasn't that true? 'You were born to dance. I am not a virtuoso,' Singaram said.

'Don't put me on a pedestal, Singaram. I was born for you. Singaram is not just a name, is it? I thought I would die when you were injured. Yet you are afraid to come near me.'

Fragments of memories and trains of thought. Her mind was unsteady and in a state of utter confusion.

The carriage stopped. Had they arrived at the palace already? She drew the curtain back and looked. This was a different building. A whitewashed patio, blooming garden, and liveried attendants at the entrance. She was taken aback.

'Where are we, Arumugam?'

'Raja is expected here. He asked me to tell you that he wanted to discuss the upcoming dance festival with the Durai.'

She was shocked. 'No, no! Let's go back. I have nothing to do here.'

'Raja asked me to bring you here, Akka. This is the Collector's bungalow.'

Thinking it might be true, she got down from the carriage. But why should he hold the meeting here? She looked at Arumugam. He stood still, his face expressionless and his eyes downcast. Was he uncertain himself? But she did not expect him to turn the carriage around as she had asked him to. He was Raja's servant.

She walked gingerly up the wide, expansive steps and entered through the front door. It opened into a spacious drawing room. Seeing her pause near the door, the Durai, who was sitting on the sofa, stood up, stretched his arms wide and greeted her with a smile. 'Come in!' Though he spoke with a coarse accent, she noticed that he had learnt Tamil. She cast a suspicious glance around the room.

'Is Raja not here yet?'

'Oh, you're besotted with Raja, are you?' He laughed. 'Come, come. He'll be here soon.'

He lunged forward to grab her hand, but she sidestepped in a flash. He laughed again and looked her over from head to toe, as if he wanted to strip her naked with his eyes. Nodding in appreciation, he muttered something to himself in English. The door she had entered through was now shut. All the other doors and windows in that spacious hall were hidden behind floor-length curtains, and were probably closed too. She was angry that Raja had tricked her in this shameful manner.

The Durai brought her a chalice filled with what appeared to be fruit juice and held the glass towards her. 'Here. Drink up.'

'I don't drink such things,' she said.

'It's only juice. Very expensive wine, not liquor.' As he stood there holding the glass, she thought that arguing with him would be unwise and took it from him.

He gazed at her steadily as he sipped liquor from his own glass.

'When is Raja expected to come?'

'Let him come in his own time. Meanwhile, let me play one of our songs. I heard you are a fine dancer. Let me see you dance to our music.' He went over to the gramophone cabinet and flicked a switch. Strains of Western music filled the room. Even in her distraught state, Kasturi was able to enjoy the tune. The Durai drew close to her, grabbed her waist and caught her hand with his. She came back to her senses in a flash and tried to move away. 'What's the matter? This is how we dance,' he said, and pulling her close, tried to lead her in step with the music.

Kasturi realized that he was very drunk, and began to look for a clever way to escape from him. But how? If all the doors were closed, how would she get away? Noticing that he had begun to whirl around the room while dancing, she moved her feet and whirled in step with him.

The Durai's enthusiasm grew boundless. 'Good! Good!' he cried.

Kasturi leaned backwards with a smile as they danced, determined to not let him press his body against hers. When the music picked up pace, they twirled faster. As they spun around, she kept searching for a gap in any of the doors. If she couldn't get away, she was afraid that she would be trapped with no means of escape. Even if she screamed, no one would come to her aid. Lord, how will I get out of here? Just then a curtain in front of a door fluttered in the breeze. Could the door be open?

Suddenly, loud slogans were heard outside. 'Vande Mataram! Vande Mataram!'

Vande Mataram! It was a procession of freedom fighters!

A thrill coursed through her body. Yet, at the same time, she loathed herself for being in the arms of a white man. She teared up at the humiliation. Lord, how am I going to escape?

The sound of slogans grew louder as though the procession was drawing near. The Durai's face was flushed with anger. 'Damn them!' he muttered under his breath. 'All of them will die. Such fools!' he said to her.

All of a sudden, he wrapped his arms around her and started planting kisses on her face. When she tried to push him away, he grabbed her roughly. 'Stay quiet, you whore!' he snapped in Tamil.

Kasturi was startled. Who had taught him that word of abuse? A blaze flared from her navel. She freed herself violently and slapped him on the face. Spewing some English words—what did 'bitch' mean?—he lunged towards her.

'Sir! Sir!' There was loud knocking on the front door.

'Who is that? Idiot!'

As the Durai angrily strode to the entrance, Kasturi stole away to the door where the curtain had moved in the breeze and pushed it slightly. She couldn't believe her luck when it opened wide. Emerging soundlessly, she bolted the door from outside. She could see a vegetable garden and a thornbush fence; this was the backyard of the bungalow. She ran headlong into the night.

Fortunately, it was pitch-dark all around. She jumped over the fence, tearing her sari, and entered the adjoining lane. Ignoring the rent in her sari, she continued to run. Now she could hear the slogans more clearly.

'Vande Mataram! Get out, white man!'

Her body trembled as if an electric shock had passed through her. The lane joined the main road where a large procession seemed to be on its way. Sundaramurthi Mama and Singaram would definitely be a part of the crowd. The very idea was like a shot in the arm for her. She spotted Singaram first. She ran spiritedly until she was next to him, raised her hand and shouted, 'Vande Mataram!'

He was stunned to see her. 'How did you come here? It's dangerous!' he said nervously.

She experienced an inexplicable erotic thrill. She laughed. 'But you are here, aren't you, to guard me like a fortress?' That she could laugh even after what she had experienced moments ago amazed her.

'Don't be foolish. They won't spare you just because you're a woman. They will beat you black and blue. I won't be able to do a thing.'

Kasturi could see stark signs of anxiety in Singaram's eyes. Sundaramurthi Mama was two rows ahead of them. He too was taken aback on seeing her. But then he glanced in the direction of the Collector's bungalow and she realized that he had understood her situation. She was moved by his sensitivity and intelligence. Before he could say anything though, the police charged the crowd with canes and the protesters' cries of distress filled the night.

Suddenly Singaram caught hold of her hand and said, 'Come with me. We must run. Can you?'

'Do you think someone who dances can't run?' she said and started running with him.

Singaram did not appear to have noticed the playful note in her voice. He grabbed her hand and began to run. Immediately, the surrounding chaos and screams faded away; in the warm touch of his hand, Kasturi was steeped in an intoxication she had not experienced before.

They ran through alleys the police could never enter, past the back entrance of the temple and to the opening that led to the well called Simmakkinaru. Singaram stopped beside the opening where two stone lions stood guard. 'You must hide here for some time. I will remain outside,' he said.

Kasturi looked down. There was enough space for two people to sit with their legs stretched out. And steps that led to the water below. 'How is that possible? I will sit here only if you come with me. What an idea! If the police see you standing outside, they will come after you. Both of us will be in danger.'

He must have thought she made sense for a few seconds later, he came inside reluctantly and sat next to her. As thigh rubbed thigh and breaths mingled, she realized that it was the greatest moment of her life.

21

THILAKAM SAT UPRIGHT with a jolt. Gopalaiyer and her husband were talking in slightly raised voices in the hall. She was not normally in the habit of eavesdropping on their conversations; she believed it was uncivilized. Besides, not only did the feeling of being an outsider in the house make her keep her distance, but she knew that they wanted it that way as well. Yet, today, the name that surfaced in their conversation drew her in with a fierce tug. *Kasturi*. The moment she heard that name, her whole body was swamped by a rush of affection and her eyes welled up. She listened with keen ears.

'I want no truck with their kind, which is why I've forbidden any contact with her family.'

'That's fine, son. Even now, whenever Kasturi asks me whether Thilakam will sing for her performance, I put her off with some excuse. We won't allow Thilakam to sing, but when Kasturi is performing here, it won't be proper to stop them from meeting.'

'Why not?' Kalyanaraman said. Thilakam flinched at the vehemence in his voice. 'They should be glad that we've given her a life. As someone who came to us wanting to escape from there, why does she need their kinship? If she meets them, they might latch on to her again. I don't want that to happen.'

'Let's be a bit lenient now. You can always refuse the next time.'

She realized that they had kept talking in loud voices only so she could hear.

Neither Kalyanaraman's angry outbursts nor Gopalaiyer's vague excuses affected Thilakam. If anything she was worried to know that she would be taken to Kasturi's upcoming sadir concert in Madras with her husband's half-hearted consent.

Even now, she couldn't come to terms with what she had done. Falling in love with Kalyanaraman, giving up her village and family and eloping in the middle of the night with a near stranger—it all felt like a foolhardy move, committed in a stupor as it were. Every day, she wondered in disbelief whether she was really the girl who had run away. She wondered how her mother and Kanagu Paati had taken the news. She knew Amma would never forgive her for as long as she lived. Kasturi and Sabapathi would have been devastated. Thilakam had come away without confiding her secret even to Kasturi, a close friend more than an elder sister, not because of that stupor, but because she was afraid that Kasturi would stop her if she came to know. Though she tried to appease herself with such thoughts, she was racked by guilt from the day she arrived in Madras. If she told Kasturi, 'I had no other way, Akka, to escape from that shameful life,' her sister might not understand.

'I refuse to lead a disgraceful life that gives any stranger the licence to grab my hand. You might say, "There is no connection between me and the shame visited on my body, dance is the only thing that matters to me." But the way the world looks at you is different. How long will your life as a dancer last? And when you can't dance any more, who will live with you as companion and mate? Who will come forward to give you a life? Will you wait for your man to come late at night like a thief, the way Periya Mirasu visits Lakshmi's mother? Will he take care of you till the end? Living in Dasi Street, what respect can you command? Won't random men knock on your door?'

Even as these arguments raged in her mind, her eyes teared up: Kasturi stood before her. 'Are you happy, Thilakam? Do you sing at all?'

Thilakam came back to her senses with a start. She understood only now the connection between singing and happiness.

But it hadn't seemed important that day.

'After the arrogant Durai grabbed your hand in public, Akka, I decided I couldn't live this life. I didn't have the means to educate myself like Lakshmi. If things got out of hand, I believed my only recourse to be a length of rope. I didn't tell anyone, though.'

It was strange how she had fallen in love with Kalyanaraman at first sight. When he confessed within minutes of their meeting in Madras that he was attracted to her, her heart grew wings and soared into the sky. Ignoring the sound of alarm bells ringing within, it began to braid imaginary festoons.

Eyes brimming with love, he had begged her, 'You must come out of this gutter, Thilakam.'

'How?' she had asked, her eyelids fluttering and eyes filling with tears. 'I yearn for that, but I can't find a way.'

It was then that Kalyanaraman uttered the words: 'I'll show you the way out. I'll marry you.'

She couldn't believe it. She felt overwhelmed. She couldn't ask further, 'How, exactly?' Some visitor had arrived to meet him and he disappeared. Later, on the railway platform, a boy had brought her a letter and placed it secretly in her palm. She hid it in her blouse and was able to read it only after she returned to her village. The plan he had drawn up for her escape was in the letter.

What a thrilling moment it was! A spirit of daring—there was nothing wrong with forsaking her family and running away for the sake of her lover, the man who would give her the life she wanted—permeated her entire being. She was embarking on a journey in search of a new dawn, a day when the body and mind crackled with electricity.

'Do you understand, Akka?'

'Never mind all that! Are you truly happy?'

How can I tell her that I don't have the answer to that question?

When they came home from Thiruneermalai, garlands from the wedding still around their necks, a shocked Gopalaiyer's first words were: 'So, did you use your dasi's wiles on my son?'

Stung by those words, Thilakam was silent, but Kalyanaraman stood by her. 'I was the one who asked her if she would live with me as my wife. I've made her promise that she will have absolutely no contact with her past life. Only a life of respect and dignity is important to her now, nothing else.'

'Not even singing?'

'Not even singing,' Kalyanaraman replied firmly.

Nothing had seemed amiss that day. 'Will you promise before god that you are not related to them any more?' he asked in the temple. She laughed. 'From now on, you are everything to me. I've left the past behind.'

Kalyanaraman, who had graciously tied the sacred cord around her neck and given her the status of a wife, seemed like the ideal young man she had never even heard of until then. She marvelled at her luck over and over again, and rejoiced in it.

But when Gopalaiyer uttered those words, all the malevolent angels must have chanted their approval. They must have ensured that vile thoughts about Thilakam's clan gained a permanent place in the depths of Kalyanaraman's mind. Not only the severance of her relations with her family but disturbing the very foundation of her life as well must have been their doing.

In the village, her days had always begun with songs and notes at dawn. She didn't regret that it had changed. She *needed* change; it was the only route to freedom. This was a life she had accepted willingly and she prepared herself for it wholeheartedly. However, she couldn't erase Kanagu Paati's empathy steeped in love and tactful speech, along with the affection of Kasturi, Sabapathi and Sundaramurthi Mama, from her memory. They obscured her path every now and then but she learnt to push them away.

'You have to wipe yourself clean of everything in order to live,' Paati would say. 'I can't, Paati. Forgive me.' When the tears flowed during sleepless nights, a nameless sorrow sat like a ball in her belly.

'Didn't you say you would die if someone asked you not to sing?'

The question stalked her daily. She hadn't imagined that on hearing birdsong at dawn she would have to suppress the melody that rose involuntarily from her navel, press it back into her vocal cords and direct it back to where it had come from.

'I won't sing on the stage; I have no wish to. But I can sing in god's chamber, can't I?'

'Inside the house, within you, without making a sound.'

She had laughed at first. How was it possible? It was singing only when you let your voice soar freely; otherwise, it was just whimpering.

'You are the type who would take a mile if you're given an inch. What's the guarantee that if you sing you won't start dancing the sadir?'

'The blood that flows in you is different.'

'Will a whore's character change on its own?'

'You should be a whore only at night.'

She had never imagined that words could also be used as whiplashes in this manner. Within a week, her dreams and expectations had collapsed.

She was not permitted to enter the kitchen and the puja room. She learnt that Kalyanaraman's mother had died when he was very young. There was a man who did the cooking. He was a stickler for ritual purity. Even if her shadow fell on him, he would go to the well at the back and bathe angrily before returning to the kitchen. Gopalaiyer performed the daily worship with pomp and ceremony. When she was new in the household, she had sat outside at a distance, and when the puja was over, asked eagerly, 'May I sing for the aarti?' When he nodded his assent, she closed her eyes and began to sing. As her voice rang out, her heart turned tender. The village, the temple and the deity surfaced in her mind. She felt as if Sabapathi was sitting beside her, tapping the mridangam. Her eyes filled with tears.

Someone was rapping her on the head. When she opened her eyes with a start, a furious Kalyanaraman stood before her.

'I called you so many times. Didn't you hear me? Don't I need to go to the office? Why haven't you kept my clothes ready?'

'Go and attend to him. Serving your husband is of utmost importance,' Gopalaiyer said.

Looking at the state her husband was in, she started trembling. She got up immediately and followed him. 'Please forgive me. I forgot. I'll fetch your clothes right away,' she said in an appeasing tone.

'When you start this song-and-dance nonsense, it can only end like this. You will forget all about your husband and family,' he said in a tone of irritation.

Still pleasant, she said, 'It won't happen again.'

Thilakam found it difficult to understand him. She could not predict when he would lash out in anger or when he might invite her to bed. She had never imagined that sex would be so fraught with violence. She had never spoken to Kasturi about this subject. It felt as if in return for giving her a life, he had forcibly taken control of her body. He appeared to derive a cruel satisfaction from it. Long before nightfall, her vagina contracted in fear. One night, when she lay inert, he slapped her repeatedly on the face. 'Will you only yield to a man who pays you? Are you already bored of your husband?' At that moment she had regretted not having received instruction from Kanagu Paati.

How will I face all of them? 'Are you doing well, darling?' That one question is enough to make my heart crumble. My face will betray my condition.

'You ran away, talking about respect and whatnot. Is this how your husband treats you?' her mother would sneer. 'I am not longing to see that slut who eloped without a word to anyone,' she would say, as if throwing a punch on Thilakam's face.

As she thought more about it, she decided that it would be better if she skipped attending Kasturi's concert. Every time Kalyanaraman took her somewhere, she ended up feeling depressed and regretful about having gone at all. Out on the streets, he would watch, with the alert eye of a predator, all the people on whom her gaze rested, and throw barbs at her all the way. 'Why are you looking at him? Is he known to you?' It would make her weary. 'What makes you think so? Why would I look at another man? There is no one in my heart except you. I was a virgin when I came to you.' 'But you might change your mind. Infidelity runs in your blood,' he would retort. One night, when she could not bear it any more, she dared to talk back: 'But you knew that when you married me, didn't you?' She received a hard slap on the face. Then she was stripped naked and made to lie face down while he lashed her with a belt. She could not understand why he married her.

'You ran away, talking of honour and whatnot, didn't you?'

At times she thought Kalyanaraman had married her only out of perverse lust, certainly not to give her a life of dignity and respect. But he boasted gracelessly that his acceptance of an untouchable as his wife was an immense sacrifice. Now, he expected her to serve him all life long—as a courtesan, as a slave. He had told her one day, 'What more does a destitute whore like you need? Just come and lie down.' He must have thought that as a courtesan's daughter, she would be well versed in erotic play. That she was not able to match up to his lust was the reason for his resentment.

How can I share this with a third person? How can I tell anyone that I fell for his smooth talk and was duped? If her family stood before her, she wouldn't need to tell them anything. There was no one as intuitive as Kanagu Paati. She would grasp the situation in a single glance.

'Come back with us, child.'

What if I go away from here? Instead of staying here, I can go to the village and live under my family's protection. No one will hurt me there. Kasturi will accept me without reservation. Amma is smart enough to put a lid on any gossip about me in the village. 'We believed they were a reputed family. It didn't work out. So we brought her back,' she'll say. There won't be any loose talk after that. Unlike here, I won't be slighted with constant instructions: Don't touch this, don't look there, don't step in here.

I don't have what it takes to build a respectable life, Paati. I know that now. It can happen only if some great soul is willing to give it to me. Kalyanaraman is not a great soul, just a sex-crazed animal.

The moment the idea germinated in her mind, her heart jumped with joy. Thereafter her time passed in weaving and unravelling plans of escape.

Fear had clutched at her heart all day for some reason. She had never felt so lacking in self-confidence. Before leaving for office, Kalyanaraman told her without a trace of civility on his face, 'Kasturi's sadir concert is happening today. Appa has asked me to take you. Don't disgrace me by going there looking dull and gloomy. Wear a nice sari. You should behave like a respectable housewife. Don't jump and shout when you see your people.'

Behave like a respectable housewife.

She wanted to laugh. He knew that she could only pretend to be one.

She had a dark maroon silk sari, a gift from him. It had belonged to his mother. 'A sacred garment,' he had told her, as if her body was not fit to wear it.

That day he chose the sari himself and kept it on the swing before leaving. Gopalaiyer must have asked him to do this too, she thought. She picked it up gingerly, draped it neatly and looked in the mirror. Thilakam didn't know what kind of person Kalyanaraman's mother might have been; Kalyanaraman himself didn't know much about her. Thilakam wondered if the lady would have accepted her. There was a mild aroma of sandalwood emanating from the sari. Had his mother been alive, Kalyanaraman might have become a human being.

In the evening, when he saw Thilakam wearing his mother's sari with her back fully covered, Kalyanaraman was appeased to some extent. Before setting out, he warned her in a curt voice, 'You mustn't get all excited and happy when you meet your family. Remember that. I am not coming. I have to go somewhere else.' She couldn't believe it for a moment. She hadn't imagined that she would be so lucky.

A large crowd filled the hall. Gopalaiyer led her through the back door to the room where Kasturi was getting ready for the concert. With a spate of emotions rushing through her, Thilakam entered the room. Kasturi looked like an angel in her dancing costume. As soon as she saw Thilakam, she ran towards her and embraced her tightly. Thilakam could not control her emotions. Behind Kasturi, she could dimly see Kanagu Paati, Sengamalam and Sabapathi gazing at her with tears in their eyes.

While Sengamalam spoke to Gopalaiyer about something, Kasturi asked Thilakam in a gentle whisper, 'Thilakam, tell me the truth. Are you happy?'

'Yes, Akka.' Thilakam was afraid that her voice might crack suddenly.

Kasturi's gaze bored into her. Kanagu Paati's eyes were piercing. Sabapathi was overcome with emotion. He stood by, crying silently.

'Do you still sing?'

'Oh yes. When these people are not at home.'

'Why?'

'They are afraid that the old association will continue if I sing.'

Kasturi shook her head in dismay. Seeing her eyes fill with tears, Thilakam added hastily, 'It was because I didn't want all that that I left.'

'You said you would die, didn't you?'

Thilakam smiled gently. 'Aren't we all born to die?'

Kasturi looked at her in astonishment. 'Chee, chee! Look at you. How can you talk about dying at your age?'

Thilakam noticed Gopalaiyer coming towards them. She touched Kasturi's arm with a smile and said, 'We'll meet after the performance.'

Before she could talk to Kanagu Paati, Sengamalam or Sabapathi, the secretary of the sabha came there and told them to hurry; it was getting late for the programme. Thilakam had not imagined that she wouldn't be able to talk to them at all.

As usual, Kasturi's performance was wonderful. As Sengamalam sang, Thilakam felt a thrill run through her body, as if her whole spirit had been awakened. She wanted to hum the song along with Sengamalam. Her feet tapped in time to the singing and her fingers spelled out the rhythmic structure. She did not realize that around her people were observing what she was doing. When the item was over, Thilakam felt as if she had attained the limits of ecstasy.

The secretary of the sabha appeared suddenly on the stage and asked to say a few words. 'All of you saw Kasturi's wonderful dance. Her younger sister is also present here. She is a fine singer. I am told she has stopped singing since her marriage. I appeal to her to accept our request and sing for the thillana that Kasturi will perform next. You may not know that she is Gopalaiyer's daughter-in-law. He is a fine connoisseur of the arts. I am sure he will accept my suggestion.'

Thilakam trembled. She looked at her father-in-law in alarm. Gopalaiyer's face had turned red. He appeared to be very angry. Standing up and addressing the audience, he said, 'Please forgive me. Actually, my daughter-in-law is indisposed. I brought her only because she insisted on watching the performance. We are leaving right now.'

Looking at Kasturi, he said, 'Let the concert go on.' To Thilakam, he hissed, 'Get up,' and started walking briskly towards the exit.

When she looked at the stage for the last time, Sabapathi was gazing fixedly at her. His fingers were tapping the mridangam.

Thakita thaka thimi ...

22

THE CLIP-CLOP OF the horse's hooves made Kasturi, seated inside the carriage, queasy today. For a while now, perhaps since Thilakam went away, she carried a tremor in her heart through every moment of her life. As long as Thilakam had been with her, Kasturi had had no fear that life might go off the rails some day.

It was strange, considering Thilakam was actually a few years younger than her. It was Kasturi who had earned a name and respect in the village. Like planets that revolve around the sun, other members of the family orbited around Kasturi, to support and enable her art. Song and rhythm were performed for her sake. Dance practice sessions, rehearsals, timely and nutritious meals, and Kanagu Paati's loving gaze existed only to fulfil her needs. Thilakam's sudden exit was the first sign that her world was beginning to fall apart. Thilakam had shown them that she had a mind of her own; it was a cry of revolt. To think that Sabapathi's silences too could be indicative of the changes within made her extremely anxious.

Kasturi was even more agitated after their visit to Madras. The wan expression on Thilakam's face troubled her constantly.

She was distraught when she had seen Thilakam. Though she was wearing a richly embroidered expensive silk sari, it seemed that Thilakam had buried some grief deep inside. Were those dark circles under her eyes? Had she lost weight? Kasturi couldn't remember. They had barely spoken for a few minutes. Thilakam didn't even talk to Sabapathi, Amma and Kanagu Paati. Their plan to speak after the concert was ruined by the secretary's public request.

Later, he had said in her presence, as if he was going out of his way to explain it to someone else, 'Gopalaiyer's veil was torn to shreds today. He boasts in public that he is a progressive man, that he got his son married to a devadasi and gave her a life. After his son eloped with the girl and wed her in secret, what else could the man do? That's why I put him through a small test today. "Allow your daughter-in-law to sing, just for one jathi," I said. Gopalaiyer left abruptly.'

Who knew what rivalry and jealousy the two men harboured against each other? But the picture his words painted disturbed her. Now they knew Thilakam was no better than a captive. Kanagu Paati didn't say a word. Sengamalam, too, spoke tersely, as if she didn't really want to talk about it. 'We didn't send her there, did we? It's a life she chose for herself and she should deal with it on her own.' What she said made sense.

Now I want to ask questions that I had never contemplated before, Kasturi thought. Her mind could no longer accept all that it had once held as right. Even someone from the older generation like Sundaramurthi 'felt like asking what had not been asked before'. Lakshmi, Thilakam and Sabapathi had grown up breathing fresh air. They knew how to ask questions the moment they learnt to speak. Women close to her had dared to set foot on an unfamiliar path.

Will I be able to do the same? Will I need to?

Her heart trembled again. A change was occurring within her too. It made her fearful. But the fear brought on a feeling of stupor. Realities moved swiftly to the background.

'Akka, bear in mind that he is an achari.' Thilakam was highly intuitive. She had made the remark when Kasturi was repeatedly humming the kaavadi chindu sung by Singaram.

She had smiled and evaded the subject then. 'Achari or priest, he is a genuine artist.' Even now she felt like laughing when she thought of everything that had happened the other day. How mortally shy Singaram was!

Kasturi and Thilakam had been returning to the village after a visit to the Swamimalai temple, when they heard a man singing. 'Ask Muthu to stop the cart for a bit, Akka,' Thilakam said. 'Such wonderful singing, isn't it?'

Muthu stopped the cart. 'Haven't you seen him before? It's the same achari, Akka. He has a workshop here too. Come, I'll take you there.'

They could hear the song clearly now. A kaavadi chindu. Singaram's voice was enchanting; it sounded cool and happy. When he noticed Kasturi standing before him, he stopped abruptly.

'Please carry on. Don't stop,' Kasturi said.

'Sing, thambi,' an old man urged him. 'She would really like you to sing. You know who she is, don't you?'

'I know,' Singaram said and turned to work on a sculpture. 'That's why I am hesitant.'

'Why? You are such a fine singer! My feet are restless from the urge to dance,' Kasturi said.

He looked up at her and asked, 'Will you dance to my song?'

She laughed. 'Why don't you sing and see what happens?'

His eyes betrayed a hint of surprise. When he resumed singing it was with a smile on his face. *'When a wayfarer takes Valli's husband's name, my heart turns to mush, dear one.'*

As Thilakam picked up a bronze kundaan and tapped a beat with her fingers, Kasturi mimed with her hands and face. What an amazing experience it was!

'You must not tell Amma about this. She will kill you,' Thilakam had warned, much to Kasturi's amusement. Later that night, as she had tossed and turned in bed, humming that song, Thilakam asked her, 'Akka, is it the song that's haunting you, or the man?'

Taken aback for a moment, she laughed dismissively and recovered by saying, 'What rubbish, silly girl!' It was then that Thilakam had reminded her again, 'He is an achari.'

But it never registered in her mind.

That day, after she had run with Singaram and taken cover from their pursuers, she felt that she had come a long way with him. It was a journey fraught with danger. Yet, her crazy heart was ready to ignore it. Memories of the erotic thrill she had experienced as they dashed through the darkness took her back to that night.

To the question in Sundaramurthi Mama's eyes—'Why have you come here, child?'—she replied flippantly in sign language, 'Vande Mataram.' She whispered gently in Singaram's ears, 'Do you think only you can be patriotic?' She could understand the tension that spread on both their faces on seeing her there. Even as she agonized over the trouble her visit might have caused them, the furore started.

'Come, we have to run,' Singaram said and quickly grabbed her hand.

It seemed like yesterday when she had laughingly said, 'Do you think that a woman who dances cannot run?'

They were fleeing at breakneck speed. Once, when she stumbled and was about to fall from the momentum, he caught and steadied her.

'Oh my. I never imagined you were so patriotic,' he said.

'Is there a measuring scale for such things?' She laughed.

'Enough to come out into the street and raise slogans?'

Though she knew that it was a probing question, she said softly, 'Yes, today I was forced to come out into the street.' He couldn't have seen in the dark that her eyes were shiny with tears. Her eyes downcast, she added, 'By a white idiot.'

He looked at her in confusion for a moment, then muttered, 'We have to walk another four miles. I don't think we'll find a cart or carriage at this hour.'

Suddenly they heard voices: 'I see someone over there. It must be the girl.'

Quickly, she pulled Singaram close and took cover behind a bush. After waiting for the furore to die down, she removed the silver anklets on her feet and the gold waistband strung with tiny bells, and tied them in the free end of her sari. 'Come, let's go now,' she told him.

The sounds that followed them were full of menace.

'Come, let's go inside that stone well,' he whispered to her.

Together they entered a cavernous passage guarded by two stone lions. As he sat on the flight of steps inside, she sat on his lap with his hand supporting her.

Meanwhile, after a thorough search of the surroundings, their pursuers decided to leave. 'It looks like they didn't come this way. They must be hiding somewhere in the coconut grove. Let's go and find them.'

Singaram seemed lost in some reverie.

'Where do these steps lead?' Kasturi asked.

'There's water below. There will be moonlight too. Come, I'll show you,' he said. He took her hand again and led the way.

At the base of the stairs, they could see water in the well. A piece of the moon seemed to have fallen on it. The soft light created an unearthly ambience. It seemed to her that all the perversities, inhibitions, impediments and insults inflicted on her had lost their meaning and sunk to the bottom of the well. This was a paradise in which only Singaram and Kasturi existed. Having sensed the same thing, Singaram was overcome by emotion. It was evident from his hot breath. He was a shy man; it was a trait his birth had instilled in him. She knew that he would not take the initiative to move closer to her—his inhibition had erected a fence around the desire that raged inside. She stroked his neck gently. When her hands reached out and embraced him, he was vanquished. He bent and pressed his lips against hers. As if they had been waiting only for this touch, their two bodies became passionately intertwined. His manhood seemed to have come alive. She was not a courtesan today, but a slave to him. They were lost in a dream where the water, moon and solitude were performing a song together. She had not realized until now that sexual union could be a source of such magical ecstasy.

When they returned to the street, Singaram had become his former self again. He said with his head bowed, 'It's best that you forget what happened today.'

'That's difficult,' she said lightly. 'I can only forget what my heart doesn't like.'

She could not put the incident at the Simmakkinaru out of her mind. Raja Rajendra Chola, who had conquered Bengal, had filled the well with water brought all the way from the Ganga. It was a well that offered redemption for one's sins. Her body tingled as if she had been cleansed.

Suddenly she came back to her senses. She had to quell Raja's anger. Of late, he had been venting his ire on her. She imagined that he was in some trouble with the Collector. When he told her that the Collector Durai had been fuming ever since she escaped from him, she dared to argue with Raja for the first time.

'When Arumugam told me that you would come to the Collector's bungalow, I believed him and went there. Why didn't you come?'

'I could not. I had a headache suddenly. You can ask the physician. Why, what happened because I couldn't come?'

As Kasturi had described the incident, Raja listened with evident lack of interest. She was shocked when he blithely said, 'He is a big man. If you were pleasant to him, it wouldn't mean the end of the world, would it?'

She was furious. 'Doesn't it make you angry? Don't you feel that I belong only to you? It looks like you sent me to him deliberately, without even seeking my consent. He is a wretch, a foreigner. He is sitting in our country and making a show of his arrogance.'

Raja had covered her mouth in alarm. 'If you speak like that once more, he will shove you into jail. Hold your tongue! As it is he is angry with me because you ran away. Your mother knows that. Didn't she tell you?'

Kasturi found Raja's words revolting. They filled her with distaste. This prideless Raja wouldn't understand the humiliation she had suffered. Her own mother did not, so how could she expect it from Raja? After she escaped from the Durai and reached home at midnight, Sengamalam, who opened the door and greeted her with 'So, you're back', had had an expectant half-smile on her face. Kasturi realized immediately that her mother had known about the invitation from the Collector.

'Yes, I am back in one piece. Amma, don't become greedy. If you do, you will destroy me. Did you or did you not know that the carriage was for taking me to the Durai?' she exploded.

'Yes, I knew. What about it?' Sengamalam said stubbornly. 'Raja is a king only in name. What have you got from him? Nothing by way of jewellery or ornaments. Even the plain women around here are flaunting their gold.'

'For money will you send me to a dog? Don't push me into that situation. He is a white British dog. The very thought turns my stomach. People are shouting "Vande Mataram" in the streets, ready to die for the country—'

'Let the fools die! There is nothing in it for us. They will drive Raja away in nothing but his loincloth.'

'Chee! Nothing good ever comes out of your mouth,' Kasturi had said angrily.

It seemed that Raja was also beset by the same worry, and was trying to work out a deal with the Collector. Did he send me to the Durai as a part of an agreement, like throwing the dog a bone? What a shameful life!

The more she thought about it, the more bewildered she felt. Where is it all going to end? *You were born to dance, the deity is your husband*—Paati had told her. Yet He has completely abandoned me and is looking on in amusement. I consented to sleep with Raja as an arrangement. If Raja himself wants to trade me around, what can I do? She thought it was an ordeal that god had sent her way to test her.

You are not a chaste woman, are you? Raja himself thought of her like that. Cha, what an ignominious life. Did Singaram think so too? Suppuni? He, too, might think the same of her.

This is a wretched clan. We need to enact a law to eliminate it. It was only after thinking everything over that Lakshmi had said that.

Kasturi was feeling agitated again.

When Sundaramurthi Mama had come home yesterday he had told Kasturi that Lakshmi's name was gaining fame in the newspapers. 'That girl is waging a struggle even bigger than the freedom struggle,' he said expansively.

'I heard that she was studying to be a doctor?' Sengamalam said as she joined them.

'She finished that and then went to England to get an advanced degree. Now she is back and working as a doctor. In appreciation of her work, the government has made her a member of the legislative council. What a big honour! Her speeches in favour of a law to abolish the devadasi system are covered in all the newspapers.'

As if she had suddenly woken up, Sengamalam had asked, 'What did you say? What kind of nonsense is this? When?'

'As soon as possible.'

'If there is a law to abolish the system, will it mean that Kasturi can't dance in the temple?'

'I can't say when it will come into force. But once it does, I think she won't be able to,' Mama said in a calm voice.

Kasturi was stunned. Though Lakshmi had subtly hinted at it, Kasturi couldn't believe her influence could have climbed high enough for her to bring in a law.

'Then the grants will stop?'

'Yes.'

Sengamalam was sitting with both hands on her head, looking as though she was mourning the death of a close relative. 'But what's in it for us, Sundaram?'

'You mustn't think only about Kasturi, Sengamalam. Think of it as freedom for the whole clan. Nobody can force any of us to carry on the traditional occupation. They can't talk about us with contempt.'

Sengamalam's voice had sounded as if she was mumbling. 'If the grants from the temple are stopped, what do you think people will do for their livelihood?'

Kasturi drew back the satin curtain in the carriage and looked at the street. She could see Singaram's workshop. Unable to resist the temptation to meet him, she said, 'Arumugam, stop the carriage here for a bit. I have to ask the achari to make an aimpon statue.'

After stopping the carriage, Arumugam asked her politely, 'Do you have to go there yourself, Akka? Or should I ask him to come over?'

'No, no. He is known to us. It would only be proper if I went there and spoke to him,' she said and got down from the carriage.

Arumugam noticed that there was a spring in Kasturi's step as she walked towards the workshop. 'This won't end well, thambi,' he muttered to the horse.

Singaram was humming while he worked on a statue. Someone ran up to him and whispered in his ear. He looked up and saw Kasturi. He hurried over and said in a gentle voice, 'Why have you come here?'

'Only to see you. Are you saying I shouldn't?' she asked softly.

'Yes, you shouldn't. People will get suspicious and talk.'

Suddenly she raised her voice and said, 'I don't know how you will do it, but I need a Paravai Nachiyar figurine a month from now.'

He gave her a smile tinged with mild surprise and said, 'How tall?'

'A foot and a half.'

'Oh my.' He laughed. Then he turned to his colleagues. 'They want a Paravai Nachiyar figurine, measuring a foot and a half—in one month, it seems.'

Some of them said that it could be done. She waited, smiling.

'We will try,' he said.

'When do we meet again?' she asked in a low whisper.

'No need for that any more,' he said urgently.

'I'll be waiting by the tree in our backyard at eleven tonight,' she said and walked to the carriage without a backward glance. Two men stood near Arumugam, talking to him. On seeing her, they moved away. One of them wore the uniform of an attendant.

Later that night, she waited under the mango tree in her backyard. The moment she heard the soft strains of a kaavadi chindu, her body was aflame.

23

THE BLAZE OF anger lying dormant like ash-covered coals in her heart exploded suddenly, and an indomitable force born of the scattering embers came to possess her. This must be the true manifestation of Kali, the fierce goddess, she thought.

The wrath of Kali was a metaphor—for a woman's awakened selfhood. I am an elaboration of that metaphor. To liberate me and my community from slavery, Kali became omnipresent. In that unearthly ambience, I was in a trance, unable to discern whether the self was real or imagined.

Once she sat down after her speech, an abnormal silence, like that following a blow from a sledgehammer, pervaded the session. The men seemed to be collectively paralysed. Was it real, or merely an illusion? Why were all of them sitting like stone figures? The words that had rolled off her tongue were not hers alone; they had lain buried in the minds of women through countless generations. Today, they had come surging up. Her stinging speech impaled those guilty hearts. The men needed some time to digest it. There was a cruel satisfaction too, along with the excitement that she felt. She found consolation in having delivered whiplashes to these elite men who had assumed the right to make society dance to their whims. When she looked around she saw that everyone in that assembly of men had turned pale.

The hate that she had nurtured all through her conscious years had taken a definite shape today. She knew that opposing tradition would mean a struggle fraught with enormous risks. From the day she was made a member of this council, she had waited for this moment. Before initiating the debate, she had to work for many months to garner support. She had been warned about the hostility of upper-caste members. She was prepared for it.

'How arrogant she must be to talk like this?' she heard a member say. Ignoring his remark, she remained silent, watchful. The gentleman who had pontificated just a little earlier on the need to continue the devadasi system sat red-faced before her.

'They are rendering a social service. According to the agama rules, the temple needs their services. Without them, devotional service would be incomplete, and their art would be destroyed.' As he began thus, many heads nodded in agreement.

'A whole community is being exploited in the name of god and the arts. We can't allow it,' Lakshmi said.

'Devadasis serve as the balm that relieves men's fatigue. How can men do without them?' Many laughed and banged noisily on the table to show their approval.

Lakshmi's anger knew no bounds. She felt herself transported back in time. Lakshmi and her mother waiting in the backyard of Periya Mirasu's house. The cook asking, 'Why are you here so early?' Amma spreading the free end of her sari and collecting the food packet … Mirasu sneaking into their house … Amma's shameless face betraying her pride. The Durai grabbing Kasturi by the hand. Kasturi saying, *I am a courtesan only of the Lord.*

Kanagu Paati waiting at the feast. *Girl, we will get to eat only along with the last batch of guests.* Lakshmi wanted to shake everyone—Amma, Kasturi, Kanagu Paati, the man who had spoken a short while ago. She was gasping for air. Beads of sweat appeared on her forehead.

Addressing a row of arrogant men, she said, 'What a pity. For a change, why don't you send women from your family to do that job?' It resulted in an uproar in the assembly.

Finally, towards ending the lifestyle imposed on temple devadasis, a resolution was passed to enact the Devadasis Abolition Act. The resolution said that the power to cancel grants of temple lands to them would be given to the Hindu Religious Endowments Department.

To Lakshmi's disappointment, several devadasis got together and raised their voices against the resolution. These were distinguished artists. Bangalore Nagarathnamma, Veenai Dhanam and her daughters, along with a few others, claimed that what she had done was unjust. It is a humiliation meted out to us, they said. Devadasis are equal to priests; sanction of land and grants is for our devotional services to the Lord. How is it fair to snatch it away from us and evict us from the temples?

But Lakshmi was firm. Their connection with the land was what tied them to the temples, kept them hostage and prevented them from breaking free. It was psychological imprisonment devised by upper-caste men. Through that land, the women of the community signed the bond of their own enslavement. It was a system that promoted rivalry and jealousy between famous, genuine artists and those without talent. As gossip, hatred and betrayal turned into life strategies, these women were also, on top of being exploited by upper-caste men, victimized by the dance masters. No one understands this better than me, Lakshmi said.

'The arts will be wiped out!'

Let them be destroyed.

Lakshmi felt a surge of blind rage. In any society, the destruction of the arts was not a greater horror than the erasure of honour. Whenever the sound of singing and ankle bells fell on her ears, she was filled with distaste. She learnt later that at the time this furore was going on in the council, a sabha had invited Kasturi and organized a sadir concert. While praising Kasturi's recital to the skies, a newspaper report noted that there had been stiff opposition to her performance the first time. The small mention of Thilakam surprised Lakshmi. It referred to her as the former secretary's daughter-in-law and said that Gopalaiyer had not allowed her to sing. Why did this snippet of news perturb her? She was perplexed. She wondered how Thilakam had got married to an upper-caste man. Did it mean freedom for Thilakam or was it just another prison? Were men becoming magnanimous enough to marry a woman born in the devadasi community? She knew that Thilakam had hated the life led by Kasturi. Was change imminent in the village too?

After she had passed the exam and found new accommodation, Lakshmi had got busy with her job. Her mother and Periya Mirasu would come to see her regularly, giving her no opportunity or cause to go back to the village. During one visit, her mother said, 'No one knows how Thilakam got friendly with that boy. One day she ran away to Madras without telling a soul. Sengamalam covered it up by saying Thilakam had got secretly married to a rich man. The girl sang very well. It's a great loss for Kasturi.'

'Singing was not important to her. I know she yearned for a life of dignity,' Lakshmi said.

'I won't go into what is honourable and what isn't, kannu. My life is over. I was worried about you but you have carved your own path. Not many can be so determined about what they want. I still don't know whether it's good or bad. But things we have never heard of are happening now. It's all very disturbing. Our people are very angry with you. They are worried about what will happen to them if the grants disappear when the act comes into force. Why are you getting involved in this business? You were adamant about studying to become a doctor. You are one now. Why don't you stop with that?'

Lakshmi realized wearily that there was nothing to be gained in arguing with her mother. Yet, she continued, 'Have you heard of this person called Gandhi? He could have kept on earning money as a lawyer and stayed happy, couldn't he? Why has he involved himself in this freedom struggle? He undertakes fasts, gets beaten by the British and is sent to jail. Why?'

'What do you have to do with that man?'

'A lot. If we don't raise our voices now for issues that need resolution, this struggle for freedom would become meaningless.'

'Are you going to take part in that struggle?'

'I may or may not take part, but I will definitely extend my support. The time for the white man to leave our country has come, Amma. But merely driving away the white man isn't enough. We must throw out the demons that live in our society and in our hearts. We have to do all that *now*.'

Thulasi laughed. 'I don't believe it.'

'That is the problem with you. You never believe anything I tell you.'

Her mother said something else too. 'This Gandhi must be a big leader. Even in our village people wear that Gandhi cap and march in processions, shouting "Vande Mataram". Even that nadaswaram player Sundaramurthi has been thrashed many times and sent to prison. Our Konar boy told us that he saw Kasturi too, marching in a procession one day.'

Lakshmi was astonished. 'Kasturi? Excellent! Eventually, she will also support my struggle.'

'I don't know about your struggle,' Thulasi said wearily, 'but it seems you've become very obstinate.'

Lakshmi's obstinacy kept escalating. If I fail to make a serious attempt, an incomplete victory would be more dangerous, she thought. Much to her frustration, people in Madras, who had shown little interest in dance till then, had started inviting devadasis to major functions and weddings, especially in the households of rich men, often advertising that a certain eminent devadasi would grace the occasion. In sabhas, members of the Brahmin community held conferences and declared that dance ought to be supported. A man from that community had learnt the art from devadasis and begun to give performances dressed in female garb. She wanted to laugh. Why, it's excellent! Devadasis don't need to dance any more.

Lakshmi worried that the sadir of devadasis was becoming popular in a way she had not foreseen. She had an idea: if they were stopped from performing in temples, their dancing careers would come to an end. Immediately, she got to work with furious determination. British officials and friends extended their full cooperation. They had been shocked when they heard about the devadasi lifestyle from her. When she tried to bring a resolution in the legislative council that the tradition of devadasis dancing in temples should be done away with, there was opposition again from upper-caste members. In the end, the resolution was passed.

Kasturi appeared in her dreams that night. 'What do you think I will do now?' she wept.

'Join the freedom movement. Gandhi is going on a peaceful protest march against the salt tax. Let's go, too. A new world is going to dawn, Kasturi!'

There was a letter from Yogu.

'My exams are over. The cold weather has turned and Kodaikanal is quite pleasant now. The sun in Madras must be scorching hot. Why don't you come and stay here for a few days, Akka? How much longer will you push yourself to work all the time without taking any rest? I want to meet you in person. When I read about you in the newspapers, I feel proud. Once I finish my education, I want to do something useful. Mother Superior says I can work right here as a teacher. Akka, all the people here are so kind and full of love. It feels like a different world here. I'll be beholden to you for the rest of my life. You gave me a new way of being. You gave meaning to my life.'

Whenever she got a letter from Yogu, Lakshmi was very pleased. Proud too. She didn't know when the nation would get its freedom, but a new world had dawned for Yogu. Seeing her develop into a new person with incredible wisdom gave Lakshmi immense satisfaction. She felt that this was the one substantial task she had accomplished in her life.

She could go to Kodaikanal. But with the freedom struggle growing stronger by the day, she was reluctant to even think about taking a holiday. Mahatma Gandhi had set out on a journey to Dandi to perform salt satyagraha. Hearing Gandhi's call, those in the south were going on a journey by foot to Vedaranyam under the leadership of a Brahmin called Rajagopalachari. It was to protest the tax levied on common salt by the British. They would go into the salt pans themselves and extract salt. Unable to comprehend that salt was the symbol of their revolt for freedom, the government laughed derisively at the idea of the protest. But when the whole nation gathered and walked behind

Gandhi, an old man who wore only a loincloth, the government was frightened. What a wonderful strategy it was to use salt as a weapon to rouse the common people and daily-wage earners! Lakshmi marvelled at the idea. Ranganathan, her colleague at work, told her that he was going to Vedaranyam. 'Why don't you come along too, Lakshmi? Many women are participating,' he said. She also wanted to join the march, but she could not leave her work at the hospital and travel to Vedaranyam.

The British government was watching Gandhi's activities nervously. They had not imagined that confronting an unarmed, non-violent protester would be so difficult. Day by day, Gandhi was becoming more of a nuisance. There were instructions from the top that there should be no threat to his life. Rows upon rows of people marched behind him and raised slogans. When you are slapped on one cheek, turn the other cheek, Gandhi said, just as Jesus did. *If we extract an eye for an eye, a tooth for a tooth, the whole world will become blind.* Gandhi's word was gospel now.

'Thrash the idiots! Shove them in jail!' The salt protesters, who marched ahead shouting 'Vande Mataram!' were beaten ruthlessly. Gandhi was jailed for creating a law and order problem.

Lakshmi heard about Gandhi's incarceration just as she was leaving for the hospital. She was in a rage. She could think of only one way to express her opposition to the British government's cowardly arrest, without any plausible grounds, of a great man who had engaged in a peaceful protest. She decided that continuing as a member of the legislative council of the Presidency, which functioned under the authority of the colonial government, would be a disgrace. She had nearly completed the task that she had intended to perform as a council member. The resolution she had proposed had been adopted. All that remained was for it to be enacted as a law and brought into force.

She was confident that it would happen in due course. After giving her resignation to the Speaker in writing, she proceeded to the hospital.

Ranganathan had returned from Vedaranyam. His face shone with a new radiance. 'It was a wonderful experience, Lakshmi!' he said, becoming emotional. 'Do you know how it felt when we fell down and stood up again and again while the police kept beating us? It was as if every blow added more strength to our resolve. Faced with the inherent power of our peaceful protest, the force behind the cane charge and police firing will become shaky. I am confident that the British don't have any other option; they will have to leave.'

'When I say the same thing, my mother refuses to believe me,' Lakshmi said, smiling. Ranganathan's words evoked a tenderness she had never experienced before.

'There are many who fear that their security will vanish if the British leave,' Ranganathan said in a conciliatory tone. 'They think we don't have the necessary administrative skills. Another fear that has reared its head here is that instead of the British, now the north Indians might enslave us. They don't believe me when I tell them that after we become independent everyone will enjoy equal rights.'

She looked at Ranganathan with renewed interest. He continued to talk about many other things.

'In Vedaranyam, I remembered you often.'

She was taken aback. 'Why?'

'I felt it would have been nice if you had been around.'

Lakshmi laughed. 'You're talking as though you had gone on a picnic.'

He laughed shyly. 'I know it was not a picnic. You would have got beaten too—and I wouldn't have been able to prevent it. But it was an experience. I am truly impressed when I see your selfless service. You are a born satyagrahi. You should participate in the freedom struggle. Would your being a member of the legislative council stand in the way of that?'

'Oh, I resigned my seat as soon as I heard the news of Gandhi's arrest,' she said with a smile.

Ranganathan's face lit up. 'Really!' he exclaimed, eyes widening. 'You've done a great thing, Lakshmi. Not many would give up their position that easily. You are an honest fighter. I don't know how to express my happiness.'

All of a sudden, he grabbed her hands and shook them. It seemed to Lakshmi that there were many unsaid messages in that handshake.

She found it funny. Whenever the two of them met for professional reasons or during the protests, which was often, their conversation was usually limited to medicine and the state of the country. Ranganathan was different from the other men she had encountered. It was a big relief that he avoided unnecessary banter and gossip. As for her, she knew nothing of his antecedents. Beyond the fact that he was an intelligent and honest doctor, she had neither the time nor the interest to find out more about him.

Gandhi was set free. An excited Ranganathan came looking for her.

'Mahatma Gandhi is going to address a meeting today on Marina beach. I am going to attend. Will you come with me?'

She nodded eagerly, infected by his enthusiasm.

The sandy expanse of the beach had turned into a sea of human heads. The road was dotted with police caps. Gandhi's words had magical power.

Seeing Lakshmi overwhelmed by emotion, Ranganathan told her tenderly, 'We are really fortunate, Lakshmi, that we are living in the same age as Gandhi. This is truly a golden age, an era when so many great intellectuals, patriots, ascetics and sages are among us, sharing the very air we breathe.'

'That's true, Ranganathan,' Lakshmi said. 'But we are surrounded by enormous ignorance as well.'

'There will be a solution for everything. I am hopeful.'

She walked in silence. She wanted to believe him. Ranganathan had the ability to give hope to someone who was rudderless. She laughed gently. 'You make me think that anything is possible as long as I am with you.'

'Only if you think something is possible does it become so. You are a living illustration of that principle.'

'You don't know whether I have struggled.'

'That is true. But I believe you have. Nothing can be achieved without a struggle, Lakshmi. You too do not know about my struggle.'

She looked at him in surprise. She could not read his expression in the darkness. The crowd on the beach had dispersed. Strands of her hair flew about in the chill breeze. She wrapped the free end of her sari tight around herself and combed her hair back with her fingers.

'What struggle?' she asked gently.

He walked on without replying. 'Didn't you just say that when you are with me you feel that anything is possible?'

She was intrigued. She could not understand what he was trying to say.

'What if you stay with me?'

She was astonished. 'What do you mean, doctor?' she said, mildly angry. She suspected that he was asking her to be his mistress. Cha, these men!

'Don't be angry, Lakshmi. I am asking you if you will be my wife.'

She was amazed. 'So, you are not married yet?'

'No! What did you think? That someone who claims to be a disciple of Gandhi is actually a loafer? I was firm that I wouldn't marry unless I found a woman who had a broad outlook and believed in Gandhi's path. Until I met you, I had concluded that finding such a girl was impossible.'

'What do you know about me? What do you know about where I come from?' Her voice was hoarse.

'I don't need to know your antecedents. You are an idealist. Only your true image is important to me.'

'No. You must know where I come from. My mother is a devadasi. My father would be ashamed to admit in public that I am his daughter. I am a woman who can't name her father.' Before she finished, her shoulders shook, and tears of humiliation streamed from her eyes.

Ranganathan was silent for some time.

He was shocked, surely. A Gandhian needs this shock, she thought, and walked briskly ahead of him, ran almost.

For some inexplicable reason, she thought of Thilakam.

24

THERE WAS A basket of flowers in front of her. Oleander, jasmine, crossandra and tulsi conspired to give off a heady fragrance. Gopalaiyer performed puja in the evenings as well. Thilakam would string the flowers daily and keep them ready for the evening rituals. That day he said he had asked for a special puja at the temple. The flowers were to be sent there. Thilakam's fingers mechanically strung the flowers. Back in the village, Kanagu Paati's artistry at this task was something special. One type of braiding for jasmine; a different one for oleander. Chrysanthemum, dhavana and oleander were woven together into a thick garland. When Paati described it as a unique offering to Lord Siva, her face would light up with a special radiance. When she chose flowers of different colours and strung them together with an aesthetic eye, it mirrored the beautiful way in which voice and feet added rhythmic pauses to a train of jathis; the hands working with the flowers turned into floral strands themselves. After seeing Gopalaiyer offer worship daily with loose flowers, she had happily taken on the task of stringing them into garlands. When Gopalaiyer appreciated the garlands and

praised her, it felt like she had received a big award. Seeing the
garlands resting on the idols of the gods, her heart was enthralled,
and she was moved to tears. While stringing the flowers,
Thilakam would often feel like singing. Since Kalyanaraman and
Gopalaiyer were usually not at home at that hour, her heart shook
off the fetters and soared high.

Today too they were not at home. Yet her mind flinched,
as it had taken to doing for many months now. Whenever she
started to sing, she stumbled on the words, forgot the lines. She
wondered whether she might also forget how to speak some
day. 'When the land is lost, the language is lost,' Kanagu Paati
often said. On many occasions, when she wanted to string words
together, the syllables folded back into her tongue. She was in a
panic that some enormous change was happening within her. She
became fearful of movements. If she heard footsteps, she would
want to withdraw into her room. The image in the mirror was
not hers; it was someone else's. No voice emerged from its throat.
'Thilakam has a unique voice. A voice that drips honey. A voice
that glides and moves like silk. It has the magic of a gold strip of
zari that sparkles like glittering stars. Girl, you have earned this
voice now only after performing worship to the gods through
many births,' Paati would say. 'You must look after it.'

'It is lost, Paati,' Thilakam said, joining crossandra to jasmine.

'Find it, then,' Paati said, with a smile white as jasmine.

'I can't, Paati. They've chased it away.'

'Stupid girl! Did you think they would celebrate it? What
were you seeking when you went over?'

Thilakam slowly nodded to herself. I couldn't get what I was
after. That is why my heart yearns for what I lost of my own will.
On the day of the concert, they forced me to leave before I could
meet you, Paati. If I had, I might have blurted out my secret.
Come away with us, girl, you would have said. I would have left

immediately. Now I have no one to protect me. You should wipe yourself clean of everything in order to live, you always said. I will try, Paati.

She sat up abruptly. Someone was singing. On closer attention, it turned out to be a familiar song. It was the one by Bharathi that Sabapathi had sung for them: '*Chinnanchiru kiliye, kannamma*'. Her heart instantly grew lighter. Her folded wings opened out slowly. Her voice rose unfettered from the throat, surprising her. '*When you come running to me, my heart is pleased.*' A cool drizzle fell in her heart. A smile appeared on her lips. She started humming the song along with the singer. Since the singer sang each line twice, she learnt the song quickly. She was brimming with zest, as if that feeling was beyond her control. Her voice assumed a gigantic shape, moved away from her and became a sovereign entity that enslaved her.

'*A kiss on the cheek, and my heart is drunk as if on toddy.*'

How would Kasturi portray it with her hands and expression?

'*A kiss on the cheek, and my heart is—*'

The basket of flowers in front of her toppled suddenly and landed a few feet away. Only then did she notice a pair of feet and the zari border of a veshti. Startled, she looked up. She wondered why Kalyanaraman had such an ugly expression on his face.

'What are you staring at? Get up and go inside,' he said in a guttural voice. She was frozen with fear. As she tried haltingly to gather the flowers and put them in the basket, he gave her a fierce kick. 'Go inside, you shameless bitch!'

To protect herself from falling, she gripped the wall, got up quietly and walked in. Her heart was pounding. Her brain had stopped functioning. He followed her inside. Her panic deepened. What was he going to do?

'Why were you sitting at the entrance, singing obscene songs? Were you looking out for customers?'

She blinked back her tears and said, 'It's airless inside.'

'Oho! She is a princess, it seems. There is an open courtyard in the rear bay, yes? You can sit there. Why should you sit near the doorway? That too while singing a song like that? Your innate traits won't leave you, is it?'

'It's a song by the great poet Subramania Bharathi, not some lewd song,' she muttered softly.

'Showing off your genius, are you? How come you don't know any other songs written by him? Of all his songs, *this* is the one you picked. Why?' He took a towel, draped it over his shoulder and went to the well.

Thilakam closed her eyes. 'Oh Lord!' Through how many births would she have to carry this stigma? She could not stop the tears from flowing down her cheeks. Hearing him coming back inside, she wiped her eyes quickly.

'That's enough. Don't keep crying all the time like some goddess of ill luck. Don't you know that Appa has arranged for a laksharchanai at the temple? He asked me to bring you. Come on. Wash your face, change your sari, and get ready. Don't embarrass me with your dull and gloomy look,' he said irritably.

Mechanically, she did as instructed. Her mind was numb once again. For a few minutes today, when she heard that song, it had been alert, but it froze the moment he entered. With Gopalaiyer leading the way, she followed Kalyanaraman and entered the temple, her head bowed. As she stood on the ladies' side of the deity's chamber and gazed at the idol in the inner sanctum, she was reminded of her village. The head priest and his son, Suppuni. Sundaramurthi Mama elaborating '*Saraguna Palimpa*' on his nadaswaram. The idol being taken out in holy procession. Kasturi dancing while she stood behind and sang.

The priest held the plate with lit camphor in front of her and said something. She collected herself, swept her fingers above the

flame and raised them piously to her eyes. When he got no reply
from her, the priest turned to Gopalaiyer and said, 'Tell her to
sing a couple of songs, Anna.'

Startled by the request, she froze. Gopalaiyer glanced at her,
then said to the priest, 'She doesn't sing at all these days.'

'I am not asking for a concert, am I? Our oduvar hasn't
come in today. It will please the Lord if she sings "*Thevaram*" or
"*Thiruvachakam*",' the priest insisted stubbornly.

'All right. You may sing one hymn,' Gopalaiyer said to her.

She looked awkwardly at Kalyanaraman but his attention
was elsewhere. The crowd was watching her expectantly. To her
surprise, her diffidence vanished instantly. Her husband could
not stop her from singing in god's chamber. She closed her eyes
and her voice surged up from the navel and rose like a serpent
awakened from the kundalini.

'*Nada bindu kaladhi namoh namah ...*'

As she sang on, a thrill coursed through her body, as if
countless celestial maidens were raining a shower of petals on her.

When the song was over, she stood with her eyes closed, dizzy
from exhilaration.

'Aha! Most respected sir, hers is a divine voice. Don't ask her
to stop singing.'

The priest's words brought her back to the present. She
received the votive offering from him, piously touched her eyes
with her fingers and turned. Kalyanaraman was frowning at
her. Lord, where did the love in his eyes before our marriage
disappear? As the women around her began saying 'You sing so
well, 'ma. Who are you learning from?', she started walking. She
realized with embarrassment that the men there were eyeing her
with interest.

It was dark. There was not much light on the road. Their
home was walking distance from the temple. She had no idea

of Kalyanaraman's state of mind. The joy she had experienced while singing in god's chamber pervaded her whole body. Some people, who may or may not have noticed Gopalaiyer's family walking ahead, were talking as they followed.

'Did you notice the girl's voice texture? Such a cool, enchanting sound.'

'Whatever anyone might say, only women from *that* clan can produce such dazzling art.'

'What do you mean?'

'Don't you know? She is Dasi Kasturi's sister.'

'Really? No wonder her voice is so seductive. She is even pretty as a painting. Did Gopalaiyer get her married to his son? How broad-minded of him!'

'Broad-minded, my foot! What else could he do after his son eloped with her?'

Thilakam's whole body began to shake and tremble. She couldn't see Kalyanaraman's face, but his fury was evident in the quickening of his stride. Oh Lord! Why didn't it occur to her that she might have to live such a frightful life? Leaving home without confiding in Kanagu Paati was a mistake. She would have definitely warned Thilakam. But on that day, her mind had been a plaything in the hands of a devil. Filled with lust, frenzy and the audacity to sever ties, it wouldn't have heeded warnings from anyone.

As soon as they entered the house, Kalyanaraman slammed the front door shut. Gopalaiyer had told them that he had to go somewhere else. Kalyanaraman dragged her roughly to the bedroom.

'Did you have to use that podium to show off your charms when you were asked to sing, you whore?' he said.

Seeing him remove his belt, she said in panic, 'I sang just one song, and only because your father had asked me to sing.'

'Are you talking back to me, bitch?'

A stinging lash fell across her back. 'Amma!' she screamed, unable to bear the pain.

'Shut up or I will thrash you some more.'

'What did I do wrong? Please tell me.'

Blinded by rage, he got ready to swing the belt again.

'Did you marry me only to torture me like this?'

'You are tortured, you say? *I* am the one who is suffering.'

Suddenly, to her surprise, he began hitting his head with both hands again and again, like a maniac.

'*I am the fool here!* Marrying you was a mistake. I was seduced by your sweet talk. I thought there would be no connection between me and your clan. But it follows me everywhere. Lurking in the streets, in the office, inside the temple, on people's tongues—it reminds me of its presence. Elei, she is a courtesan, it taunts me. Deceiving you is her clan's vocation, it tells me.'

Tears filled her eyes. Thinking of him, she even felt pity.

'After all these days, do I seem unfaithful to you?'

'What can we do about what's in your blood? How can we change that?'

Not knowing what to say, she moved away quietly, tired of it all.

'Where are you going?'

'I need to change my sari.'

In a daze, she began to remove her sari. He sat gazing at her.

'Um. Take off your blouse.'

Thinking he wanted to have sex with her, she told herself that she had to appease him today, be submissive and loving, soothe his wounded ego.

She stood before him, completely naked.

He looked at her for a second from head to toe, and said, 'Lie face down on the bed.'

She lay down obediently. As she waited for him, he gagged her mouth with a piece of cloth and tied it tightly behind her head. Realizing what he was about to do, she closed her eyes in fright. Without a word, he started to lash her, swinging his belt again and again. Her body shook all over and her eyes burned as if they were being singed by flames. Her howls of pain were lost in the rolled-up cloth.

Thilakam could not move for the next four days. At midday, when it was time for lunch, their maid Anjalai would leave food for her on a plantain leaf and go away. After that no one asked whether she needed anything, or how she was. She did not know what Kalyanaraman might have told them. She yearned to speak to someone, anyone, but she was not acquainted with any of their neighbours. Even Anjalai had begun keeping her distance.

She had had a bit of strength left in her body then. Now even that thought had faded from her mind. The very ability to think had been blunted. Her body had turned into a machine. It nodded like a puppet at Kalyanaraman's every word, stopped speaking, ate when food was offered. When she closed her eyes, the streets swayed, and Kanagu Paati, Sabapathi, Kasturi and Sengamalam engulfed her mind. There was only the past, no present or future.

Suddenly, her senses became alert. Somebody mentioned dasi. Had they come to abuse her? She curled up and hugged her knees tight.

'Her name is Lakshmi.'

She got up instantly and stood near the door. In the hall, Gopalaiyer was speaking to someone.

'You're telling me she is a dasi's daughter?'

'Yes.'

'And she has studied medicine and become a doctor? I can't believe it.'

'Sounds preposterous, I know. Not only that, she is also a member of the legislative council. What a fine orator she is! She even has the courage to argue against the redoubtable Satyamurthi. Imagine that!'

'What did she say?'

'She is making a lot of noise about passing a law to abolish the devadasi system. Our man had argued that the elders have created such a clan so that men who are exhausted in mind and body need not wander around seeking relaxation for both. How would men survive if the Devadasis Abolition Act came into force, he asked. Very well, she said, but the devadasis have served these men for long. They need rest now. Since that too is a need, please prepare Brahmin women to provide such service, she asked in return.'

Thilakam smiled to herself. Lakshmi was indeed capable of talking like that. Had she become such an important person?

'My god! How dare she!'

'It's arrogance, sir. Pure and simple. Arrogance that comes from being educated. Suppose they pass the abolition act, then all the agama rules in our temples will be destroyed.'

'As will the art!'

'That's what I'm saying. If the law is passed, then the land and grants they receive from the temple will be gone too. Then, what will the women of that clan do to survive? How many people are as broad-minded and generous as you?'

Thilakam's heart started beating fast.

'They will be reduced to destitution,' Gopalaiyer said. 'Else, they can always take up prostitution. Those who did it secretly will hang up a shingle now.'

There was a cruel edge to his voice. Thilakam felt dizzy. She thought her head was going to explode. Holding her head in both hands, she sat leaning against the wall. Was it true? Would their lives become even more shameful than before? Would they be reduced to destitution? All kinds of images danced before her eyes. Kasturi and Sengamalam standing at the corner of a street. Sabapathi playing his mridangam. 'Come, come, gentlemen. See how beautiful our akka is. You'll know when you sleep with her. My mother too is not that old. Come, come.' 'Whore! Whore!' Kalyanaraman coming to beat her, swinging his belt like a whip. Raja laughing. 'Go to anyone who gives you money. I can't do anything for you.' The Durai saying, 'Come, come.'

Why do you go and sit near the doorway? Are you on the lookout for customers?

She wanted to wail and weep her heart out.

We have lost all protection. There is no hope of redemption. We have been duped, Akka. This clan must die. It should die with us, Kasturi Akka.

The food left by Anjalai remained untouched. The edges of the plantain leaf turned brown and curled inward.

When he entered the bedroom that night, Kalyanaraman was stunned. 'Oh, you wretched woman!' he groaned in a whisper.

25

Wʜᴇɴ I ᴅᴀɴᴄᴇ for the dawn puja in the temple, my heart is always spotless and pure. The thought that when god wakes up his first glance will fall on me fills me with joy. Today, I wonder for the first time whether there is a rationale behind that naive sentiment, whether I actually receive a special benediction. That a nameless sorrow has inhabited my heart since daybreak could be the reason for my anxiety. Before god's sacred form, I am overcome by an unprecedented sense of my own frailty. I feel I am a speck of dust before that power which is imperceptible to the eye and all other senses. Its inscrutability makes me fearful. Lord, I am not mature enough to endure your trials. Punish me for my transgressions and I shall endure it. Please don't punish those who love me. I won't be able to bear it, Lord. Will my prayer even reach you?

As the head priest waved the sacred flame in front of the three idols and spread the light, the temple bells began to ring as if to wake the world from its slumber. Kasturi shivered and tears filled her eyes.

'What's wrong, Kasturi?' the head priest said as he held out the platter with the camphor flame to her.

She wiped her eyes quickly, swept her fingers over the flame and then touched her eyes. 'I don't know, aiya, but for some reason my mind feels perturbed,' she said, tearing up again.

'These are bad times, Kasturi. What can you or I do about it?' the head priest said soothingly. 'Riots and scuffles have become routine now. I pray to god each day that it should pass without incident. I heard that Sundaramurthi was beaten up yesterday. That's why he wasn't here to play the nadaswaram. Didn't you notice?'

Kasturi was astonished. 'Really? I was preoccupied. I'll go and see him. Was he the only one who took a beating?' she asked with some hesitation.

'These days an achari boy is always with him. He is also injured, I believe.'

'Aiyaiyo!' Kasturi said, her eyes widening in panic.

Surprised, the head priest said, 'Do you know him?'

'I've met him, aiya, I even gave him an order for an aimpon figurine,' Kasturi said, trying to calm her fluttering heart.

'I see. This freedom frenzy has gripped everyone. If Suppuni didn't have this temple regimen to follow, he too would have gone to Vedaranyam.'

'What's happening there?'

'Haven't you heard? Gandhi is leading a march to Dandi to protest the salt tax. Aligned with it, an Iyengar Brahmin here has gathered a lot of people and headed to Vedaranyam. Just when Sundaramurthi was all set to join the march he was beaten by the police. He is laid up now. Suppuni went to see him early this morning.'

'I have to see him. I'll take your leave, aiya,' she said as the head priest looked on with concern.

Seeing a visibly agitated Kasturi approach him, Muthu asked anxiously, 'What's wrong, Akka?'

She climbed on to the cart immediately and said, 'I heard Sundaramurthi Mama is badly hurt. I want to see him—hurry!'

Muthu drove the cart for some time without speaking a word. 'I was with him at dusk yesterday. He wasn't injured then,' he said softly.

Kasturi was not listening. This must be why her mind had been perturbed since morning. How many more crises are in the offing, she wondered. Had Singaram been beaten up badly? One would be lucky to die in the struggle for freedom, he told her once. But if freedom wasn't won even after lives were sacrificed, how did it benefit anyone? Just when she was beginning to taste the ambrosia of true love for the first time in her life, she sensed a variety of unsettling vibrations spreading around her. Before diving headlong into the affair, she should have thought seriously about the possible consequences. She should have kept her heart locked up instead of allowing it to be stolen. But her heart had not waited for instructions from her mind. Though her instinct warned her now and again, and those around her expressed their concern with gestures, her naive heart had stood at a distance, clapped its hands and laughed, and paid them no heed. Her body yearned to be held captive within his broad shoulders. Her breasts heaved in anticipation of his touch.

His warm hands had magical powers. Though Kanagu Paati had schooled her in the deft manoeuvres of sexual frolic, it was Singaram who revealed the secret doorways that were unfamiliar even to her. She had never imagined that physical union could take her to such heights of ecstasy. This was truly the gateway to heaven that Kanagu Paati had lured her with. Sleeping with Raja was a mere arrangement, an artful deception she practised while keeping her emotions at bay.

But Singaram brought her femininity a wholeness of meaning. Her relationship with him was fraught with danger; she felt it every moment. When Kanagu Paati had cautioned her the other day, Kasturi was able to laugh and evade her warning. Now she was afraid. How much longer could she hold out against the inevitable?

That night, after Singaram had freed himself from her embrace and left, Kasturi closed the back door gently and entered the house. Kanagu Paati stood there, blocking her way. Somewhat taken aback, Kasturi recovered quickly and said in a soft whisper, laughing, 'Who are you planning to meet, Paati, standing here in the middle of the night?'

'That's exactly what I want to ask you,' Paati replied in the same tone of voice.

'I'll tell you if you promise to keep it a secret,' Kasturi said. There was a wooden bench in the backyard. Holding Paati's hand, Kasturi made her sit on the bench and sat next to her.

'Paati, if I want to express romantic passion, shouldn't I experience it first?'

'Girl, what are talking about? Don't try to fool me,' Paati said.

Kasturi sighed wearily. 'All my romantic feelings disappear when I see that Raja. Didn't you say it was an arrangement? I think the same.'

'Come to the point, girl.'

'I am ... It is only now that a man has taught me what romance is.'

'Why should he come through the backyard instead of the front door?'

'If he comes to the front door, you people won't let him in.'

'Is he that kind of man? Who is he?'

'The achari who makes idols of gods.'

'What?' Kanagu Paati's shock was palpable in her tone. 'Foolish girl! Do you have any brains? With your status, you had to find yourself an achari of all people?'

'He is an artist, Paati. A genuine artist.'

'Rubbish!' Kanagu Paati said angrily. 'You dance for the gods in the temple. It's an honour not given to anyone else. Do you not know that it involves a lot of restrictions? You can't have relations with anyone from the lower castes. If word gets around, you will not only lose your status, but also become an outcaste, girl. They will break his leg, and maybe even kill him.'

Kasturi covered Paati's mouth with her hand. 'No, please don't say that. I can't help it, Paati, he is the one I want. He was diffident at first. Forget it, he told me. But I didn't know how to control myself.' Before she could finish, she started crying.

Kanagu Paati would not yield. She said sternly, 'Look here, you can't become emotional and fool around in such matters. Get that into your head. You are a temple devadasi. A woman who doesn't know how to control herself cannot occupy that position. This won't end well, I'm telling you. It's a transgression against god, girl.' There was genuine anxiety in her voice.

After that day, with Paati keeping a watch on her movements, Kasturi was unable to meet Singaram for a long time. What Paati had said was right. Kasturi was a responsible person and she knew the rules. But she could not agree that it was a crime against god. Was it not a rule framed by upper-caste men? When the head priest gave her the news today, her body had trembled and she had set out involuntarily to see him.

Oh god, what shall I do?

When they arrived at Sundaramurthi Mama's house, Kasturi got down quickly and went inside. Mama was lying on a mat in the courtyard, a bandage around his head. Singaram was nearby, leaning against a wall. His head was heavily bandaged too. On seeing her enter, he sat upright.

'What happened?' she asked anxiously.

Sundaramurthi opened his eyes and tried to sit up.

'Please, don't get up. What happened? Did they beat you in the procession? Did you march again?'

Without a word, Sundaramurthi closed his eyes.

'We were thrashed during the procession,' Singaram said slowly. After a glance at Sundaramurthi, he bowed his head.

'What is this, aiya?' Muthu asked as he joined them. 'I saw you at dusk yesterday. The march ended quite early, right?' he said, looking alternately at Mama and Singaram.

Kasturi gave them a suspicious look. 'What really happened, Mama?'

'It's nothing, Kasturi. By now, this body is used to blows,' Sundaramurthi said.

'When did this happen? Who hit you?'

Sundaramurthi's wife, who had come from the kitchen, said, 'Last night, after the police charged them and everyone dispersed, these two were returning from the riverbank when some people who were waiting there attacked them.'

'Who were they?' Kasturi asked, eyes widening in fright.

'Who knows? Who knows what enmity they harboured against whom? Or on whom they wanted to exact revenge? Luckily, these two were destined to live, so they got away.'

Kasturi was startled to see the tears pouring from Mami's eyes. 'This happened because of you'—had she left the words unsaid?

They will break his leg, maybe even kill him.

Terrified, Kasturi looked from Mama to Singaram and back. She covered her eyes with her hands and sobbed.

'Why are you frightening the poor girl?' Sundaramurthi Mama scolded his wife. 'There is no rhyme or reason behind such incidents, child. The police were angry that we were the ones who shouted the loudest. Cowards! They didn't have the guts to hit us when we were with the crowd. They hid in the dark and attacked us. We will be careful in future. Go home, Kasturi.'

She cast a glance at both of them and said, 'Take care, Mama. I heard you were going to Vedaranyam?'

'We were planning to leave tomorrow at sunrise. Meanwhile, this happened. Who told you?'

'The head priest.'

'Oh, it figures. Suppuni was here a short while ago.'

'Come, Akka,' Muthu said. 'The police are keeping watch.'

'Careful,' she said again.

As she headed for the entrance, Singaram said, 'The Paravai Nachiyar figurines will be ready in a couple of days. I'll send them here. Ask Muthu to come by and collect them.'

Again, her eyes filled with tears. When she returned home in the cart, her mind swung between various thoughts.

The police are watching us.

Why? Is it solely because those two are freedom fighters? Why am I being watched? By whom? The police were under the Collector's authority. That Raja was aligned with him spelt trouble. They were jointly spying on her.

'It would be unwise to antagonize the Collector,' her mother had cautioned her. 'A devadasi shouldn't have relations with a lower-caste man,' Kanagu Paati had said. Kasturi was guilty on both counts.

Muthu did not say a word. He probably thought that she was responsible. The respect he had for her must have diminished. She was immersed in serious reflection.

She could only practise for form's sake that day. Sengamalam
too was in a slump. After lunch, Kasturi had the unusual urge to
sleep. Exhausted in body and mind, her eyes closed involuntarily.
Caught between sleep and wakefulness, like sand trickling
through the gaps between fingers, her mind kept sliding into
some remote depth. It groped through cavernous openings. She
heard Thilakam's voice from a cave and ran eagerly towards it.
Thilakam's figure appeared as a silhouette, but as she ran to it,
the figure receded further.

Was it a song or a plaintive cry?

'Was I born a woman for this?' Thilakam's voice melded all the
sorrows of this world into Saveri raagam …

Thilakam, Thilakam!

Kasturi woke with a start. Her body was soaked. Her heart
was pounding like a hammer. She felt like crying her heart out.
Hearing the sound, Kanagu Paati got up. 'What is it, Kasturi?
Why are you crying?' she asked.

Kasturi recovered her composure instantly. 'It was a dream,
Paati. I saw Thilakam in it.'

'Why should you cry over it? She'll come. Maybe she is
pregnant or something.'

'No, Paati. She looked very sad. She is not happy, Paati.'

Kanagu Paati sighed. 'She has brought it upon herself. What
can we do?'

'Let's bring her here, Paati.'

She spent the whole day thinking about it. Once Thilakam
came back, all their problems would be solved, she was sure.
I'll be able to bring my mind under control. I've had enough of
being wounded; and of others being punished on my account.
I won't cause such suffering any more. Thilakam is definitely
unhappy. I must tell Lakshmi the next time we meet. I must let

her know that it's not easy for a woman from this clan to lead a normal life—unless, like Lakshmi, she is able to study and change her life.

That night, she heard a knock on the door. Was it Thilakam? Kasturi's mind leapt in excitement.

'Thilakam?' she asked as she opened the door. A stranger was standing outside. 'Who are you?'

'My name is Panchapakesan. I have come from Madras. Gopalaiyer sent me.'

'Come in,' she welcomed him with a smile.

The man entered the hall with some hesitation and sat on the swing.

'Who is it?' Paati and Sengamalam asked, entering the room.

'Gopalaiyer has sent him, it seems,' Kasturi told them.

'Welcome, aiya. Will you have some milk?' Sengamalam asked. By then, Kasturi had gone to bring the milk.

Panchapakesan was quiet for a very long time, or so it seemed. On seeing Kasturi walk in with a tumbler of milk, he said with his head bowed, 'I don't want milk or anything else, 'ma. I don't know how to say this. Your daughter Thilakam is no more.'

The metal tumbler in Kasturi's hand dropped to the floor and the milk spilled, branching out haphazardly.

'What! What are you saying?' Both Sengamalam and Kanagu Paati screamed in unison.

Unable to speak, Kasturi crumpled to the floor and began to weep.

Did you appear in my dream only to tell me about it?

'What happened, aiya? Was she ill? She was never laid up in bed, not even for a headache. How did she die? Couldn't that Brahmin send us a telegram at least?'

'If it was a normal death, he would have.'

'What do you mean?'

'Your daughter hanged herself.'

'What—' Sengamalam started in a loud voice, then, as if realizing the horror of the situation, moderated her tone and exploded in a surge of grief, 'I don't believe it! Why should she hang herself?'

'Gopalaiyer couldn't understand it either. He is a generous man. He did not select the bride and conduct this marriage. Though he knew society would disapprove, he accepted the girl publicly as his daughter-in-law.'

As Kasturi and Sabapathi, who was sitting close to her, shed silent tears, Kanagu Paati cried out in sorrow, 'Poor child. You wretched girl. I really can't bear it.'

'I can't believe it,' Sengamalam repeated. 'You still haven't told us when it happened.'

'Four days ago.'

'Four days! And you've come only now to give us the news? You didn't even give us a chance to see her face one last time,' Sengamalam raged.

'There's no use being angry with me. It became a big scandal, with the police and others getting involved. Because of Gopalaiyer's reputation, everything had to be settled discreetly, without attracting attention. Gopalaiyer instructed me to tell you not to come there and trouble yourself.'

Kasturi was livid. 'If they had treated her right, why would she have hanged herself?' she burst out. 'She was a very proud woman. Who knows what really happened! Gopalaiyer is feeling guilty. That's why he says we need not come. Anyway, what's left there for us? If there had been no wrongdoing, he should have come here personally to console us.'

'Leave it, Kasturi,' Kanagu Paati said. 'There's no use saying anything to this man. You may leave, aiya. You've given us the news. That's enough.'

Panchapakesan left immediately.

Kasturi's anger did not subside. 'It was not a suicide. It was murder.'

'What do you mean, girl?'

'They killed her, Amma. It was murder! I know that her husband forbade her from singing. He broke her heart. Who knows what else he did to her! She couldn't talk about it. So, she killed herself.'

'When my girl ran away wanting respect and whatnot, eloped without telling anyone, I warned again and again that this wouldn't work. Which upper-caste man would treat us with respect? Even Periya Mirasu came to Thulasi only in secret. Has he ever openly said that she is his mistress, that Lakshmi is his daughter? It was only because she couldn't stand it that Lakshmi went off to study. She didn't go away believing that marriage and whatnot will give her freedom, did she?'

Kanagu Paati continued to shed tears but did not say anything. Kasturi went up to her and said, 'Don't cry, Paati. That's all we had in our destiny.'

At midnight, they heard a noise in the backyard. Sabapathi hurried over to check.

'Akka! Amma!' he shouted. 'Paati has had a fall.'

Kanagu Paati had fallen on the ground near the well.

Sabapathi made her lie face up. Holding a finger below her nostrils, he said, 'She is not breathing.'

26

Kodaikanal. Amma was born in this town. I didn't know it until now. Since Paati had had a job in Madras, I assumed that Amma was born there. Why had Paati come all the way from Madras to deliver her child here? She was a doctor herself. This town couldn't have had better facilities than the big hospital in Madras where she worked. It made no sense to me. From whatever I heard, Paati was a strong, determined woman who didn't mince words. Amma had told me that her mother accomplished things which were deemed impossible for the women of that era. I was in awe of her. Yet, I didn't get too many chances to interact with her. My life was spent mostly in hostels up north. Since Amma held an important job in the government, taking leave and going home was often deferred for some reason or other, and she never sent me alone to the south. Had she kept me away deliberately? My family history seemed to hold many secrets in its depths. Perplexed, I kept turning the pages of my mother's old passport.

I remembered a newspaper item that Joan had mentioned to me. 'Did you know that Charlie Chaplin always claimed that his birthplace was London? When he died, even his obituaries said that he was born in London. But recently his daughter or grandson discovered an old diary from one of Chaplin's locked cupboards. In it, Chaplin has written in his own hand that he was born in a gypsy camp. When I think of how he had hidden his gypsy provenance till the very end, I understand why my mother lied about her birth.'

I came back to the present. It was a strange coincidence that I should recall that conversation at this moment. There was no connection between that snippet of information and Amma. My mother had no reason to hide her place of birth. It was recorded in her passport. She didn't tell me about it because I never asked her. Nor was I inclined to ask why she had bought a house in Kodaikanal. It was no surprise to me that as someone born in the south, she wanted to spend her summer holidays in a cool hill station in the region.

Place of birth: Kodaikanal.

Could there be a connection between the Christian seminary and her birth? The people who ran the seminary might have been Paati's friends. Paati might have come here for the delivery because May, when Amma was born, was a month of scorching heat in Madras. It could be the reason for Amma's large donations to them. Apart from their address, there was no other note in her diary. Thinking that Appa might know more, I went downstairs. He was not in the drawing room. To my surprise, he was standing near the gate and shouting at someone. I went outside to see who it might be.

'Run, boy! Don't come this way again.'

As I walked to the gate I saw a young boy dash off. When he turned and looked at me, I was stunned. It was the boy I had seen with the old woman the other day. Why did he come here?

Appa turned to walk back towards the house.

'Who was that, Appa?'

'Some loafer!' Appa said angrily. I had never seen him so upset.

'Seemed like a young boy, didn't he?'

'Young or old makes no difference. They are all out to make mischief. He stands in front of the house and stares curiously at it, as though he is searching for something. Why should he stand there?'

'Has he come here before this?'

'Yes, of course. I've caught him twice earlier and chased him away.'

'Why did that boy come here?'

'Who knows?'

I was surprised. What did the boy know? Who was he waiting for—me? Did he want to tell me something? I was intrigued. If only I hadn't missed him. I wasn't sure I'd be able to spot him during my walk that evening.

There was no point in talking to Appa about anything while he was in his present mood. But I couldn't understand why he was so agitated on seeing that boy.

'Let's go, Appa.' I held his hand and led him inside. 'Why are you so upset over this? He might be an acquaintance of our gardener or maid.'

Appa didn't say anything. He was lost in his thoughts. Then he told me softly, 'I'll lie down for a while.' A few minutes later, before entering his room, he said, 'I'll go back to Delhi. You can stay here if you want. This cold weather doesn't suit me.'

I looked at him in surprise. Why had the boy's visit affected him so much? It troubled me. What had happened to Appa? I followed him inside and waited until he had removed his shoes and stretched out on the bed, then I covered him with the blanket that lay folded at his feet.

'Thank you,' he said with a faint smile and closed his eyes. I sat down on a chair near the bed and gently stroked his forehead. Two small nerves at the edges of his forehead throbbed lightly.

'Relax,' I said without knowing why. 'Relax, relax ...'

As I sat there, I realized that I didn't know my father even to the extent that I knew my mother. Clearly, this environment affected him badly. Since my mother had met an abnormal end here, it was understandable. He had been quite reluctant to come here. It might even be a mistake to have compelled him to accompany me. Contrary to what I had imagined, his presence wasn't helping my investigation. He contradicted himself all the time. When I asked him something that he ought to have known about, he would say he did not remember. He did not seem to be pretending. I wondered whether he had developed amnesia as a matter of course or if he had brought it upon himself. Or, was this a symptom of Alzheimer's or Parkinson's? Instead of sorrow, Amma's death seemed to have created feelings of extreme vexation in him; inflicted a burden. He had no desire at all to talk about Amma; her death was too great a tragedy for him.

'She has taken revenge on me, 'ma.'

What for, I wondered.

'What did I do wrong, 'ma?'

I could not understand it either. It seemed like a problem that could never be solved. Appa and Amma certainly had differences of opinion. But they were not deep and divisive, rather the healthy disagreements that were normal between two intellectuals. They did not rupture the bond that existed between my parents. Appa was a liberal. Amma did her work, which included travel to many countries, with complete freedom. I was reluctant to connect her death to the state of their marriage.

'I cannot walk with my head high any more. When I heard the news, it didn't make any sense to me.'

'How was Amma on that day?'

His eyes became clouded; I could see him floundering in an emptiness. 'I don't remember at all. Had I known she would do this, would I have watched her more closely? Perhaps. I was stunned when I got the news, as though my brain had come to a standstill. Yet everyone looks at me with suspicion.'

People in this town did indeed have a tendency to be suspicious. It was evident in what the old man had said the other day. *Who knows what happens inside those big bungalows?*

Appa fell asleep. I left the room and strolled in the garden for some time. Palm-size roses in full bloom swayed happily in the breeze. Amma used to be mad for roses. She was a person of cultivated tastes—in the way she dressed or decorated the house. She would hum sometimes. Her voice sounded beautiful, but it was obvious that she had had no formal training in music.

'My mother hated song and dance,' she said with a laugh when I asked her why she had not learnt to sing. From then on I lost the respect I had had for Paati. She seemed to have been a rigid, narrow-minded woman. Even Aurangzeb was hated by avid connoisseurs of history for having rejected music. Paati must have been a difficult person. Every time we met, a frown, as if from deep reflection, would appear on her face. It irritated me immensely whenever Paati told me to cut my very long hair short. Being really proud of it, I refused outright. Even today, there was no one I knew in America who did not admire my thick long hair.

'Why did Paati hate song and dance?'

'That's a long story!'

'Tell me ...'

'Look, I don't have the time now. After you grow up, maybe ...'

'After you retire ...'

Amma laughed.

All the things that Amma never got around to telling me could add up to an epic or a Puranic tale. There was no doubt that Paati was a rare woman. She possessed abnormal courage. I had heard Amma say proudly at times that Paati had a place in the history of the nation. But I never displayed any eagerness to learn more about her. She seemed to shun me for some reason. There was a disquiet in her eyes whenever she saw me—one I felt threatened by. Lately, however, I had been thinking about researching her and her activities while I still had the time, just as Joan had done with her ancestors.

I mulled over what Appa had said. He wanted to go back to Delhi. Yes, it would be better for him to leave. The driver, cook and everyone there were used to him. I wouldn't have to worry on his account. But it was essential that I stayed on in Kodaikanal. I had to make one more visit to that C.S.I. Centre and find out what I could.

I intended to go to Thanjavur as well. Thanjavur or Madurai—I should check that page in the diary more closely and enquire about this person, Sabapathi.

I got ready in the evening to set out on my usual walk around the lake. I wanted to let Appa know, so I went to his room to check if he had woken up from his nap. He had. Sitting on a chair by the glass window, he was gazing at the garden outside or at the sky. I felt a strange sympathy for him. I walked over to him silently and placed my hands on his shoulders. He was not startled. As if it was something that happened every day, he said without turning his head, 'Your mother peeked out from that cloud.'

Hiding my surprise, I laughed amiably. 'Where, Appa?'

'Look. Over there. I saw it just now. It's gone.'

'I keep seeing her too—in the water, in the sky above.'

'If I could speak to her, I'll ask her: Why did you do it?'

'Leave it, Appa. There is no use dwelling on it all the time. But there's some mystery behind her death. I only wish I could make sense of it.'

Appa nodded in dismay. 'It'll be difficult. Your mother was a mystery herself. I couldn't understand her till the end.'

An idea came to me all of a sudden. 'Come, Appa. Let's walk for a bit. If you get tired, we can rest on one of the benches facing the lake.'

'All right.' Appa stood up. He put on his shoes slowly and carefully. When he was ready—muffler around his neck and woollen cap on his head—we told Ganesan that we were going out.

'Don't you want tiffin and coffee?'

'We'll eat after we're back,' I said quickly. Now that Appa was finally ready to go for a walk with me, I didn't want to let the opportunity slip away.

The area around the lake was filled with gaiety. The lively banter and laughter among the cyclists. The brisk gait of those who walked for exercise. Those who smiled at everyone, strangers or acquaintances, they encountered on the way and greeted them with a 'Hi!' or 'Good evening!' before moving on. We ambled along, watching all of them. Only Appa and I seemed to walk as though we were weighed down by a burden, immersed in our own worries. I was saddened by the thought of Amma, who had reduced us to such a miserable condition. Appa strolled in silence. He smiled gently at the schoolboys who passed him. After we had walked for some time, we went down to the lake through a gap in the fence and sat on a bench. The lake sparkled like a diamond in the evening sun. Ripples spread out from a stone someone had tossed into the water. I gazed at the lake for some time with the crazy expectation of seeing Amma's face.

'Your mother was a mysterious woman,' Appa said, as if he hadn't realized that our conversation had been interrupted midway. 'Do you know this story from the Mahabharata? When Maharaja Shantanu lusted after Ganga and wanted to marry her, she laid down a condition: You must not question anything I do. When Shantanu questioned her, she left. Till the end, I never questioned your mother. Then why did she leave?'

As Appa continued talking, I became numb with shock. It felt as if he was inadvertently revealing a secret about which I had no clue.

'Did Amma lay down a condition? What was it?'

'Something inane. "We should both protect our respective privacy. I won't ask you about your antecedents or meddle in your affairs. You must not interfere in mine. Only if I am assured of complete freedom will I consent to this marriage," she had said. It was all right by me. I liked her a lot by then. I had grown up without parents in an orphanage. I had no religious faith. None of her ideas struck me as wrong. Your grandmother was already famous. Everyone knew she was the daughter of a devadasi. I never tried to discuss it with your mother.'

I was astonished. 'Was Paati's mother a devadasi? I had no idea. But then, wasn't Paati seriously involved in enacting a law for the abolition of the devadasi system?'

'She was serious exactly for that reason. But I didn't speak to your mother about such things either.'

'Where did you first meet Amma?'

'At a conference. She spoke very well. When we were introduced later, I liked her instantly. We met often after that. Your mother liked me too. Once we got married, we abided strictly by her condition. I didn't want to send you to a hostel. But she was adamant. I agreed to that as well.'

I listened to him with a growing sense of alarm.

'Once, she said she was going to Thanjavur to meet someone. I didn't ask her anything about it.'

I was taken aback. 'Thanjavur? When?'

'I don't know if she actually made the trip. It was four months before she came to Kodaikanal. I was in Indonesia then. I forgot to ask her later. Who knows? She might have wanted to visit her grandmother or uncle.'

I sat upright. 'Do you know someone called Sabapathi?'

Appa knit his eyebrows and tried to remember. 'Sabapathi? No, I don't know anyone by that name. Nor do I recall Amma mentioning a person like that.'

'I found an address in a notebook, written in Amma's handwriting. The name Sabapathi, and a Thanjavur address.'

Appa nodded without interest. 'Could be. Right now, I have no desire to know more. She is gone forever. What's the point of finding out? "Don't interfere in my affairs," she said. Perhaps I don't even have the right to ask why she decided to kill herself.'

I sat beside him, still in a state of disbelief. They were such an odd couple. How could such a relationship, bereft of intimacy, have endured between a husband and wife? Was it because of Appa's abundant patience, or his love? But in the end, even he could not help feeling that she had deceived him. If he hated her now, I wouldn't be surprised.

'I have no interest.'

As I listened to these words, born of extreme weariness as they were, I realized that bringing him to Kodaikanal was a mistake.

'You can go back to Delhi like you wanted. I'll stay here for a few more days,' I said.

He turned and looked at me with clouded eyes.

'Don't torment yourself about her passing, 'ma. Some deaths do happen this way, for no particular reason. We can't analyse them like psychologists. You should think about your own life from now on. Let's leave together. Come and stay with me for a while.'

'I'll come, Appa. Give me some time.'

'As you wish,' Appa said wearily.

I spent the next few days making arrangements for Appa's return to Delhi and helping him pack his belongings. Though I kept up my morning and evening walks, nothing remarkable occurred; that boy was nowhere to be seen. I postponed my visit to the C.S.I. Retreat Centre. On our drive to Madurai, Appa was asleep most of the time. At the airport, shortly before departure, he squeezed both my hands and said, 'Take care. Don't go alone to unfamiliar places. You are the only one left for me.' He added, 'You must understand one thing—trying to solve the mystery can only lead to more trouble. You shouldn't get hurt.'

My eyes filled with tears. Appa had never displayed such affection with me. 'Don't worry. If I can't find anything, I will come soon.'

'I don't understand what you want to find, 'ma.'

'I am confused myself,' I said with a weak smile.

The car headed for Kodaikanal. The police station was on my way home. On my two previous visits, there were only two constables there. They were new to the town. When I asked them about Amma's case, they looked up old records. 'It was a suicide, 'ma. They have closed the case. Many such incidents take place in this town,' they told me, clucking their tongues in sympathy. Thinking I would drop by, I asked the driver to stop. Today the inspector was also present. I came directly to the point.

'Oh, that case! I was the one who handled it. What do you want to know? We have closed it already. Once it was determined to be a suicide, what else could we do?'

I asked hesitantly, 'How can you be so sure that she died by suicide?'

The inspector was instantly provoked to anger. 'Are you saying it was murder then? Do you have a suspect in mind? Or do you think your father killed her himself? You should have seen him that day. He was speechless from the shock. There is a witness who can attest to his presence in the house. You come from America after two years, at your own leisure, and ask me how I came to such a conclusion? Do you think we are fools?'

'Sorry,' I mumbled, aghast that he should have got so angry. 'I learnt only recently that she died by suicide.'

Rolling the paperweight on the table with his fingers, the inspector said, 'A reliable person informed us that your mother was not in her right mind.'

I was stunned. 'Who said that?'

'Go and ask them yourself. Who knows whether they are alive or not?'

'Who? Where?'

'Do you know that C.S.I. Centre? There was a very old woman there.'

'Who—Mother Superior?'

'No. She is not a nun. She is a teacher. I forget her name ...' The inspector scratched his head thoughtfully.

My heart trembled as I waited.

'Ah, I remember now. Her name is Yogambal.'

27

As Kasturi rode in the twin-horse carriage from the palace, sitting on a silk mattress, her mind was empty. No matter who came and went, steered by an invisible hand, life seemed to follow its own course, like a blinkered horse. The absurdity of having to submit to Raja's invitation amid personal bereavements and the various upheavals around her sapped her energy.

She had been disgusted by her birth for the first time in her life when Raja indicated that accommodating her mourning for Thilakam and Kanagu Paati was a nuisance for him. Chee, chee! What a shameful way to eke out a living! Would she be able to discard the trappings of this life and get out some day? Her dance, the agama rules and rituals at the temple, her service to the deity, Raja's patronage—they were all intertwined. If she rejected one, she would lose the others. Raja presided over the temple administration. Her position and status continued under his benign gaze; she was his slave. If she behaved in a way that displeased him, she would lose her position just as Kanagu Paati had warned her. She would be prohibited from dancing in the temple. It could happen to her even before Lakshmi got a law passed.

Singaram had told her once, 'We live in this society. Confronting it in a big way would cause more damage to you than me.' On one of their secret trysts in a mango grove, he had sensed that someone was spying on them.

Kasturi was certain that Raja was having them watched. There was no telling what he might do. Wondering how she would cope with the consequences, she got down from the carriage and walked slowly towards Raja's room, where he sat reclining on the sofa, keen with anticipation. He looked intently at her impassive face, but pretended not to have noticed her greeting.

'Welcome, Kasturi,' he said. 'These days it seems you come here against your will?'

The words quickly brought Kasturi back to her senses. Giving him a radiant smile, she said, 'Aiyo. Not at all, aiya! It is just that dance practice went on for a long time today. Perhaps my face looks tired from the exertion.'

'You practised the whole day?' There was a note of derision in the question.

Paying it no heed, she said, 'Yes, aiya.'

'Of course, that would tire you out.'

She realized that she had to manage the situation with utmost care. From the small container she poured fragrant saffron-infused milk into a tall silver glass, handed it to him and said lovingly, 'Shall I show you the new item I learnt today?'

But today, he was not the man she knew, who would soften at once. 'No. You are tired already.'

Kasturi laughed adoringly. 'Aiyo, I could never be too tired to dance for you! It's a very fine varnam,' she said and started dancing flirtatiously. 'The joy of love is crossing all boundaries.'

Raja began to enjoy the performance despite himself, until suddenly, as if he returned to his senses, he said stiffly, 'No, no. Stop. I need to talk to you about something.'

She cast him a plaintive glance. 'What's wrong? Why does my Raja seem to be angry?'

Giving her a sharp look, Raja said in a tone of mild anger, 'I am told that you are seen in all kinds of disreputable places these days.'

'What! Who do I need to visit apart from you? Do you really believe these stories?'

'How can I expect a woman of your clan to be faithful? If you betray me, I can't help but get angry.'

She felt a sharp stab of fury at this violation of her self-respect. It is absurd of him to use the word betrayal, she thought. Not only does he treat me as his slave to satisfy his lust, but also as his property. He can use me in any manner he chooses, including pimping me out to others. He is not a patron, but an invader.

'Aiya, does it seem fair to you? If you feel this way, why did you send me to that Collector Durai? Did you think he wouldn't touch me? Didn't he tell you what happened that evening?'

Raja calmed down a little. 'He only said that he wanted to see you dance. But you ran away from there before he could, which was insulting to him. He is very angry with you.'

'Had I not escaped that day, he would have torn me apart. He said, "Come, you whore." You are my patron. How could you push me into such a disgraceful situation? You did know his intent when you sent me there, didn't you?'

Covering her face with both hands, Kasturi began to sob. All of a sudden, a terrible weakness overwhelmed her. Kanagu Paati's warning loomed over her like an apparition and threatened her.

Raja was silent for some time. Then he said, 'All right. At least the Durai is a white man; he rules over us, and I am bound to obey him. But I am told that you have been roaming around with some low-caste fellow.'

Immediately, she took her hands away from her face and looked at him. Because of the tears, the kohl in her eyes had run and streaked down her cheeks.

'Once you give in to suspicion, everything will look wrong. Yes, I went twice to see the achari who makes aimpon figurines. I have asked him to make a Paravai Nachiyar idol. Why don't you check and tell me if it is true?'

Raja gave her a piercing look. 'So, you're saying there is no other relationship between you?'

'No.'

'Will you swear before the deity?'

She looked at him, startled. Oh Lord, what fresh trial is this! Her eyes filled with tears again. 'There can be no greater insult to me, aiya, I can't. Please don't humiliate me.'

She sat by the wall, with her face buried between her knees. How could she swear this in front of the deity? She had never imagined that she would be trapped in such a crisis.

'If everyone believes that the temple devadasi is having relations with a lower-caste man, the temple administration will take your position away. You will be forbidden from dancing in the temple ever again.'

'You must believe me! You are the one who presides over the administration,' she said feebly.

Kasturi was afraid that the temple administration might have already taken the decision. Shouldn't the temple administration have said something when the Durai had grabbed her hand? Was he not a foreigner of impure birth? Her tongue curled back, unable to utter the questions. No matter what, she couldn't swear in god's chamber that she had no relations with Singaram.

After a long time, Raja came to her and helped her to her feet. I've got away today, she thought. That night, Kasturi tried to please him by using all the tricks she knew. As she was leaving, Raja told her gently, 'The relationship between us will remain like this. But I can't interfere in your issues with the temple. If you insist that you cannot stand in god's chamber before everyone and swear that you've done no wrong, it would mean that you are guilty. And I will have no option but to agree that the administration has taken the right decision. I can't change rules that have endured for generations.'

Not having the strength to look her in the face, he turned his eyes away.

On the journey home, Kasturi trembled uncontrollably. Raja hadn't asked her who it was. He must have known ... *If you betray me, I can't help but get angry.* Raja's words echoed in her mind, frightening her. *I can't change rules that have endured for generations.* This too was true. The agama rules at the temple were extremely strict. But who had set down these rules? Men who controlled the administration of temple affairs: upper-caste men, big landlords, kings. Were they not rules that gave these men exclusive rights to enjoy the devadasis? Was it not a trick to keep her under their control?

Lakshmi's ideas were making a very late entry into her mind, she realized dejectedly. 'If you had suffered the humiliation that was my lot, you would understand my anger,' the other girl had said often.

The disgrace being visited on me now would never have happened to any devadasi in the past, Kasturi thought to herself. But the ecstasy she experienced while dancing in god's chamber was genuine and true. It was a spiritual vision, one that liberated her from earthly woes. Wasn't the Lord of the Universe aware of her dedication and devotion? Was it a crime to love a being that the Lord himself had brought into the world? Was this not a punishment meted out to her by petty, envious men? I can't change the rules of the temple, Raja said, but the relationship between you and me will continue like this. Her whole body cringed with shame. It was like the padmavyuham, the battle formation in which Abhimanyu was trapped. Could she emerge alive? Tears poured from her eyes. She drew the curtains back and looked out. The day had dawned. The peal of the temple bells was a sign that the dawn puja was about to begin. Today her service was slated for the evening, when the smaller idol was to be taken on a ceremonial procession around the temple. She dropped the curtain back in place and said, 'Arumugam, stop the carriage in front of the temple. I want to pay obeisance to the Lord.'

Without a word, Arumugam drew the carriage to a halt.

She ran to the well, took the pot of water that someone else had kept there and poured it over her head. Her whole body was drenched; tears kept pouring from her eyes. She wrung the water out of the sari's folds and hurried to the deity's chamber. Her wet sari clung to her and dripped water on the ground all along the way. Instead of the head priest, Suppuni was performing the deeparadhanai to the deity. No one was present in the chamber. A shiver ran through her—it felt as if the deity was granting a sighting meant exclusively for her. After sweeping his fingers above the flame and touching his eyes with them, Suppuni turned around and was taken aback to see Kasturi. Holding the plate with the flame in front of her, he said, 'Kasturi, why have you come here in this state? What happened? Why are you crying?'

Receiving the votive flame, Kasturi looked at him with immense sorrow.

'Suppuni, they've told me that I cannot dance in the temple from now on. They say I am a sinner. Before anybody comes, please allow me to dance one last time, Suppuni.'

Suppuni looked at her in shock and disbelief. 'Who says you can't dance here? Who could have a greater right than you?' he said indignantly.

'They've taken away all my rights, Suppuni. They're doubting my character. I've broken the temple rules, they say.'

Suppuni looked at her in confusion. 'I don't understand. My father didn't tell me anything about this. He has fever, so I came today for the dawn puja.'

'I am sorry to hear that, Suppuni. But all the same, it allows me to ask you a favour. Please, Suppuni ... just once. Let me offer my tribute here, in the chamber, in front of the deity. One last time ... I can't bear it, Suppuni. I feel as if my heart is going to break. There is no place for me anywhere ...'

Suppuni looked at her sorrowfully. 'Dance, Kasturi. If you don't, the Lord himself won't stand for it. Dance.'

A bright smile appeared on Kasturi's face. 'Thank you, Suppuni Aiya.'

She started dancing. '*Coral red lips and dimpled smile ...*' As if the Lord himself was present, a rapture spread within her.

Suppuni sat watching her with teary eyes. 'There is a divine aspect to your art. What right have they to tell you not to dance?'

She gazed at him with a wan smile, said, 'Thank you, Suppuni,' and left.

Sengamalam was taken aback to see her daughter enter the house with wet clothes and hair. Afraid that her mother was going to be difficult, Kasturi went inside quickly to change her clothes. Her tears had dried up once she danced in the temple. Nothing was to be achieved by crying and moaning any more. She couldn't sit and wait for a miracle to happen. She had learnt long ago that it would be foolish to do so. This was not the early medieval era of Appar and Sundarar, the Saivite saints. It was a highly volatile age. God must have disappeared after handing over charge to humans.

As she changed her clothes, she remembered Paati. You deceived me, Paati. You are the one to blame. You addled my brain, saying that the temple was my world and the Lord my husband. You are an eternally auspicious wife, you told me, and all other bonds are untrue. Now my relationship with the temple has become a lie. I have lived like a fool, not realizing that the position given to me is merely an arrangement for the convenience of others. I didn't know that I wouldn't have the freedom even to love someone. Why didn't I think it over like Lakshmi?

When she came to the hall, she found Sundaramurthi Mama sitting on the swing. Sengamalam sat next to him, looking as if she had encountered a ghost.

She burst out on seeing Kasturi, 'Sundaram has some news. Is it true?'

'What is Mama saying?' Kasturi said evenly.

'That they have taken away the position of temple devadasi ...'

'That's what I hear too.'

'Did Raja tell you?'

'Yes,' she said, bowing her head.

'What was the reason? What wrong did you commit that Raja himself could not intervene and set matters right?' Sengamalam's voice brimmed over with anger and grief.

'I don't know, Amma. As far as I know, I haven't done anything wrong.'

'Why didn't you tell him that you will place a flower in front of the deity and swear on it? Won't the administration believe you then?'

Kasturi looked up instantly at her mother. 'I can't. Doing so would be demeaning.'

'And losing your position and becoming the laughingstock of the village is not?' Sengamalam asked in anger.

'Ask Mama. They have passed a bill to abolish the devadasi system. When it comes into force, this position will be lost anyway.'

'She is right, Akka,' Sundaramurthi said.

'Then it will be taken away by the law. But now it is as if you have ruined your reputation and been fired from that position. I feel so ashamed I want to die.'

Kasturi could no longer control her fury. Forgetting that Mama was present in the room, she lashed out, 'Didn't you want to die when you sent me to the Durai who has enslaved us? Or while you wait for the next filthy rich zameendar to send for me? You and Paati deceived me into thinking that sleeping with Raja was an arrangement. Last night I wished that I could pluck out my tongue and die!'

Sengamalam was dumbstruck. She didn't ask Kasturi again what wrong she had committed. No one said anything. Mama seemed lost in deep thought. He could not have been unaware of her friendship with Singaram, yet he never tried to stop it or warn her against it. If Sengamalam found out, she would consider it a terrible humiliation, more grievous than all the others.

'I never thought such things could happen to us, Sundaram,' Sengamalam said softly. 'I always worried that antagonizing the Collector, Raja and other big shots would do us no good. Let her say whatever she wants, but a woman born in this clan must give up honour and self-respect. Thilakam's life ended the way it did. I never imagined that this one's career would collapse in disgrace.'

Kasturi sat in a daze as if none of this was reaching her ears.

Sundaramurthi Mama spoke: 'You must understand one thing, Akka. It is this life which is disgraceful. For a long time, we accepted it without protest, but now the situation has changed. Movements against the temple have sprung up. Atheism is rearing its head. There is talk of freedom everywhere. "Freedom for the Paraiyars and Pulaiyars", a Brahmin poet sings. Where everyone is deemed equal, there is no place for such systems. They *should* be abolished. Bringing in a law will be good. We will be in disgrace only if we despair about our livelihoods and take the easy path. We can try our hand at other work— singing on the stage, playing the nadaswaram, dancing. What's wrong if we earn that way? The children of our clan should study from now on. As that girl Lakshmi did, they should learn new professions, show that we are not dependent on anyone. When the country gets independence, everything will become possible.'

Sengamalam shook her head stubbornly. 'You are saying all this, but the future looks bleak to me. It's a good thing that my mother is not alive any more.'

Sundaramurthi nodded in agreement. 'For a few years life will be hard. It's not enough for the nation to be free. Freedom should come to all communities. Slowly, we will rise.'

'What's this freedom you talk about? I have no clue.'

The next evening, Muthu came by at sunset and whispered to Kasturi, 'Akka, the Paravai Nachiyar figurine you had ordered is ready now. It's at Sundaramurthi Mama's house. Should I go there and bring it for you?'

'From Mama's house? I'll come with you,' Kasturi said. After a quick word with Sengamalam, she set out with Muthu.

Somewhere in the distance, they could hear loud cries of
'Vande Mataram'.

'Is it a procession? Mama could be marching with them.'

'We'll see. He was the one who asked me to come so he'll
surely be at home. I forgot to tell you something else. Lakshmi
Akka is visiting from Madras.'

'Really?' she said, surprised. 'It's been a long time since
we met. After collecting the figurine, we will call on her.' She
needed to meet Lakshmi. Everything you predicted has come to
pass, she would tell her. Lakshmi would advise her on what she
needed to do.

Inside the house, Sundaramurthi Mama was absent. But
Singaram was there. Kasturi's face lit up. Faltering a little, she
said in a feeble voice, 'I have lost my position at the temple,
Singaram.'

'I know,' he said, his head bowed. 'I understand how
distressing it must be for you. Not just grief, but humiliation
too. I also know it happened because of me. Please forgive
me! I've committed a grave mistake. I played with fire without
appreciating my situation. There can be no forgiveness for me.'

His voice cracked, and his face crumpled in anguish.

'You shouldn't have any regrets, Singaram. They say the
regulations are strict, but now I realize they are actually cruel. In
a way, this is liberating. Maybe the Lord himself has arranged
it, who knows? If I don't have to dance in the temple any more,
no one can object to our friendship.'

Singaram looked at her in amazement. Laughing ruefully, he
said, 'It's not that easy. Only when the country becomes free will
there be any salvation for my community. I don't know if I'll be
lucky enough to see it happen.'

She felt a knot of fear in the pit of her stomach. Why was
he talking like this? She wanted to go near him, clasp his head

to her bosom and console him. 'You and I are the same now—not just as human beings, but socially as well,' she wanted to tell him, but he stood a little apart. It was as if he wished to erect a wall between them. He uncovered the figurine that was wrapped in an old cloth and gave it to her. 'I've finished it. You can take it home.'

The figurine glittered in the dark, a work of extraordinary beauty.

'How beautiful you have made it! You are a divine artist,' she said joyfully.

'Thank you. While I worked on the face, I could only remember yours. So I made it in your image. Let it be with you to remind you of me.'

Why was he saying such things?

Kasturi was dying to embrace him, but he moved away suddenly.

'Elei. They are about to leave. They want to know if you are coming,' someone called him.

'I must leave for the procession,' Singaram said, and after pausing for a moment to look at her, went out.

'Be careful, Singaram,' she said.

He entered again, wore the Gandhi cap that was hanging on a nail, shouted 'Vande Mataram!' and disappeared.

A feeling of emptiness assailed Kasturi as soon as Singaram departed. With heavy steps she walked to the entrance with the figurine in hand and got into the cart. She realized she was being watched by many pairs of eyes. Paying them no heed, she said, 'Let's go, Muthu.'

The procession wound its way along the main road. Shouts of 'Vande Mataram!' reverberated across the sky.

'Hearing this slogan gives me goosebumps every time, Akka,' Muthu said. 'Shall we duck into this alley and go home?'

'Station the cart on the side of the road and come back, Muthu. Let us join them.'

'Aiyo! No, Akka. It will be risky for you.'

'Nothing of the sort. Come! I hear a lot of women are marching with Mahatma Gandhi.'

Wearing the Gandhi caps that Muthu had secretly stashed in the cart, both of them joined the procession. When the crowd roared 'Vande Mataram! Quit India!', Kasturi also shouted with gusto. Though the rumble of a police jeep and the shrill sounds of a whistle followed them throughout, the protesters marched forward fearlessly. Suddenly, someone began singing.

'Vande Mataram is our chant! We salute the mother of our great land!'

Singaram's voice rang out clearly in the night, brimming with emotion. A thrill ran through Kasturi, giving her goosebumps. She tried excitedly to move ahead, but Muthu held her back. 'It's dangerous! Don't go.'

Suddenly the sound of gunfire was heard. A cloud of tear gas rose into the air. The crowd dispersed in panic and started to run helter-skelter. The song continued—*'Vande Mataram is our chant!'*—spreading and thrumming through the universe. 'Vande Mataram' ... He was but a lone man, holding a flag in his hand ...

'No! Don't go, Singaram!'

'Shoot the bastards! Shoot him!'

Shots were heard again and again. Abruptly, the song stopped. The jeep's rumble and sounds of gunfire ceased. The procession disappeared. Kasturi and Muthu were the only ones left. They could see nothing through the pall of smoke. As they groped their way through it, her eyes fell on them.

Four or five corpses lay on the ground. Singaram lay separately a short distance away. His dirt-coloured shirt had turned blood-red. His eyes were closed. His mouth seemed to be smiling. Muthu held a finger below his nostrils and stuck out his lower lip. Eyes bulging, Kasturi stared at his lifeless body. A strangled sob escaped from her as though her heart had been rent in two. He had deliberately embraced death. She bent down to touch his face.

Hearing the sound of an approaching jeep, Muthu pulled her into the alley. Hugging him, she began to weep convulsively. When they came back to the road, the police had taken the bodies away.

Muthu bundled her into the cart.

'Take me to Lakshmi's house, Muthu,' she said suddenly. Her brain had stopped functioning. She sat with her eyes closed.

It seemed only moments had passed before Muthu stopped the cart and knocked on the door of Lakshmi's house.

'Kasturi!'

Hearing someone call out to her in a voice that brimmed with all the compassion in the universe, Kasturi opened her eyes.

'Come, Kasturi!' Supporting Kasturi with her arm, Lakshmi helped her get down from the cart and led her inside.

Kasturi fainted. When she opened her eyes, Lakshmi was sitting beside her, checking her pulse. Something that looked like a snake was hanging from her neck. Feeling distraught, Kasturi clasped Lakshmi's hands tight.

'Lakshmi, please take me away somewhere. Some place far away. At least for a few days.'

28

I AM DRIFTING BETWEEN sleep and wakefulness. A ray of ashen light has crept in through the window. My life appears to be suspended in limbo, at the end of a string held in a puppeteer's hand. If he relaxes his hold, the puppet will collapse to the floor, its life will expire and mingle with the sky. It's strange, the way he sits tight without relaxing his grip. Enough! Why is my life still hanging by a thread? Unable to withstand that one shock, Kanagu Paati died instantly. Why, then, is my life still glued to my body even after enduring so many blows? I remember dancing to 'Naan oru vilayattu bommaiya' (Am I a play doll for you?) aeons ago. Still, whenever I hear the song, my feet and hands automatically keep time to the rhythm, my limbs move as if they are beyond my control.

I had heard that even in his dying moments our dance master raised his hand as though he was about to fling the kattai at someone. When I told Lakshmi, she had a hearty laugh. 'He was lucky that I didn't study to be a lawyer. If I had, I would have sent him to jail. Ruthless man! He would take out his disappointments on us.'

'What disappointments?'

'He didn't lack for them, did he? For someone with his vast knowledge, what status did he have in society?'

Lakshmi analysed everything clearly, and laid out precise causes and effects. The more Kasturi listened to her, the more awestruck she was. She understood some of Lakshmi's arguments, but a lot went over her head—and there were some she couldn't accept.

'Forget everything, Kasturi. Learn to renounce all ties and affection. Learn to think that nothing belongs to you,' Lakshmi had said.

I can't, Lakshmi. I am not an ascetic. I live with a lot of self-control. Still, I simply cannot. Song and rhythm are in my blood. All the agonies I suffered are unrelated to my art—it is distinct from them. I can't forget anything or anyone. Even now, it is as if Thilakam is sitting before me and singing. When she does, no memories haunt me; the whole world seems full of joy.

I fought with you all the time. I thought you would destroy my life. Please forgive me, I wanted to tell you, bury my head in your lap and weep. I couldn't do it because you moved away. God alone knows how much I yearned to see you till the end. But you died without coming to see me. It seems you were the one who gave up all ties and affection. It was possible for an atheist like you. Isn't that amazing?

In the patch of sky visible outside the window, many faces appear like shadows and fade out. 'This be the gate, this be the gate,' Kanagu Paati says. 'It's the gateway to heaven, girl.'

Paati, I see no gate. Everything is shut.

'Even if a wayfarer takes the name of Valli's husband …' It's *kaavadi chindu*, Akka. How beautifully that man sings it! Is it Singaram who is singing? *Ada, ada, what a fine voice …* Her whole body trembles. *'Vande Mataram is our chant! We salute the mother of our great land!'* Listening to this song gives me goosebumps, Akka …

Come, Muthu, let's go …

No, Akka. It's dangerous, Akka.

Gunfire. The sound splits my eardrums. A river of blood is flowing. *No, Singaram, don't leave me and go.* A sob rises from the depth of her stomach. Her back heaves and trembles.

'Is Aththai crying? Aththai, why are you crying?'

'What's it to you if the old woman is crying? Maybe she is mourning someone long dead. We won't shed a tear when she dies, though.'

'Somu, don't carry so much cruelty in your heart.'

Kasturi didn't hear anything. On the table in the corner, someone had covered the Paravai Nachiyar figurine with a cloth. She felt the urge to remove the cloth. *I made it in your image.* The kaavadi chindu played in her ear. She heard the taps of the chisel.

How well you sing!

I am not a learned person like you. All I know is only what I've heard.

She wanted to giggle. *That is knowledge too, isn't it?*

'Aththai is laughing now. As if making us the laughingstock of the town weren't enough.'

Her eyes were waiting for someone. She was not certain who it could be. Lakshmi would know. A host of memories appeared like shards in her mind's eye and spun around. But there was one thing that was not clearly visible, that kept slipping from her mind. The later part of her life had been erased totally from her memory. How? She was bewildered. The early phase kept unfolding without a strand out of place. The body lying in the middle of the road, chest drenched in blood—that seemed like the final chapter of her life. What happened after that? Why was that section lost? She couldn't remember a thing. But the life in this body was waiting for something.

You. It must be waiting for you.

Lakshmi, please tell me, when will you come to see me? I know you won't come. I can't say what would happen if you came and stood before me. I am not even fit to tell you what a piteous creature I am. I can't die either. I don't understand how I have lived for so long. There must be a reason for that.

I dimly remember fainting in your arms on that day. Thoroughly exhausted, my mind and body were like worn fibres, frayed. I couldn't even take care of this body of mine.

Kasturi didn't know what Lakshmi told Sengamalam, but her mother didn't come to see her before she left with Lakshmi. Sabapathi came alone, carrying a suitcase filled with her clothes. He stood there, crying. 'Come back home, Akka. I will take care of you ...' She could not say anything. It felt as if she had forgotten all the words.

Sabapathi was a fine boy. He had a lot of affection for her. All that is old-fashioned now. His son, Senthil, hates me. It's a wonder that he hasn't killed me yet. If he comes by when I am alone, dread pools in my stomach. What can I do, boy? Is it my fault that I was born in this clan?

'Ei, old woman! How many more years do you plan to stay alive?'

What can I do? Give me poison, if you want …

'It looks like I'll be forced to do it …'

Lakshmi took her somewhere in a vehicle that she drove herself. Everything was like a fog to Kasturi. Nothing registered in her mind. A mountain road wound upwards through many bends and curves. She vomited all along the way. Lakshmi kept putting something sweet on her tongue.

'Lakshmi, why is this place so cold?' Her body shivered and trembled.

'Yes, it's a cold place, but you'll be safe here. Like you said, a remote place, out of everyone's sight. See this girl? Her name is Yogu. She will be your companion. She works as a teacher here. She has also suffered a lot. Listen patiently to her story.'

Yogu? Who was she? That detail was also fogged over. A face exuding kindness, always bending over her, smiling, arms embracing her.

Yogu was a talkative girl. What a fine girl. I don't remember her story.

'If it weren't for Akka, I would have died long ago.'

'Me, too.'

'Lakshmi, you have given life to so many people. When will you build one for yourself?'

'What do I lack in life?' Lakshmi laughed. 'I wanted to study to be a doctor. I did that. Now I am working, doing everything I can to provide childbirth facilities to women. I even brought the legislation as I had planned, though it scares you to death.'

'All that's fine, but don't you need a life of your own?'

'Why are you asking in a roundabout way? I am going to marry a doctor who works with me.'

'That's wonderful. Who is that brave man?'

Lakshmi smiled. 'Like the hero in some story, the man asked me if I would marry him. I goaded him by asking him, "What do you know about me?" Then, I gave him a shock and announced that I am a devadasi's daughter. As if that weren't enough, I left for my hostel immediately without a backward glance. I thought he wouldn't step in my direction ever again. But he stood before me the next day, persistent as blame. "I don't care whose daughter you are. Should I begin to love you only after enquiring about your lineage?" he said. "Poor man. He is pining so much," I thought and agreed to marry him.'

Kasturi laughed. 'Please tell me the truth! Don't you love him too?'

'I wouldn't have said yes if I didn't love him, Kasturi!'

'Will you call me for your wedding?'

'I am not going to call anyone. It will be a registered wedding.'

'How ludicrous! I wanted to sing laali at your wedding, push the swing, and feed you fruit and milk.'

'I want no such fuss. Forget it.'

Lakshmi, why did you die without seeing me? You never allowed me to meet you either. Did you not realize that I was pining for you all these years?

Her eyes stared vacantly, looking for something. Her ears perked up at the slightest sound.

'Who are you looking for, Aththai?'

'I don't know.' Her head lolled from side to side on the pillow. Her speech faltered.

Lakshmi. Lakshmi.

'Who is Lakshmi, thatha? Aththai keeps muttering her name.'

'It's been many years since Lakshmi passed away, 'ma.'

'She won't come, Aththai. She is no more.'

Her head lolled again from left to right.

'Aththai doesn't believe me.'

'Someone's at the door. Senthil, see who it is.'

Her senses were roused immediately. Someone is standing in the doorway. Who is it? Lakshmi? Yogu? So both of them remembered me, finally?

'Who is it?'

'Is Mr Sabapathi at home?'

'Who are you?'

'I am Dr Lakshmi's daughter.'

'We don't know anyone by that name.'

'Mr Sabapathi would know. Is he here?'

'What do you want?'

'I want to meet him.'

'About what?'

'Why are you asking so many questions, thambi? I have come all the way from Delhi to meet him.'

'That is why I am asking you: what for? This is what journalists do ... They show up with their tall stories and then print all kinds of rubbish.'

'I am not a journalist. I work for the central government. I am about to retire. What else do you want to know?'

'Who is Senthil fighting with? Who is it?'

'Greetings, Mama. You are Sabapathi, right?'

'Who are you, 'ma?'

'I am Lakshmi's daughter, Dharini.'

Sabapathi didn't speak for some time. He kept stroking his bald head in disbelief as he stared at the woman before him.

'I see,' he said at last. 'Come in. We have never met. What brings you here?'

'I heard that Kasturiamma was very ill and laid up in bed.'

'Senthil, will you go inside for a bit?'

'Who is Dr Lakshmi, 'pa?'

'Aththai's friend.'

'Appa, you are inviting trouble for no reason. We should have no truck with the old contacts. Send her away now.'

'Senthil, leave us alone for a while,' the man called Sabapathi said. 'You mustn't think ill of him. Come in. These days Akka is not fully conscious. She hasn't been for several years. Her condition is precarious. I am surprised that you've come now.'

'Is she able to speak?'

'Very rarely. She only remembers a lot of old incidents. Witnessing the commotion and the riots during the freedom struggle traumatized her. She lost her mind. Your mother had kept her in another town for some time. Then I brought her here.'

The light that had entered the room through the window split into four or five beams that touched the floor.

An angel is standing in that spot. Is it Lakshmi, or Singaram, or Thilakam?

'Akka, Lakshmi's daughter Dharini has come to see you.'

Her sunken eyes looked in the direction of the voice.

An angel, surely. She comes closer, smiling, and joins her palms together in greeting. She takes my withered hands in her grip, as though holding a packet of jasmine flowers.

An electric current passed through Kasturi's nerves. Who, who, who? Her eyes widened. It felt as if a light unfamiliar even to her was spreading in the room. 'It's me, Kasturiamma. It's me.'

I want to say 'Don't cry'. I want to wipe away the tears streaming down the girl's cheeks. Don't cry.

The face bent down and kissed Kasturi's cheek. It felt like her whole body was being anointed with rose water and raindrops.

So, you've come. You're here. Don't leave me again and go away.

She didn't want to release those hands.

'Aththai, let go of her hand. This akka will come every day.'

Who is this, trying to stop me? Her head lolled left and right.

'Aththai doesn't want you to leave. Stay for a while.'

Those hands kept stroking Kasturi's arms. An extraordinary peace pervaded her heart. A smile appeared on her lips. She wanted to keep gazing at that loving face which looked down at her. Gradually her senses relaxed and she was overtaken by sleep.

'Please give me a photograph of Kasturiamma if you have one.'

'We have thrown them all away, 'ma. We were fed up; we didn't want even a single marker of the past.'

'Even now?'

'Of course, yes. The moment anyone talks about those days, my son gets very angry. That revulsion won't fade away for at least two more generations. No one sings or dances now. Such was the stigma we suffered. Here, take this with you.'

'What is this?'

'It's a Paravai Nachiyar figurine. Akka's.'

'I will come to Kodaikanal again after two months. I'll come and visit her, if she is alive then.'

'Who is this, Appa? After staying away for so many years, why does she come now and weep? And you gave her the figurine too!'

Sabapathi was quiet for a long time. 'She came, finally. Leave it. Don't talk about her visit any more.'

Someone was standing before him. His meditation interrupted, Subramania Gurukkal opened his eyes. It was Shanmugam.

'I heard that Kasturiamma has passed away.'

Gurukkal got up slowly. 'Has the gateway of heaven finally opened, Kasturi?' he muttered, and closed the doors of the sanctum sanctorum.

29

EXCITEMENT MADE MY steps falter, slowing me down. The last time I had visited the C.S.I. Retreat Centre, the nun told me that no one who might have known my mother was there now.

However, the inspector claimed that a Hindu woman who was a teacher there had spoken to him about Amma. 'She may or may not be alive now,' he added for good measure.

She must be old now. If, given my bad luck, she was dead, an opportunity for further investigation would have slipped away. Why hadn't the nun told me about this woman? Did she withhold the information deliberately? Or did she not know about the woman? It was unlikely that she didn't know. Theirs is a small world. I had studied in a convent school myself. My friends and I would zealously analyse the various incidents that happened in the seminary. The women who entered the seminary with total dedication, renounced their youth, and spent their lives as nuns amazed me. But there were disappointments in that world too. It didn't take them long to realize that renouncing desire and affection was not that easy. For that very reason, to divert their minds, they ran schools and worked in hospitals.

Yet, for them life was lonely, full of secrets and fears. It made them live with extreme caution. Had this Yogambal been a nun, I doubted she would have taken the trouble to go to the police and testify that my mother had not been in her right mind.

I was for some reason annoyed with Yogambal. How could she say that my mother was not in her right mind? I suspected that her statement had prevented the police from investigating the case properly. What was she trying to hide when she said that? What was the relationship between her and Amma?

I walked fast; running nearly all the way. As soon as I glimpsed the sign—C.S.I. Retreat Centre—my heart started beating fast. I hurried along the elevated, curving pathway that led to the main building. I was nervous. I worried that if the same nun whom I had met the other day was at the reception desk she might become suspicious and ask me to leave. Mentally rehearsing how I might cope with that eventuality, I stopped near the glass door and, through a gap in the curtain, peeked inside. Luckily, a different nun sat at the reception today. I entered quietly and said with a bright smile, 'Good morning, Sister.' With an even kinder smile than the other nun, she looked at me and said, 'Good morning?' in a tone of enquiry. Her eyes were sharp.

'Is there someone called Yogambal here?' I asked in English.

'Yes. What about her?'

'May I see her?' I asked, greatly relieved that Yogambal was alive, and she was at the Centre.

'Oh dear.' The nun firmly shook her head. 'She can't see anyone. She is very ill and confined to her bed.'

Disappointment surged within me. Even though I knew I wouldn't be able to weaken the resolve of the nuns, I said, 'That's precisely why it's important that I see her, Sister.'

'Impossible, child. We can't allow that. Who are you, and why do you want to see her?'

I was reluctant to give her the background information. If I told her the truth she would probably get rid of me as quickly as the other nun had on my previous visit.

I wrote 'Dharini's daughter' on a card and gave it to her. 'I am the daughter of someone who was close to Yogambal. Never mind. Just show her this card. That's enough,' I said.

The nun glanced at it once and stuck out her lower lip. 'Do you know how old she is? She is very frail. Barely conscious these days, can't speak at all,' she said. 'Fine, I will send this to her. Sit down over there.'

I was slightly surprised that Amma's name hadn't aroused any suspicion in the nun's mind. She must have joined the centre recently. It was my lucky day, it seemed. This, too, might have been orchestrated by Amma. I had the crazy notion that whether or not Yogambal sent for me was also in Amma's hands. If I hadn't inadvertently noticed that Amma had written 'C.S.I. Retreat Centre' in her diary, I wouldn't have learnt about this place. I had begun to believe strongly that my chancing upon those words was not accidental. I waited in the reception with my head bowed, sifting through my thoughts. Some foreigners were lounging on the sofas in the hall, immersed in their books. The calm that prevailed here seemed extraordinary. Amma must have been born in some room on the campus; Yogambal would know.

Feeling someone's hand on my shoulder, I looked up. The nun stood beside me. She told me in a low whisper, 'She wants to see you. A surprise, indeed. Come. But I can give you only five minutes.'

I was overwhelmed. I took her hands in a firm grip and said, 'Thank you, Sister. Thank you.'

She led me across several verandas to a building that stood apart, and into a well-lit, spotlessly clean room. 'Five minutes only,' she said. Just before she stepped out and closed the door behind her, she touched my long braid and said with a smile, 'You have such beautiful hair, child.' Her words made me remember how my grandmother had insisted that I should cut my hair.

All of a sudden, my attention settled on the very old figure lying on the cot. She looked like a bird for a moment. There was an extraordinary glow in her eyes. Strangely, I thought of the bird Jatayu in the Ramayana. I felt her eager glance fall on me and then freeze in disbelief. I hurried over to her side. There was a chair near the bed. Still in shock, she watched my movements intently, as though I had set off a cascade of memories in her. Conscious that I had been granted only five minutes, I carefully took her hands in mine and asked, 'Do you know my mother?'

Smiling, she nodded to indicate that she did. Her bony hands eagerly reached for the braid of hair that had slid over my shoulder and stroked it. Twisting the curl at its tip through the gap between two fingers, she looked at me.

Unable to contain my excitement, I came to the point at once. 'The inspector says you told the police that Amma was in poor mental health, and it drove her to suicide. Is that true?' I asked in a regrettably sharp tone.

That she had not expected a direct question was evident from the way she withdrew her fingers somewhat awkwardly. I was ashamed that the pressure of not having much time had made me speak to her in that tactless manner.

After trying to say something, her lips closed in resignation. Suddenly, tears began to spill from her eyes. My eyes too filled with tears.

'Do you think that my mother committed suicide?'

She nodded in dismay, as if to say yes.

'It can't be true,' I said emphatically. 'My mother was a brave woman. I don't think anything could have affected her so badly that she would be driven to suicide.'

Her only reply was more tears. I felt disappointed. I realized that she was truly unable to speak. Again, she puckered her lips to say something but was unsuccessful. Defeated and tired, she moved her melancholy face as if to say 'you can't understand' or 'you don't know'.

'Did Amma come to see you before she died?'

She nodded again. Her fingers drew lines below the eyes to indicate tears.

I was bewildered. 'Why was Amma upset? What was the reason?'

She stuck out her lip and shook her head. Did that mean she didn't know? She pointed to her forehead. Or that it was written on Amma's head? With great effort, she said in a very feeble voice, 'Fate.'

I couldn't understand anything. Given that she had worked in a Christian seminary for many years, I was surprised to hear her talk about destiny and fate. Amma hadn't believed in such things. Somewhat dejected, I wondered what other information I might be able to get from her in this condition. Even before I had finished the thought, I was overwhelmed by shame. Disturbing her further would be wrong, especially when she had so kindly agreed to meet me. She must have been very close to Amma. Otherwise, she wouldn't have wanted to meet me, or shed those tears. I was moved by her gesture.

I wondered whether she knew anything about Sabapathi. Exhausted by the interview, she closed her eyes. I waited for some time. It was my misfortune that she was unable to speak—or, as she had said, it might be my fate. She probably knew many things about Amma that I didn't. After all Amma had failed to mention anything about the existence of such an intimate friend right here. Suddenly I realized that Yogambal was looking intently at me. She gestured with her hands as if to say, 'Forget everything.' She patted my hands lightly. That consolatory touch made me emotional again. I shed silent tears. For a moment it seemed that this old woman, a total stranger to me, was the only one in the world who was an intimate and who shared my grief.

How did you meet my mother? What did you know about her? The questions churned impatiently within me. She kept stroking my hands in that soothing manner, without taking her melancholy eyes off me. I sensed a kind of disbelief in her, as if she had seen Amma in my face. I wiped my tears but before I could say anything more, the nun came rushing into the room. 'Ten minutes are over, child. I allowed you in against the doctor's advice. Please leave now,' she said.

I looked at Yogambal for one last time. Her eyes were fixed on me. She lifted her hand in a gesture of farewell and then closed her eyes. I thanked the nun and walked out. Before I departed, the nun told me, 'The doctor says that she has only a few more days to live. She has throat cancer. You are lucky to be able to meet her before the end.'

On my way home, I was beset by a feeling of crushing disappointment. My confusion had grown worse after my meeting with Yogambal. Why had Amma gone and cried in front of her? What had happened to make her cry? I couldn't understand her behaviour. Even if there had been a misunderstanding between her and Appa, she was not so weak that she would complain and cry about it to an outsider. She would have tried to resolve it herself instead of discussing it with an older person, however intimate. I simply couldn't reconcile this incident with my mother's personality.

Dark clouds moved swiftly across the sky and a cool wind started to blow. Anticipating that it might rain, I quickened my pace. Every now and then I looked up and watched the clouds roll by. Do you know anything about Amma, I asked them. They kept moving. They turned the whole sky dark, shed tears in the form of raindrops. I ran towards the house. Ganesan was standing near the gate. Seeing me, he smiled with relief. 'I was worried because it looked like rain and you had not come home yet.' He laughed. Do *you* know anything about my mother? I wanted to ask him. He had joined us only recently. Why was my mind running chaotically like this? I felt troubled. No one who had worked with us earlier was around now.

'When will you have tiffin?'

'What's for tiffin?'

'Idli, dosai, chutney, sambar. Let me know if you need anything else.'

'This is more than enough. I'll come down at eight,' I said, heading upstairs.

Once again, I wandered into my mother's study. 'You are playing hide-and-seek with me. I still don't understand why you died,' I said aloud, as if Amma was present in the room. I was angry with her. She had lived a life filled with so many mysteries—and, finally, had even attained a mysterious end. Without sharing anything with her daughter or husband ... like Ganga who extracted a promise from King Shantanu. I marvelled at how patient Appa had been.

What could have happened to her that compelled her to take her own life? I could not digest what Yogambal claimed. Why had the old woman gone out of her way to give a statement to the police?

I had the police inspector's mobile number. I dialled it immediately. Once he came on the line, I said, 'I met Yogambal today.'

'Oh, is she still alive? What did she say?' he said.

'She couldn't speak. She said through gestures exactly what you had told me.'

'Drop the matter, then. Our decision is right, isn't it?'

'Perhaps, but I am surprised that she came to you of her own volition to provide information.'

'Oh, no. She didn't come to us. When we heard that your mother visited the Centre fairly often, we went there and made enquiries. She spoke to us quite reluctantly at the time. At first, we had suspected your father. You know ... a domestic quarrel of some kind. It was Yogambal who told us that the husband had done no wrong and there was no domestic quarrel. "I knew that her mind was perturbed," Yogambal said. "Sometimes, it happened suddenly." I understand Yogambal had studied psychology and earned a doctorate in the subject.'

I was astonished. Had Amma weakened in some way that I had no inkling about? Had Yogambal come to her conclusion *after* hearing that Amma's corpse was floating in the lake? Could she have said what she did to protect Appa? I was even more perplexed. I realized that I was back to square one in my quest to discover the reason behind my mother's suicide. All the signs that I thought Amma had shown me were mere figments of my imagination.

Again, I searched the inner drawer of the desk. I opened the diary at random; it opened on the page that had Sabapathi written on it along with a Thanjavur address. Immediately I glanced around the room, checking eagerly to see if Amma was present. The curtains flapped back and forth in the wind and rain. A curtain was caught on a beautiful aimpon statuette in a corner of the room. I released the curtain and looked closely at the statuette. Amma must have bought it in the south. It was the statuette of a woman. Possibly a character from the Puranas. It was a very old figurine.

I came back to the desk and flipped through the pages of the diary again and again. There was nothing apart from those lines written on the day Amma died. 'Rain is pouring down like wires drawn between the sky and the earth.' The page for the previous day was wrinkled, as if it had been torn off in a hurry. Who could have torn it? Was I right to exclude Appa completely from my investigation?

I groped about in the desk's lower drawer. My fingers felt something in the gap between the desk and the drawer. I pulled it out in excitement. It was the page that had been torn from the diary. Crumpled and rolled up, it bore the slanting script of Amma's handwriting: *Kasturiamma passed away.* The sheet was from the day before Amma's death.

Used to the cooler climate of Kodaikanal, I found the heat in Thanjavur unbearable. I stood in front of the house in the address and stared at it in wonder. It was a very ordinary lane. The house was very old, with a front pyol. I knocked on the door and waited. 'Who is it?' I heard an old man's voice before the door opened. An elderly man stood there.

He must be Sabapathi.

I found it strange that he staggered visibly, as if he was astonished to see me. I pushed my braid hanging down my front to the back and said, 'Mr Sabapathi?'

'Yes. Who are you, 'ma?'

'I am Maya, Dharini's daughter.'

Still in shock, he muttered, 'I didn't know that Dharini had a daughter.'

Growing impatient, I said, 'May I come in?'

'Come. Come in. What's the purpose of your visit?' he said in an uncertain tone. 'There is no one at home. My granddaughter has gone out.'

It was dark inside the house. The old man fetched a mat and spread it on the floor for me to sit and parked himself on the only wooden chair in the room.

'Did my mother come here?'

'Ah, yes, it was a long time ago. Must be two years now.'

'Why did she come?'

'Why are you asking me? You can ask your mother, no?'

'She passed away.'

He looked at me in shock. 'Is she dead? When?'

Keeping my emotions under control, I said, 'Over a year ago. Why did she come?'

'She heard that my elder sister was very ill and came to look her up.'

'Who is your elder sister?'

'Her name was Kasturi. Your grandmother Lakshmi and my sister were close friends. I suppose your mother heard the news from somewhere and paid us a visit. I gave her a statuette as a memento of my sister: a figurine of Paravai Nachiyar.'

I was taken aback. It was the statuette I had seen in Amma's study. 'Had she ever come earlier to meet you?'

'No. I had never seen her before. Soon after your mother's visit, my sister passed away. Your mother called once, asking whether she could drop by. I told her that there was no need, and informed her of my sister's death. She never called again. I forgot all about Dharini. My son was killed in a road accident. He had gone to Vathalagundu on business. On his way back, his bus fell into a ravine. I heard it rained heavily in the area that day. We got the news only after three days.'

He spoke without a pause about the accident. Poor man. He must be in great shock.

I said wearily, 'Your son died in an accident. My mother took her own life.'

'What!' he cried out, eyes bulging. 'Why?'

'That's what I don't understand. I came here wondering if I could find an explanation. My mother had written down your address in her diary.'

Tears pooled in Sabapathi's eyes, which were filled with dread. 'I don't understand anything. This house is being knocked about by all kinds of forces. It's fate, 'ma. Our fate,' he said and slapped his forehead repeatedly with his hands. 'I don't know whose curse has befallen this family. In my youth, my other akka, Kasturi's younger sister, hanged herself.'

Feeling perturbed, I went over to him and touched his shoulder. He started to weep with great heaving sobs. 'What other horrors do I have to witness still.'

I kept looking at him awkwardly. I felt that I might also go mad in that dark environment. 'Don't be upset, aiya. I am quite stunned myself.'

He didn't hear a word of what I said, just shook his head in disbelief. 'It's like an evil curse. It's affected only my family ... the other families somehow managed to cope. They went to college, got married ... But here, we were stranded without any means. My son married late, and then died before his time. It feels as if we've been carrying this burden of stigma throughout our lives ... for a transgression against god committed by someone else ...'

I did not understand what he meant.

'Do you know someone called Yogambal, in Kodaikanal?'

He gave me a startled look. 'Who? I don't know anyone like that. You had better leave.'

I got up, feeling a sharp tug of frustration. 'Please forgive me. It looks like I have upset you.'

'You have your troubles, and I have mine. Your mother was an educated woman. How would I know why she took her own life? We have a thousand things to worry about. The burden of the past is unbearable in itself. I can't engage with any fresh trouble right now. My son often said that we should completely cut off all the contacts from the past. He didn't like it when I allowed Dharini to enter the house.'

'Why?'

'I told you just now, didn't I? Be off, now.'

Seeing a telephone in a corner of the room, I said, 'May I have your phone number?'

'What for? There is no need for all that,' he said hesitantly. Softening moments later, he said, 'It's written on the phone itself. You can note it down from there.' After quickly copying the number, I said, 'I am sorry, sir. Please forgive me for disturbing you,' and walked out.

The fog of confusion that I was trapped in today was thicker than what I had encountered in the forest that day. I was deeply bewildered by what Sabapathi had said. Why did he cry, hitting himself repeatedly on the head? He said something about 'a transgression against god.' Had Amma been here, she would have laughed, taking him to be a proper lunatic.

Your mother is an educated woman. Why did she commit suicide?

Exactly. That's why I am at my wits' end, unable to understand it.

Sometimes the mind suddenly loses control, the old woman said. She is an expert in psychology.

Yogambal was presently not in any condition to explain. Why should the death of Paati's friend drive Amma to suicide? Just as Sabapathi had hit himself on the head, I too wanted to do the same in my frustration and despair.

My mouth had gone dry. There was a shop at the street corner selling soft drinks. I bought a Fanta and started to sip it slowly.

'From out of town?'

I looked up, startled. I stared at the shopkeeper in silence, not sure whether I should respond to his question.

'It looks like you visited Kasturiamma's house?'

'Did you know her?'

'I never interacted with her. My father said that once upon a time, Dasi Kasturi's dance was very famous.'

Swallowing my disbelief, I gave him the money with a smile, and moved on. The sight of Sabapathi hitting himself repeatedly on the head, haunted me throughout.

Once I reached home, I bathed, changed into fresh clothes, ate the breakfast that Ganesan put before me and set out. With no thoughts in my head, I let my feet take me to the C.S.I. Retreat Centre. Luckily, the same nun I had met the other day was at the reception desk. She gave me a weak smile tinged with sadness. 'Yogambal passed away,' she said.

I could not hide my shock. 'Oh god! When?'

'Within two days of your visit. Wait, it's a good thing you're here. She left an envelope for you.' She opened a table drawer and held out an envelope to me. 'To be delivered to Maya' was inscribed on it.

Dazed, I opened it. There was a very old black-and-white photograph inside, set in a photo frame. In it were two women, one of them holding a small baby of two months or less. One thing struck me immediately. The woman with the baby. Her face. The plaited braid that hung down her front.

Peering at the photograph with interest, the nun said in wonder, 'Who is this woman? She looks just like you, doesn't she?'

I was astounded. In no condition to reply, I removed the photo from the frame. On the back was written in English: Kasturi, with her child Dharini, and me.

The nun said, 'She must be your grandmother.'

Still in shock, I muttered, 'It would appear so.' I looked up with a smile, said, 'Thank you, Sister,' and walked out.

Amma was Kasturi's daughter. Kasturi must have given birth to her secretly in Kodaikanal. Why? I remembered Yogambal stroking my braid and looking at me in disbelief. I understood now why Paati had wanted me to cut that braid—because she was afraid it would betray my lineage. On seeing me, Sabapathi too had stood transfixed, as if he had seen a ghost.

I became so unnerved that my legs started shaking. This was a completely unexpected discovery. Still, something bothered me. Why should Kasturi's death drive Amma to despair? That too, when she had not been in touch with Kasturi at all?

Unable to walk, I pushed through a gap in the fence around the lake and sat on a grassy knoll adjoining the bank. I drew up my knees and buried my face between them. It was dark inside. I couldn't understand anything. Sabapathi was Amma's uncle. Sabapathi had said that Kasturi's younger sister had killed herself. Was suicide a tendency that ran in their blood? Was Amma pushed to suicide by this genetic trait? She was educated. Why would she take her own life? Don't educated people commit suicide? Many famous writers and intellectuals have ended their lives—often at the brink of some disappointment, in a moment of revulsion against life. The more I thought about it, the more I felt suffocated, trapped inside a labyrinth where no path was clear.

I was startled by the feeling that someone was sitting beside me. I raised my head. It was the boy, the one who had run away when he saw me, the one whom Appa had chased away. He was looking intently at me, his dark eyes steadily widening. Soon, it seemed, his eyes would cover his whole face. I felt inexplicably agitated. Why was he looking at me like this?

'What is it, boy? What do you want?' I asked.

To my surprise, he asked, 'The woman who fell into the lake, was she your mother?'

I nodded.

'I saw a man push her.'

I was stunned. I dreaded what he might say.

'What do you mean?'

'I am telling the truth,' he said in a low whisper, as though he was scared even now. 'That day a fog came down suddenly, and I couldn't walk at all. My grandmother and I were waiting for the fog to clear. We had to go to Dindigul. My grandmother had a cyst in her belly, and I had to take her to the hospital. If we didn't catch the bus that day, we couldn't see the doctor for another two days.'

I waited patiently as he continued with his tale in a leisurely fashion. My heart was pounding. What was he going to reveal?

'It looked like it was going to rain too. Because of the mist, there were no people on the road. We couldn't even see the people standing next to us. When we started walking briskly, it got really cold and my teeth were chattering.'

'Um, and then ...?'

'See that mound over there? The water is very deep at that spot, my grandmother says. Someone was standing there, looking at the lake ... a lady. But we couldn't see her face. There was a man with her. I was watching idly, wondering why they were lingering in the fog. They must have come for a walk and got caught in the mist, my grandmother said. While we were watching, we heard a big splash, as though someone fell into the lake.'

The boy performed the incident, gesturing with his hands. I watched him carefully, without interrupting.

'The moment we heard the noise, we knew that the person who was standing there had fallen into the lake. Since there was mist everywhere, we couldn't see anything. My grandmother stepped aside quickly and told me to take cover. A man ran past us and headed towards the bus stand. No sounds came from the water. I told my grandmother that the woman who'd been on the mound was missing. I told her the man must have pushed her. "It could be something we imagined, so keep quiet," she said. "We must not get into trouble."'

I was very annoyed to hear it, but I suppressed my feelings and remained silent, waiting eagerly for what he was going to say next.

'I was scared. My grandmother had to go to the hospital, so we walked fast, hoping to catch the bus before it left. The man was still at the bus stand when we reached. The mist had lifted by then. He had a blue woollen cap on his head. I remembered that very well. When I told my grandmother, she asked me to stay quiet. A little later, the man got into a bus and left. It was a bus to Vathalagundu.'

I looked up, startled. 'Bus to where?'

'Vathalagundu.'

I had heard that name recently. I wondered where— Oh, Sabapathi had mentioned it.

The boy continued diffidently, with his head bowed, 'When we came back from Dindigul, a lot of policemen were standing around the lake. They had taken a body out of the lake and laid it on the bank. My grandmother warned me to keep my mouth shut. She is very scared of the police.'

I was utterly shocked. If what this boy said was true, then my hope that my mother hadn't committed suicide wouldn't be belied. I found it oddly consoling. But try as I might, I couldn't find the connection between Sabapathi's son and Amma's death. The very thought was absurd; Amma had met them only once in her entire life.

The boy started to leave. I was moved, as if a new relationship had been forged between the two of us. I tousled his hair and said, 'You are a smart boy. You could become a big police officer some day. What are you studying?'

He smiled shyly. 'Fifth class.'

I stood up and headed home. All of a sudden, I felt abnormally weak. Even walking seemed difficult. I sat on a bench and dialled the number of Sabapathi's residence, which I had saved on my phone. Luckily, Sabapathi himself came on the line.

'This is Maya speaking, sir. Forgive me for disturbing you. You said your son was killed in an accident—what date was it?' I was embarrassed at the note of agitation in my voice.

'Fourth of July.'

The day Amma died.

'Why are you asking now, 'ma?'

Without replying, I disconnected the call. I couldn't believe it. The more I thought about it, the more depressed I became. In all my life, I had never heard of such an absurd murder.

I remembered Sabapathi's benighted house and the way he had slapped himself on the head and lamented his fate. Though there was no apparent connection, I also recalled Oshima's explanation and warning about the maze to Kafka Tamura, the protagonist in Murakami's novel. Amma, who was highly educated and enjoyed a good position in life, must have unintentionally set foot inside such a labyrinth.

We couldn't bear the burden of history.

Though I had no idea what it was, I realized that Amma had in some manner become its symbol. Would the weight of this burden haunt many generations to come? The burden carried by that young man whom I had never met could have been the burden of humiliation. Amma wouldn't have felt that way. What Joan had told me about gypsies was more or less similar. I sent her a brief email message: 'I have chosen the topic for my next research project. It might even be a novel. Its protagonist will be a devadasi called Kasturi.'

Then I dialled my father's number in Delhi. 'I am coming back tomorrow, Appa,' I said with a warmth I had never felt before.

Afterword

VAASANTHI

≡

Translator's Note

N. KALYAN RAMAN

≡

Glossary

P.S.

Insights
Interviews &
More . . .

AFTERWORD

A CONTEMPORARY NOVEL WOULD not normally require an exposition on its theme or an elaboration of the factor(s) that inspired the work. However, I feel that the reader of this novel could indeed benefit from an afterword.

Though *Breaking Free* is entirely a work of the imagination, it is also connected to history. The narrative is braided through a few actual events during a turbulent period in Tamil country, when the whole nation was waking up to the call of freedom from foreign rule. The customs and rituals that governed the social and religious life of Tamils, designed mostly by the upper and dominant castes, were always unjust to women; worse, they were not even perceived as such. In various forms, they remain unjust even today. While there is much argument and debate about the many disgraceful customs and rituals that were prevalent in our society, there is deep-rooted reluctance to talk about the devadasis (or servants of God, connected to the temple and the arts). In fact, as I learnt purely by chance, members of this community are seeking to erase its existence completely from their memory.

I discovered how the wounds, agonies and humiliations suffered by those women—some of whom were great artists—over many generations had made a profound impact on their descendants, and how the latter have sought aggressively to reject the markers of their past. The shock of that discovery and the effect it has had on me over the years, along with my research as a journalist into the devadasis' art practice, gave me the impetus to write this novel. Although some of the incidents described herein are real, the people who inhabit these pages are fictional and have no connection to anyone who lived during that period.

Many years ago, when I was working as editor of the Tamil edition of *India Today*, I spoke at length about the devadasi system with Mr S. Guhan, former Indian Administrative Services officer and connoisseur of the arts. A casual remark he made during that conversation affected me deeply and left me eager to find out more about the subject. He said, 'Bala [the celebrated danseuse T. Balasaraswathi] took the art of dance to supreme heights, but no one talks about her these days.' He added, 'Even worse than the erasure of the contribution made by the devadasis of yesteryear, who looked upon service to the arts as a lifelong penance, are statements made by upper-caste dancers of today that the dance of the devadasis was vulgar and obscene.'

'The dedication, immersion and knowledge with respect to the arts that was the norm in those families, where art practice was a part of daily life, couldn't have existed in other families,' Mr Guhan said emphatically.

Initially, my curiosity was limited to meeting, interviewing and writing about the surviving devadasi women who were famous dancers and singers at one time but had since been forgotten by the arts community. I was not deeply familiar with the Tamil environment at the time. Raised in Karnataka, I had lived most of my life in north India. But I was keenly interested in the performing arts of Tamil Nadu, having learnt Carnatic music and Bharatanatyam as a young girl myself. On the pretext of writing an article for the magazine, I got the opportunity to meet and talk to a few highly distinguished artists. The famous singer Sathiyakkudi Meenakshi Sundarathammal of Thanjavur; the genius of dance, Jayalakshmi, famous for her Kutrala Kuravanji, in Thiruvidaimarudur; Thirukokarnam Ranganayaki, a mridangam player, who lived like an ascetic in Pudukkottai; Thiruvarur Kamalambal who lived in Chidambaram—meeting and having long conversations with them was a memorable, scintillating experience. The extraordinary glow that appeared on their faces when they talked about their art, and the way they readily sang, or mimed gestures even while seated, brought me an ineffable joy that was equal to a sighting of god. All of them were past eighty at the time.

Today, no one speaks about the service rendered by these artists to the music and dance of Tamil Nadu; their own descendants do not wish to talk about it. Even after the name of the community was changed—from 'chinna melam' and 'devadasi' to the respectable 'Isai Vellalar'—and the passage of several decades after the enactment of the Devadasi Abolition Bill, no one born in that community wishes to turn the pages of their history. One of the main reasons for their aversion is the injuries the community received from society. I saw with my own eyes that those wounds were still raw and bleeding, to the extent that the younger generation refuses to go anywhere near music and dance. It is evident in the way their blood, which had sustained the tradition of developing and nurturing the arts, has frozen, hardened and become subsumed in the mechanical way of life of the larger society.

My article about these forgotten artists and their unique forms of art met with massive opposition, which came mainly from the men of the Isai Vellalar community. It was interpreted as advocacy for the revival of the now defunct devadasi tradition. At first, I was shocked by the resistance. But later, upon reflection, I concluded that perhaps the *way* I had written the article was what might have been objectionable. (What was prominent in the essay was a wistful lament that their arts have been destroyed.) There was a strong undercurrent of revulsion in the opposition, which I naively believed was aimed at me. Over time, however, I realized it was directed against the social institution that they wanted to forget. I thought it likely that there were many tragic stories behind that total rejection. My journey in search of those stories formed the seed of this novel.

I haven't written a social history of the institution in these pages. Rather, I have tried to understand its impact on the lives of the people and the era through my fictional characters. Many details that I had collected in the course of my research went into the narrative. It grew into a story of the life struggles of three generations of women. Kasturi, from the first generation, is its protagonist. Hers is a time of great upheavals, an era in which many important questions about our social structure are raised. There is revolution in the air and an abiding thirst for freedom. A sense of political urgency affects everyone. Detached from all this, Kasturi lives her life with the conviction that nothing can be more important than art. I experienced the joy that dancing gives her and the shock she suffers when her hopes are dashed.

Lakshmi, who takes the first steps towards revolution, is a character modelled after Dr Muthulakshmi Reddy, who has a special place in the annals of feminist history. Dr Reddy was from the devadasi community, yes, but the narrative draws only on certain historical details of her public life. There is absolutely no connection between Dr Reddy's actual life and that of Lakshmi, a character of my imagination. I took advantage of the freedom available to a writer of fiction, and nothing more.

In Tamil Nadu, where caste privilege and prestige still control social life, the devadasi tradition is a delicate subject that few want to remember, let alone discuss. Their aversion to the past is so deep that their contribution to it has been summarily erased. It is this erasure that prompted me to explore, through the prism of fiction, the underlying sociological reasons and their impact on the community.

I felt the pain of all my characters at various levels and in different periods, and underwent a metamorphosis along with each of them. It was a difficult journey, one that connected me intricately to the women I had created, all of whom became real for me. I realized in the end that this was the story of women, then and now—and of the women of tomorrow.

Many people have helped shape this novel; experts with first-hand knowledge of the community provided anecdotes, facts and references. I thank them all. Most importantly my thanks are to the remarkable devadasi women, stars of a bygone era, who opened an unknown treasure chest guilelessly before me and permitted me to dive deeper into their past.

I express my heartfelt gratitude to my dear friend and publisher, Sethu Chockalingam of Kavitha Pathippakam, who readily published my novel written in Tamil under the title *Vittu Viduthalaiyagi*.

I am very grateful to N. Kalyan Raman, my friend and an excellent translator, for translating the novel into English. His translation, *Breaking Free*, has exceeded all my expectations. It was exciting to see how involved he became with the narrative and the characters. My thanks to HarperCollins India, publishers of the English translation.

March 2022   Vaasanthi
New Delhi

TRANSLATOR'S NOTE

VITTU VIDUTHALAIYAGI (2012), the Tamil original of this text, was the first novel I read that deals with the complex history of the devadasi community through the device of fiction. The novel form allows the author to explore not just the subjectivities of these hereditary dancers in relation to their art practice and life, but also the web of social relations in which they are entangled, often in a context of unequal power. Lakshmi's mission to actualize a life of freedom and dignity for members of her community brings about a transformed social reality that disrupts and destroys many lives. The novel portrays the turn of events at this particular juncture in history as a labyrinth where the way out is blocked by both external and internal barriers.

Although several attempts have been made to address this complex history, it remains a polarized and polarizing discourse. On the one hand, the effort is to justify what happened—the 'appropriation', as it were, of the devadasi art form of sadir and its modification into Bharatanatyam that was practised exclusively by women from Brahmin and other upper-caste communities. On the other, it is to valorize sadir as the true art, which gives full expression to an erotic culture that is our proud legacy, and denigrate Bharatanatyam as the manifestation of a repressed, moralizing nationalism. The discourse has predictably stagnated because neither side is willing to take cognizance of realities that do not suit their purpose, more so the realities of the hereditary dancers themselves. When I read the novel in 2014, I found it path-breaking in its ability to actually come to grips with the diverse subjectivities and precarious social locations of devadasis during that period of upheaval and change. I wanted to translate it into English.

Unfinished Gestures: Devadasis, Memory and Modernity in South India, a landmark study of the community by Davesh Soneji, an academic based in the United States, was published in 2012. A few years later, two novels in English that dealt with the same milieu and history—*The Undoing Dance* by Srividya Natarajan and *Girl Made of Gold* by Gitanjali Kolanad—came out respectively in 2018 and 2020. I am hopeful that *Breaking Free*, an imaginative, feminist retelling of the same history as told by an accomplished writer and veteran journalist, will be a worthy addition to these ongoing narratives and discourses.

Translating another work by an author one has translated before is always a pleasure. There is a greater ease and depth to one's engagement with the work. *A Cusp of Ages,* my first translation of a novel by Vaasanthi, was published in 2008. Like *Breaking Free,* that too was about the lives of three generations of women, and traversed the distance from a Brahmin agraharam in a village to a completely metropolitan setting at the turn of this millennium. Working on it made me familiar with the author's language and narrative styles and gave me insights into the nature of her concerns as a writer engaged with society, especially the condition of women.

By the time I started working on *Breaking Free*, I was used to dealing with texts populated almost entirely by women. And that helped me capture the author's nuanced portrayals of Kasturi, Lakshmi, Sengamalam, Kanagu Paati, Thilakam, Yogu and others with a measure of empathy and understanding. Having been born in the first decade after Independence, I am quite familiar with the culture of Tamil country, with its music, dance and temples, the freedom movement and the rousing poetry of Subramania Bharathi, important ingredients in the narrative.

Translation from an Indian language to English involves two main challenges: modifying sentence structures to suit the narrative flow in the target language and observing certain rules of brevity that are simply not an aesthetic requirement in the source language. Given the emphasis on description and drama in the Tamil literary tradition, one of the oldest in the country, prose fiction tends to rely even today on an accretion of qualifiers, phrasal nouns and supplementary clauses to convey substance and depth of meaning. Modern narratives in English are less than hospitable to such 'quirks' and hence the challenge of writing the sentence anew while keeping the many strands of meaning intact. Brevity involves no more than an alert ear for the unrhythmic or superfluous, but the skill is in choosing the words to excise without betraying the spirit of the original text.

There are many Tamil terms, unique to the culture, that have been left untranslated in the text. Usually, the meaning is clear from the context, but for certain arcane-sounding terms, especially related to music and dance, the reader can refer to the glossary provided at the end of the text.

I am grateful to Vaasanthi for the opportunity to translate this remarkable novel and for her forbearance in putting up with delays in the execution of this project. I would also like to thank Shatarupa Ghoshal for her sharp and splendid contributions as my editor at HarperCollins India, and Rahul Soni for his patience and wisdom in guiding the publication of this book in its present form.

26 March 2022   N. Kalyan Raman
Chennai

GLOSSARY

Abhinaya	Expressions, mimed using hands and face, in Bharatanatyam
Achari	Person belonging to a community of sculptors/carpenters/blacksmiths
Adavu	Basic unit or building block of steps in Bharatanatyam
Agama rules	Rules of liturgy governing rituals and worship in south Indian temples
Aimpon	Alloy of five metals: gold, silver, copper, iron and tin
Akka	Elder sister; also term used to address older women
Alarippu	The first item in a Bharatanatyam recital
Amma	Mother

336 GLOSSARY

Andal	A woman Bhakti poet of the seventh or eighth century CE and one of the twelve Alvar saints of the Vaishnavite tradition; author of *Tiruppavai* and *Nachiyar Tirumozhi*
Angavastram	Stole worn around the shoulder(s)
Appa	Father
Aramandi	Half-sitting position, a basic posture in Bharatanatyam
Aththai	Aunt; father's sister
Bharatanatyam	Dance form evolved from Sadir in the early twentieth century; also said to be of ancient provenance
Brahadeeswara	Main deity in the eleventh-century Chola temple in Thanjavur, Tamil Nadu
Chinna Gurukkal	Junior priest; son of head priest
Chinna Melam	Term for a branch of the devadasi community (now obsolete)
Chithirai	Tamil calendar month from mid-April to mid-May
Dasi	Female servant; also, short for devadasi
Deeparadhanai	Worship of the deity with votive offering of sacred flame
Devadasi	Servant of God; female member of the devadasi community

Drishti	Evil eye; refers also to the ritual to neutralize it
Durai	British overlord/administrator
Gopuram	Temple tower
Gurukkal	Head priest
Jaavali	An expressive item in Bharatanatyam with colloquial lyrics that describes love at the human level
Jathi	Sequence of syllables, of percussion or intoned vocally by the nattuvanar, in Bharatanatyam
Kaathu karuppu	Ghosts and spirits that are believed to cause harm to humans
Kaavadi chindu	Light compositions in Tamil which are popular for their simplicity, emotional content and appeal
Kannu	Term of endearment, especially for a younger person
Kattai	Short stick and a block of wood on which the dance master keeps time
Khaddar	Handspun cotton, a fabric that symbolized nationalist sentiment during the freedom movement
Kolam	Decorative pattern drawn every morning with rice powder at the thresholds of houses
Konar	Person belonging to the caste or community of dairy farmers

Kudumi	Hair worn in a tuft by men
Kundaan	Large vessel
Laksharchanai	Worship by recitation of the Lord's name a hundred thousand times
Manai	Raised plank of polished wood, offered to an honoured guest
Mandapam	Open stone-built hall made up of a raised platform, roof and pillars
Mangalam	The last item in a music or dance performance, bringing it to an auspicious end
Mel thundu	The upper cloth worn by a man over his chest
Mirasdar, Mirasu	Landlord with hereditary rights over cultivable land in a village
Muhurtam	Auspicious time-slot for ceremonies
Naayanam	Another name for nadaswaram
Nadaswaram	A pipe instrument used to play Carnatic music, similar to the north Indian shehnai
Nattuvanar	Dance master and choreographer in Sadir and Bharatanatyam
Oduvar	The traditional chanter of Saivite devotional hymns in temples
Oththu	Drone to provide tonic support to nadaswaram players

Padam	An expressive item in Bharatanatyam, narrating divine love or the pain of separation from the beloved
Padmavyuham	The lotus battle formation in which Abhimanyu was trapped in the Kurukshetra war in the Mahabharata
Pallankuzhi	Board game played using tamarind seeds or cowries
Pallar	A depressed caste community
Panchakacham	Prescribed style of wearing a five-yard veshti. Mandatory for men performing religious rituals and ceremonies
Paraiyar	A depressed caste community
Prasadam	Votive offering distributed after worship
Pulaiyar	A depressed caste community
Pyol	Raised platform flanking the front entrance of houses; also known as thinnai
Raagam	A melodic framework for improvisation and composition in Indian classical music forms
Sabha	Association to organize music and dance concerts in cities, funded through subscription of members
Sadir	Dance form developed and performed by the devadasi community

Salangai	Strips with bells worn around ankles by dancers
Shruti box	A small bellows-like instrument used to provide drone notes
Shruti	A drone of basic notes
Sombu	A mug-sized metal container with a narrow mouth
Taalam	A pattern of rhythmic structure in Indian music and dance
Tambura	A plucked drone instrument used to accompany instrumental or vocal performance
Tevaram/Tiruvacakam	Poems to Lord Siva that form part of the Tamil Saiva canon; sung as part of the temple liturgy
Thambi	Younger brother; also familiar term of address for boys and young men
Thangachi	Younger sister; also familiar term for younger women
Thatha	Grandfather; also familiar term of address for old men
Themmangu	A kind of ditty sung by rural folk of southern India
Thillana	The final item of a Bharatanatyam recital, almost entirely an abstract dance number, with a lively tempo and a dynamic quality to the movements

Varnam	The central item in a Bharatanatyam recital, includes abstract and expressive dance in specific patterns, and a full exposition of the song, so the audience experiences its flavour
Veena	A long-necked pear-shaped lute, with a pear-shaped neck
Veshti	A two-to-four-metre unstitched fabric wrapped and secured around a man's waist that extends to his ankles
Vibhuti	Holy ash worn by worshippers of Lord Siva
Yalis	Dragon-like beasts in Hindu mythology
Zameen	Term for agricultural estate with a designated ruler under the British Raj
Zameendar	Designated ruler of a zameen under the British Raj

ABOUT THE AUTHOR

VAASANTHI is a renowned author and journalist who writes in English and Tamil. She has been writing in Tamil for more than forty years and has published thirty novels, six short-story collections and four travelogues. Her books in English include *Cut-outs, Caste and Cine Stars: The World of Tamil Politics*; *Amma: Jayalalithaa's Journey from Movie Star to Political Queen*; *The Lone Empress: A Portrait of Jayalalithaa*; *Karunanidhi: A Definitive Biography*; and *Rajinikanth: A Life*. Her works in Tamil have been translated into Malayalam, Hindi, Telugu, Kannada, English, Norwegian, Czech and Dutch. Two of her novels have been made into films in Malayalam.

She is the recipient of several awards in Tamil Nadu including the Best Short Story Writer award, Best Novel award for *Ammani*, and the Gyana Bharathi award. She has received the UP Sahitya Sansthan award and the Punjab Sahitya Akademi award for the Hindi and English translations of her novels, respectively.

She was the editor of the Tamil edition of *India Today* for nearly ten years in Chennai. Now a freelance writer and journalist, she lives in Delhi.

ABOUT THE TRANSLATOR

N. KALYAN RAMAN is a translator of contemporary Tamil fiction and poetry into English. Over the past twenty-five years, he has published thirteen volumes of Tamil fiction in translation, by important writers such as Asokamitran, Devibharati, Poomani, Perumal Murugan, Vaasanthi and Salma. His translations of contemporary Tamil poets have been published widely in journals and anthologies in India and abroad. His translation of Perumal Murugan's *Poonachi* was shortlisted for the inaugural JCB Prize in 2018 and nominated for the National Book Foundation Award in the US in 2020. In 2017, he received the prestigious Pudumaipithan award for his contribution to the cause of Tamil literature through his translations. He lives and works in Chennai.